THE Soul Midwife

Ursula Benjamin

SONTHEIL PRESS

Published in 2017 by Sontheil Press
'Edwin Pittwood'
Poplar Dock Marina
Boardwalk Place
London
E14 5SH

www.sontheil.com

www.ursulabenjamin.com
email: soulmidwife@ursulabenjamin.com

A catalogue record for this book is available from the British Library.

ISBN 978-0-9570955-3-3

Cover image: © The British Library Board. Cup.401b.14.
(Dante Gabriel Rossetti, from title page of *Goblin Market and
Other Poems* by Christina Rossetti, published 1862)
Design and layout: Julie McDermid/Punaromia Publications
Printed by Witley Press Limited

Dedication

To my crazy husband, Phil
For your love, patience and encouragement.
If you weren't mad before you married me,
you most certainly qualify now.

Thank you

Raphaël Denis for opening the doors of Fontaine-Daniel to me,
and Nicola Denis for keeping them open.
Carrie Britton for your grace under fire, Chris and Bill Walton
for lighting fires and feeding me, Rina Gill for being utterly
grounded, Tony and Mary Bowers for taking me in, and those,
of course, who allowed me to use their names:
Lorraine Flaherty, Margaret Burton, Ana-Marija Kozuh,
Valerie and Bruno, Denise Tiran, Linda Thorne and the
wonderful Geraldine Beskin whose existence really does prove
that fact is often stranger than fiction.

My love to you all.

'Soul Midwives' is an organisation set up by the inspirational
Felicity Warner (End of Life Care Champion of the year 2017)
and was formed to facilitate safe and gentle environments for
the dying. You can find information on their work here:
www.soulmidwives.co.uk
They are neither the inspiration for, nor are they in any way connected
with, or associated to, the events or characters in this book.

CHAPTER I

REBECCA FIRST SAW an angel when she was quite young. A real one, I mean, not the stone monstrosities which draped themselves simpering around the headstones in the graveyard behind her home. Rebecca didn't think much of it at the time. Well, you wouldn't, would you? She lived among the dead anyway, spending many of her waking hours amidst the tombs. Walking. Sketching. Dreaming. The dead kept her company. They weren't *her* dead after all, so they couldn't harm her.

She had been an only child for the first ten years of her life. Her six sisters had all died before taking a breath in this world. How (and why) she – a useless female – had survived was an ongoing source of irritation to her father. Rebecca was a shy, solitary, and now, motherless child, her mother having only followed her children into the grave with her final offering of a longed-for son.

It was now October and the grounds of the Ramsgate churchyard she walked through crunched with dry, dead leaves. She stopped in front of a particularly large grave, pulling her collar closer to her neck to protect it from the wind which had now begun to howl around the gravestones. The sky was grey and dismal, the same colour as the fat and (in her view) ugly cherubim on the headstone closest to her. The angel baby stared back at her, its plump hands reaching out to, what looked like, a bunch of grapes. She stared back. Her father would have called these images blasphemous. He wouldn't see them, of course. He wouldn't be caught dead in a Christian cemetery. She smiled to herself. Of course he wouldn't. A good Jewish man like him? As a respectable, well-integrated and financially secure man of substance he had Gentile colleagues and, perhaps, some he would even call friends. But deep down he drew away from the potential embarrassments of anything he didn't comprehend, anything which was different from him, and that included Rebecca herself.

Even though years had passed since her death, Rebecca missed her every day, but couldn't help feeling that the memories of her mother were already slipping away. She used to remember how she laughed, but now the sound was fading, more an echo than a sound now. Rebecca felt suddenly much colder, and started to walk deeper into the graveyard. As she did, she reached inside her coat for and wrapped her hand around the locket hidden there. It was warm, and its weight comforted her. This was her only link with her mother. It contained a lock of her hair, cut from her head as she lay dead. She opened the locket and touched it. It felt coarse now, it might as well have been horsehair, but it was her only link and she closed the locket with a click before tucking it back beneath her blouse. It was all she had of her now and she reached for it like a talisman whenever she was afraid. Not that she was afraid now, but there is always fear of the unknown, and the woman she was about to meet back at her home was unknown to her as yet. Would this woman be a good mother to her? Would she be kind to her and treat her as a daughter? Rebecca had no way of knowing this, but she did know that her father had chosen to remarry and that his bride, Anna Coren, had been chosen by him for a reason, and that reason had nothing to do with providing a mother for her.

She walked as fast as she could now, the cold air forcing its way into her lungs. The wind grew stronger, and the leaves started to swirl around her. Small and wiry, she pushed her way through the weather as if it were a physical thing, her large eyes slitted against the onslaught. The wind suddenly dropped, and Rebecca stopped to catch her breath. Her feet had found their own way to her safe place. Before her was a small, well-tended grave with a simple headstone. Here there was only one angel, and she stood beautiful and proud. This angel was more of a warrior than a heavy-headed mourner. Rebecca stopped to read the inscription as she had done many times:

Gathered into the arms of our Lord
on the 14th of January 1884
Bertha Laxton and her newborn son
An angel whose feet never touched this earth
Mourned in this life by her loving husband Elias
and faithful daughter, Beatrice.
We will be reunited

She liked it here. Sometimes she would pretend this was her mother's grave. She wasn't allowed to attend her mother's funeral, nor had she ever been taken to see the grave, so for now she used this as her surrogate. A place to come and talk to her mother. A place to feel her love. When the real family visited, she would hide herself away. When the gentle widower appeared with his surviving child, Rebecca become a watcher in the shadows. Once, last summer, she had watched Elias bring his toddling daughter to visit her mother and brother and place flowers onto the grave. The little one was a chubby child, perhaps three or four years of age, and prone to tripping on the path. Elias was always so patient, and if she fell would scoop her up and swing her high into the air with a bright smile before sitting her on his shoulder to be carried. Rebecca was surprised. He did not seem to have any servants with him. His clothing and demeanour suggested he would have a household of servants, or at least a maid-of-all-work to care for the child while he came to visit the grave, but it seemed to Rebecca from her hiding place that, in his grief, he did not care about social convention. She found herself warming to this man, especially when he stood before the grave and talked to his wife. He told her about his life, and how little Beatrice was progressing. How their daughter was learning to walk, learning to talk, getting into everything. Rebecca would listen to the minutiae of their lives from her viewing point behind a nearby oak tree. She loved to hear how he talked so softly to his dead wife, and sometimes, when the child fell asleep or wandered off to chase a butterfly, he would stare silently at the angel. One time she watched as he knelt on the damp earth of her grave, hung his head and cried. She had never seen tears like that before. They were forced out agonisingly from some dark space deep inside this man. These were tears of searing, visceral pain – like an animal. Rebecca watched herself move as her body stepped out from her hiding place and softly called out to this stranger. He started violently, turning to see who had spoken. 'Elias,' she repeated, quietly. 'Do not be sad. Love does not die. She does not want you to be sad.' She could hear her own voice but the sound seemed to come from a place far away from her. Rebecca and Elias looked at each other as the stone angel watched them impassively. The moment was broken by the sound of the child's crocodile tears. She had fallen again and demanded his attention. She was not part of this exchange and wanted her father back so he could carry her up high into the sky and home. Elias scooped up the child and turned back to look for his interlocutress, but she had disappeared. Shaken, he pulled his attention to his beautiful daughter and opened his tear-filled eyes wide to bring a smile to her face. They headed home.

Rebecca pulled herself away from this memory back to the here and now. The church-bells were chiming four and she realised she was going to be late, very late. She started to run now, still thinking about her own mother. Alma had given her lifeblood in the final act of submission to her husband's will. She had produced the son and heir for her – oh so proper – husband, and in this act had turned from an object of his continual loathing to one of eternal veneration. The doctors had told her father that he should not put his wife through another pregnancy, but the hate with which he looked at her each time a child died gave her no choice. In the last few years she had been virtually absent from Rebecca's life – illness and pregnancy, visits to clinics in Europe, trips to doctors and healers. Prayers said and offerings made at alternate altars of faith and science. She tried them all. She had still died. Part of Rebecca believed her mother had chosen her own death rather than be suffocated day after day by a religion that dictated her every action, and a man who saw his will as the personal extension of Elohim *may he be forever blessed*. Rebecca knew little about the life beyond her home and the graveyard that she hadn't learned from her mother, or from books. Alma Zimmerman, her dear dead mother, had been well-read, musical and vibrant, and had taught her daughter to speak her own native language of German fluently and to be able to converse comfortably in French. Rebecca could read and write in three languages by the time her mother died, not that anyone really paid it much attention.

Three years had passed since then and now her mother was nothing more than a flat image safely trapped beneath its glass in the drawing room. Even now she made her final escape as the image became ever more metallic and transparent in the sunlight as each month went by. With it, all memories of her faded from the house. She had hated that house anyway. It was never her home, and now it was about to have a new mistress. One who would eradicate any traces of its previous inhabitant. A different life for all those who remained there.

Rebecca pulled her jacket closer around her and watched the warm air escaping from her mouth. It would be time to go back to the house soon. To meet her future mother. She walked slowly, thinking of all the other children who were gone too. Agnes and Ruth, Marion and Evelyn, Judith and Ida and then – when all hope of a son and heir to be proud of was almost spent – Zachary finally arrived. Zachary – remembered by God. Why this name? Perhaps, she mused, her father had believed that God had forgotten him, punishing him for some unknown transgression by giving him only daughters and not the son he prayed for. Zachary was his prize now. His trophy.

Looking back, Rebecca saw that the birth of each female child had etched another line of contempt onto the face of her father until it became as rigid and unyielding as those of the stone angels in the graveyard. That final time, as the doula tightly wrapped the precious boy-child and handed him over for Father to display to the powerful men waiting to congratulate him on his son, he could not hide his victory. She had watched him as he made his triumphant entrance into the drawing room with the nervous midwife hovering in the doorway – her hands twitching to take back the baby. He was exultant – raising the child before him in biblical style for approval. 'A son. Finally. An heir to my work. A son to stand shoulder to shoulder with me so I will no longer be hag-ridden.' The latter spoken as a shadow of contempt clouded his features. The men around him stepped back to allow his moment of exaltation in the circle before Zachary was taken from him by the doula. He would be returned onto his father's lap eight days later for the ceremony of the Brit Milah. His circumcision. Zachary's first lesson in the pain of being a man. But Father – she struggled to call him *my* father since that time as the words had come from him with such venom, such deep-rooted anger. It was not just about the lack of male children, but also about the softness and weakness of women, about his wife and all those children who had died. I, mused Rebecca, the survivor, had learnt to stay out of his sight, in the shadows of his consciousness. I was too much of a reminder of the son I could have been if God granted him the gift of a male child instead of me. As for me, I was small for my age, dark of hair and pale of skin, and I had learnt to receive the gift of silence. Father was close to taking me for a mute, and I was happy for him to think that way. Besides, the dead didn't need words, and I conversed with them much more readily than to anyone living.

So it was on the day that Zachary was born, I stood by the foot of Mother's death-bed holding onto the railings there, like a prisoner clutching at the bars of her cage. It was Mother who now looked like she was in prison. Not for long, though. I watched her as she slowly bled to death in exchange for Zachary's life while father carried his prize down into the drawing room where the other men had waited in respectful silent court to his prowess. Father, and the downstairs regions, the public rooms, had claimed Zachary and he would be lost to me and the upper regions of women and softness for many years. However, that is not part of my story. For now, caught in the strands of this memory, I remain in the room of my brother's birth and my mother's death, and watch the life ebb slowly from her body. It was not a raging death, such as those I saw since, nor was it a fight for life, but a peaceful return to her home. Mother's home was not here in this house with the man who married her for her position and her money, but far away in Europe. Mother's home and accent were German and she was proud of her homeland. As she lay dying I heard her parched voice murmuring the songs of her homeland. Only once did she open her eyes and look towards me. Even then it was not me that she saw, but the angel who stood beside me. In those days I only saw the light, but as my experiences of death increased I saw this figure with greater clarity and darkness and learned to give him a name, a space, and reason for existence. The Angel of Death. My books told me to call him Azriel. Companion. Saviour. Destroyer. Again I run ahead of myself.

The shape of the angel leaned over the narrow bed on which the figure of my mother lay and I made myself small and insignificant in the corner of the room, sitting on the floor with my hands clasped tightly around my knees to prevent myself from fetching help. I watched until I could no longer see her. Eventually the light around Azriel became blackness and I knew my darling mother's imprisonment was almost over and she would be free.

On the ceiling of the drawing room below, a bloom of blood

appeared. Its drip, drip, drip painted the gift of pure white lilies red. A centrepiece of lilies which stood stiffly in their fat, ugly vase on the mahogany table. Staining the lilies red. So prominent yet unnoticed. For many years after that time I waited and wanted for lilies to grow on her grave. I wanted it to be known that she was innocent of any crime and her execution was unjust. Time taught me to look for signs and wonders elsewhere. I soon stopped believing in childish legends created by man to comfort the weak-minded. I could inhabit the narrow space between darkness and light, between life and death. Of course I was afraid. Wouldn't you be?

Rebecca heard the chimes from the church as she ran onto the gravel path of the house and launched herself through the half-open front door. She saw the scene before her as brightly as if it was illuminated by a sulphur flare freezing it in a moment of tableau.

In the vestibule before her were her father and the woman she was to welcome as her new mother. His head was bowed before her and he had raised her hand to his lips to kiss her in obeisance, to invite her to become the Angel in his home. Arranged around them, dim in the shadowy hallway, were people she didn't recognise, all faces turned towards her. All were staring at her. All movement frozen in that second.

A daguerreotype of the moment in her life when her childhood would be lifted to reveal the reality of life from now on.

CHAPTER 2

THE MOMENT WAS shattered by the low growl of her father's voice. 'Have you no respect?' Rebecca raced away from the voice up the curving staircase, and looking up she caught sight of the maid and the housekeeper leaning over the banister, watching the scene. They pulled back as soon as they saw her look, but they had seen, and they had heard, and as much as they were always kind to her she knew that they were angry with her. Angry because when Master was upset, there was no doing right in the household. They feared, with good reason, that he would deliberately find fault now, regardless of whether there was a problem.

Rebecca stamped grudgingly up to the second floor, and threw herself onto the iron cot in her room. She lay there, looking at the ceiling and wondering whether anyone would remember to feed her today. Probably not. To distract herself as she had many times before, she took the temperature of the house. This she did by closing her eyes and willing her consciousness to float out of her body. This released her to move unseen from room to room, person to person. She preferred to move systematically from the top of the house downward, but sometimes if she found someone she would track their progress from room to room, floor to floor, sometimes jumping to someone they met and following them. On the floor above her now were the servants' quarters, fed by the back stairs. They were empty of life. This was another world to that of the rest of the house. Once, a long while ago now, she had been discovered in the hallway outside the kitchen door, another hidden space connected to the servants' quarters by the back stairs. Rebecca was listening in fascination to the noises and scrapings coming from within the kitchen. She heard the low rumble of a male voice and what sounded like a woman laughing. This wasn't a sound she often heard in that house. She closed her eyes and rested her head back onto the wall to better absorb the feeling and was abruptly dragged out of her reverie as the kitchen door opened and she found herself being pulled into the kitchen. The housekeeper hauled her onto a chair, flushed and dishevelled. She demanded to know what had been heard, what she had seen, what she was doing there. Rebecca froze, and stared down at her feet, remained silent. She had quickly learned over time that this was the safest way. Freeze, fight, flight. Stay frozen. Much better to wait. Let the situation blow itself out. Slowly the fearful raging of the woman subsided, and the man gently pulled her away by the hand. 'Annie! Can't you see she isn't all there?' He spoke quietly and drew her into his arms. She rested her head on his chest, her arms crossed before her forming a barrier. He looked over at Rebecca. 'Are you hungry?' She looked up from her shoes and nodded. Food arrived on the table and she ate happily and in apparent oblivion to the conversation taking place around her. Annie left the household soon after. No-one told her why or where, but she knew. Rebecca heard and saw much. She was learning that her silence was much like a cloak making her imperceptible to the adults. She was learning all the time.

The kitchen was fed by four ways of ingress. A door leading to the steps onto the street, stairs leading to the public rooms, the back stairs leading to the servant's quarters and the dumb-waiter, the waist-high hole in the wall designed to convey hot food up to the dining room. Zachary had persuaded one of the male servants to allow him to ride in it one day, much to the fury of Cook. Zachary was the golden child. Dark, curled ringlets and a ringing laugh to match. He was the bringer of light into that gloomy house, and Rebecca adored him for it.

There were no carpets or coverings on the floors in these hidden spaces, and the sound here was different from the rest of the house. Rebecca drew herself back into the journey and continued her exploration of the servants' floor, moving methodically from room to room. No-one was ever up here during the middle of the day, but she could feel the essence of the inhabitants of each room as she passed through them. All rooms had two beds. Narrow metal cots with thin mattresses and slightly damp coverings, and gazunders on the bare boards below, modestly covered with a cloth in the rooms of the female servants. The larger spaces had bedside tables with single drawers. Rebecca knew that in one of those drawers, wrapped in a lady-cloth, had lain a rosary belonging to Annie. A Christian curio in this supposedly entirely Jewish household. A gift from someone, perhaps? Pink and cheap with a vulgar crucifix on it, the figure on the cross made indistinct by generations of fingers praying. She moved on. The larger of these rooms also had small fireplaces in them. In the whole of her memory she had never known them to be lit. A nightstand with a jug and bowl and a screen were to be found in the room of Housekeeper and Cook. These were the only concessions to female modesty to be found here. Rebecca found this floor to be cold and bleak but full of more dreams and life at night than anywhere else in the house. Dreams of freedom. Gossip of Annie and her baker beau. She would be a woman of substance, married to a tradesman, with her own front door and freedom to go out whenever she wished, not just one half-day per week, or per month for the below stairs servants. There were twelve servants in the house in all, twelve souls in the service of a master, a female child and a toddler. Twelve servants now deeply worried about the woman who had arrived in the vestibule this morning. A woman who would be the new mistress of the household. Life would change. Change brought trouble. Rebecca realised she would have to tread very lightly from now on, until she could work out the new order of things. Rebecca turned to see the housecat ambling along the hallway between the servants' rooms, and froze in the doorway of Cook's bedroom. The cat looked up at the girl's disembodied self and hissed angrily. Rebecca sighed and pulled herself back into her body from her reverie back-stairs and brought her body upright, her stocking feet swinging. One foot of her stocking dangled emptily, and she pulled it back up, drawing her feet under her as she did so and stared blankly into space.

After a half-hearted attempt to make herself presentable she left her room, walking past her brother's bedroom, then padded across the landing to the nursery. It was a light and airy room. The windows were not as grand as those on the ground or first floor, but taller than those on the floor above. Light and wealth. Light equals wealth. The room was the most colourful one in the house too. It had an abundance of wooden toys, a rocking horse, as well as books and a nursery table that doubled as a school desk for her and for her brother. She had worked her way through all of the books on these shelves, and for some years now had been 'borrowing' books from her father's study, reading them at night, and returning them with care. She had become skilled at arranging those remaining so no gap showed. She knew, although no-one had told her this, that she would not be encouraged, or even permitted, the type of reading to which she had graduated. Rebecca preferred that she be thought of as stupid rather than attracting too much attention to herself. She had a hunger, much greater than the one in her belly, a hunger for knowledge. As long as she could keep feeding this hunger she could be content. She had a secret ally in her study, Samuel, the student rabbi. He made a choice to pretend ignorance of much of her reading.

The hot and crowded nursery contained the only other thing which Rebecca loved, and that was her younger brother Zachary. Plump and clumsy, loud and happy. She loved him unconditionally. This love made her fearful, vulnerable. She feared the day they would be separated, and she feared for his future, for what he would become if he trod the path which was being prepared for him. Would she love him as much if he turned into a snobbish prig like their father? Would she love him if he was more interested in making money and ingratiating himself with Gentile society like their father? Even though she was now seventeen years old and Zachary not quite seven, she thought she could see shades of Father creeping into Zach's behaviour with the servants. What would he become? More to the point, how was she going to protect him? She wasn't even sure what specifically she was trying to protect him from: Father, society, his own character? For the present, all she could do was watch over him, and fuel his laughter for now. She called out his name, and he pulled himself from Nanny's arms and ran over to her. She could no longer lift him up and plant him securely on her hip so he could see into her eyes as she used to. He had grown too solid, too real. For now, her only role was to watch and build up his reserves of happiness. All she knew was that in the future he would need them. In one short week her brother would no longer be in the house. He had been 'invited' to stay with Nanny's family in Eastbourne. Invited? Ha. Pushed out of the way, more like it.

A few merry hours playing with Zach and she felt more like herself. Refreshed by the nursery tea of bread and jam brought by Nanny she found herself pondering events downstairs, while Zachary slept the sleep of the innocent. Since the death of her mother she had been aware of the spectre of prospective replacements. Rebecca realised that this desire for a new wife had little to do with providing a mother for herself and Zach, and was more about the next step on the social ladder for her father. She knew he was more interested in being British than being Jewish. She knew he wanted to assimilate into his environment and keep his Jewishness a private rather than a public affair. She knew that the next wife would be a step towards that. Not a Gentile, obviously; that would be a step too far for him. Maybe for Zach, one day, perhaps. Rebecca herself would be expected to carry on the bloodline and marry a Jewish man. Thus her father would have a foot firmly in both camps, Jew and Englishman. Thankfully, any suggestion of her own marriage was far in the future. Rebecca found herself sighing dramatically, causing Nanny to open one eye as she catnapped by the cot. Nanny smiled at her indulgently and closed her eyes once more. Rebecca left the safety of the room to dress for dinner, and to greet the living woman who had taken the place of her dead mother. She stopped herself from feeling anything, and dressed with care. Her final touch was to decorate her neck with the mourning brooch. She stroked it superstitiously. Rebecca wouldn't allow her mother to be forgotten, even as her father tried to eradicate her.

CHAPTER 3

THE DRAWING ROOM was claustrophobic, noisy, full of people and smelled strongly of unknown perfumes. Rebecca stood at its threshold and tried to take a deep breath from inside her new corset. It felt like each time she breathed in, it gripped her more tightly, like the boa-constrictor which her tutor, Samuel, had shown her in an exquisitely illustrated book. Samuel lived in the house too, neither servant nor master. He was a teacher – not yet a rabbi – he was part cleric, part educator. As such he inhabited a grey area between master and servant. Samuel never spoke of himself, and she respected his wishes. He taught her much, including how to live in the grey.

Strictly speaking, Samuel wasn't her tutor, he was supposed to be teaching her brothers, but as there had been many years with no male child in the nursery he had first reluctantly, and then with growing enthusiasm, taken it upon himself to educate her. This repository of knowledge now found herself writhing at the doorway to the drawing room, trying to find a way of scratching a new itch from somewhere inside her corset, and contemplated disappearing before anyone spotted her to find a discreet doorway she could rub herself up and down against until the irritation could be relieved.

Too late for that, she had been noticed. Standing with his back to the fireplace, her father was looking directly at her. Unsmiling, he gave the tiniest of nods in her direction, bidding her to come to him. She acknowledged his signal, and then glued her eyes to the carpet as she wove her way through the strangers, hearing murmurs of curiosity as she passed. She could feel herself reddening, and her heart racing. It was too hot. She was hungry too, being too cautious to go down for food earlier. She took another deep breath and the constrictor-corset grabbed once more at her ribs.

A woman's hand touched her gently under her chin, bringing her face to face with Anna Coren. On close inspection she was older than Rebecca had thought she would be, and had a soft plumpness about her which surprised her. Her future stepmother smiled and stepped back to place a proprietorial hand on the arm of Rebecca's father. 'Good evening, Rebecca. I am sorry we did not get to speak together before now. I trust we shall be friends.' Rebecca had seen Anna Coren only once before, on the day she became her father's bride – and only then at a distance. She seemed stiff and unapproachable, caught up in the ceremony of the wedding. There had been not a soul there that Rebecca knew well enough to talk to at the feast, confined as she was in the women's area, separated as they were from the men for propriety. Once the dining was over and the women began to mingle with each other, she moved to the wall and tried to make herself invisible, wishing she were anywhere but there.

The noise in the drawing room had dropped as Anna Coren spoke to Rebecca, all eyes discreetly watching this intimate moment play out as if on a public stage. Rebecca curtsied and smiled, but found no words with which to respond to her stepmother. She looked over at her father. Once again he nodded at her, but this time he gestured towards the piano, and the servants moved silently around the room to light the gas lamps. Rebecca sighed inwardly, taking her seat at the piano, and sifted through the music on the stand. Without waiting for any other signal she started to play 'The Fairy Wedding Waltz'.

The atmosphere changed, people began to sit, and the conversation became more muted. Three remained standing by the fireplace. Her father, Anna Coren, and an unknown man by her side, who, from his looks, could only be a younger brother. As Rebecca's hands moved over the keys, she could feel herself drifting away. The overpowering warmth of the room was also making its way through its other inhabitants. Eyes started to close around the room. At the end of the piece, she watched as if from a distance as her hands fell to her lap, and, as a muted sound of applause rippled through her audience, she slid slowly and inelegantly to the floor.

'Quite a performance!' She watched as Samuel's face swam into view and took stock of her surroundings. Someone must have carried her to the nursery and deposited her on the daybed there. She had no recollection of how she had got there. 'Hot sweet tea, and a cake which I cajoled out of Cook. Drink up while it's still warm.' He put both hands around the cup, testing the temperature. 'Warmish, anyway.' She pushed herself up on one elbow and Samuel eased the cup into her hand, smiling his peaceful, knowing smile. As she ate, he recounted the dramatic scene which she had created. 'Honestly – anyone would think you were trying to draw attention to yourself!' Samuel laughed, and then filled in the gaps of what happened and how she came to be in the nursery. It seemed that with her fit of fainting she had given her father enough of a fright to rein in his anger at her late arrival earlier that day, and given herself a perfect excuse to stay out of the way for the remainder of the visit from Anna Coren. 'Thank you for carrying me here,' she mumbled, between mouthfuls of cake. Samuel smiled ruefully and shook his head. 'My strength is in my brain, not my body – Isaac did.'

'Who?'

'Your future uncle. Anna's brother. He has had his hands all over you without having even been introduced. What will people think?' Samuel exclaimed with his peculiar barking laugh. 'Hussy!' She watched him silently as he straightened his yarmulke on his head and pushed his hands down onto his lap to raise himself up from the chair. His movements were awkward and of a man much older. His face and body told a story of a different and harder life than anyone she could imagine. Small and wiry, he walked with a limp from some old, unmentioned injury. His black peyot framed a face with eyes that sparkled with intelligence. When he was deep in thought he would often pull at these ringlets. Samuel stared back at her with an odd expression.

'You are almost a woman now, Rebecca, and change is coming to this house. I will no longer be able to teach you. It wouldn't be proper.

Rebecca was paying full attention now. 'What do you mean – it wouldn't be proper? You have always taught me. There is still so much for me to learn!'

Samuel leaned down until his face was level with hers. 'Change is inevitable. Accept this fact and you will always find a place of safety.' His finger reached out and touched her gently between the eyes on the forehead. 'In here.'

Sometime later, Rebecca woke with a start. Someone had covered her with a blanket. She looked around the nursery for what had disturbed her. All was silent. Maybe that was it. She was used to the noise of her brother in here. Even when he was asleep he was noisy. She dreaded the day when he would be sent to school. She knew it was inevitable – but may it not be just yet.

She stretched out on the nursery daybed and thought about Samuel's words. He was, as he always had been, brutally honest. His words troubled her. He knew more than he was saying, and it bothered her that he wasn't being direct with her.

Samuel held a strange position in the household. She knew he was some kind of distant relation of her mother's, but he hadn't volunteered anything about his past, and when she had asked questions he was evasive. With the selfishness of her youth, she took from him what she needed. Knowledge. Her hunger for study and facility to learn had meant he had begun teaching her, and taught her much more than was usual for a girl, or even a woman. Art appreciation, music, conversation and social graces would have been considered enough. All of these bored her rigid, but she worked her way through these studies and then demanded that he teach her more than she learned from the procession of milk-weak governesses who had come and gone.

Rebecca had secrets now. With her working knowledge of French and German, was able to read the classics in each language. She badgered Samuel until she wore him down and he taught her to read and understand Hebrew. Recognising her desire and ability to learn was strong, he introduced her to the worlds of science, medicine and rudimentary law. The more he taught her, the more she wanted to learn. Samuel said he felt like the stoker on the Sebastopol Steam-Engine. The more he shovelled knowledge into the furnace of her brain the more she consumed. She valued Samuel. He was a good man, and a good teacher. He was the closest thing to a real friend she had in the household. She realised that this friendship and study was now under threat simply because she was a girl. Understanding instinctively that she needed to keep this study a secret, she had taken care to stay as invisible as possible. With her secret held close to her chest, and by going even further than Samuel would have taken her from within the walls of her father's library, her world of knowledge was expanding. She had developed far beyond the confines of her age, sex and upbringing. It wasn't a world she was about to give up easily, even if she could any more. She sat up on the daybed and began to chew on a fingernail. Whatever the nature of the change which was happening in the household, she was now convinced that it wouldn't be one with space for her to continue her studies. She wandered around the nursery, and pushed the rocking-horse absent-mindedly. 'If I could only have been born a boy. Samuel would be able to teach me *everything* and Father might, just might, tolerate me.' She channelled her frustration by pushing the horse again, this time with much more force. Leaving it racing to nowhere, she left for the sanctuary of her own room.

CHAPTER 4

THE LETTER ARRIVED two weeks later.

As she came down for breakfast, Rebecca registered the unusual occurrence of a letter addressed to her resting on top of a pile of other correspondence on the silver salver in the hallway. Her attention was first drawn to the florid writing and purple ink, and only then did she realise the letter was for her. As she reached out to it, the plate was scooped from behind her by the footman who had appeared from nowhere. She followed him and her letter into the breakfast room, where the tray containing it was ceremonially placed on the table within a suitable distance of her father's left hand for him to lay his hand onto the envelopes without having to look up. The footman bowed and placed a letter-knife into Father's right hand.

She had so far managed to evade breakfast with Father and Anna Coren, but could avoid it no longer. That morning found Rebecca walking around the breakfast table to her seated father whereupon she kissed him drily on his cheek. 'Good morning, Father.'

He turned to her. 'Rebecca.'

Seated to his right was Anna Coren. Unsure of what to do next,

Rebecca walked towards her and curtsied. Anna put down her cutlery and turned to face her. 'No formality, please, not now we are a family.' Rebecca froze, unsure of what to do next. 'You may kiss me, if you would like to?'

Rebecca leaned forward and brushed Anna Coren's cheek with her lips. She realised she was blushing. Anna Coren smelled sweet, like violets. Violets for virtue and affection, said her book. All good qualities to find in a wife. It was a totally different aroma from that which had surrounded her mother. Her scent had been a heavy one of Damask Rose. She pulled her attention back to the moment. 'Sit down, child.' Father's voice contained enough of an undercurrent of suppressed irritation to break her reverie. She took her seat and started to push the fruit around her plate with little interest.

Trying not to get caught, she watched her father closely. She studied as he continued to open the letters, scrutinising each intently before flattening then onto the table with the envelope neatly folded around them. Finally, he picked up the purple-penned letter, and opened it without even looking at the envelope. Rebecca could feel her heart beating, hard, in her chest. Her mouth felt dry. She desperately wanted to know what was in the letter, but knew that, after her failure to please over the last few days, she wasn't in a good position to ask questions. Her father preferred her silent, or, preferably, absent. When he encountered her in the house during the course of the day it would be more by accident than design. Rebecca had quickly learned his routine so as to be able to disappear. She saw him only at breakfast and before dinner, where she would come into his study to wish him a good evening before retreating into the back rooms of the house where she chose to spend the majority of her time.

The letter in his hand appeared to be long. It was at least three pages, and when he had finished he continued to hold it in his hand. Finally, he looked towards the end of the table where Rebecca was sitting. He contemplated his daughter with an unreadable expression on his face. He said nothing.

Anna Coren placed her hand gently on his right arm and, in doing so, looked down at the letter. She raised a quizzical eyebrow towards her husband. He handed it to her and she carefully pulled on a pair of spectacles to read. Rebecca found herself experiencing a strangely sad emotion on seeing this, before irritation started to get the better of her. The purple-ink letter was addressed to her. What right had Anna Coren to read it before she did? Anna Coren. Anna Coren. That woman would always be Anna Coren to her. Not Anna, certainly not Mother. Anna Coren. A complete name for a complete stranger. She continued to push her food around her plate, and felt her ears reddening with frustration. She did not want anyone to know how she felt, but somehow her body always seemed to give away her secrets, at least to those who cared to look – like Samuel, and also her beautiful baby brother who seemed to feel her distress almost before she did.

At the head of the table the master and mistress of the house discussed her letter. Quietly. Rebecca kept her head down. She heard the words 'London' and 'Miriam', and then they put their heads closer together and she heard suppressed laughter from Anna Coren. Looking up, she saw her father raise Anna Coren's hand to his lips and he started to laugh. 'Come to me, child,' he commanded, still holding his wife's hand. His words were direct, but his tone was softer than usual. Rebecca slipped off the chair and walked over to his end of the table. 'Well, it would seem you have had an invitation.' He seemed to be teasing her, but, never having heard this from him before, Rebecca was unsure of how to respond – so she stayed silent. 'Your Aunt Miriam has invited you to come and stay with her in London.' She raised her eyes from the letters arranged on the table and looked at her father to gauge his reaction to this unexpected event. 'I think it would be a good experience for you now to spend some time with your mother's sister.' He sat back in his chair and started appraising her from top to toe as if she were a curiosity. 'Time to move from childish occupations and learn what it means to be a woman.' He called the footman who was standing at a discreet distance from the table. 'Take the correspondence to my study. I will be there shortly.' He rose from the table and Rebecca made as if to leave the room with him. He stopped. 'No. You stay. Talk to Anna. It's time for you to get to know one another. After all, a house can only have one mistress!' He laughed at his own witticism, and was gone.

Anna Coren had removed her spectacles by the time Rebecca had turned around, and was reaching for the bell. She rang it once and the dining room door was opened by her personal maid who had come with Anna Coren from her past and had been waiting within earshot in the darkness of the hallway. She looked anxious and out of place. 'Ask Cook for some more tea, please, and how about some more bread and butter? Rebecca, will you join me?'

That afternoon, Rebecca was in the nursery with Samuel, her eyes devouring the drawings in the huge botany book which lay open on the desk. Samuel was at the window, seemingly taking in the scene in the street below. On the wall beside the window was a small, vibrant oil painting. The window was open, and the sounds of Ramsgate permeated the room. He was distracted. His attention already miles away. Rebecca left her book and stood beside him.

Letting her gaze follow his, she saw that he seemed to be watching the artist who was methodically setting up his easel and paints where he could see the harbour wall and the ships beyond. She pulled gently at his sleeve. 'Samuel?' It took a few moments before he appeared to register her. He pointed towards the artist, now rearranging his easel better to see the view. 'Do you see him? His name is Vincent. He teaches in the school in Royal Road. He's Dutch.' Rebecca studied the figure of the young man and his easel more closely, wondering how Samuel could possibly know so much about this man. She realised that she knew virtually nothing about Samuel's life outside of this room. Samuel continued, 'His dream is to be a painter. He is following his dream.' He suddenly turned from the window and straightened the oil painting hanging there. 'Dear, sweet Mr Van Gogh. Between you and me he isn't very good – but at least he is being true to himself!'

Rebecca closed the botany book. 'You're leaving, aren't you?' she said, flatly. He sat down awkwardly on the tiny school chair, and pulled it closer to her. He smiled, ruefully. 'I can't hide anything from you, can I, sweet Rebecca? You know what your name means, don't you? Of course you do. Snare – a trap.' Rebecca tilted her head to one side as he spoke. 'You do that only when you don't understand what is being said to you, are you aware of that? It is as if you want your ear to open more so the sound can pour in more easily. My lovely knowledge trap. Anything that comes close you capture. You are a remarkable creature. I will be sorry to leave you.' Rebecca wanted to ask why he was going, but deep down she knew the reason. Anna Coren. He continued talking. 'Your brother will be sent away to school very soon and there is no longer any reason for me to be here.' He looked at Rebecca. 'I know how you feel, and what you would like, but there is nothing more I can do here. I am a humble student rabbi, and without a student I am not even that any more.'

He picked up the botany book and returned it neatly to its place on the schoolroom bookshelf. 'I have enough money put aside to go to Paris. When I get there, who knows what I will be. Maybe I will follow my dreams – but not as an artist like dear Vincent!' He pulled out a brown paper parcel tied with string from his pocket. He smoothed the corners with his long, tapering fingers. 'A small parting gift. It was my own copy. It is time you read it. Something which will challenge your thinking. It's time for you to discover that not all knowledge is truth. Not all books agree with one another.' He handed her the package, and she tugged at the string to open it. Folding back the paper, she found in her hand a well-loved book. Opening it, she read out the words written on the title page. 'On the origin of Species by means of natural selection, or the preservation of favoured races in the struggle for life. By Charles Darwin, M.A.' She looked up quizzically. 'How am I to understand this without you?'

Samuel pushed his hands deep into his pockets. 'For me, there is no contradiction with his findings and the Torah. I want you to have it because it has been an important book for me. Darwin waited a very long time before he published his findings because they ran contrary to his beliefs. In the end, the evidence of his own research was overwhelming. What we believe and what we discover can be in complete opposition to one another. It makes life – how to put this? – interesting, for those of us who live in the spaces between contrasts, the strangers to the norm.' Samuel sighed deeply and then smiled. 'You are not alone in wishing I could be with you when you read this. I know we would have many interesting debates. However, perhaps it is best for you not to mention my gift. Or your own abilities, little Rebecca.' She opened her mouth to speak, and settled on pretending to study the volume in her hands. 'Yes, Rebecca. I am aware of your – self-education.' Without realising it, Rebecca had stiffened as he spoke of her 'abilities', and relaxed, thankful he only meant her reading. 'I am also aware of your gift of Sight. Even if you don't want it, the gift was given to you. We each have a journey to make through life. As I do. As we all do. You have the gift for a reason. Don't be afraid. Learn. Try to think. Try to understand. Then make your own choices.' She couldn't escape his gentle gaze, so instead she met it, sadly. His final lesson for her now over, he returned to the window and closed it, shutting out the sound, and with this movement, sealing his goodbye.

CHAPTER 5

TIME PASSED WITH the repetitive monotony of a ticking clock and there had been no word from Samuel. It was as if he had never existed. She had long since read every book in the house and craved novelty. Four weeks after Samuel's departure was the only time his name had been mentioned in the house, and by that time she had completed reading his gift and was already going through it again, this time underlining sections and making note of her questions as if she would be seeing him soon. She knew that with this gift he was trying to teach her more than the subject on the page, and without his guidance it was eluding her. She knew this book contradicted so much of the learning she had done before, but what was she to understand from this? She closed the book, and with it the connection to Samuel slipped a little further from her.

Earlier that day, Rebecca had come down to the kitchen to collect her tray. Unusually, Cook was seated at the kitchen table, poring over a well-thumbed copy of *The Jewish Manual; or, Practical Information in Jewish and Modern Cookery edited by a Lady*. Everyone knew 'The Lady' in question had been Lady Judith Montefiore, a stalwart of the synagogue which father attended.

Samuel had told Rebecca that in the years since it was published this book had made its way into every Jewish household and provided a guide for both kosher and 'foreign' cooking. Samuel laughed as he explained to her that in this instance, 'foreign' meant anything non-Jewish. Rebecca had been quite young at the time, and had questioned Samuel on the reasons why they ate differently, and why certain rituals were observed in the house, and others not. He answered patiently, but more often made her go and do her own research, to read the texts from the Mishnah and the Midrash. Samuel knew as a woman she wasn't supposed to read them. He seemed not to care. For him, he explained, the rabbinical explanations would be the start of knowledge, or at least give fuel to the formulation of more questions. Samuel often said to her that the true purpose of study is to learn how to think, not to just accept what is said. Questioning is the root of all knowledge. She came away frustrated from these conversations, always wanting more. He would just smile at her. Now he was gone, and she missed him more than she could admit to anyone.

She seated herself in the kitchen by the range until Cook had finished reading. Eventually, she placed a bookmarker in the page she was studying and sat back, pulling her cap off before running her hands through her wiry hair. The top of the bookmark stood out from between pages of the heavy volume. The words 'Thank you' in Samuel's handwriting could be clearly seen. Rebecca was sure she had never noticed it before. Cook replaced the cap and, as if reading Rebecca's thoughts, started to talk to her about the day Samuel had left the house. 'Heading for the Continent, for the fleshpots of Paris, he said.' Cook began chopping cabbage with some violence. 'Although why he would want to do that, I cannot imagine. Full of foreigners!' She laughed and wiped her hands on her apron, before turning to stop and look at Rebecca. 'It's better this way.' She turned back and continued her work. Rebecca knew better than to ask her to expand on her cryptic comment. She would come out with it in her own time, probably. She usually did. Cook seemed to enjoy being in possession of information which no-one else in the household had. Incredible that she knew so much about everyone, really, considering she rarely left the house – or below-stairs for that matter. Rebecca picked up the tray and left the kitchen via the back stairs. She preferred to maintain her invisibility to the rest of the household for as long as she possibly could manage – and she sensed that it wouldn't be long.

The next day, rising early, she offered to take a package from Cook to her sister, Hilda, also a cook. Hilda was in service in a much smaller household which was on the other side of the harbour. It was no more than a twenty-minute walk, and she had done it many times before, but it afforded her a little freedom. She could be out for the whole morning and no-one would really notice. Taking the parcel she allowed herself to be wrapped in Cook's cloak. 'I won't be responsible for you catching your death, thank you very much,' she muttered, portentously, tugging at the cloak around her as if to make sure it wasn't going to blow away. Placing her work-worn hands on either of Rebecca's shoulders she looked straight into her eyes. 'Now, you take care, you hear me?' Cook wasn't referring to her going out with the parcel, and she felt a sudden and deep unease. Noticing her changed expression, Cook grabbed a large red apple from the fruit basket on the table and pushed it into her hand. The older woman smiled suddenly, before spinning her young mistress around to face the door. 'Off you go then!' As she made to leave the kitchen, Rebecca felt rather than saw Cook wipe her face with her apron. 'Goodness me, child, I will forget my head next! Here you go. The parcel.' Turning to face her, Rebecca saw the smear of tears still evident on her face. She looked down, pretending to search in the voluminous cloak for a pocket to put it in, giving Cook time to compose herself. Impulsively, she threw her arms around Cook and kissed her floury cheek, grabbed the parcel and left the house via the servants' entrance.

The wind was blowing hard as she appeared at the top of the steps from the subterranean area of the house in Wellington Terrace. By the time she reached the street level, a squall of wind caused her cloak to billow around her. The parcel was heavier than she had first thought, so she decided to take the direct route to Mrs Marx's house where Hilda, Cook's sister, ruled her own below-stairs kingdom. As she walked, Rebecca wondered idly whether there was jealousy between the sisters, but as she grasped the parcel tight to her chest she knew that this package contained love from one to the other. It felt soft, as if it contained some sort of fabric. Her mind pulled at the string of the parcel and the story it might contain.

Half an hour later she was firmly ensconced in the kitchen of the Marx household. She seated herself on a tiny stool by the range in the warm kitchen as the kettle hissed beside her and the parcel was opened. She was right. It was linen – a beautiful set of bed-linen – stitched by Cook. (Who knows how she had found the time?) It was a gift for a betrothal. Hilda slowly rewrapped the parcel in its brown paper and started to roll up the string to be put away for reuse. 'This is not the celebration I would have wished for, Rebecca. I am marrying out. Do you understand what that means?' She worried away at knot she found. 'It means I am marrying a Gentile, but my family will not – cannot – accept this relationship.

I will be dead to them from now on. He is such a good man, you know. A really kind and gentle man. He doesn't really understand what this means. It's not as if I am religious. Religion is all very well for the likes of them,' with this she nodded angrily upwards to the rooms above, 'but if you are poor you have more important things to worry about than lighting candles and what sort of food you eat – food is food when you are hungry.' All the time she spoke she worried away at the knot in the string. Finally, she gave up, and, picking up a kitchen knife she cleaved the string into two pieces. Rolling each into separate skeins, she lay them neatly side by side on the table before her. She stared at them with unseeing eyes, as she continued to talk.

'We met when he used to deliver the coal to this house. Last year he took a position as lock-keeper on the Grand Union Canal, and now has permission to marry. We will live in the lock-keeper's cottage and, if we are to be fortunate, we will be blessed with children – but hopefully not too soon! I have been saving hard. It won't be easy for us to manage at first with only one wage coming in, but I will get a position, and I can always sew, so we will be fine.' She smiled ruefully as she continued. 'My family turned their back on me when I told them about William. Our children will not know them or their heritage. I cannot care for a god who separates families – and creates sorrow.' She ran her strong fingers around the edge of the parcel. 'Only my sister still stays true to our blood bond. I will miss her terribly when I leave Ramsgate.' Rebecca said nothing as Hilda told her that Cook wouldn't be able to visit her for fear of losing her own situation. It made no sense to Rebecca. Perhaps she could talk to her father and explain. 'No! Please don't do that. Even if he did understand he would have to do what is seen to be right and proper.' Hilda stroked Rebecca's hair. 'So young –

but soon a woman. Life is changing for you too, Rebecca. I pray the changes will bring you joy.' Suddenly she took both Rebecca's hands in hers and pulled her up from her stool, and started to dance her around the kitchen, smiling broadly. 'May they bring you a man who will give you joy in *every* room of the house, and children to make it sound with laughter! L'chaim – to life!' Rebecca swirled around the room with her, laughing, caught up in Hilda's sudden gust of happiness.

As she left the house she selected the longer route home, one which took her close to the harbour and Pier Yard. She walked past the Obelisk, commemorating George IV's safe return into Ramsgate Harbour, past the Customs House and onto the Clockhouse where she paused. There was much activity going on around her, a five-masted vessel was docked on the slipway nearby, and she could count at least another ten of similar size further out in the harbour. Luggers and merchant ships, steamers and tiny pilot vessels. It was a different world out here to that of the Ramsgate streets, and the people on the quayside seemed different too. They seemed to be people more on the edge somehow. Perhaps it was always this way by the coast. The proximity of the element which could take life at any moment made people aware of life itself, perhaps. She felt melancholy and alone. Everyone here seemed to be on the way to somewhere else. They all seemed to have a purpose.

It was cold by the water too, and she positioned herself with her back to the Clockhouse, so as to better take in the sights of the ships tall and small, the sounds of the many voices, local and foreign, and the smells. Overwhelming some of them, but different and exciting in their own way. She suddenly remembered the apple in her cloak pocket, and pulled it out, slowly rubbed its skin with her sleeve until it shone with a red, mirror sheen. The movement lulled her, and she found herself yawning. In that moment she realised just how bored she was growing without Samuel's lessons to help her structure her day. Thoughts of the morning she had recently spent with Anna Coren had been pushed into the back of her mind like half-finished knitting into a bag. She wanted time and solitude to work out what she thought and felt about that encounter. Tucking the thought back into a corner of her mind, she raised the red fruit to her lips to take a bite.

Her awareness started to slip away from her immediate surroundings and she felt, rather than saw, the eyes of the child beside her. A boy, filthy and small, his large eyes stared out at her as if in terror of the light. He was staring at the apple. She watched herself pulling her cloak away from him. He continued to stare at her. Repelled by the sores around his mouth, the apple lost its appeal. She looked at the fruit, then him, and, opening her hand, let it fall. His eyes had stayed on the apple and he caught it before it hit the hay-strewn cobbles. Immediately, he pushed it into his ragged shirt and darted into the crowd. A chorus of jeers followed him, as did the myriad boots kicking out towards him as he careered into the boatmen working on the quay. She watched him plough his way through this sea of humanity, and then she first sensed, then saw the tall, cloaked figure come into focus beside the boy. It was Azriel, the Angel of Death. The figure seemed to momentarily surge towards her, then turned swiftly in the wake of the urchin. Both disappeared into the crowd and Rebecca felt her heart pounding with fear.

Shocked back into her body, she felt deeply ashamed and shaken. As fast as she could, she ran for the safety of home.

CHAPTER 6

ALL WAS NOT well between Father and Anna Coren. They spoke little, and Anna Coren ate less. That evening she had been invited to join them and Isaac, Anna's brother, for dinner. She didn't get as much chance as she wanted to observe the situation between them, as Isaac seemed intent on monopolising her, and the conversation. Perhaps he was aware of the chill between his hosts, or maybe he was just nervous. She found him hard to read. She had not seen him (and furthermore had tried not to think of him) since the evening he had carried her unconscious body from the drawing room. She blushed deeply from the memory, and tried hard to pay attention to him as he talked about his life in London. He was polite and formal with her, but seemed to be trying too hard. He was also consuming large quantities of wine. Rebecca tried hard to focus on his words, but she failed. Uncomfortable and bored, she resigned herself to listening to him and nodding in agreement in what she thought were all the right places, while she took her mind for a walk in the dark corridor outside to try to collect her thoughts about the events of the last few days. She just wanted to be alone to think. Since returning to the house she had been dragooned by Cook into helping chop vegetables. The kitchen maid had disappeared and with the news of an unplanned visit from Isaac, and the subsequent requirement for a more formal dinner, the kitchen had suddenly become a hive of activity. Cook didn't work well under pressure, as the over-salted meal she had produced for the evening demonstrated. No-one was eating much, least of all Rebecca, whose gnawing thoughts were eating away chunks of her peace of mind even as she (tried) to listen to Isaac tell an interminable story about the Lord this and Lady that who had been guests at some grand dinner Isaac had attended in London the week before.

The meal was coming to a close, and so she hauled her sulky shadow-self back out of the corridor and tried her best to focus her attention fully on Isaac. As she did, she remembered Samuel's words to her, what seemed like years ago but could only have been months now. *Allow people to talk about themselves and they will believe you the most scintillating and intelligent individual.* She realised this was definitely the case. She smiled at that thought, and Isaac, who was deeply involved in his story, took her smile as encouragement. 'I would be delighted to show you their home one day, from the outside, of course. That is, when you are in London.' At those words, her father looked up sharply, and signalled to Isaac that it was time for the gentlemen to withdraw. He stood immediately, dropping his napkin carelessly onto his plate where it started to turn pink as it soaked up the juices from the cherries. Cook won't like that, Rebecca thought. More work for her. Cook oversaw the cleaning of linen from the kitchen, just as the butler oversaw the starching of her father's collars. So many rules. So much work for the invisible people of the house. Rebecca found herself mesmerised by the sight of the napkin turning darker and darker, and the colour of her mother's blood seeped back in her consciousness. She felt herself start to slip away from her own body once more.

'Rebecca, can you hear me? Are you unwell? Rebecca!' With a jolt she realised that Anna Coren was now standing beside her. 'Here, drink this.' She felt the small crystal glass being pushed into her hand, and guided up to her lips. She drank, and started to cough. 'I coughed – just like you – when I first tasted alcohol! I still don't like it very much!' She took the glass from her gently and placed it back onto the table. The servants were hovering around the room, nervously, unsure of what to do as this scene played itself out. 'Rebecca, let's go and sit in my dressing room. It is much more comfortable.' As they left the room, the servants started to clear the table, the atmosphere palpably changing among them as each went about their allotted tasks.

Rebecca perched uncomfortably on the low dressing-room chair in the chamber which had been her mother's sanctuary, and looked slowly around. The embroidered seat, she recalled, used to be by her mother's bed, and was now positioned by the window so the occupant could have a view of the sea. The curtains were drawn now, against the cold, and the fire had been lit in the grate. She felt her eyes sting. Rebecca was unsure of whether this was from the smoke of the fire, or from being in this room. Her mother had died in this place. She wondered if Anna Coren was aware of this fact, but then she realised that it must be the case. To marry a man who had been espoused before was to be in the constant presence of ghosts. With sudden and unexpected empathy, she realised that it couldn't be easy for Anna Coren living here in this house, in a home where everything from the curtains to the cutlery was chosen by a dead woman. In some sense Anna Coren was the ghost in this household. Almost all the current household had been here when her mother was alive, and Anna Coren was the outsider – the interloper.

She sat in silence as Anna Coren poured out the hot milk which she had ordered for both of them. Rebecca studied her hands as she arranged the cup perfectly in its saucer before handing it to Rebecca. Her hands were small and pale, not the hands of a cook or a servant, but the hands of a lady. The rings on her fingers seemed loose, and the amethyst bracelet around her bony wrist seemed far too heavy for her. She attempted to unclip it, failed, then pushed her wrist towards Rebecca. 'Would you, please?' Rebecca busied herself with the clasp, and let the bracelet fall into Anna Coren's other hand. 'Thank you.' Anna Coren rubbed her wrist and dropped the bracelet carelessly onto her dressing table. Rebecca drank her milk in silence, and Anna Coren did the same.

In bed later that evening, Rebecca allowed her thoughts to flow like water over the events of the last few weeks. The letter addressed to her, about which nothing had since been mentioned. Cook's sister… Isaac… Her feelings about each of these followed her thoughts around like a hungry dog. There was nothing here to feed her, just more questions, more hunger. Finally, she allowed her thoughts to come to rest on the urchin at the harbour. She knew in her heart and with a fierce certainty, that the boy was certainly dead by now. The Angel had pursued him and the Angel *never* turned away from his prey. She had handed the apple to the child, like the witch in the fairy tale, and the boy had died. By slipping into the space between worlds where her dismembered self could explore, she had somehow alerted the Angel. As she slipped into his world, he had moved into hers. It was as if her visit to the space had created a vacuum into which the Angel could move, and once he was here he could feed.

She knew now for certain that she and Azriel were linked. Through her revulsion to the urchin, she had unconsciously called the Angel and he had come. Since her mother had died, she had seen this figure from a distance on a number of occasions. Each time she knew that death had followed. Now she was convinced that – somehow – she was the one who was summoning him. Maybe, deep down, this time, she had believed that a creature like the urchin would be better off dead, and the Angel knew her thoughts. The boy was probably alone and lived off the street like an animal. She attempted to rationalise her feelings. Perhaps if she had called the Angel to take him it was for the best. She pressed her palms deeply into her eye sockets and tried to block out the vision of a desperate child screaming in pain.

CHAPTER 7

WHEN REBECCA AND Anna Coren left for London it was still dark. In the carriage from Wellington Terrace to the railway station they had passed by the harbour. Rebecca craned her neck through the carriage window to catch a glimpse of the Clockhouse. The landscape at the quayside teemed with humanity, and the soundscape was full of noise. Anna Coren watched her, misinterpreting her action. 'Don't worry – you will see Ramsgate again!' Rebecca chose silence as a suitable response.

Since the evening of Isaac's visit, six more tedious months had gone by. Months without Samuel, months without her brother who had been taken straight from his visit to Eastbourne directly to boarding school in Brighton. Quite a neat move by Anna Coren, Rebecca thought drily. No fear of dramatic goodbye scenes in the circumstances. She was restless and unable to settle down. Not even *On the Origin of Species* could distract her from the emptiness caused by her brother's absence. This was now a home without the boy child to remind Anna Coren that she wasn't the first mistress in this house, and now she herself was leaving for a visit to London. She continued her musings. Perhaps this would become a permanent move, as well. Thinking now of Zachary and her deep fear that he would soon forget her filled Rebecca with a sadness so strong its pain was physical. He had been gone for over a year now, and she wondered whether he thought of (or even remembered) her. She reached for the hidden locket to check it was still there. Her talisman connecting her to the past. Her past. Her mother. Her brother who had never known his mother. Without being conscious of it, Rebecca had tried to be a mother to Zachary. Not that he had seemed to need or want her ministrations, but he was ever present, there in her thoughts. As was the Angel. She tried to shake off the darkness of this image as she watched Ramsgate reveal itself in the pale morning light.

They travelled into London by train. The London, Chatham and Dover Railway was a matter of pride to Ramsgate, allowing its wealthier residents direct access to London. Escorted by a uniformed guard along the platform and through the throng to their First Class carriage the women stepped aboard, took their seats and waited patiently for the train to leave. Rebecca found herself staring out of the open sash-window at the crowded station. There were the travellers themselves and weaving among them she could see the station lads carrying on their heads the open wooden boxes of produce left that morning at the station by a farmer which would now be carried to London to go to Covent Garden market. The coming of the railways had meant fresh produce could go from field to table before a day had gone by. This was a place constantly in motion, a little like the docks, but faster, more crowded, more urgent. There were uniformed porters pushing trolleys and clearing their path with piercing whistles. So much going on. It seemed hard to believe that the train would leave on time, but it did. As the train pulled away from the station, its cloud of steam rose to hide the crowded platform, and it seemed to Rebecca that the form of the Angel Azriel rose momentarily from its midst, the illusion only dispersed by the station master stepping forward through the smoke and signalling the departure of the train. She slumped back into the seat, letting her fingers push into the space made by one of the buttons in its plush surface. The train gathered speed, and its rhythmic movement and the early start from home gave her the excuse she needed to close her eyes and process recent events.

She hadn't wanted to admit it in front of Anna Coren but Rebecca was finally allowing herself to get excited. Excited to be on the train, excited to be leaving Ramsgate, excited to be going to London to stay with her Aunt Miriam, excited that *something* was happening to her. The purple-penned letter which had been addressed to her and, as far as she was concerned, been forgotten, had contained an invitation to visit her aunt in London.

One week ago, Anna Coren had again invited her to drink hot milk with her, as she seated herself as before at the dressing table, and Rebecca on the window chair, she handed over not a drink, but the flattened pages of the letter for her to read. These sheets were now safely in her trunk which had already gone ahead by road to Aunt Miriam's house in Gower Street. Since Isaac's visit, she had noted an improvement in the atmosphere between Anna Coren and her father. Now it seemed to be as it had been before, with father being once again attentive to his wife. Rebecca watched the display of affection as he kissed his wife's fingertips that morning at breakfast. Unlike before when she felt anger, she now felt nothing. Her resentment of this woman was fading, and after what she had heard from Cook she realised she had Anna Coren to thank for this visit to London happening at all. When Rebecca had gone below-stairs to tell Cook all about her new adventure, it appeared that everyone in the household had known the contents of the letter apart from her. Cook now took great delight in telling Rebecca that her visit to London was the reason for the discord between Anna Coren and Father. Now the invitation had been accepted, Cook told her the whole story as she started to prepare luncheon.

'Miriam Blumenkranz as you know,' Cook said, 'is your mother's older sister. Went back to her maiden name when she was widowed. Odd that, don't you think?' She shook flour and the detour from her head before continuing. 'A lovely woman, at least, so I hear from her cook, and she would know!' Cook continued, before reminding her of other things she already knew – the fact that Aunt Miriam was a widow, and her only surviving relative in England. Cook warmed to her subject. 'There may be others abroad, for all I know, but that's not important.' Rebecca smiled from her perch on the stool by the range. Cook's intense dislike of anything *foreign* was an ongoing theme in her conversations these days. It seemed that since receiving the letter her father had gained new information about Miriam. Since the last time they had met some five years ago, Miriam had developed some unconventional opinions. It was widely known that she had refused any further proposals of marriage, but as a woman of independent wealth she could afford to be selective. However, instead of embracing the notion of remarrying, it appeared she had instead espoused some very radical ideas. Firstly, she had declared herself non-conformist. She no longer had any intention or inclination to adhere to Jewish observance, ritual or dietary rules. Miriam drew the line at eating pork, however, preferring to become a vegetarian. 'I ask you,' laughed Cook, 'who would want to live on radishes? If I had her money I would eat meat every day if I could!' The final horror, Cook said, came when the master found out that Miriam took great delight in having a constant stream of visitors parading through her home, without care for introductions or even a chaperone. 'Liberals, free-thinkers, even Spiritualists!' Cook exclaimed in disgust. 'Can you imagine! All those hungry people, traipsing to her door, and all expecting to be waited on hand and foot, without two pennies amongst them!' Cook's flurry of words had momentarily taken her breath away, and she leaned forward, placing both elbows onto the kitchen table, allowing her heavy bosom to rest there. Her head was now level with Rebecca's, and she pushed her cap to the back of her head as it slipped forward and tried to obscure her view. 'Anyway...' she continued in a quieter, more conspiratorial voice, 'Master said he wasn't going to have you going to that place – who knows what ideas you might come back with! The mistress disagreed with him, and gave him the silent treatment – no fun for us below-stairs, I can tell you – and that's why they weren't speaking for weeks, in case you were wondering! In the end the master gave in – there is no peace for a man with an unhappy wife – and here you are now, off to London!'

Cook left Rebecca alone in the kitchen to digest this unexpected piece of information, and returned with a laden basket which she lifted onto the kitchen table. 'One last errand, miss, before you leave us?' Cook had rarely called her that before. Life was changing around Rebecca, whether she wanted it to or not, and she now realised that she did want it, and this change in particular. Staying with Aunt Miriam would be – interesting – and, with any luck, she would be able to visit the museums and the galleries, and the wonderful libraries. Yes. She was excited. Rising from her seat she dragged the fully laden basket from the scrubbed table, allowed Cook to bundle her in her cloak one last time, and set off on her errand.

Rebecca found herself avoiding the harbour altogether this time. When she finally arrived at the Marx household, she found Cook's sister in her walking-out clothes, viciously jabbing a hatpin into a tiny straw hat. 'You have just caught me – I'm leaving this place, and I can't say I'm sorry!' These last words were shouted up the stairs from the kitchen. Rebecca followed her into the street, still carrying the basket. A cart stood outside, with a patient horse before it, and even more patient-looking man holding the reins. He reached down to take the basket from Rebecca, and she drew away. 'Its fine, miss, this is my William.' Hilda then climbed up beside the quiet man and took the proffered hamper from Rebecca's hands. 'William is my husband now.' She blushed with pride with those words. We got married last week. When Mrs Marx found out she let me go. After five years of service – service – ha! Hard labour more like!'

Once again Hilda was shouting, this time at the blind windows of the house, and Rebecca heard the gentle accent of William saying to his new wife, 'Now then, Hilda. We just get to start our life together earlier. It will all work out for the best.' Hilda leaned close to him and squeezed his arm as he flicked the reins and the cart pulled away with a lurch. Rebecca watched as another part of her life changed forever. Suddenly Hilda jumped down from the cart, almost being hit by an omnibus, and ran back to Rebecca. She pulled an envelope from her sleeve. 'Please take this to my sister – it will tell her everything!' She hugged Rebecca tightly. 'Shalom!' Rebecca watched until the cart disappeared around a corner, and headed back for home.

CHAPTER 8

Rebecca was woken suddenly from her reverie by the jolt of the carriage and screech of the wheels as the train pulled into Holborn Viaduct Station. She had arrived in London! Anna Coren smiled at her as she reached towards the leather handle of the carriage door. 'Wait. The platform is too crowded. We can give it a few minutes and we will find it much easier to make our way out.' Anna Coren seemed perfectly at ease, and for some reason this surprised Rebecca. She sat back in her seat, clutching her purse, and studied her surroundings. From what she could see of it through the window, the station seemed huge to her. She could make out at least five platforms. Above their train was a canopy which kept in the sound and the steam as it billowed out along the platform. She could feel her breathing accelerating, her heart pumping harder. This was a place of technology, of science and industry. This was London. She could imagine no place for the Angel Azriel here. She pushed the thought from her mind and the carriage door open as she took her first step into the thundering heart of the British Empire.

Once they were out in the street, she froze, unable to move because of the overwhelming array of sights, sounds and, most pungently, smells assailing her senses. The buildings around the station seemed immense, perhaps seven or even eight storeys tall. The viaduct itself spanned the street, which was teeming with traffic. She could see people, private carriages, hansom cabs, double-decker omnibuses with their curving staircases at the back, the top deck open to the elements. She stared. Where had all these people come from, and where could they all be running to in such a rush? Suddenly Anna Coren pulled her away from the road, just before a cab rattled by and splattered the pavement where she had been with a liberal dollop of straw and horse dung. Rebecca found her hand in that of Anna Coren and herself being guided away from the pavement's edge and through the portico of the hotel located directly behind them. Instantly the hubbub died away, to be replaced with a more subdued set of sounds, muffled by the carpeted entrance hall. Anna Coren called to a nearby bellboy. 'We wish to take tea.' She looked down at her hand as if surprised to find Rebecca's was still there. Both women released their grip simultaneously, and followed the bellboy into the lounge, where they seated themselves on a low settee close to the fireplace.

Fortified by a pot of Darjeeling, Rebecca took in her changed surroundings with more care, and studied the change which had taken place in Anna Coren. She seemed more at ease, more commanding, and strangely younger than she seemed in the home. She suddenly realised that she knew virtually nothing about this woman, and made a mental note to discover more about her from Cook when she got back – whenever that might be.

As Rebecca mused quietly, Anna Coren had somehow summoned the waiter, paid their bill and ordered transportation to Miriam's house in Bloomsbury. Once installed safely inside the growler, they headed through the crowded streets towards the final destination for the day, Gower Street – and Aunt Miriam.

Both women stayed locked within the thoughts of their own head for the journey. Rebecca tried to take in the sights of the now darkening winter streets, and Anna Coren watched her – wondering whether this young woman would be a friend or an enemy to her in the future. For now, she mused, it would have to be enough for neutral ground to be established, and for Rebecca to be safely elsewhere. For now, at least. Anna Coren smiled over to her companion, and leaned towards her so as to look out of the same window at the streets around them. 'I do believe we are almost there! Are you excited, Rebecca?' Rebecca smiled with her lips but not her eyes, saying nothing, and turned her head away all the better to feast her eyes on the sights of the London streets.

The house in Gower Street was imposing, positioned as it was on the corner of Henry Street. Rebecca waited on the pavement while Anna Coren reached up to pay the cloaked cabbie and watched as he tipped his cap to her and then clicked his tongue to signal for the horses to walk on. With the darkness the fog had descended, and the sound of hooves seemed louder on the cobbles as they clopped off into the deepening smog. She turned now to look at the house. The bricks on the facade had been blackened by soot. The tall windows were shuttered from within. The front door was at street level, unlike their home in Ramsgate. Above she saw a semicircle of glass, the wooden frame within describing a sunrise, an impression deepened by the pale yellow light which could be seen through it. The pathway from pavement to the door itself was like a bridge, tiled in black and white, and surrounded by spear-topped railings which continued along the front of the whole building. As Rebecca crossed the bridge to her next life she looked below to see dim lights showing from the servants' quarters, and a momentary vision of two figures down there, seated closed together at the kitchen table, seemingly reading the same book.

As Rebecca stood at the threshold, the door opened suddenly. The draught from within pulled a low curl of smog into the hallway from the street which momentarily swirled around the woman standing there holding the door open, making her look eerily insubstantial. The voice, however, immediately dispelled the impression of any ethereality, loud and strident as it was. 'Come, come, *do* come in! This pestilential air is *lethal!*' This extraordinary figure stuck her head out of the doorway, seemed to look down the street from left to right, nodded swiftly and then pulled Rebecca into the hallway, before signalling to Anna Coren that she had better hurry inside too. Aunt Miriam – for it was apparently she who had opened her own front door – then turned her back on them before marching down the corridor. She headed directly for the end of the house and then down the back stairs. 'Do come! Come, come, come us on!' Rebecca found herself smiling in spite of the numerous lapses of protocol. No, actually, she was smiling *because* of them. She had a sudden realisation, she was going to enjoy it here. It was certainly going to be different from Ramsgate.

Now ensconced in her bedroom, she reviewed the events of the day. Aunt Miriam had indeed taken them both below-stairs, where they ate at the scrubbed kitchen table, next to the warmth of the range. There was no sign of the two figures she thought she had seen from the street. 'It's vegetable curry,' exclaimed her hostess, lifting the lid from the pot which was simmering away atop the range. She opened a small iron door beneath the hob and, using her skirt to protect her hand from the heat, brought out three warm bowls, which she proceeded to fill herself with a ladle which was hanging on the wall. There appeared to be no servants around, in fact the house seemed empty apart from them, and Miriam seemed to know her way around the kitchen quite competently. As if in response to her thoughts, her aunt said, 'Yes. I made this myself yesterday. I always find it tastes better the day after!'

Once the bowls of delicious-smelling soup were on the table, Miriam seated herself down before leaning over to roughly tear off a piece of the loaf which was sitting there, covered by a towel, smelling wonderful and evidently fresh out of the oven. 'It's okay, Anna, you can eat it. Nothing to offend your kosher sensibilities on this table.' Rebecca watched this exchange between the two women. It was obvious to her that Miriam knew Anna Coren, and from the way she elected to tease her, knew her quite well. She watched as the two women chatted amiably enough, topics veering from enquiring about each other's health, about the talk of more and deeper railway lines being dug beneath London (Miriam vehemently asserted that enough was enough and London would certainly collapse if this happened), about the various merits of a vegetarian versus meat diet, to other minutiae of life in general. Even so, Rebecca could feel the conversation was brittle. Both women were on thin ice and seemed to be keeping a distance from one another for fear of being pulled by the undercurrents below.

She found herself suppressing a yawn. It had felt like a lifetime since she had left Ramsgate, and she was now warm, full and the tiredness which had threatened to overwhelm her was now winning its battle. Miriam looked up at her from her seat at the other end of the table, a piece of bread used to wipe out the remnants of her soup momentarily dropped into the bowl. She pulled it out, thoughtfully, and, slowly lifting it to her mouth she began to chew, unhurriedly, studying Rebecca as she did. After what seemed like an age she addressed Rebecca for the first time since she had pulled her over the threshold. 'You have your mother's eyes, Rebecca. She had the same expression that's on your face now. Like she was seeing into your soul.' Suddenly she rose and clapped her hands together. 'Come, come, come us on! Bed for you, young woman. Immediately. We have a long and *very* busy day ahead of us!'

From her bed, Rebecca looked once more into the unfamiliar shadows of the bedroom where she had been taken. Someone had emptied her trunk and put her clothes away neatly on the shelves and hanging spaces of the small garderobe. She smiled, remembering how she had read the word in a book of medieval poetry and discovered that it was also the name for a toilet in those days. She had already checked beneath her bed for the reassuring shape of a chamber-pot, and was comforted to see a brightly glazed gazunder covered delicately with a bead-edged cloth in readiness in case she didn't fancy the journey to the bathroom in the darkness.

The other contents of her trunk had been placed around the room. The mother-of-pearl-backed hairbrush and hand-mirror were on the night stand next to the bowl and jug that she would use for her ablutions. Her small collection of books she had selected to accompany her had been placed within easy reach on her bedside table. Her mother's *Baedekers Guide to London*, *The Sentiment of Flowers*, and Samuel's last gift of *On the Origin of Species* were all piled neatly together. The fire had been recently lit, the bed had fresh linen, and someone had thoughtfully placed a tiny posy of red and yellow wild roses; some of the petals had already fallen by the books. *Excitement,* she yawned. *Red and yellow roses together mean excitement.* This was the last thought in her mind as she fell into a deep and dreamless sleep which lasted all night long.

CHAPTER 9

THE FIRST MONTH in London had flown by. When Rebecca woke from her first night in the house she discovered that Anna Coren had left the previous evening to stay at her brother Isaac's house before leaving the next day to return to Ramsgate. A scented note wishing her a pleasant stay had been left by Anna Coren for her to read at breakfast, and that was all. Rebecca felt a pang of emotion, not one which she could easily identify. Apart from anything else, she had a feeling of things left unsaid which should have been said by her. She hadn't even shown her gratitude to Anna Coren for bringing her to London, nor had she thanked her for persuading Father to let her come. She shook off the thoughts and applied her attention to breakfast instead.

Her days soon settled into a sort of routine. She would breakfast in the dining room, either alone or with Aunt Miriam, and the rest of the morning would be hers to explore her surroundings. On foot and with her mother's tattered German Baedeker guide to London in hand, she attempted to navigate the streets immediately surrounding the house. She very quickly learned that to walk around with a book (or a map) in her hand marked her out as a tourist and prey to street urchins, so she spent the first few evenings of her stay learning the map of the new locality off by heart. Miriam delighted in testing her on this. 'I swear with this knowledge you could be the first woman hansom cab driver – handsome driver indeed. Ha!' It wasn't long before Rebecca learned that Aunt Miriam was given to making pronouncements in a high voice, repeating words and expostulating loudly at the end of sentences. On the other hand, she rarely expected any commentary from Rebecca, and she soon got used to these monologues. Miriam was tall, thin, and – Rebecca thought – beautiful. True, she wasn't what you would call conventionally beautiful, in fact at some angles she could seem positively ugly, but she carried herself like a wild creature, her head and neck straining as she pushed the words out. Most wonderful of all, she dressed herself in loose, flowing robes. 'Rational dress, Rebecca. *Rational* dress. Away with the corsets and ridiculous frippery, frills and frou-frou! I will *not* have you fainting from lack of air! It's hard enough to breathe in this London fug without encasing your ribs in whalebone!'

Subsequently, the whole of the afternoon of her first day was taken by a visit from Miriam's dressmaker, who measured Rebecca for, as she put it, 'Clothing for a goddess! Clothing you can breathe, think, and feel in – a wardrobe for freedom! Rational dress – for rational women!' Rebecca stood on the chair, being prodded and pulled, as Miriam and the dressmaker busied themselves around her. They talked until they were breathless, but beneath all this movement Rebecca could feel that this was something quite important. Rational dress. No more corsets, no more physical restrictions. She smiled as she wondered what would be the look on Father's face when he saw her new London wardrobe. Miriam and the dressmaker reflected her smile and she raised her arms as instructed, a compliant goddess of rationality giving silent benediction to her acolytes.

For the first few days, Rebecca saw no-one else in the house except her aunt. She sensed rather than saw the two small figures she had seen on that first evening. Then, a few days after her arrival, the house burst into life. Noisy servants repopulated the below-stairs and Rebecca suddenly found herself the centre of attraction. It transpired that, once a year, Miriam would send her household to the seaside – to take the waters and enjoy the invigorating effects of long walks and fresh air. Whatever they had actually been doing, they all seemed in good spirits. 'Lovely woman, Madam is. We is all very fortunate to be in her employ. Seven years, me. Seven years in this house and never a cross word with Madam. Mind you, we is all in accordance with Madam. We is all of one mind here. Not everyone would be so accommodating to Spirit as she is.' Rebecca smiled awkwardly, and backed out of the kitchen, allowing the well-organised traffic of the household to continue undisturbed.

She elected to spend the next morning in the Reading Room of the nearby British Museum. She wore her travelling clothes, complete with corset. As she walked she pondered whether she would ever feel comfortable enough to venture out in the street wearing the new rational-style clothes Miriam's dressmaker had made for her. Taking a deep breath, she walked up the steps to the Reading Room. Entry required a library ticket. This was a much desired item, and had to be applied for in advance and in writing. It transpired that the recipient of this prized access would be asked to explain why they needed access, and even then their request might be rejected. Somehow, Aunt Miriam had predicted her need to read and had written on her behalf. With no small anxiety, Rebecca entered this temple of words without a sound.

Once inside, she handed in her letter to the silent doorman who disappeared noiselessly into an inner office, closing the door behind him. She took a seat, noticing all the other occupants of the room were men. As calmly as she could, she opened up her purse and pulled out Samuel's book – and started to read. After some minutes, the door opened again, and all eyes went to the clerk as he walked to Rebecca and reverentially handed her a coveted ticket with which she could use the library. 'Be so good as to follow me, miss,' he intoned, and led her through the door into the library itself. Rebecca could feel the envy following her out of the waiting room. She hurried to catch up with the clerk who was now winding his way through desks occupied by silent readers. 'Here you go, miss. The Ladies Section.' He pointed to a single bookcase, and a row of three tables with a painted sign saying *Ladies only*, next to which a single woman was seated, almost hidden behind a pile of heavy, old volumes. Rebecca stared at the sign, momentarily transfixed. She turned to speak to the clerk but he was gone. Feeling dejected and angry, she turned to leave. 'Don't pay any attention to the sign. It never stopped any of us.' The seated woman looked up and swept her hand across the empty tables as if they were fully occupied. 'Well. Blow me! There were more of us when I last looked.' She leaned back and rubbed hard at her neck. 'Here, let me show you round. No bugger else will round here.'

Clarissa Fanshawe – for this was the name attached to this curious woman – was studying to be a teacher at Bedford College, the renowned London teaching establishment for ladies. 'Teaching is nothing more than a route to give me access to knowledge, though, my dear. My passion is religion, dear Rebecca. None of that Judeo-Christian nonsense,' she declared, before filling her mouth with more teacake. 'Goddess worship – Earth religion. Far more logical – after all, woman is the creator of life!' She and Rebecca had spent a surprisingly companionable morning in the Reading Room speaking in whispers to each other and ignoring the glares from the male occupants as they flagrantly ignored the 'Ladies' Section' and drew down books from all around the library. After a few hours of glorious immersion in these volumes, and watching Clarissa scribble furiously in her notebooks, Clarissa suggested that they make their way around the corner to Grape Street and the comparative seclusion of a tearoom there where they could talk more freely. Clarissa, Rebecca had noticed, like Aunt Miriam, was wearing rational dress. On her it looked nice, womanly. It seemed to really suit her, mainly, Rebecca decided, because it allowed her to move differently from women in corsets. She began to review her feelings about her new wardrobe and decided that once the dressmaker had finished her work she would contemplate giving it a try for herself.

Squashed together in the cheap tearoom, she observed her new friend as she chatted to her of her life in London. Clarissa lived in 'The Residence' in York Street with her fellow students – *So convenient for college – all I have to do is walk downstairs!* – which she described like a boarding school for women, ruled, apparently, with a rod of iron by a formidable matron, Mrs Margaret Burton. An indomitable and elegant figure with a shock of beautiful white hair. *She is more of a housemother, really.*

Always to be addressed as Mrs Burton, never Margaret, or Maggie as the students called her affectionately behind her back, she was an ever present feature of Clarissa's stories about life at Bedford College. 'She is supposed to teach us home-management and accounts, and suchlike, but basically we all pitch in with cooking and cleaning. She is an Owenite – a respectable Socialist – don't you know. Amazing woman.' She looked down at her empty plate and then up at Rebecca. 'Would you think me terribly rude if I order some more food?' She called over the waitress as Rebecca watched her. There had been no mention of family and Rebecca thought it would be impolite to ask. Besides, from the look of Clarissa's clothing, and the alacrity with which she allowed Rebecca to pay their bill, it was fairly obvious that she did not have much money. No matter. Rebecca did and she was more than happy to spend it in the company of her new friend.

When Clarissa had finished eating, she sat back in her chair and rubbed her stomach appreciatively. 'So. How about you signing up as a student at Bedford next year?' Rebecca stared at her. 'Me? I … well … I don't know. What would I study?' Clarissa leaned over and rested a hand firmly on her shoulder. 'Anything you want, Rebecca. This is London – the centre of the Empire – of the world – and the world is changing!' Once outside in the street, Clarissa invited her to walk around the corner to Museum Street to collect a book which she had ordered from a specialist bookshop there. They walked companionably, making occasional comments about the others in the streets. As they neared the British Museum itself the foot traffic started to change. 'Tourists!' exclaimed Clarissa. 'A bloody nuisance if you ask me!' As they rounded the corner to Museum Street, a blackened street-Arab ran full tilt into Clarissa, knocking her down. The next moment a surprisingly agile matron came into view who then shook her umbrella into the crowd in the direction the boy had taken. 'Damn thieves. Almost had him too!'

She looked around her and saw Clarissa on the ground. 'What you doing down there, Clara, old thing?' And with that wonderful pronouncement she reached out her hand, hauled her upright and dusted off her skirt. 'No bones broken, I take it? Your book arrived, by the way.' Without waiting to find out if Clarissa was fine or not, she turned to the road and pushed out her umbrella, before stepping out into the path of an oncoming hansom which gave no indication it was going to slow down. 'Well come along, ladies. What are you waiting for?'

CHAPTER 10

THE ATLANTIS BOOKSHOP on Museum Street was small and plain enough to be ignored by the passing tourists, but suitably central for it to have become a hub for all things esoteric said Clarissa. *If you seek knowledge, it will be given to you here – but choose carefully what it is you wish to learn.* This pronouncement sounded oddly rehearsed. It was, however, said with no small amount of pride.

Once within its door Clarissa made a half-hearted attempt to brush the street dirt from her shoes, and Geraldine Beskin, the owner of the establishment, put down her umbrella, hung up her cloak and positioned herself into the rattan chair in the far corner of the shop whence she could watch both the shop itself and the streetscape. When she had first come into view, bearing down on them and berating the thief, she had seemed both large and formidable, but here in the shop she displayed a different aspect. Motionless. Serene. Smaller and less visible – somehow. In some ways she seemed oddly cat-like. Rebecca realised immediately that this was not someone to underestimate. She noticed with surprise that she really wanted Geraldine to like her, but felt that this was probably unlikely to happen. The best she could hope for was for her respect. On reflection, she would prefer it.

Rebecca took in her surroundings properly now. By the chair was a small, baize-covered table on which sat a reading lamp, a small pile of tattered volumes, and a teapot. The light from the lamp created an aura around Geraldine's plaited hair. She made no attempt to speak, but watched closely as Rebecca proceeded to fill her eyes with the extraordinary titles on the spines of the books around her. *The Pythagorean Triangle – Or the Science of Numbers* by George Oliver; *The Occult Sciences – The Philosophy of Magic, Prodigies and Apparent Miracles, Vol. 1 of 2* by Eusèbe Salverte; *The Rosicrucian Dream Book – Containing Solutions of Over Three Thousand Different Dreams* by Paschal Beverly Randolph.

She continued to study the shop, watched now by both Geraldine and Clarissa. It seemed to be little more than a room, albeit one filled to the ceiling with books. It had the smell of the Reading Room, but somehow it felt more appealing, more alive. Geraldine had not moved since she had taken her seat, in fact she was extraordinarily still. Only her sparkling eyes moved as she watched Rebecca walk around the room, touching some of the books gently. As if reading Rebecca's thoughts, the statue spoke. 'The books can come to life when you read them. Not before, and not everyone can understand them to make it happen. That's the beauty. That's the magic.' From the shelf by her side Rebecca pulled out a small volume. Geraldine's eyes narrowed, but she still didn't move. Rebecca read the title. Out loud. In Hebrew as it was written on the cover. Geraldine leaned forward in her chair and touched the teapot as if testing its temperature. 'Jonathon,' she called, summoning an as yet unseen individual from a back room. 'Tea for three, I think.'

By the time Rebecca left Atlantis, it had become dark outside, and the smog was rising around her. She hurried back to Gower Street, vowing not to let time slip like that again. She had no desire to be out in the streets when she could no longer see the pavement before her. She arrived at her aunt's house just as the door was being opened to a large and bearded gentleman. Unlike the night of her arrival, the door was opened by a slight, dark-skinned youth. He was dressed in Indian robes and wore a turban on his head. Behind him was another stranger, a strikingly similar young woman. A twin, perhaps? She, in turn, took the cloak and cane of the unknown visitor, while her brother held the door open for Rebecca. The bearded visitor seemed to know his own way around the house, and headed off into the drawing room, from where a substantial amount of noise was now emanating.

'Good evening, miss. I trust you had a good day?' chimed the twins, bowing and introducing themselves respectively as Karim and Aisha. She realised these were the two shapes she had seen in the kitchen that first evening. Without waiting for her reply the door was closed behind her and they indicated that she was to follow the bearded gent into the drawing room. Rebecca stared back at this exotic pair, and wondered what other surprises she would encounter in this house. She didn't have to wait long to find out.

Peeping into the drawing room, she could see six people in there: four men and two women, and all of them seemed to be talking at the same time. Her aunt was not among them, and Rebecca had no idea who any of these people were, or indeed what they were doing in the Gower Street drawing room. She stood by the doorway, undecided as to whether to go in, or retreat to her room before anyone had noticed her. Deciding retreat would be the most sensible course of action, she took a step back and found the doorway blocked by her aunt who had just appeared. 'Excellent, excellent, dear girl! So glad you made it back in time. We need you to balance the energies. Now then everyone, come us on!' With that the room quietened, everyone rose and started to seat themselves around the large pedestal table which usually resided at the corner of the room, but had now been arranged in the centre. Rebecca was thoroughly perplexed. What was going on? The table was not set for a meal, nor for a game of cards; besides, the table was really quite crowded with everyone sitting there. Three chairs had been left empty, one of which had a posy on the table before it. Rosemary *for remembrance*, white chrysanthemum *for truth*, and a piece of oak with acorns on it. That was one she didn't know. She would have to look that up later in her copy of *The Sentiment of Flowers*. Her aunt led her to the two empty chairs which were next to one another, and motioned her to sit down in one. Surprisingly, Aunt Miriam seated herself in the other. Rebecca had assumed that she would take the place where the posy had been put, but it remained empty. The turbaned youth then entered the room and closed the thick, heavy curtains, plunging the room into virtual darkness. As he did, his sari-clad counterpart walked into the room carrying a lit candelabrum, her dark features illuminated in flickering candlelight. It was placed on the sideboard, and through the mirror behind it, Rebecca could see the girl's face clearly. Although the girl Aisha had very dark skin, she had blue eyes. Startlingly blue. Momentarily they looked at one another through the dim mirror, before the girl reached up and covered the glass with a black cloth. The only other light in the room was from the fire in the grate. Rebecca felt her senses heightening. She wanted to ask her aunt where the twins had come from, and indeed what they were doing here, in this house, but as she turned to speak, the servants left the room, closing the door behind them.

At this, everyone around the table reached out onto the table-top and joined hands with their neighbour, bowing their heads as they did. Rebecca felt her aunt reach out for her, and the person to her left do the same. Her hands were guided to the table-top. Suddenly she felt frightened. The clock ticked loudly, the fire hissed, and the inhabitants of the room stayed motionless. This tableau was interrupted by the mantle clock chiming seven. The door was opened, all looked up, and the light from the hallway flooded into the room. The silhouette of a woman stood there. Nothing more than an outline framed by the light, she paused dramatically before sweeping into the room with Karim walking slowly in front of her. He pulled out her chair and she took her seat, grasping the hands of her neighbours as she did so. 'Bless this circle and all souls within. We welcome all who come to communicate in good spirit. Surround us herein with light and peace and all who choose to enter this light must leave their darkness elsewhere...' She continued for some moments, while the Indian boy walked slowly around the table, periodically bringing together tiny cymbals which made a discordant chiming sound. '...We invoke all angels of light to come to us this evening and surround this circle. Protect us from any harm from within or without.' Rebecca felt her body spasm at the mention of angels, and her aunt opened her eyes to stare at her quizzically. She felt her hand being squeezed reassuringly, but Rebecca's panic was starting to rise. She tried to pull her hand away from her aunt, but instead of allowing this to happen, her aunt gripped harder, closed both eyes and bowed her head.

CHAPTER 11

IT WAS SOME weeks later, and finally Rebecca had plucked up the courage to go into Atlantis Bookshop without Clarissa. In fact, she had seen very little of Clarissa since their first encounter in the Reading Room. 'I have to study, dear girl, and you are far too much of a distraction! We can go and have tea together again in the Christmas holiday, that is if you will still be in London?' Her question had now raised one of her own – no-one had actually mentioned how long she was going to be there with her aunt. It was now the last week of November and the street smells of the capital had started to change. The scent of roasting chestnuts heralded a different phase in the city. When she had first arrived here she had thought that – unlike in the countryside around Ramsgate with its changing crops and colours – it would be harder to distinguish the changing seasons in London. In fact, it was just that the signs were different. Smells changed, the people walking around the Museum changed, as did the visitors to Gower Street. The more able she became in blindly navigating the streets, the more she grew to enjoy being in this smelly, noisy but exciting place. Ramsgate really was a different world, narrow and dark.

Since that first experience of a séance, Rebecca had attended three more. Once a week, the same group met in the drawing room and, with the steady mediumship of Mrs Fairbrother, they tried to make contact with their dead loved ones. After the séance, tea, biscuits and sherry were proffered. Those who preferred their spirit 'in a bottle' were offered a glass of sherry. This joke was a constant at each event. She hadn't found it amusing the first time and repetition had failed to improve its flavour. Rebecca found herself trapped between Mrs Tiran and Mrs Thorne, the vocal widows who were having a heated debate about the current seating arrangements for the circle. In the end, Colonel Burbridge, the ever present bearded gentlemen, stepped in and settled the discussion. 'My dear ladies, you are both very aware of the necessity to alternate those with a passive energy with those of a more active one in the circle.' He raised his hand as both opened their mouths as if to speak, '... And no. I do not believe that passive necessarily equals female. Some of the most passive individuals I have known have been men – let me tell you – even in Her Majesties Armed Forces, and some of the most ferociously active have been women. Dash it all!' He teased them both until they became united in flirting with him, and all was well once more. Privately he believed that men were more suited to active power, while women were inclined towards passive influence, hence the predominance of female mediums. However, Colonel Burbridge was a lonely man, and the desire to be liked was stronger than his need to be correct so he kept his counsel.

Conversation post-séance veered from the mundane, such as the increasing numbers and varying qualities of Spiritualist periodicals, to the numinous, such as whether one advocated a Swedenborgian approach as opposed to Owenite values. Rebecca was not interested in the former and didn't understand the latter so she quickly learned to make herself scarce by claiming tiredness, once the formal part of the evening was concluded. She intuited that this was not the sort of event which her Angel Azriel would be inclined to attend. At no point had she ever felt herself slipping away. She remained fully engaged with the present.

Her aunt did not talk about the séances and strangely nor did Rebecca ask. Once she grew accustomed to the events it seemed almost rude of her to start asking questions. So it was that a month after her arrival she decided to go and ask the only other person whom she felt might be able to shed some light on these happenings.

A few days after she made her way to the bookshop in Museum Street. The Museum being closed that day, the streets were relatively quiet. Rebecca pushed open the door of the Atlantis Bookshop and walked in. The shop was empty, but the sound of the doorbell announced her arrival. She waited for some moments, and looking around noticed that there had been a change since her first visit. Another, smaller chair had been brought into the shop and was now located at the other side of the small, baize table. The table was bare of books, and the teapot was also missing. Only the reading lamp and a single book waited. Feeling in no small way like Alice in Wonderland, she walked slowly over to the table and picked up the book. No-one had appeared yet, so she sat down and started to read the volume in her hands. *Spiritualism – Its Facts and Phases; Illustrated With Personal Experiences by J. H. Powell.* On the frontispiece her eye was caught by a quote from Milton: 'Millions of spirits walk the world unseen.' Geraldine appeared, and Rebecca started to rise from her seat. 'How did you know?' Geraldine smiled momentarily and signalled for Rebecca to be seated, took her seat on the other side of the table and settled into her rattan chair as the silent Jonathon slid a tray onto the table with everything necessary for tea for two. Tea was poured and drunk, more tea was ordered. An hour or more passed while Rebecca read about Spiritualism, its relationship to theology and to science, and finally about the spirit medium. Neither woman spoke. One man came into the shop, and left almost immediately. Another walked in, and Jonathon attended to his request, his voice rarely reaching more than a whisper. The shop had the atmosphere of a church rather than a retail establishment, and those who came in seeking knowledge seemed to instinctively respond to this atmosphere. Rebecca felt safe here.

Finally, she looked up from the book. Geraldine spoke first. 'So. What are your questions?' Rebecca paused before speaking. There were so many of them. First of all, how did Geraldine know what she wanted to learn about? How did she know that she would come? Why did people want to communicate with the dead? She had many more to ask, but, on reflection, she knew that the quality of her question would be important. That is if she wanted to have a teacher. If she asked the right question, she would be able to ask more. She closed the book on her lap, her forefinger trapped between its pages as a bookmark. 'Who is Mr Home?'

Geraldine laughed. It was a surprising sound, more like a child than a matron. 'Now then, you're enough to make a stuffed parrot laugh!' She paused and looked Rebecca in the eye. 'On reflection, young woman, it *is* the right question to ask. Mr Daniel Dunglas Home, to give him his full moniker, is a spirit medium. A real one. Not one of these charlatans who pretend to connect to spirit and make vague and ridiculous pronouncements about life on the other side. Disembodied hands and fruit falling from the ceiling? Ridiculous! Nothing more than smoke and mirrors!'

Over the next hour, after more tea and a swift visit to the

privy, Rebecca told the bookseller about the séances at her aunt's house. Geraldine said little, only interjecting to ask the name of the medium. She snorted in derision, but made Rebecca continue her recitation of the evening's events before eventually speaking. When she did, her question took Rebecca by surprise. 'Did you feel anything?' Rebecca reviewed her emotional experience of the event. 'No. Should I have?' Geraldine rose from her seat. 'Time for a perambulation around the park, don't you think? Clear the tubes.'

A silent circuit around Russell Square brought them in front of a cab shelter, with four, driverless hansoms on the street. The drivers congregated under the shelter were chatting and laughing with one another. On seeing Geraldine, they went silent. 'Mistress Beskin,' said a tall, thin man touching his cap. The others followed suit. 'Master Kepple. How does your youngest boy?' A genial conversation ensued with the driver enthusiastically telling how the boy was now in the rudest of health, and back to terrorising his siblings. As the two women walked away from the shelter, Rebecca took a sideways glimpse at Geraldine. 'Not everyone can afford a doctor, and there are many in this city whose memories stretch into the past when their families lived a simpler life in the countryside. There is still a room for Cunning Women even at the heart of the Empire.' Rebecca's face remained impassive. It would seem her companion was a witch. 'Yes. I helped the boy recover from fever. Some simple suggestions and a tincture. That's all I gave the family – apart from hope – and that is priceless. Who knows,' she continued, her eyes twinkling, 'he could have recovered without my help. Sometimes the best thing to do is to do nothing and let nature take its course. Try telling that to a parent, though.' Suddenly she turned and headed back to the cab shelter. 'Master Kepple, we need to get to Mornington Street, post-haste. Can you oblige?'

The journey to Camden Town took almost an hour. While they travelled, Geraldine gave Rebecca her thoughts on the 'craze' of Spiritualism. There are genuine mediums, and there are charlatans, she said. Sadly, the charlatans outnumber those who can truly see spirit. Rebecca felt her cheeks darkening with anxiety as her companion continued to speak. Geraldine continued to look out of the window. Without turning, she said, 'I know you have the sight, Rebecca. It isn't something you can hide from those who are willing and able to look.' She drew her gaze back from the street scene and looked directly at Rebecca. In an action which echoed Samuel the last time she had seen him, Geraldine touched Rebecca's forehead between her eyes. 'You have an eye here, a third eye. One which, I feel, has opened many times before, and you have been afraid of what you saw. There is nothing to fear if you are willing to learn. To open all your senses. There are more things in heaven and earth than are dreamed of in your philosophy. Shakespeare knew. Some say he had the sight too, but chose to channel it into his art.'

The hansom cab had not moved for some time. Mr Kepple craned his head around. 'Apologies, ladies, there is a dead 'orse in the road. Dropped dead pulling the number seventeen omnibus from Regent Street. Mr Atchelor's meat-men haven't come yet to clear the carcase so I suggests you walk from here. It ain't far.' Helping them both down onto the pavement, Geraldine reached for her purse. Mr Kepple took off his hat and, gripping it in both hands, he said, 'Wouldn't dream of it, Mistress. Our Bertie would be in his grave by now if you hadn't come. I will wait for you at the 'ouse.' Geraldine nodded imperceptibly, and they headed off towards Mornington Street, leaving the cabbie on the pavement wiping his forehead with his sleeve with a distinct look of relief on his face. Geraldine laughed when Rebecca mentioned it. 'Some folks are only glad to see you when they have a problem. For the rest of the time they would rather you disappeared!'

As they continued along the street, they passed the corpse of the horse which had impeded their journey. Its ribs were pronounced and the chaffing of harness was in evidence all along the body. It wouldn't be in the street for long, though. Already the body was being cut up by passers-by alert to the presence of fresh horse-meat. A scuffle broke out between two women who both laid claim to the flank. Rebecca shuddered as she looked away from the scene and watched the blood of the wretched creature pour out into the gutter.

As she crossed the road after her companion, pulling her cloak away from the gory pool, she realised that she had no idea where they were going. As if in response to her unspoken enquiry, Geraldine said, 'We are off to find you some answers – or perhaps to create more questions.' She turned to look at Rebecca's still puzzled face. 'Why, my dear,' Geraldine smiled at her confusion, 'we are going to see Mr Home of course.'

CHAPTER 12

Number 20 Mornington Street was a surprisingly noisy establishment. Part residence, part laboratory, the sound of the doorbell seemed to be a constant during their visit, creating an impression of urgency and efficiency within its walls. This was not Mr Home's home – how many times had that play on words been made, Rebecca wondered? – but the home of Mr William Crookes, scientist and investigator. After a short dialogue with the surly butler, the visitors were ushered into the hallway.

The aforementioned Mr Crookes did not seem at all surprised when Geraldine arrived at the house to see Mr Home, nor did he enquire as to why she had brought Rebecca, but, with great pride, he proceeded to take them through to the back of the house along a corridor which displayed a number of barometers, and showed them to his laboratory rooms. 'I will prove the existence of spirit! I know and have seen and felt its presence for myself, many, many times, but there are those in the scientific community who will only believe it when these events are subjected to rigorous scrutiny.' Here he flung open the door to a room on one side of the corridor which had a weighing-scale with some sort of bed fixed to it, and another room opposite in which could be seen a table that appeared to have some kind of metal cage. It was the sort of cage you would usually find chickens in, but in this instance there was nothing more than a large accordion. Mr Crookes wandered into the room and touched it reverentially. He began to explain the purpose of this contraption (in unasked for and laborious detail) – that it was a mechanism to demonstrate that the accordion could be played by psychical influence alone – when a delicate woman's face appeared around the door at the height of the doorknob. 'William! Where are your manners? Ladies, please do follow me and forgive my husband's dreadful lapses. He does get *so* caught up in his investigations he would forget his head if it were loose. We shall take tea in the drawing room.' With that, she ushered both women out of the laboratory, just as their host began to tinker with the cage. Simultaneously and with a backward push of his foot he closed the door behind them carelessly. He appeared to have completely forgotten their existence. Rebecca stared at the closed door with a great deal of bemusement.

Mr Crookes, his wife Esther explained with a gentle sigh, had a compulsion to investigate. With a resigned air she cleared away copies of *Chemical News* which were strewn on various chairs and added them to a growing pile in the corner of the room. She signalled for them all to sit, and while they took tea, she expounded on her husband's theories about spirit, and how it would eventually be proven scientifically through the investigation of plasma and the suchlike. It seemed thanks to his publication of his findings that she was used to random people turning up to the house at odd times of the day and having to explain the goings-on therein. Emboldened by her hostess's openness, Rebecca asked her if they themselves were Spiritualists. Esther put down her cup and saucer carefully, wiped away some invisible crumbs from her dress and looked hard at Rebecca. Yes, she replied. They were *both* Spiritualists. It helped and supported their Christian faith, especially after Philip she explained, William's younger brother, had 'been gathered into the arms of the Lord far too soon'. After his brother's death from yellow fever, William had attended a séance and spoken with him, and from then on both man and wife had become active in the Spiritualist movement. 'Although William is more active than me.'

That phrase had stuck in Rebecca's mind, and she asked Geraldine about it during their cab ride back to Museum Street. It seemed that William had not endeared himself to the Spiritualist community when he had become somewhat possessive of one of the better known (some would say notorious) mediums, a certain Miss Florence Cook, and her spirit guide Katie. He insisted on being present at all of her demonstrations, and, according to some of the matrons (of both sexes), he would take liberties with Katie. William Crookes would touch her astral body and allow her to sit on his lap and kiss him on the mouth. According to his wife she 'fully comprehended' his actions, as it was done all in the spirit of scientific investigation, and not by way of sensual titillation. Others weren't so sure about that, and he had been somewhat ostracised for his behaviour. However, Geraldine continued, these activities were not uncommon at demonstrations of mediumistic skills. Mediums were frequently women, and so were their spirit guides. For some these 'demonstrations' were little more than a way for a working woman to make some cash by letting wealthy men have a fondle of their bodies in a nice dark room. 'Obviously a spirit wouldn't wear a corset, and the more diaphanous and otherworldly a garment, the more believable a spirit they made.' There were others who specialised in materialising fruit, or vegetables, smells, or faces and hands of dead relatives. Tricks. Nothing more. These were much worse than the women who encouraged the tuzzy-muzzy-fondlers, she expounded, warming to her subject. At least those women provided a service and they weren't lying to vulnerable folks mourning their dead. Rebecca didn't dare ask what a tuzzy-muzzy was, but she had a good enough idea to smile at her companion's colourful outburst.

During tea, their host William Crookes wandered into the drawing room and absently helped himself to a large slice of sponge cake from the tea tray and a *Chemical Times* from the top of the pile. 'In the accordion room,' he mumbled through a mouthful of crumbs. 'Daniel is expecting you. Do go on through.' Turning to thank their hostess, Rebecca saw Mr Crookes throw himself down on the couch by his wife. Esther Crookes turned her head away and studied the carpet, acknowledging the visitors' gratitude for the tea with the limpest wave of her hand.

'My dear Mrs Beskin! How completely excellent it is to see you on this dullest of days!' The figure who, until moments before, had been sprawled wanly across the table, leapt up and grasped both Geraldine's hands in his. 'You radiate positive energy. Always. Wonderful!' and with that he slumped back onto the chair, as if exhausted by his own enthusiasm. 'I have brought someone to meet you. Mr Home, may I present Miss Zimmerman.' He turned towards Rebecca, looked straight past her, and, stretched out his hand, fingers splayed, eyes wide in fright. He began to scream.

The door burst open and William Crookes threw himself into the room, closely followed by his wife. 'Daniel?' he cried 'What is it? What is happening here?' The figure of Daniel Dunglas Home seemed to have been petrified. His mouth was still contorted into the shape of a scream, but no sound emanated from it. His body stiff and unresponsive, he continued to point towards Rebecca, who by now felt extremely uncomfortable. Unsure of what to do next, she took her cue from Geraldine and stayed motionless, as the Crookes took over and began their ministrations on the unresponsive figure. It seemed that this had happened before. They gently rubbed his arms and legs, and, taking a hip flask from his pocket, William forced a liquid into Daniel's mouth. He moved suddenly, and started to splutter. 'William! You know it must always be whisky! I am a Scot after all!' With this, the charged atmosphere had been earthed, and everyone seemed to be more normal. They all repaired to the drawing room once more, fresh tea was ordered and some semblance of social normality arrived around the same time as the fortifying beverage.

It seemed that Mr Home had no recollection of his momentary 'fugue', nor did he seem now to be anything other than charming to Rebecca. She wasn't convinced that he was being honest, but she had nothing but her instinct to base that on. So much so that when asked by William Crookes if he would be prepared to demonstrate the accordion experiment in front of them, he seemed enthusiastic and very willing to do so. Disappointingly, nothing happened. Nothing at all. Not a sound came from the accordion, and Mr Home seemed very dejected indeed.

When the companions had almost arrived back at Museum Street, Geraldine turned to Rebecca. 'He could see it – the shadow which travels with you. You do realise that, don't you?' Rebecca nodded, her lips becoming numb at this thought. She continued her journey to Gower Street on foot, navigating easily through the fog on the streets. If only she could find her way through the fog in her mind as easily. She put the events of the day to one side, and hurried to dress for the evening. She was to attend a lecture.

Apart from mealtimes, visits from dressmakers, and the séances, Rebecca had seen relatively little of her aunt. Slowly she had come to realise that Aunt Miriam was very self-contained, to the point at which she found herself wondering why she had invited Rebecca to stay with her, so little time did they spend in one another's company. However, as the weeks went by, Rebecca became aware that she and Miriam had traits in common. Both loved to read, both enjoyed solitude and were happy to stay silent. She suddenly came to the realisation that she felt more comfortable with her aunt than with anyone else. Perhaps it would have been different if her mother had survived. Rebecca had grown up without a female influence and in some ways she hadn't really known how to behave around them. Now, with Aunt Miriam, Geraldine and Clarissa in her life, she felt she could allow herself to come out of the shadows a little. So, that morning, instead of eating in silence and leaving the house for the day, Rebecca asked Miriam what she would be doing. Her aunt looked up quizzically. 'I have my paperwork to attend to this morning, and this evening I am going to a talk at the Swedenborg Centre.' She paused and looked over at her niece. 'Would you like to come?' Even though she had no idea where that was or what it would be about, to please her aunt, Rebecca responded in the affirmative, and then left Miriam to her paperwork. The 'paperwork' in question consisted of writing up the events of the previous evening's séance, as she had done diligently on numerous occasions since Rebecca had arrived at Gower Street.

A few weeks before, Rebecca had come across some dated sheets of paper headed *Minutes of the Circle* which had fallen by the table in the sitting room, and had felt compelled to read them before handing them back to her aunt. It was interesting, she thought to herself. The events of the séances as retold by Miriam had been somewhat – well – embellished. Rebecca could state this as a fact as she had attended all of the séances since that first one and, to her, there had been nothing remotely spiritual to report. They all seemed to follow the same pattern, with a prayer, dimmed lights and irritatingly vague pronouncements about the afterlife. The medium always took herself into a state of communication with her guide, at which point they took her over and she spoke in the wheedling tones of a child. There were occasional unusual scents, and, once, even out-of-season flowers had appeared on the table. The medium, Mrs Fairbrother, speaking with Rebecca over tea after the circle was over, said that she rarely had any recollection of the events of the séance itself, nor could she remember the words which had apparently emanated from her mouth. Her apparent piety seemed somewhat diminished when Colonel Burbridge, who was a constant feature of these gatherings, explained to Rebecca that the circle would always have a collection which they gave to Mrs Fairbrother. 'She has a gift, to be sure, and the fact that she chooses to share it with us should be rewarded, in this life as well as the next,' he said, somewhat affectedly. She liked the colonel, though. He always responded graciously to her questions and took care to look her in the eye when responding. She liked that.

Rebecca had studied the shabby state of Mrs Fairbrother's cuffs and her scuffed shoes, and realised that there were more layers to this story than she was likely to uncover. The woman worked hard for the few shillings' collection. Furthermore, Rebecca had heard how some of the other women had spoken about her, and they hadn't been kind. 'She calls herself Mrs. Mind you, we have never seen nor heard of the so-called Mister Fairbrother. Five children living she has and three in the grave...' Quiet and awkward once the circle was concluded, the medium was usually ignored by those who, minutes earlier, had been breathless and silent to catch the words from her mouth as she channelled spirit within the circle. It soon became obvious to Rebecca that she was not of the same social standing as the others. Once the circle was broken, the stronger bonds of social hierarchy quickly stepped in. She vowed to be kinder to this elusive woman next time she saw her.

It was true that the evenings when there was a circle were all very convivial, and Aunt Miriam seemed to get pleasure from hosting them. Those who took part seemed to get genuine comfort, no matter how fake the content seemed to Rebecca. She herself had asked to be excused from the last séance after a red-faced and rather portly gentleman had decided to try for a different type of comfort when he took the dimmed lights as an opportunity to try to fondle Rebecca's knee. She wouldn't find *that* in the literature at Atlantis Bookshop. Rebecca found herself smiling. She was starting to relax. There was nothing to be afraid of either, and since Ramsgate she herself had not seen the Angel. Perhaps London was too crowded with its own spirits. Mr Home had sensed *something*, though, and with this memory she shuddered involuntarily.

CHAPTER 13

THE LECTURE WASN'T due to start until the evening, so Rebecca and Aunt Miriam spent the best part of the afternoon walking around the Ring in Hyde Park. 'The lungs of London, my dear. Breathe in deeply. People these days don't get enough exercise. So important to be fit in body as well as in mind. Come us on!' Miriam marched off, swinging her arms vigorously. It was true that the air quality was different here, as were the people. There were carriages cutting through the park, but, in the main, people were on foot. There were, however, a surprising number of cyclists, some of whom were women. Rebecca found herself laughing at the balloon-shaped outer-garments which they wore. 'Don't laugh, Rebecca. I considered buying such a vehicle myself.' Rebecca looked askance at her rangy aunt and smiled. 'Yes, yes I know.' Miriam countered her thoughts with the words, 'I would look like a deranged heron!' They laughed companionably and slowed their pace. Miriam pointed out an empty park bench and they settled themselves down there in silence, amicably watching varied scenes of human interaction playing out before them. It was a typical January afternoon and the wind was swirling the leaves from the naked trees, occasionally forcing a lady to grab onto her hat. The sky was clear and blue, although it was already starting to darken.

Without turning to look at Rebecca, Miriam began to speak. 'You are in no doubt of my involvement in Spiritualism, by now, and I appreciate that thus far I have not exactly been forthcoming with you. I have many reasons for my reticence, not least of which being the fact that I didn't know you. For all I knew you could have been one of those milk-weak girls with no interests outside of music and embroidery.' Both women continued to study the people in the park before them, keeping their eyes steadfastly on others, creating a safety net around their conversation. Rebecca started to relax and rested her back on the wooden bench and allowed her feet to swing freely.

Here in the open air she began to speak. The words which came first from her mouth surprised her. 'I miss my mother. What was she like, as a girl I mean?' Miriam smiled gently but did not turn to look at her. 'She was a kind, gentle and extraordinarily intelligent woman. If she had been born to another generation I am sure she would have gone to university. You are a lot like her, my dear. A lot like her. She was always studying, and asking questions.' Miriam turned and faced Rebecca. 'I liked her. No. That isn't quite right. I loved her and envied her both in the same measure. When she married your father it was a love match, and he adored her. Anyone with half an eye could see that. She also had the gift of sight – and I envied her for both.' Miriam reached over to Rebecca and tugged away at the chain around her neck, before gently stroking the locket which hung from it. She continued, quietly. 'Our matrilineal line stretches all the way to the gates of Jerusalem, to the days of the Crusaders – hence the design on this locket. Your mother had it made to remind you of who and what you are.'

Rebecca stared at the design. She had never considered it as anything more than an abstract pattern, but on studying it saw it contained the form of a figure eight with a line through the middle. She had fleeting memories of her mother's voice telling her bedtime stories about love and death, chivalry and sorcery. Stories to soothe a child into sleep. Rebecca ruminated. From the fragments which floated into her mind the stories weren't so innocent after all, but perhaps that was the German way. Rebecca pulled herself back to the present as her aunt pushed herself up suddenly from the bench. 'Perhaps tonight's lecture will help you to understand her better – and also, perhaps yourself.'

The day had slipped easily into evening. The Swedenborg Centre was a short walk away, and they left early to take a detour through the British Museum on their route to Bloomsbury Way. There they spent a pleasant hour wandering through the galleries with no aim in mind. Rebecca suddenly registered that all this history and majesty was incomplete – all the relics, all the collections were of men and about men. She could find no objects of women, or at least none in praise of them. It was as if they hadn't existed, other than as a passive mirror in which men would reflect their own glories. Detecting her change of mood, Miriam suggested that they head off to the Swedenborg Centre so as to get good seats at the lecture. Rebecca saw through the ruse but appreciated her consideration.

The atmosphere at the Swedenborg Centre was much more convivial. It felt exciting and alive, and the men and women (mainly in rational dress) were mixing freely around the tea-urn. The conversations were interspersed with laughter, and the unease of the museum dissipated in the sound of the lively banter between intelligent individuals exchanging ideas. Miriam had been drawn into the crowd by the ladies Tiran and Thorne, as they had someone for her to meet. Rebecca made her way towards the tea-urn, only to be intercepted by a young, bespectacled man who enquired whether it was her first time at the Swedenborg and if she knew of its history. On seeing her expression, he took pains to assure her that he in fact worked there, and would be delighted to give her the tour before the lecture started. Rebecca smiled at this young man's discomfort, and shortly after found herself following him around the building. 'Emanuel Swedenborg was an amazing man. Inventor, scientist and not least of all, philosopher.' Her guide warmed to his theme as he walked her through a corridor resplendent with copies of paintings and sketches by the great man himself and upstairs into a small but elegant library. 'His revelations about spirit are still to this day unsurpassed. I am a humble student of his works.' At this, Rebecca tilted her head to one side. He blushed deeply, and the sound of a bell ringing announced it was now time for the lecture to start. They hurried towards its sound, to be greeted by the upturned faces of Mesdames Tiran and Thorne (both beautifully turned in their corseted finery) at the foot of the stairs. No rational dress for these ladies – they were conservative in all things apart from their shared love of Spiritualism, and Rebecca wondered how much of that was due to the convivial nature of the evenings rather than any manifestations. Intelligent women both, she mused. She shook the ruminations out of her head, smiled and waved down at them. Confusingly, they pretended not so see her, turned quickly away and disappeared into the crowd now moving towards the lecture room. She stood for a moment, before realising what they must be thinking about her sudden appearance with a young man. Rebecca smiled to share her insight with her companion but he too was gone. She was surprised to feel disappointment. She didn't even know what he was called. Her reverie was broken by the sight of her aunt frantically waving her handkerchief to signal her to an empty seat in the front row.

Squashed tightly next to Miriam, she took a few moments to take in her surroundings. All the seats were taken, and there were people standing at the back of the room. The chamber itself was unusual. The walls were white and unadorned, with faux wooden pillars at regular intervals. The ceiling was arched but surprisingly low, adding to the impression of being aboard a ship of some kind. The dais before her was carpeted in a beautiful blue which was echoed by the arched panel behind it. At the centre of this platform was a solitary lectern. The room grew quiet, and Miriam took Rebecca's hand and squeezed it gently, before settling herself back into her chair.

After hearing so much about the speaker, Rebecca had expected him to be tall and imposing. The Reverend John Page Hopps was, however, small and slight and his hair had a reddish tinge to it. Book in hand, modestly and soberly dressed, he seemed unremarkable, but when he spoke his words were nothing short of spellbinding. Without raising his voice, he held the room enthralled. Rebecca felt herself leaning forward even from her place in the front row to make sure she didn't miss one word of his talk. She drank it all in like a parched flower. He could have been reading her mind.

'...Science is carrying us in every direction into an unseen universe, and that this unseen universe is everywhere felt to be the sphere of causes and the source and centre of all the essential elements and activities of creation...'

He spoke of future lives, of living beyond death, of consciousness and, above all, he spoke of 'the unseen universe' – a place where

Rebecca knew she could, and had, travelled to when out of her own body. She was no longer alone in her experiences.

Riveted by his words, time passed rapidly, and she was stunned to realise that nearly two hours had swept by since the talk had begun. Rebecca and Miriam rose with the audience in polite but sustained applause which the speaker barely seemed to register. He picked up the well-thumbed volume which he had carried with him and, walking slowly, left the room. The atmosphere immediately changed, and conversation broke out all around them. 'I want to speak to him, if I may?' Rebecca asked tentatively. 'Of course, my dear. You and everyone else in this room! But let's see what we can do.' With this Miriam politely but firmly began to use her elbows and height to barge her way through the crowds which were heading towards the door. Following in her aunt's wake Rebecca found herself face to face with her young guide. 'I expect you would like to meet him?' he smiled. She nodded, suddenly shy. 'Follow me.' He turned, and Rebecca signalled to Miriam to change direction, much to the irritation of the people she had just pushed past.

On entering the library, Rebecca could see nothing more than a bottom and a pair of legs. The Reverend Hopps was on his knees attempting to pull a particularly large volume from the lowest bookshelf. She couldn't help it, but she burst out laughing, and with a start, the object of her humour spun around and began to laugh too. Like Geraldine, he had a much younger laugh than his years, and when he smiled, Rebecca could tell it was genuine. He gave up his efforts to extract the book, and advanced on the trio with his arms open wide.

Tea was ordered, and the party sat together companionably at the large library table. Rebecca felt suddenly tongue-tied, but the Reverend waited patiently, and eventually Rebecca poured out her questions. 'How could it be that spirit survived? What if no-one could find the evidence? Were those people who could see "beyond the veil" insane, or were they special?' Delicately he placed his teacup back onto its saucer, and pushed the handle neatly to the right. 'Why did you do that?' she asked, and could feel Miriam squirming awkwardly in her chair beside her. 'I turned the cup to face me because it was designed to be seen that way, and I choose to respect that. Some people would turn the cup upside down, or not notice either way.' He paused. 'We all make choices in every action we take. Each action comes from a thought, and each thought from a feeling. What we pay attention to or ignore all go to make up the reality in which we exist.' Rebecca started to nod, realising that he was no longer just referring to crockery. 'And yes, there are some people who are able to sense more than others. It could be a yet undiscovered sixth sense, or it could be a synthesis of the five of which we are already aware. Either way, Rebecca, I am of the same mind as Darwin with regard to this, and that is to say that the human as he now exists in his current form has not finished his evolution. He continues to transmute. Swedenborg saw this process as one which is of the progression of the individual, and thus permits each spirit to continue its existence beyond death. Babbage postulated that the divine ran programmes which allowed each species to move forward when the environment was conducive to this change. Perhaps now, in this industrial age, when man has the potential to be freed from his hard labour and society changes to permit the individual to think, act and believe freely, perhaps now this is the time for humankind to feel their way onto the next step of development.' He paused and studied his cup one again. Raising his head, he looked deep into Rebecca's eyes. 'You are of the future, Rebecca. Your way of perceiving may one day be understood and shared by all. I hope and pray that I will be still alive to see that day.'

It was late. The main entrance had long been closed and bolted after the departure of the crowds, and aunt and niece were escorted out of the building through an inconspicuous side door which was promptly locked behind them. The sound of the bolt being thrown was loud, and Rebecca couldn't help feeling it was significant. She had felt safe at the Swedenborg, and the Reverend's words had comforted her. She wanted him to be right, that her ability was a natural part of human progression and she happened to be slightly ahead of the group. She wanted his reassurance that her visions were not a sign of madness and that the Angel, however much she feared it, was a natural phenomenon and therefore not inherently evil. If this was the case, then she only needed to learn about and then understand the Angel to release herself from the debilitating fear of it. She decided that she would be rational from now on, and approach her experiences in the light of science. Perhaps it was even time to experiment, to be a student even.

Winding their way back home to Gower Street they took the route along Museum Street. Glancing at the Atlantis Bookshop, Rebecca fully expected it to be dark and closed, but the reverse was the case. Illumination spilled through its window onto the dark pavement, and Rebecca saw that the room itself was full of people. Turning to speak to Miriam, she realised her aunt had already disappeared into the welcoming light. Once inside she discovered that most of the people in the shop had attended the lecture. She waved at Geraldine, who raised her hand but not her head as she continued her transaction with a small woman who was buying a large stack of books. Geraldine was too busy to talk. Rebecca would come back another time. She wanted to ask her about the symbol on her locket, but now was not the time. Finally at ease with one another, Miriam and Rebecca walked silently home arm in arm.

CHAPTER 14

THE INVITATION FOR Rebecca to dine with Isaac had come completely out of the blue. She had not seen or heard of him since the tedious dinner in Ramsgate. Rebecca put little thought into why he had invited her. He was probably fulfilling some sort of social obligation which he had made to his sister to pay some attention to a newly acquired niece while she resided in the same city as him. She found herself yawning as her body was pushed, scooped and moulded into a corset, an unfortunate action as it gave the maid who was helping her to dress additional leeway to pull tighter. Her aunt was sitting in Rebecca's room, watching the process critically. She spoke little, apart from asking her niece what she thought of Isaac. Rebecca responded by telling her about him carrying her unconscious form to the nursery, and then recounted their conversation at dinner in Ramsgate. The torture of dressing complete, Rebecca pulled herself up onto the bed and lay flat with her legs straight out in front of her. Breathing was going to be difficult. She had spent too long in rational clothes now, and her body was rebelling against the confining prison of the corset. Miriam prompted her for a response to her, as yet unanswered, question. 'I have no feelings either way. He is now my uncle. I know nothing about him, except he appears to be somewhat of a snob.' Miriam looked intently at her. 'He talked only about himself and his life, and didn't even feign an interest in me. I don't expect him to have changed.' Miriam rose and walked over to Rebecca. She touched the mourning locket and made an unnecessary movement as if to straighten it around her niece's throat. 'Keep an open mind, my dear. You may be pleasantly surprised.'

Despite her aunt's assurances, it turned out the evening was quite as tedious as she had feared. Isaac had arrived scrupulously on time, and had hired a private hansom cab to take them to dinner at Verrey's in Regent Street. On the way there, he explained that Verrey's was an excellent French restaurant – although expensive. As much as Rebecca had little social experience, she didn't feel that was an appropriate comment to make. As they travelled, she noticed how he frequently wiped sweat from his upper lip. Was he ill? Or could he be nervous? None of this made any sense to her, and she decided that remaining silent and smiling in all the right places would be the safest way to get through the evening.

As her wrap was taken from her, she took a moment to look inside the restaurant. It *was* beautiful, not unlike the foyer of the Theatre Royal where she had been to see a Christmas spectacular with Clarissa and some of her fellow students. It had gas-lit, gilt-framed mirrors all along one side, with red plush booths below. Each one accommodated six people, and had a cosy, semi-private feel about them. Other tables for four and two were arranged across from them. The format seemed very deliberate – those in the booths could be seen by few in the room, and watch the room itself with impunity. Rebecca was momentarily puzzled when Isaac took her elbow and guided her past the entire restaurant to a door at the end of the room. The maître d'hôtel opened the door to reveal a narrow wooden staircase, and signalled for her to climb the stairs. As she raised her skirt slightly to do so, a flush of anger spread through her. She did not like the way she had been looked at by the patrons of the establishment, nor did she appreciate the expression on Isaac's face as he echoed the signal of the maître d' for her to proceed.

At the top of the stairs, a waiter bowed, and pulled aside a curtain to reveal an elegant circular dining room with only one table in it, set for two. This room was candlelit. The centre of the table contained a magnificent silver candelabrum with twelve white candles flickering, and tall, single candlesticks were arranged around the room, creating pools of light. Isaac rested his hand nonchalantly against the back of his chair and smiled at her while the waiter helped Rebecca to her seat. Rebecca felt awkward and irritable. It was obvious that Isaac was setting out to impress her somehow, but for what reason she plainly had no notion. Perhaps by looking after her in London he was ingratiating himself with her father, she thought. After all, Isaac is in banking and, now he is a relative, Father would help him if he needs it, surely. Before taking his seat, Isaac once again dabbed his upper lip with his pristine, monogrammed handkerchief. 'I felt sure you would prefer to dine in private rather in the public area. It's easier for us to talk in here.' Talk *he* certainly did. A lot. Through each interminable course. Rebecca ate and drank little, in contrast to her host, who became more loud and expansive as the evening went on. All he seemed to talk about was money, and the people he knew who had money, and what they had bought with that money. He talked about their houses and horses, their artwork and their décor. Finally, he talked about their charitable works. Or, to be accurate, the salve with which they eased their consciences.

Spending time with Clarissa was fine-tuning her already burgeoning social conscience to recognise that life was extremely hard for some. Only a few days before Christmas they had accompanied Mrs Burton to visit the vicar at the Holy Trinity Church in Shoreditch to take parcels of clothes and bed-linen to the mission there. Rebecca had never seen such darkness in those narrow streets, nor so many children. The quietly spoken and surprisingly youthful priest had told them that as many as ninety souls lived in each dwelling house, consisting of little more than four rooms. The smell was overwhelming, a mixture of excrement, rotting vegetables and more insidious smells coming from the furniture and toy workshops occupying the same buildings. All the same she was surprised to see how clean, neat and curiously playful the children were. Seeing the boys playing together gave her a shock as she thought about her brother. How tall would he be now? She wrote to him conscientiously each week but no reply ever came. Was he happy? Did he remember his sister? She felt a physical pain at the thought of him.

It was at that moment when Isaac looked over at her, and, thinking her expression related to his conversation, said. 'Yes, of course, my dear, we shall talk of happier events. I can see that my talking about those poor wretches has distressed you. I can assure you that his Lordship does all he can to alleviate their suffering.' I bet he doesn't, Rebecca said to herself. She had heard from the colonel that this particular Lordship was a parvenu whose family made its money in the slave trade. She shook herself. When had she become so judgemental? For all she knew he was a good man among many who were putting their money to a different use rather than just pomp and show.

Trying to keep up with Isaac and his conversation was proving increasingly difficult. Not only was the room very hot, and her constricted stomach painfully full, but Isaac had taken her silence as agreement to his ordering a cigar and brandy to complete his meal. She realised that he was still speaking and she hadn't registered his words 'Excellent, my dear Rebecca. I trust that wasn't too much of an ordeal, was it? I'm sure we rub together just fine, don't you think?' Without waiting for a response he leaned across the table to light his cigar from the candelabrum and winked at her slumped back casually in his chair, one arm slung over its back. He continued to stare as he puffed on the noxious tobacco. An unreadable expression on his face.

The interminable meal was now over. Isaac waived the waiter away and took Rebecca's elbow to help her to rise from the table. She couldn't help it, but she flinched. A more perceptive man would have noticed (the waiter did), but Isaac's senses were now well lubricated and he cheerfully guided her back down the stairs and through the now half-empty restaurant. Along the way he was hailed by the gentlemen in one of the booths, and stopped to have a conversation. A conversation that looked set to take some time. In fact, she watched as Isaac slid into the booth beside his interlocutor, becoming sufficiently absorbed to seemingly forget that she was waiting for him in the vestibule. Calmly, Rebecca turned on her heels, pulled open the door, stepped out into the street and from there into the waiting carriage. 'Gower Street, please.' As the carriage lurched to pull away, the door was wrenched open and Isaac jumped in. 'Steady on, old girl! You will need to learn a little more patience. Bad form – don't you know – to walk out when a gentleman is conversing with business colleagues. Very bad form. Not the most auspicious way to behave at an engagement.' And with that pompous pronouncement he folded his arms, and soon fell asleep leaning against the carriage wall. Rebecca managed to disembark from the carriage at Gower Street without disturbing its snoring occupant.

CHAPTER 15

ENOUGH TIME PASSED for Rebecca to put the incident out of her mind, and for her to return to her routine. It had been around a month since she had gone for dinner with Isaac, and that morning at breakfast, Karim entered the breakfast room with a tray, on which was a letter. He carried it directly to Rebecca. Before taking it from the proffered tray, she paused and looked over at her aunt. Miriam was, as usual, poring over the latest copy of *The Spiritualist* newspaper which was propped up against the teapot. With one hand she was diligently making comments about the lead article, 'Mr Crookes and Spiritual Phenomena', into a vast ledger and eating toast with the other. Without appearing to look up, she waved the toast at Rebecca to open the letter.

What a difference from Ramsgate, she thought drily. Once she had realised that no-one had discussed a date for her return, she decided to stay silent on the subject, rather hoping that she had been forgotten, or at least she would now be free to make her own plans. She now had a friend in Clarissa, who seemed determined that she would join her as a student. The idea really began to crystallise after she had been invited to spend a whole day with her at Bedford

College. There were both tutors and students present, and the conversation was both fast and thrilling – with discussions and debates between the women about education, society and the law. Rebecca realised that here was a place she could feel comfortable. She decided to discuss the idea with Aunt Miriam first before putting it to her father. She was sure now that there was no place for her in Ramsgate, and that she only served as a reminder of his past. Surely he would agree. Rebecca was aware that her mother had left a small sum of money in trust for her. She would ask Father if this could now be released and used for her education.

She was prodded out of this reverie by Aunt Miriam, who was now looking across the table at her with folded arms and an amused expression. 'Your letter?' Rebecca laughed and picked up the envelope, taking it over to her aunt so they could open it together. Miriam handed her a still-buttery knife, with which she slit open the envelope. The contents were surprising. It was a letter inviting her and a companion – 'Of course I shall come with you, dear girl. You try and stop me!' smiled Miriam – to attend a 'select gathering of like-minded individuals' that evening in the London residence of Lord Hawsley where Mr Daniel Dunglas Home was currently a guest. The letter had been hand delivered, and the post-boy was waiting for a response. 'My dear girl, how extraordinary!' It would appear you have captured the interest of dear Mr Home. I have heard so much about him, levitations and the like, but never had the satisfaction of seeing him in person. I can't wait to see him at close hand. How wonderful!'

Miriam signalled for the letter's contents to be acknowledged and the post-boy to be sent away with an affirmative from the excited inhabitants of Gower Street. Her aunt chatted enthusiastically about Mr Home's communications with spirit and his other exceptional feats of mediumship. Rebecca decided that this probably wasn't the most auspicious time to get her aunt's full attention. Any discussion about her staying in London and studying at Bedford College would have to wait.

That evening, Rebecca, her aunt, and her Indian retainers rode by hansom cab to Victoria Street, Westminster. All were dressed in finery (including Karim and Aisha, looking beautiful and exotic in full Indian prince and princess garb) and for one evening even Aunt Miriam had decided to bow to convention and wear a tightly corseted gown, something which was obviously causing her no small amount of discomfort. 'The demonstration of Mr Home's is to be at Lord Hawsley's house where he currently lodges. Interesting chap, Hawsley. Stars and stamps – ha!' With this cryptic pronouncement she suddenly drew Rebecca's attention to the view through the cab window. Piercing the fog were the most brilliant white lights she had seen – all in a row. 'Electric. Fabulous, aren't they? Illuminating the darkness here on the Embankment.' Miriam's eyes shone brightly with excitement. 'This truly is a remarkable time to be alive, my dear, and living here in the heart of so much innovation! Men have seen the invisible through their microscopes, and identified the elements of the atmosphere itself. All now accepted as fact which were not long ago dismissed as fantasy. It will only be a matter of time before spirit itself is proven. It will be quantified and measured. Yes, Rebecca. We truly live at the forefront of change!' From the gloom of the seats opposite, Rebecca saw the unblinking blue eyes of the twins, staring back at her. Unnerved, she drew herself closer to her aunt as if to get a better view of the lights outside.

The evening itself started conventionally enough. Rebecca was pleased to recognise someone she knew. Mr and Mrs Crookes were also in attendance and, after introducing them to her aunt, she took stock of the room. It was large, and on the first floor of the townhouse. There were around thirty men and women in the room, chatting casually. All appeared well dressed and seemed to know each other. As Miriam was deep in conversation with Mr Crookes, Rebecca sought out a place from which to observe the room. She partially hid herself behind one of the long, heavy curtains which were elegantly draped around the four tall windows that looked out onto the street. From her hiding place she could see the fog swirling below, giving her the feeling of looking out from a ship at the sea. Occasionally she saw movement in the fog, presumably from a vehicle in the street, or some poor soul attempting to feel their way back home. A voice close enough to her ear for her to feel the breath of the speaker startled her.

'Miss Rebecca? Forgive me, we have not been introduced. I am Osborne, but do call me Win. Daniel asked me to see if you would be good enough to allow him to explain and apologise to you before the evening gets under way.' Rebecca nodded slowly, and started to follow her companion through the crowd. She realised that the Indian twins were following her. 'Of course, quite correct,' Osborne smiled, when he saw them. As he turned away and they headed into an elegant library, Rebecca had a sudden echo of Isaac smiling at her in the same way. She shuddered. She knew why. Both men only smiled with their mouths – baring their teeth like a lapdog taught to beg for treats from its mistress. She hated those dogs.

Osborne closed the door behind them, and the twins positioned themselves on either side of the doorway, like statues. The room itself was small and intimate, more like a lady's private sitting room. Mr Home greeted her like an old friend, silently taking both of her hands in his before guiding her to sit beside him on a low couch by the fire. There were two women in the room, one compulsively stroking the fabric of her stole, and one other figure, an older man. He introduced himself as Hawsley, the owner of the house. He made no attempt to introduce the two shadowy women. He remained silent after that, nor did either of the women attempt to speak to Rebecca, although they all seemed to be watching one another intently. The women hovered around Hawsley, constantly in motion like insects drawn to a flame. Repelled, attracted, repeated. Most odd. Rebecca realised she was staring so pulled her eyes away from this fascinating sight to take in the room and its other inhabitants. Osborne was now standing by the fireplace, posed and elegant. He retrieved a sherry glass from the mantelpiece, and idly began to sift through a number of requests for Mr Home to visit various grand establishments which were displayed there. Casually he picked one up and threw it into the fire. Rebecca found the action shocking, and somehow intimate. By what right did he destroy Mr Home's invitations? Home stared at Osborne, but without any emotion. He seemed not to register the action. Turning to Rebecca, Home begged an apology for his outburst at Crookes' laboratory, and told her that there were occasions when he sensed things of which others had no awareness. His words were kind, but she quickly realised that he was speaking to her in a very condescending manner. He obviously had no idea that Rebecca saw the Angel herself. Suddenly, and unexpectedly, her anger began to become tangible, starting with her discomfort with Osborne and building from her irritation at the realisation she was being patronised. She felt her cheeks begin to burn, and not from the heat of the fire. Irrationally, she wanted to show them all. Impulsively, she forced her eyes and ears closed to try to summon the Angel. Nothing happened, then suddenly, involuntarily, she felt her hand start to twitch uncontrollably. The twins broke their statue-like poses and moved towards her in unison. Home guided her to the table, pushed a pen into her hand, held paper beneath it, and the shadowy moths drew closer as she started to write, rapidly.

Later, the formal part of the evening itself had been a revelation, and not at all like the cosy circle which took place at Gower Street. Rebecca found it surprisingly, well, theatrical was the only appropriate word for it. The revelation for Rebecca was not in the events themselves but in the audience's reaction to them. It was as if some alchemical transmutation had occurred between what actually happened and what the viewers believed they had seen. Most curious. It was obvious that Mr Home was held in great esteem, and that the people all present believed what they were told they had seen, but Rebecca wasn't convinced. With only candlelight in the room now, and Mr Home and a select few guests seated around a card-table, everyone else gathered round them in a loose circle. For some time, very little occurred, except the medium's breathing became deep and then staccato, and he pushed himself far back in the chair, stretching away from the table in an unnatural movement. Oddly discordant bird sounds then started, and the room quietened. Rebecca ungraciously thought they sounded rather wheezy, although to be scrupulously fair, any bird which existed in the London atmosphere would probably be breathless by now. With this practical thought in her mind, she was as startled as everyone else when a loud crash came from the corner of the room, and a seemingly heavy sideboard was now overturned. Several women (and one of the men, she noticed) shrieked in alarm, and all attention moved to the table. 'I saw it raise itself two feet in the air before it came crashing down', 'I swear it was five feet, or more!' said another. A murmuration of sound swept erratically through the group, and the table at which Home and the others were seated seemed to move spontaneously, jumping erratically from one leg to another as if it was trying to levitate. Just like the table, Rebecca thought suspiciously. As this flock of words started to subside, another took flight, and she heard talk of visions of Mr Home appearing to elongate himself unnaturally, but all she had seen was a perfectly normal man, stretching. Was everyone else in the room having visions, and not her?

After the table had been righted, the demonstration was to be cut short. It would seem that Mr Home was feeling 'enervated' and 'unable to maintain a connection at this time with such strong influences in the room'. Those gathered there were obviously disappointed while simultaneously secretly thrilled that the atmosphere was so potent, and the rest of the evening was spent in discussion about various experiences of spirit. Mr Crookes happily stepped into the entertainment vacuum as he announced Daniel's recent successes in his laboratory. Rebecca noticed that there was a slight drop in the temperature of the convivium in the room as Mr Crookes started to talk, which warmed slightly only when his wife Esther took his arm, and leaned in as if in rapt attention to her husband. Miriam caught Rebecca's eye. 'Polite society never really forgave him for his shenanigans with Florence Cook. He is fortunate in having such a devoted wife to support him. There are many here who saw his physical examinations of Katie, her spirit guide, as little more than, well...' With a straight face, Rebecca finished the sentence for her with, '...Little more than tuzzy-muzzy fondling?' Caught unawares by her niece, Miriam let loose a bray of loud, unselfconscious merriment which caused a small group of women nearby to turn and stare at her in horror. Miriam waved her hand graciously to them, as if acknowledging applause. 'Really, my dear. Your vocabulary has expanded considerably since you came to London.'

Daniel Home had disappeared back into the library, from which inner sanctum he invited select individuals to enter and have private sittings with him. Aunt Miriam was disappointed that she didn't get chosen to join him. Rebecca just wanted to go home. She surreptitiously rubbed her wrist. It ached. She had written upon sheet after sheet of paper, and had little or no recollection of what she had written. It was as if she was in a dream, but one which was almost reality, but not quite. Her trance had been broken by the voices of the twins, suddenly appearing before her, and saying her name gently, one after the other, then in unison, until the pen fell from her grasp.

Aunt Miriam looked over at her niece. 'You look done in, my dear. Let's go home.' She squeezed her hand, causing Rebecca to wince. '...And we need to have a tête-à-tête about the future.'

The feminine chimes of the mantle clock had struck the hour of two in the morning before the small group at Victoria Street had dispersed. By then, the pages on which Rebecca had written had been pored over in great detail. Home had made his excuses and retired to his room some time before, leaving Osborne, Hawsley and the two silent women hovering in the shadows. The men were both seated by the fire, and were most animated. Finally, Osborne declared, 'Exceptional example of passive writing, wouldn't you agree? Some apparently in Hebraic script it would seem. It will take some effort to decipher but we have time. The Cipher is ready to be enacted soon. I feel it. Now we have found her. Now we have the Virgin to complete our circle.' In his excitement he crushed the papers he was holding. The tallest of the women leaned forward and, easing them out of his grasp, took them over to the small writing table where she carefully smoothed them out. 'I do wish you would refrain from using that term in this context. I would prefer if you call her Maiden, if you must call her anything at all,' she announced in a high, nasal voice. 'We are not pagans!' Still seated by the fire, he turned his body around until he was facing her. 'My dear – do forgive me! No-one would ever dream of calling you "Crone" or, indeed, calling Virginia "Mother", but in this context I beg you to understand my meaning. We absolutely need the third feminine divine to complete the circle – to undertake the ritual. It specifically states in the Cipher. After that – well. I can envisage no further use for her, can you?' He looked around at the others for confirmation. 'Be assured, I have already made arrangements for her. When her virginity has opened the gate to the Portal, care will be taken of her. We are all agreed?' Silence greeted this pronouncement. Sighing with impatience he checked his pocket-watch as if by doing so he could force time to move forward.

Rebecca sat on her bed in her nightclothes, her toes tracing the pattern of the bedside rug. The fire in the grate was little more than embers now, and she was cold. Instead of climbing into bed, she stayed there, allowing the prickling texture of the carpet to tickle her feet. It was very late, and she was exhausted, but she did not want to sleep just yet. She needed to process both the evening's events – and not just the passive writing. Something far more significant had been revealed to her by Aunt Miriam when they had returned home. There were plans for her future. She was to become a bride.

Rebecca felt the world she had created here in London slipping from her grasp. Climbing into bed, she lay there trying to think what she could possibly do to hold onto this version of her reality – her life in London. She turned to face her bedside books as exhaustion quickly overtook her body and she fell into a deep, dream-filled sleep.

CHAPTER 16

THE FOLLOWING MORNING the breakfast table had been laid out differently. Her place setting was now to the right of Miriam's. Nor were there any journals or notebooks populating the tablecloth. When Rebecca walked into the breakfast room, Aunt Miriam rose from her own seat to greet her and swept her in her arms. Rebecca did not respond. 'My dear. Come us on, come us on. Sit here by me. I do understand that this has come as – well – a shock to you, but I thought that you had realised, or at the very least that Anna Coren had discussed this with you.' Rebecca sat, and stared at her plate, bile rising in her throat at the mention of Anna Coren. No. She thought resentfully. No. At no point did Anna Coren bring up the possibility of her brother Isaac as a potential husband. At no point did anyone bother to include her in conversations about her future. She watched as if from a distance as a tear dropped from her eye onto the flower pattern of her plate. Celandine. Future joy. Her eyes narrowed as she looked up at her aunt. Miriam looked at the plate and hurriedly exchanged it for her own – on which there was the design of a single cherry blossom. Cherry blossom for education. Noticing this, Miriam tried to pick up the plate and change it again. Rebecca stayed her hand. 'We could be here all day. There will always be signs. It is us who choose whether to read them or not.' With that, she indicated for her aunt to sit, and they ate together in silence. Not quite at peace yet, but there was a truce. At least Rebecca understood that her aunt was truly upset and wasn't complicit in the changes which were about to occur. She felt a sudden rush of love for her aunt, and vowed to try to be the perfect niece and spend more time with her for however long she was to remain as her guest in London. That would have to wait, however. Today, she realised, she had something important to do.

After breakfast, she wrapped herself up warmly to leave the house. The fog outside was dense (and the smell particularly acrid), but by now Rebecca could walk the London streets surrounding Gower Street with her eyes closed. Miriam offered to come with her, but Rebecca had already made plans to meet Clarissa in the British Library, and then go together to take tea with Geraldine. She wanted to talk freely with her friends, and was now ready to do so. She recognised that by doing nothing to prevent it, her future life in Ramsgate had all been planned for her without her knowledge or input. Miriam quietly told her that Isaac was to make preparations to leave London and his employ there and move to Ramsgate and work for Rebecca's father. She was to become his devoted wife and present him with a suitably appropriate number of children. Rebecca could not think of anything worse than to live in a town she despised, with a man she hardly knew, and become a nurturer of children – and all of this just as she felt life was developing some meaning for her in London. Her future was to be mapped out as inevitable as the route of the steam train which would carry her there. No deviation, no opportunity to change direction, no choice. Unable to imagine her life back in Ramsgate as a corseted, restricted wife, with no outlet other than her home, husband and children, she was determined to make the most of the time which she had in London. Perhaps, she imagined, some idea would reveal itself to her through the fog which swirled within and around her – that there would be some way of finding a different path. Until then she would take advantage of every opportunity. This was not a time to allow fear to get the better of her. Leaving Gower Street, she threw herself gratefully into the anonymity of the fog. Behind her, two pairs of blue eyes blinked from beneath hooded cloaks and followed her path.

Clarissa's (gratifying) outburst of fury on hearing Rebecca's news about her imminent engagement had blown its course. Slumped in Geraldine's chair in the bookshop, her friend stretched carelessly for her cup and drained the now cold contents. On arriving in Museum Street, Rebecca had repeated the conversation with her aunt which had taken place the previous evening. According to Miriam, the die had been cast when Isaac came to dinner at the Ramsgate house. Since then, Anna Coren and he had persuaded Father that Isaac was a suitable match, and would make a good husband for Rebecca. Rebecca thought silently for a moment. The 'understanding' which Isaac had spoken of when they had dined together now made sense. Father had agreed, and it was a foregone conclusion that she would accede to his wishes. Realising that Geraldine was speaking to her, Rebecca pulled her attention back to the present. Suitably fortified with tea and righteous indignation, it was now time to reveal her secret. It was time to tell her friends about the Angel Azriel.

When she had finished speaking, the three women sat in silence, interrupted only by the hiss of the gas coming from the central light. A customer came to collect an order. A few, muted words were exchanged on greeting, and she was soon gone. The atmosphere in the room had become oppressive. Once again the bell clanged and the shop-door opened, heralding a coil of fog and the figure of Jonathon, holding a brown paper bag containing a bottle. Three sherry glasses soon appeared, followed by Jonathon's disappearance into the back room, and the contents of the bottle were soon poured into three delicate vessels. Rebecca stared blankly at the table and its contents. The sherry looked golden through the cut crystal of the glasses. She held hers but did not drink. Unlike Clarissa (now seated cross-legged on the Persian rug), who emptied the contents of her own glass in one gulp – and then stared down into it as if surprised to find it empty. Geraldine raised her own glass delicately in Rebecca's direction, took a minute sip, pursed her lips, sat back into her chair, and then smiled. Immediately, Rebecca felt her shoulders drop. Unconsciously, she had been holding herself as still as a statue so as not to disturb her friend's train of thought. 'Unlike our unconscionable Lord Byron, you are neither "mad, bad, nor dangerous to know"!' Geraldine reached for the sherry bottle to replenish Clarissa's glass, which was being held out expectantly, and, having filled Clarissa's glass to the brim, proceeded to speak, quietly.

'Throughout the ages there have existed those who saw visions. Some were praised and given power, others driven out and destroyed. They have had many names. Seers, shamans, witches, prophets, saints. For those who live with this ability it is never an easy life.' Rebecca had told her friends everything, including her belief that she was able to summon the Angel to kill. Geraldine reached across the table and laid her hand on top of Rebecca's. 'Child, it is very unlikely that you can control the Spirit.' Rebecca opened her mouth to contradict her, '...or Angel, or whatever it is you choose to call it.' Geraldine continued. 'For some these abilities are a curse, for others a blessing. It all depends on you and how you choose to use them.' Rebecca remembered the words from the lecture by the Reverend Hopps. Was her ability part of man's evolution? Was her capacity to see beyond the normal range of others one which would become more common, or, like those creatures less suited to their surroundings, would it die out altogether through natural selection. Is this what Samuel was trying to teach her when he gave her *On the Origin of Species*? Although they had never got to discuss the book, she felt sure that he would have wanted her to ask questions – to experiment and learn from her own experiences. Rebecca rubbed her eyes viciously. Was her ability a throwback or part of the future? Suddenly tired, she realised she didn't care. She didn't want this ability. Furthermore, she didn't want to get married. Nor did she want to leave London. Expressing these feelings to her friends, they asked her the obvious question: If these are the things which you do not want, what exactly *do* you want? She looked down at the figure of Clarissa, who had now uncrossed her legs, and was unselfconsciously inspecting the hole beneath one of her boots with her forefinger. Clarissa looked up, her attention drawn by the sudden silence. 'What?' Geraldine started to laugh. The sound spread and soon Mother, Maiden and Crone were united in this joyful sound. Drawn by the sound, Jonathon's surprised features appeared through the arch to the backroom. He smiled and shook his head, bemused by the laughter, and left them to their merriment.

It was not only foggy now, night had also fallen. Rebecca concentrated on navigating through the streets by sound alone. She could detect the proximity of the road from the sound of the horses' hooves, and oncoming pedestrians from the sound of their footfall.

The thickening fog acted as both barrier and repellent. There would be fewer people out on the streets now, and the songs and calls of the street sellers were in abeyance for now. It would start again soon, this time with the men who sold hot cooked potatoes from a cart. The only smell she could detect now was that of steamy horse, and nearby at that. A figure appeared within arm's distance from her, oblivious to her presence. Cloaked and tall, momentarily she thought it was the Angel, but it was only a man, and a drunk one at that. She could smell the alcohol fumes as he passed by. She found the wall and pressed her back to it, until her pounding heart slowed once more. Choosing the right words with which to tell her friends had not been easy, but in the end it hadn't been the ordeal she had thought it would be. First of all, they had believed her. Furthermore, she felt less alone now she had shared her experience. Finally, they had both seemed more interested in helping her find a way to stay in London and study at Bedford College. Perhaps – they suggested – her father could be persuaded to allow her to study for a year *before* her marriage. In the interim, Isaac might change his mind, or other ways of extending that freedom could be found. She would speak to Aunt Miriam. Rebecca had felt both heartened and invigorated by her friends' enthusiasm for her idea of studying and also by the very fact of their companionship. Having had no experience of friendships before, and, now discovering what it felt like, she had no desire to relinquish this joy. She found herself at the corner of Gower Street, where she observed a private carriage with a curious crest on its door was waiting. A sleek, black horse pawed the cobbles impatiently. Casually committing the image to her memory, she ran to the front door, eager to initiate her conversation with her aunt.

CHAPTER 17

THE TWINS OPENED the front door to her before she had a chance to ring the bell. She was no longer surprised by this as it seemed to happen often. Rebecca had got used to their presence among the other servants, and even though they seemed removed from the day-to-day running of the house, they seemed to seamlessly anticipate her aunt's wishes, and now her own. She thanked them as they removed her cloak, and was rewarded by a rare smile from both. She made a mental note to ask her aunt more about them. Having Indian servants was not unheard of, but it was still quite unusual. She wondered how they had come to join the household. Removing her cloak and handing it to Aisha, she was about to enquire as to the whereabouts of Miriam; however, she could hear her aunt's voice from the parlour and followed the sound. Any thought of asking about the origin of the twins, or even her more pressing request about permission to study, was wiped from her mind as soon as she entered the room. Her aunt was not alone. Two other women were with her, taking tea.

'Good evening, Rebecca,' the taller of the women uttered carefully. 'It is delightful to see you again.' Rebecca stood in the doorway of the room and found herself staring at the speaker, confused. She had no recollection at all of ever having met these women. The silence stretched uncomfortably and the clock ticked portentously in the background, filling it. The other figure whose face was in half shadow and had not yet spoken started to smooth the fabric of her dress, nervously. The movement sparked Rebecca's memory of the same fastidious, almost hypnotic motion the shadowy woman had used when stroking the fabric of her stole that evening in Victoria Street. Aunt Miriam coughed gently, breaking Rebecca's reverie. 'My dear, it seems you are to be honoured with another invitation. May I present the Honourable Mrs Osborne and Lady Hawsley? These ladies,' here Aunt Miriam swept her hand expansively towards the two women, 'they tell me that they met you at the soirée in Victoria Street. It would seem you made a great impression on them. You are invited to a very exclusive gathering in Piccadilly. It transpires you are to be invited into the inner sanctum itself.' There was a distinctly sarcastic inflection in her aunt's voice at the end of the sentence, one which Rebecca noted but to which she decided not to react. Still standing in the doorway, she kept her head bowed and her voice and expressions became masked as she thanked the visitors for their unexpected invitation. She was just on the point of declining when Lady Hawsley sat forward in her chair. Rebecca could now see her face, which was tired and strained. 'Please, do say yes, Rebecca. You cannot imagine how important this is. We have waited for a female energy as extraordinary as yours for some considerable time. Please do not make me wait any longer.' Rebecca looked sharply up at her as her speech changed to 'me' from 'we'. Why was this so important to her, particularly?

The speaker sat back into the chair and re-entered the shadows, seemingly exhausted by the effort of her words. Miriam raised a quizzical eyebrow to Rebecca and patted the seat of the settee next to her. 'Do come in properly, Rebecca, and sit down. I am fascinated to hear what this is all about.'

Cautiously, Rebecca told her about the spontaneous passive writing that had taken place at Victoria Street. Although the conversation was between Rebecca and her aunt, the two guests were also listening intently. They remained silent, as if hoping their presence in the room had been forgotten. Miriam spoke little, but listened attentively. Hungrily, she occasionally prompted her niece with questions about how the experience had felt. Rebecca knew she had had the sensation many times before – when she had 'travelled' through the house, or taken herself elsewhere – but had not ever put these experiences into words. When her hand had started to twitch in that room in Victoria Street, and then the writing had started, it was the first time she had the awareness of both stillness and movement simultaneously in her body. She tried to describe this to Miriam as if her very being had become both 'thick' and 'thin'. She tried to elucidate this comparison – it was as if you were looking at a piece of paper from the side and it became absent from view and almost disappeared, and yet if you looked at it face on it was present and obvious. The room started to feel oppressively warm, and she was overcome by a strong desire to just get up and leave. She tried to continue in her description, but found herself becoming frustrated at her inability to convey the intensity of this sensation. She stared into the flames in the grate. She began to believe her attempt to explain was as ineffective as trying to describe the events of a dream to someone who had never dreamt themselves. It would always be a pale reflection of the reality. She gave up the attempt, and bowed her head. Rebecca had the feeling that Miriam was somehow disappointed in her. In response she felt her aunt squeeze her hand reassuringly. 'It's fine. You haven't done anything wrong, my dear. I just wish I had known that you have the gift. I, myself, have tried for many long years in private contemplation to develop passive writing. Perhaps I have tried too hard.' She sighed, resignedly. Then suddenly she jumped up from her seat. 'Ladies, how remiss of me to ignore you in this way! I am sure that you have far more important things to do than listen to our familial chit-chat. Come us on! Don't let me keep you.' With this she took the extraordinary step of practically manhandling the two women out of the room and into the hallway. Karim and Aisha were waiting there motionless, already holding out the fur-edged outer-garments and gloves to help the women to dress. As they did, Mrs Osborne turned to Rebecca. 'You will consider our invitation, Rebecca? Do. Please think about it.' Even though her manner was imperious, her tone was curiously humble – pleading even. Rebecca was on the point of saying she would think about it, when Miriam spoke for her. 'My niece is engaged to be married – and will be leaving for Ramsgate soon. I am not sure whether she will be able to accept this invitation – gracious though it is.' Rebecca felt as if she had been slapped in the face, and, without waiting for the guests to leave the house, stormed up to her bedroom. She threw herself onto the bed, and cried out hot, angry tears of frustration.

It was some hours later when Rebecca woke, and this was only in response to the persistent, gentle knocking at the door. Slowly the handle turned and Aisha's face appeared through the opening. Making a curious mime of someone eating with both hands, she signalled to Rebecca to come with her and then smiled. Rebecca sat up on the bed, suddenly aware of how hungry she was. Aisha led her past the dining room, down the corridor, and into the kitchen where she had eaten her first meal with Miriam and Anna Coren. Rebecca smelled the vegetable curry which was warming away on the range and felt suddenly very sad. She had not realised how much she had grown to love this house, her life here, and her aunt. Tears welled up in her eyes as she sat down at the scrubbed table. Miriam, meanwhile, busied herself around the kitchen, taking bread out of the oven and filling two bowls with the nourishing stew. By the time she sat down beside her niece, Rebecca had composed herself. Any animosity she had felt towards her aunt as a result of what she had said in the hallway was gone. 'I just don't want to go. I don't want to leave here. I want to stay with you. I want to go to Bedford College and become a student.' Rebecca's words poured out of her in a tumble, not at all how she had rehearsed it. She could hear her voice sounding more like a petulant child wheedling for a new toy than a young woman putting forward a reasonable argument for how she wanted to live her life. Eventually she ran out of breath, and words, and with her heart racing she let the silence take hold in the room. Miriam slowly finished her curry, tore a chunk of bread from the loaf as she had on the first evening, and broke it in two, handing half to Rebecca. With her half she proceeded to wipe her bowl clean, slowly chewing the curry-laden morsel. Rebecca held her piece of bread in her hand feeling unable to swallow, so full of emotion was she at that moment.

When Miriam finally broke the silence, her words surprised Rebecca. 'When I was sixteen, my darling Papi died. Your mother – my dearest sister – had already married your father. This was at home, in Germany. Life was different then. We really did not have a choice. Before he died, Father had arranged for my betrothal to a much older man. Older than he, even. He was, however, rich. I did not love him, but I did show him respect, and somehow we rubbed along quite decently for the first two years or so. When what passed between us as intimacy on that first night occurred it was a great distress to me. I cannot describe the confusion I experienced, nor how my self was forever changed by his actions. I said nothing, believing this was to be the norm, and the price I would have to pay for being respectable. I am sorry to shock you by speaking to you in this way but you are a woman now, and are to be married. There are things for you to learn and you have no mother to teach you.' Miriam rose and went to the kitchen dresser, from whence she lifted a rustic-looking flask with a narrow neck, and with it two goblets made from the same earthenware. She placed them awkwardly on the kitchen table and, removing the cork stopper with a satisfying sound, poured liquid into each of the vessels. 'Cider. Good for your health.' Miriam drank deeply, and refilled her goblet. Rebecca remained motionless. 'Then one day a man came into my world. He was young, vigorous, and he loved me. I felt the connection with him before we had even spoken to one another. It was as if there was a thread connecting us, and only us, to one another. He made love to me – with me – in a way that I cannot describe. Just as you had difficulty earlier when you tried to describe passive writing to me. It is for the same reason you will not understand me when I tell you that I left my body during lovemaking with him, and have never experienced such sensations since. My husband discovered our affair, and had him removed from the household. Yes, Rebecca. He was a servant. He was the coachman. Not an intellectual, not a wealthy man, not even a Jew – but I adored him with such a passion I cannot begin to name.' Her voice became thick with emotion, and she stared into her goblet, pushed it away and thrust the stopper back into the flask. 'He died less than a year after. He would have been twenty years old. My beautiful Erich. My beautiful boy.' Rebecca rose and stood beside her aunt's chair then gently cradled Miriam's head on her breast. Stroking her aunt's hair, she silently waited for all those long-stoppered tears to run their course. Eventually her aunt pushed her gently away, and fumbled in the sleeve of her blouse, extracted a delicate, lace-edged handkerchief from it, and blew her nose vigorously. She breathed out, hard, and signalled for Rebecca to take her seat once more before she continued. 'Obviously my husband and I never spoke of this. Not a word. If anything he was even kinder to me afterwards, but we never shared a bed again. For that I was grateful. Once I had known what lovemaking could be like, I couldn't bear the thought of my husband touching me ever again.'

Miriam cleared the table of its contents and, fetching the metal milk churn from the pantry, began to prepare a hot drink for them both. Rebecca broke the silence. 'So it is Erich you are trying to contact? He is the reason you are part of the Spiritualist Circle?' Miriam turned to her from the stove where she was stirring the milk and wiped her hand slowly over her face. 'No. I'm trying to make a connection with my husband. I want to know that he forgave me.' Rebecca's face betrayed her confusion. 'There are many types of love, Rebecca. I now understand that. My husband could have ruined me. He could have left me on the street, penniless. As a woman I had no rights, no property, nothing. He could have made sure that I suffered for what I had done. Instead he left me all his wealth. Everything. He left me with everything including my guilt. I feel the weight of it every day, and the burden becomes heavier as I contemplate my own existence on this earth.' Rebecca did not know what to say. While her aunt had been speaking she had unconsciously rolled the piece of bread into tiny crumbs. She pushed them into a little pile with her forefinger. As she watched, she felt part of her mind drift apart, and, like the day in the Ramsgate churchyard, she heard her own voice speaking as if from a distance. It was her voice, but lower, and more breathless. Seemingly unaware, she rose from the table. Her aunt grasped her arms with both hands. *'Bitte, noch einmal, bitte sehr!'* Miriam was shaking her hard now. 'Rebecca, please, say that again!'

CHAPTER 18

REBECCA HAD A disturbed sleep that night. The location of her dreams seemed to be real and tangible enough, but she was the ghost. When she tried to touch something or someone, she passed through them. They were unaware of her existence, except for a small, ugly lapdog which bared its teeth at her as she passed through a doorway. She floated through a dismal house surrounded by a stark orchard. It felt strangely familiar – was this somewhere from her memory, way back in her memory, perhaps from when she had been a child? Everyone was speaking German. It must be her mother's childhood home, perhaps. Perhaps not. Part of her mind stood apart from this thought, and concluded logically, *it can't be, I hadn't been born when this household existed, it must be Miriam's home – where she lived with her husband. I don't understand...* She heard conversations drift around her, distorted as if she were at the bottom of a lake, she floated through walls, then watched as the sun rose and set in an instant.

The previous evening, when Aunt Miriam had shaken her, Rebecca had pulled herself back into her body and had no apparent recollection of what she had said. Miriam was hysterical, and

Rebecca confused and disturbed by the sight of her aunt's distress. Aisha's silent appearance comforted Miriam, and she allowed herself to be taken to bed. Rebecca found her own way to her dark room; for once the fire was unlit and the room felt unwelcoming. She climbed into bed and undressed herself under the covers, before lying awake listening to the night-time sounds of the house around her. For the first time she could remember, she wanted – needed – the comfort of another person around her. Sleep was elusive, and enervating when it finally came.

She had woken parched and feverish. Reaching out for her water carafe, her hand touched Samuel's gift, *On the Origin of Species*. It had become a talisman of logic, and it grounded her thoughts. She pulled herself into a sitting position in bed, and plumped up the pillows behind her. She needed time to think, to remember, to work things out. She wasn't going to have that luxury.

'Excellent, dear child, you are awake!' Miriam burst into Rebecca's bedroom, followed by Aisha and Karim carrying trays laden with food. 'Come us on!' she said, nudging Rebecca sideways to make space for herself to sit alongside her. 'We are going to have a picnic!' And with that, the smiling twins raised two cloches, each containing two boiled eggs, ham and toast.

On conclusion of this impromptu meal, Miriam cosied up to Rebecca, placing an arm over her shoulder to pull her closer. 'Now. I expect you want to know what happened last night? Well, my dear, it appears the interest of others being paid to you is for a reason. You do have a gift. Last night you spoke to me in German...' At this, Rebecca tried to speak but Miriam held up her hand to interrupt her. 'Yes, I am well aware you speak the language – this was not spontaneous xenoglossy – but it is not the language you used, rather the words you spoke to me. You called me *mein klein*

Eichhörnchen, my little squirrel. It is the pet name my husband called me – before – before...' Her voice tailed off with emotion. 'I understand the message. He has forgiven me. I now know it is true that when we die we move through the circles ever higher. He has moved onwards and upwards, and so must I. He has freed me from my guilt.' Her eyes shone. Rebecca tried to prepare her words. She wanted to say to Miriam that she could have heard this expression from her mother, or even when she was a baby in Germany. At the look of pure happiness on her aunt's face the words dried in her mouth and she stayed silent. Suddenly Miriam pushed Rebecca away, so she could look her fully in the face. 'I have treated you like a child, and that was wrong of me. Allow me to explain why I refused the harpies' invitation. Get dressed. Let's go shopping.' Rebecca recognised the allusion and smiled at the thought.

It was noon before they left the house, heading by cab for Burlington Arcade. Gloved hand in gloved hand, the women walked through the arcade before stopping to buy a beautiful Chinese shawl for Rebecca. She tried to refuse the gift, but it would seem that Miriam was on a spree and nothing was going to stop her from treating her niece. Rebecca found herself caught up in the excitement, and had a morning like no other in her experience. Clutching various boxes and bags, they repaired to the tearoom at Fortnum and Masons. Rebecca was grateful that she had worn accommodating clothing as, after numerous cups of tea, countless exquisite sandwiches and a selection of cakes and drop scones she felt ready to explode – or sleep – whichever came first. Miriam was in great form. Her eyes sparkled as she laughed noisily at some of the more ridiculous fashions they had seen as they had walked around London. Both aunt and niece were in rational dress that day, and, after the third glance from a table of two corseted women seated nearby, Miriam whispered, 'They're only jealous. Shall I give them my dressmaker's details?' Rebecca smiled, pleased to see her aunt so unrestrained in her happiness. She had only just realised that prior to this moment Miriam had been as constrained by her memories as she had once been by her corset, and now she was free. There could be no possible advantage, only harm, in Rebecca explaining away the cause of Miriam's pleasure. Rightly or wrongly she had no intention of taking her aunt's happiness away from her now.

Miriam poured the last drops from the teapot, and summoned a waiter to replenish it with more hot water. 'Now,' she began portentously, 'it is time I gave you enough information to make up your own mind about the invitation from Mrs Osborne and her sister.' The recitation took enough time for another teapot to be drained and then refilled again. Once concluded, Rebecca summarised, just to be clear on what her aunt had actually told her. It appeared that the two women she had met on the evening of Mr Home's demonstration considered themselves to be serious spiritual researchers, and that they had formed some sort of esoteric research group with their husbands Osborne and Lord Hawsley. The latter appeared to be some sort of sponsor of the whole club. It was a very exclusive group, one to which even Mr Home was only incidentally associated. They kept their meetings private, and their research too. Hints from Daniel Home and passed to Miriam via Mrs Crookes that evening in Victoria Street were that the group were receiving extraordinary spirit messages via passive writing. These messages spoke of a codex for Spiritualism – one which would fuse together both eastern and western philosophies. The group had a particular interest in all things Kabbalistic, and this was, Miriam believed, why they were prepared to extend an invitation to the group to Rebecca. Obviously they had become aware of her gift somehow.

At this point she felt it was prudent to confess what had happened in the library. Before she had chance to start, Miriam waved her words away. 'I already know. Aisha and Karim told me. Besides that I saw the ink on your fingers. You are not the only one who is able to observe and say nothing,' she concluded, tartly, but with a smile on her face. Rebecca felt her shoulders sag. She hadn't wanted to lie to her aunt, and felt saddened that she hadn't told her about her sudden expression of passive writings. Or about the Angel. To be truthful, to try to explain it now, in the bright and modern tearoom, felt incongruous. She would save that particular recitation for a more appropriate time. Miriam delicately folded her napkin and indicated to the waiter that they had finished. 'Don't worry, my dear. I am aware that the Gift chooses you, not you the Gift, and that for some it is unwanted and creates fear. There is little to be afraid of if you trust Spirit. Besides, when the ladies came to visit me they did speak of helping you to explore your Gift, and share it in a scientific environment. It is, of course, entirely up to you. The choice is now yours.'

Rebecca felt strangely tired. It was probably the combination of sleeping poorly the night before, the unaccustomed walk around the arcade, and the considerable amount of food which she had just consumed. On returning to the house, she gathered Samuel's gift from her room, took it into the sitting room and soon fell into a deep sleep over its pages.

She woke to find Aisha standing silently before her, but instead of being startled, she was comforted. Aisha and Karim were almost like a part of the house, like automata. Apparently unspeaking and unresting, they seemed to exist only to serve the household. What was behind those startling eyes? she wondered. 'Where are you from, Aisha?' The young woman bowed her head and spoke in a clear and surprisingly unaccented voice. 'We are of here, Mistress Rebecca.' Riddles. Rebecca did not believe Aisha was deliberately avoiding her question, but decided that she would ask her aunt later instead. She was learning that everyone seemed to have their reasons for what they told, or didn't tell, and what they showed or hid to the world. Reality, she was learning, was elective. She recognised this in herself as she behaved differently when she was with Clarissa and Geraldine than when she was with Isaac. It was not beauty, she mused, that was in the eye of the beholder, but reality. We become what the person with us believes us to be. I think too much, she said to herself, shaking her head to dislodge her philosophical contemplation, and quietly left the servants to their tasks as preparations for that evening's séance began the transformation of the drawing room.

As it turned out, she did not get the chance to speak to her aunt that evening, and so it was at breakfast the next day she broached the subject of her invitation. 'You must choose for yourself, Rebecca. It is not for me to decide.' Just as she was about to respond, Karim entered the room with the morning post. There were two envelopes, one for Rebecca, one for Miriam. Both were addressed in the same firm, masculine handwriting. They looked across the breakfast table at each other. There was only one person it could be who was writing to them both. Rebecca's father.

CHAPTER 19

NEITHER LETTER WAS of any great length. Miriam's consisted of a one-page formally worded expression of gratitude for allowing Rebecca to stay, and a date specifying her return to Ramsgate. Rebecca felt like a parcel being claimed from the railway left-luggage depot.

Rebecca's letter was only slightly longer in length, telling her that she had two weeks to prepare for her return to her home (even the word jarred her), and that the date for her marriage to Isaac had been set for the autumn, allowing a six-month period in which she would be engaged in the organisation of her wedding. The dress, if she wished, could be purchased in London, giving her the opportunity to visit Miriam once more before she became a bride.

Both women sat in silence, with the letters side by side on the table in front of them. Finally, Miriam spoke. 'I take it from this that Isaac did propose to you?' Rebecca recalled the tedious evening with him and responded hotly. 'No, he did not!' She silently reviewed the events of the evening, including his cryptic remark in the carriage home. Was it possible he had asked for her hand in marriage and she hadn't really noticed? Limited in her experience as she was, she had read enough of the Railway Library books with their romantic heroes and heroines which were hidden away under Miriam's Spiritualist periodicals to know that she should at least have noticed it was happening – and at best been swept away on a wave of euphoria at the thought that all her dreams had come true. Reading the novellas was a guilty pleasure shared by both women, but never mentioned. They were pure slush, she knew, but a wonderful way to spend a rainy afternoon. She shook her head to shake it free of these irrelevancies and tried to clear her thoughts. There was *no way* she was marrying Isaac. Apart from anything else, he was her uncle, wasn't he? She felt her panic rising. Miriam explained that avuncular marriage, especially if they were not related by blood, was perfectly acceptable, common even. In the circumstances, she mused, she wouldn't have been surprised if Anna had it in mind all along. Rebecca was momentarily confused. Anna? Anna Coren. Of course. Anna Coren. How cosy that would be. Father, Anna Coren, Isaac and her. Forever. It was *not* what she wanted, not what she planned.

She poured out her heart to Miriam. Her dreams of staying in London. Her dreams of studying at Bedford College. Words escaped her like birds from a cage and she did not try to stop them. Miriam could see her distress. She let Rebecca speak until there were no more words. The cage was empty, and with no more prisoners to flee, Rebecca sat in dejected silence. Then, taking her in her arms, Miriam promised that she would write to her father on her behalf. Rebecca stayed in her aunt's embrace until she was pushed away. 'Now, my dear, I have a missive to compose, and you have London. I suggest you enjoy its pleasures while you are still able. Oh, and before I forget, the invitation from the harpies. What have you decided to do?' 'I shall go, of course! I shall accept every invitation I can. I intend to experience as much as possible before, before...' Miriam said nothing, but squeezed her niece's hand gently in response.

Miriam listened to Rebecca's footsteps as her niece ran up the stairs to her bedroom. She hoped her optimism would last, but knowing her brother-in-law he was unlikely to bend once he had made up his mind. Even if he agreed with Miriam, it would be a matter of pride with him to stick to his decision. She would have to handle him carefully. Pulling out her writing box from her bureau, she began writing the first of many, many drafts of her petition to Rebecca's father.

Although Rebecca had accepted the invitation from the Honourable Mrs Osborne and Lady Hawsley, now she was on her way she was having second, and even third thoughts about it. Four days had passed since their visit and it was now early evening on the fifth day when the two women had come to collect her from Gower Street in Lady Hawsley's carriage. The women were exquisitely dressed in evening gowns. Rebecca knew enough now after her visit to Burlington Arcade that her own dress was somewhat provincial, but that wasn't what was really bothering her. The weather was particularly unpleasant, the smog thick and the stench intense. Neither women seemed to be aware of it. Rebecca's eyes, however, were starting to sting terribly. Once in the private carriage, Mrs Osborne leaned over to Rebecca. 'Eye drops. Here.' She pulled a brown bottle from her purse and handed it to Rebecca. She squeezed the rubber stopper and drew out a measure into the glass vial. She dropped three into each of Rebecca's eyes before carefully returning the glass dropper to the bottle. Through blurry vision she thought she caught the merest hint of a smile pass between the women. Rebecca was starting to wonder whether they were laughing at her. A momentary fear passed through her that the whole evening was just some elaborate ruse designed to humiliate her. She dabbed her eyes. They felt better. She essayed a small smile at Mrs Osborne who responded with a small smile of her own before focusing her attention on the window. So dense was the fog outside that nothing could be seen apart from a reflection of the women inside. Each woman retreated into her own silence and the journey passed without another word exchanged.

Arriving in Piccadilly, Rebecca stepped out of the carriage to a stunning sight. Before her was a magnificent building, unlike any of the others in the street. Indeed, she had never seen anything like it apart from in the pages of a book. The yellow brick frontage was illuminated by two tall metal posts topped with bowls of flame. The building was laid out symmetrically, with two stone pillars on either side of the door. Each of these tapered up through the first and to the second floor until it reached a point topped by a flat keystone. This made the doorway itself seem the size of the building. On either side of this entrance were elegant windows which tapered in a similar manner. These characteristics gave the building the weird illusion of being a pyramid, rather than the rectangular shape of those abutting it. Rebecca stood before this extraordinary edifice and stared at the final oddity. The doorway was topped by the statues of two huge female figures. These figures faced forward with arms raised, their bodies covered with a sculpted diaphanousness through which their naked forms could clearly be seen. Rebecca was rooted to the spot, and felt a sudden wave of disorientation pass over her as she stood in the street. Her companions quickly took her each by the arm and guided her into the building.

Once inside, she seated herself on a marble bench in the vestibule. 'Here, drink this. It will help.' Rebecca tried to take the glass which was offered to her, but found her hands were shaking. Mrs Osborne brought the glass to her lips, gently cupping the back of her head as she did so. Thirstily, Rebecca took a gulp of the contents and started to cough. She looked up at Mrs Osborne. 'Sherry, my dear. It will revive you.' Both women were now standing in front of her, watching intently. She didn't like the taste at all. She remembered the flavour of the sherry which Anna Coren had given her – what seemed like a lifetime ago now – and this was different. It had a strangely bitter aftertaste. Feeling more composed, she looked at the remainder of the liquid, before raising the glass again and thirstily draining its contents.

'Excellent, excellent my dear!' Both women smiled broadly. 'We really are most delighted that you chose to take up our invitation to come.' Suddenly animated, both women began to talk at once. 'First, a tour of the house!' Both women seemed equally at home here, opening doors and proudly displaying the contents. Now she could hear them speak, their physical similarities seemed more pronounced too. There were certain inflections and idiosyncrasies which bonded them together. As they continued through the rooms, she suddenly realised that these sisters were close, able to finish one another's sentences, and comfortable enough to interrupt one another.

The house itself was considerably smaller than it seemed from the outside. The rooms on the ground floor were conventional enough apart from the paintings. These seemed to be an odd mixture of landscapes and dark figures. The first floor had two large rooms. One more like a museum, with an eclectic mixture of sculptures all around and heavy oriental drapery hiding the windows. The other was dedicated to books, which were everywhere. Scrolls and manuscripts were piled high. There was only one chair, next to a bureau which had a lectern and a book open on it, papers and writing utensils still strewn on its surface as if a student had suddenly been called away from his desk in the British Library. She paused, fascinated. Inexorably drawn into this room, Rebecca found herself scanning the titles. Many of the books were too large and heavy for her to even attempt to take down from the shelf, but she was excited. This was a place of learning after all. Her aunt's fears would be unfounded.

Rebecca turned to her hostesses. 'This is wonderful, really.' This time the smile was more genuine, and she was invited to sit down on an exotic ottoman, draped in a rich silk fabric. Lady Hawsley spoke for the first time. 'We truly are so very thrilled that you are here, Rebecca. There are so few who have the appropriate – how can I put this correctly? – qualities, to appreciate what we are attempting here. Yes. We are a select group, an hermetic gathering, as it were, but this secrecy is for a good reason. The knowledge which we share is not for the masses and most would shrink in fear at the implications. Our study is at the forefront of human understanding. We are here as interpreters of the Cipher. We strive to the betterment of all humankind, whether they are willing to accept it or not.'

Rebecca opened her mouth to ask what was mean by the 'Cipher', but no words came from her lips. She suddenly started to feel incredibly drowsy, her limbs lethargic and tired. Perhaps she was coming down with a chill? She raised her arm speculatively, and watched her fingers as they seemed to merge and separate. She became aware of colours seemingly flowing around her fingers. She turned her hand over and studied it. It was her hand but didn't look or feel like her hand. Calmly she studied the sensation from a distance. These were the sensations of her dreams, a kind of floating, a slowing down of time, a disconnection... She could hear – or was she imagining? – the sound of deep chimes, as if a huge gong was being struck repeatedly somewhere in the building. The sound became a sensation; the sensation became a wave of feeling which started to pulse through her, then a sudden lightness overcame her. She felt fine now, in fact better than fine. She felt energised and alert. Whatever it was that had come over her earlier had now gone. So had the women. They had left a note and sweet-smelling madeleine cakes beside a sherry decanter, inviting her to partake of both until their return. She found herself very thirsty, and with nothing else to drink she poured herself more of the bitter-tasting sherry. At least the madeleine should take away the taste, she mused, hopefully, picking one up and biting into it tentatively. It was sweet and moist.

With nothing else to do, and with a great deal of curiosity she could now select a companion from the manuscripts with impunity. Momentarily content, she picked up the slim volume which had until now occupied pride of place on the lectern and started to read it. It seemed old and worn. The cover felt like skin of some kind, and the pages were thick and parched. With nothing else to do she read on, absorbed. At least an hour had gone by, and no-one had disturbed Rebecca. She wasn't concerned. She was more than happy to be left alone here. Her reading, however, had both stimulated and disturbed her. The 'Cipher' of which her hostesses spoke was, it appeared, a work in progress consisting of (seemingly) feverish and unintelligible passive writings of various kinds, and a handwritten and leather-bound journal which had been written in German. According to the date inscribed on the top of the first sheet, this volume was more than two hundred years old. It was a slim volume, and Rebecca read it cover to cover, then turning it over in her hands she pondered the contents. Contained in its pages were predictions and visions of the writer set down in graphic and sometimes gory detail. It made very little sense to her. She flicked the pages and realised that the figures which she had first taken for page numbers around the corners of each page were, in fact, Hebrew characters. Taken one after another they formed words. Each break before the next word was denoted by a blank corner. Gathering the writing materials that she had seen on the bureau, she began to piece the words together. Contentedly she applied herself to her self-imposed task. She had just completed the translation of the last word when she gratefully gave in to the lethargy that had been threatening to overcome her. With the pen still in her hand, she lay her head on the bureau and fell into a dreamless sleep.

CHAPTER 20

S HE WOKE TO the sound of the gong once more, close by her in
the room. This time it was much louder and more insistent. She
realised that she was no longer in the library. This was a room she
had not been taken into on her tour. It was small and windowless,
and the walls were decorated with murals highlighted with gold leaf.
Pools of darkness crowded the chamber, making it feel forbidding
and tomb like. The obscurity was alleviated only by sconces of
flame in each corner and the large light-well above her, a curious,
pyramidical construction of varied colours of glass. She could see
little through it but momentarily caught sight of the full moon
through the clouds. The room must be at the top of the edifice.
As her eyes became accustomed to the darkness, she could see
more detail in the paintings surrounding her. The walls to the right
and left of her appeared to be decorated in designs of fantastical
creatures. She could pick out a male figure in a toga with a dog's
head, holding some sort of staff in his hand. There were winged,
semi-clad women in attendance around him. In the flickering of
the firelight they looked for all the world as if they were moving.

Trying to stand, she found her legs would not support her.

She tried to think. Think. Think. Her mind was foggy, her head throbbed painfully. The room began to spin around her. Slumping back into the ottoman she took stock of her surroundings. Someone must have carried her and arranged her in this high-backed golden throne, her hands had been limply arranged on the lion head hand-rests. She could see her shape reflected in the dark mirror on the wall before her. Another mirror behind the chair reflected her back. She could feel her sense of self being eroded, drawn into the mirror, trapped into an endless expression of anguish. Eternally diminishing selves. She was both present in the chair and walking around herself, inspecting, judging.

As she turned, her loosened hair stroked her shoulder and, with panic rising, Rebecca realised that someone had removed her clothes and she was now dressed in a diaphanous blue robe, which had been tied over one of her shoulders. Her limbs were naked apart from a serpent bangle gripping her right upper arm. She tried to reach up to pull it away, but her body felt just as heavy as lead. She could move her head only. Her frame felt as unresponsive as a statue. The panic now flooded through her body, and she began to shake. The sound of the gong was coming from directly behind her. It grew louder, faster, more insistent. She could sense the sound pulsing through her body. It was all she could feel now. Suddenly, when she felt she could stand it no more, out from the space from which the sound emanated, four figures separated themselves from the shadows and walked slowly around the chair, two female forms from the left, two male forms from the right. They stood in front of the mirror, unspeaking, doubling her fear.

The four figures were known to her, but dressed in their robes they were almost unrecognisable, but there they stood, Lord and Lady Hawsley, Mr and Mrs Osborne. All were dressed in ceremonial garments. The women were robed in simple shifts of pale green, their hair curled loosely and dressed with flowers. Both wore heavy necklaces and arm bangles. Around their head, one wore a triple moon tiara, the other a crescent moon. The cloying and intense aroma of incense forced its way into Rebecca's nostrils. Nauseated, she tasted the bile rising in her throat as she fought to stay conscious.

She tried to focus her thoughts. Where had she seen these moon designs before? Now she remembered. She recognised the forms from a book which Geraldine had, only recently, given her permission to open. What was their significance here, she wondered. Thoughts of her friend gave her courage. This was not the time for weakness.

Rebecca could not speak, and even if she had been able, she had no words. Hawsley had stepped forward out of the line and began to speak to her. 'We welcome and honour your presence here at this time, in this, our temple of Hermanoubis. Here we celebrate the son of Set and Nephthys.' He pointed to the dog-headed figure painted in the wall. 'He is both Hermes and Anubis. It is his power as the conductor of souls which we channel. It is he who is the conduit between this life and the next, and when all rituals in the Cipher have been completed, then we will have his power. We brought you here for an initiation.' As if exhausted, he dropped his head and crossing his arms across his body he stepped back into the gloom. Osborne took over, even now speaking with a supercilious drawl, as if in emphasis of Rebecca's ignorance. 'The Manuscript was passed to us. We are its inheritors. This knowledge is not for the masses. There is no-one else who could understand its contents, nor how to unlock the secrets. The power to transcend death itself will be within this circle.' Finally, he intoned. 'We brought you here for elucidation.' As Hawsley had done before him, he stepped back into the gloom. Unlike him, however, Osborne's hands were planted firmly on his hips, and his stance was arrogant. He stared blatantly at Rebecca's body and her anger started to displace the fog within her brain, giving it fuel like oxygen to a smoky fire.

The next to step forward to speak was Lady Hawsley. Any pretence of kindness was gone from her face. 'You are here for your gift, and your gift alone. Once the ritual is over you will remember little, and wish to recall even less. You will leave your gift here. The ritual will ensure that.' Rebecca was puzzled, and not only by the words. Her Ladyship had almost spat out the words, this speech did not seem rehearsed like those of the men. As she stepped back into the gloom, Mrs Osborne stepped forward awkwardly. She looked back at her sister who steadfastly refused to return her gaze. Instead, Mrs Osborne turned to Rebecca, seemingly completing her sister's sentence with the words, 'We brought you here for perpetuation.' She continued impassively. 'You are the link. Now you have interpreted the words of the Cipher and so the final ritual can be performed. We can complete the circle, and bring both worlds closer.' She stepped back, and Rebecca saw a fleeting glimpse of sadness in her eyes as she intoned. 'We brought you here for transformation.'

The women circled slowly around Rebecca, scattering handfuls of sand from copper bowls until the floor was lightly covered. Both stopped beside her, one to the left, one to the right, flanking her in an echo of the carved images outside the building. The entire process had a stilted, poorly choreographed feel to it. Next, and in a perfect mirror of each another, both men drew a short dagger from the belts of their robes with their right hand and each raised it to their forehead. '*Ateh...*' they intoned. Next they lowered the dagger to their chest. '*Malkuth...*' Then, with the point resting on their right shoulder, '*Ve Geburah.*' With each word the women scattered handfuls of sand onto the floor around Rebecca. '*Ve Gedulah... LeOlam... Amen.*'

Then, with Rebecca at its centre, they traced the outline of a pentagram into the sand.

Hawsley took a step towards Rebecca and raised his hands up to the full moon shining now through the skylight. 'Beneath me flames the pentagram. Above me shines the six-rayed star,' he declaimed. Then, pointing his dagger in each direction to amplify his words, he continued. 'Before me Raphael. Behind me Gabriel, at my right hand Michael, at my left hand I make sacred space for Azriel.'

Finally lowering his arms, he stepped forward and aimed his speech directly towards Rebecca.

'With this purification ritual we cleanse the space herein, and absolve all those here participating. We are merely vessels of the energy we espouse, and as such, subject to its desires. With this symbol here below, we dedicate the events that are to happen here to the higher power and thus remove them from all limiting earthly constraints. We are here to free you from your connection with the Angel of Death, Azriel himself, and to take that charge unto ourselves so he can take his place among his true peers.'

Rebecca watched, transfixed by events. How could they possibly know anything about the Angel? Did they truly have some supernatural power? She felt no more connection with anything otherworldly here than she did at home in the Spiritualist Circle, but she did feel fear. Intense, numbing, and very much present here in the chamber of darkness. Her mouth tasted metallic and dry, her lips parched. Her body was paralysed and she could only move her head to watch as events unfolded around her. She wanted to close her eyes and block out the madness, but Rebecca compelled herself to watch as the four figures circled now around her chair, chanting words she could not hear. Round and round, their words filled the air, the heavy smell of incense increasing the feelings of nausea which were coming to her in waves now. Round and round, round and round, the four figures merged and separated in her blurry sight and she fought to stay conscious. The words she heard were nonsensical, gibberish, but somehow they were familiar to her. Where was the Angel now, she wondered? Would he come soon? This is what they wanted. This is why she was here. They wanted the Angel for themselves – but how did they know? How could they know of his existence? She tried to think when, suddenly, with a single strike of the gong the chanting stopped, and once more they stood before her. The silence dragged at the air around them, increasing its weight with every passing moment.

Eventually, Hawsley turned to Osborne. 'I, I can't. Old man. I just can't. After all she is little more than a child.' Osborne smiled his little dog smile and twisted his body towards Rebecca. 'If you aren't man enough, Hawsley, then I will just have to claim the prize for myself, won't I?' He approached the throne where Rebecca sat, frozen, and with one hand he pushed her down until she lay prone, inert. With the other he pulled aside his robe, exposing his genitals. He brought his face close to hers until she could taste the whisky fuming on his breath, roughly pushing her legs apart with his own. He whispered, almost gently, 'Don't worry about the future, my dear, you will not be ruined. Isaac will still take you. We have an – arrangement.' Rebecca turned her head frantically towards the two women for help, but they were in each other's arms, faces turned away from her. Hawsley stood rooted to the spot, watching openly, but with shame suffusing his face. Rebecca began to scream hysterically but Osborne continued to push up her robes relentlessly. She could feel his engorged penis blindly pushing its way around her groin. Terrified, she called desperately to the Angel to appear and take him into the darkness. Before she could reach out her mind to him, her thoughts were suddenly splintered into a million pieces and she watched as the glass pyramid above them gave way and glass showered the room.

CHAPTER 21

IN HIS HASTE to save his own skin, Osborne had upturned the ottoman where Rebecca had been. It was now lying on its side in the corner of the room and Rebecca had been thrown behind it. Her brain finally registered pain, and looked down at her clothing to see her blood seeping through from between her legs. Its intensity shocked her body out of its catatonic state, and she tried to pull herself upright. The sisters were both now screaming hysterically and, emanating from somewhere else in the house, she could hear shouting, and a gunshot. Suddenly, the door to the chamber was flung open and light flooded in. Aunt Miriam and Colonel Burbridge filled the doorway. She was aware of other people crowding behind them, and it was clear that some kind of altercation was still going on in the hallway. Miriam raised a pistol. 'The first thing to move I will shoot.' Osborne raised his hand as if in protest. The reverberations of the shot were stunning. Rebecca ducked down and hid herself behind the ottoman, and, when the echoes had subsided, she tentatively raised her head to see Osborne supine in the corner, blood pouring from his hand.

The rescue itself was, in retrospect, rather shambolic, with

Rebecca being bundled in a cloak and half carried, half dragged down the staircase and out to Colonel Burbridge's waiting carriage. With her head resting on Miriam's lap, and the colonel seated opposite, she watched as Miriam refused to relinquish the gun to its rightful owner. She folded it carefully into a handkerchief and placed it into her pocket, all the while continuing to look across the carriage at her companion. He relented. 'I take my hat off to you today, madam. That was an extraordinary shot. I do believe you took his finger clean off!' Miriam breathed in sharply, her cheeks still suffused with rage, and responded tartly. 'Not, really, dear colonel. I was aiming for his tallywag.' He sat back in his seat and grinned across at her. She responded sheepishly.

Rebecca herself didn't care about anything. At that moment she felt more loved than she had ever done in her life. She tried to raise her head to tell Miriam that she loved her, but instead she promptly puked profusely over her aunt, herself, and the carriage window, before lapsing into insensibility.

The brougham soon pulled up outside St George's Hospital, and the coachman leaned in and spoke to the colonel. 'Quite so,' he responded. 'Change of plan, m'dear.' With that he directed the coachman to make post-haste to the house in Gower Street, back along Piccadilly where the sound of policemen's whistles now added to the general chaos of a London evening. The doors to the Egyptian House were wide open, light flooding into the street along with various police and servants who now congregated on the doorstep. Pausing for only the briefest of moments to take in the scene, an indistinguishable carriage conveyed its insensible and rather smelly cargo along with her rescuers safely home to Gower Street.

Soon after, the renegade group reconvened in Miriam's drawing room, returning to the house separately or in pairs to avoid appearing too conspicuous. It would seem that Rebecca's deliverance had been a somewhat public affair in which most of the members of Miriam's Spiritualist Circle had participated. The rescue itself had been hastily organised by the colonel, and led, by general consensus, by Miriam herself. After all, it *was* her niece they were liberating. The sound levels in the packed room were surprisingly high, and highlighted an unexpected bonhomie. Even among those for whom there had been rivalry there was, for now, consensus. Nothing unites a group like a common enemy, the colonel thought to himself on more than one occasion during the evening. He noted Mesdames Thorne and Tiran deep in reprising their own account of events. Both were pink and flushed with excitement. It appeared that between them they had 'accidentally' managed to give Mrs Osborne a bloody nose during the altercation in Piccadilly with the judicious use of an umbrella and a hefty volume of poetry which they happened to have about their persons that evening. It would seem a personal score had been settled. It transpired that Mrs Osborne had previously snubbed both women. Not a good move as it turned out. The triumphant pair now chatted amiably, praising the other for their audacity and courage and occasionally touching each other on the arm affectionately. That truce won't last long, mused the colonel, smiling inwardly.

The evening ended much later than usual, without so much as the smallest prayer or summoning of Spirit. By the time Miriam had said her thanks and goodbyes to the last of her group, she could feel the emotional exhaustion of the evening's events threatening to overcome her. The front door closed, leaving herself and the colonel alone in the drawing room. 'How is she? I mean, did he...?' began the colonel, tentatively. 'No. No, he hadn't. No. Rebecca is still intact. The blood was from a cut on her thigh.' With that,

Miriam felt her knees buckle, and she started to sob, silently. 'Oh, Hugo. What kind of a woman am I? This child has been entrusted into my care and she almost... almost...' Hugo Burbridge guided Miriam to the settee and sat beside her. 'You had absolutely no way of knowing what those unspeakable people were intending. Even in my military days I have never seen or heard of the like! These people have no right to call themselves Englishmen, and aristocrats too! Old money would never had behaved in such a despicable manner. Never. Never.' Miriam looked at her companion. Through all his bluff and bluster he was a good man, with a kind heart, and she knew that he loved her and would marry her tomorrow if she had encouraged him even in the smallest way. His monologue gave Miriam time to gather her thoughts. Rising, she said, 'You must go, now. We can't have people gossiping about you now, can we?' The colonel rose, bowed deeply, and put his hand out to Miriam. 'What?' she said, innocently. 'My revolver, Miriam. Think about it. It would be difficult to explain how you just happen to have a recently discharged pistol in the house on the same day as Osborne gets himself shot. I cannot allow you to be involved in any scandal.' Miriam went to her bureau and retrieved the weapon, still wrapped in cloth. 'I will keep your kerchief, m'dear. A souvenir of an exciting evening.' He looked suddenly serious. 'One which, I pray, will not have made too deep an impression on Rebecca. She is young. Youth has remarkable facility for recovery. You will see. She will be fine, I am sure. It would have been too risky to take her to see a physician at the hospital around the corner from Piccadilly – not when there were so many police around. Besides, I'm sure that rest will be better for her than any quack.' He bowed and raised Miriam's hand to his lips. 'I will visit you again as soon as I have gathered intelligence on how the events of this evening were presented to the police. I will make the appropriate enquiries at my Lodge and I am sure I will be able to find out discreetly. Don't worry, Miriam. I doubt you will have the Detective Branch knocking at the door of Gower Street. I will, as ever, be discreet in my enquiries. We need to know what story they concocted before deciding on the best course of action – the best path for Rebecca, I mean.'

Once the colonel had left her alone with her thoughts, she reviewed his words. Miriam shuddered at the thought that Rebecca might have to undergo an interview by the detectives, or even worse that this happening might in some way become public knowledge and cause her untold distress and humiliation. Rebecca's father would be incandescent, and Isaac may even withdraw his proposal of marriage. Miriam calmed herself with a small sherry. She knew that no-one from the circle would utter a word, and only she and the colonel saw the inside of that dreadful room, so they would have very little to tell. Gratefully (and somewhat unsteadily) she made her way up the stairs to Rebecca's bedroom. What the colonel didn't know, and Miriam had no intention of telling him, was at this moment Rebecca was already being attended to by someone whose ministrations she trusted more than any doctor.

Although Geraldine Beskin and Miriam Blumenkranz had never formally been introduced, they knew quite a lot about one another. Geraldine knew about Miriam from talking to Rebecca, and Miriam of Geraldine through her reputation within the Spiritualist brother and sisterhood. Although avowedly not a Spiritualist herself, the bookseller was highly regarded – and somewhat feared – by those who took their study of all things esoteric to the next level. At this present moment, Geraldine was half-marching, half-carrying a listless Rebecca around her bedroom. 'Whatever drugs they gave her, they were strong. We need to keep this up for two or three hours.' Rebecca's teeth were chattering. 'The window must stay open. The cold will help rouse her. Here. You take over now while I go to the kitchen.' Miriam took hold of Rebecca, who seemed ready to drop to the floor. 'You *must* keep her walking. Prevent her from sleeping.' Miriam gritted her teeth and set about her task.

Time passed in the silent house, punctuated by the chimes of the grandmother clock in the hallway downstairs. The patient was now in bed, Miriam now watched as Geraldine lifted up Rebecca's unresisting head to encourage her to drink a brown liquid. Miriam was surprised to find she was more than a little nervous in Geraldine's company. 'May I ask is this one of your own decoctions, madam?' she asked, politely. Geraldine turned to her with a serious face. 'Not mine own, no, but a well tried and tested remedy. Hot, sweet tea. Do have some.' She nodded to a tray with a teapot. Miriam tested it. The pot was cold. Turning to call for Aisha to fetch a fresh brew, she saw that the silent servant was already standing noiselessly by the door. Miriam saw that there were tears in her eyes. 'Come us on, Aisha! We will have none of that. Rebecca will be back with us soon and everything will be fine.'

Aisha nodded imperceptibly, collected the tea tray, and left the older women alone. Miriam felt her shoulders sag. 'She will be, won't she?' Geraldine walked over to the washstand, poured water into the bowl, and soaked a flannel with the water. She carefully wrung the water from it and used it to wipe Rebecca's sweat-soaked brow. 'The night is not yet over and we will know more in the morning.' She reached down into her voluminous carpet bag and pulled out a pack of cards. Miriam grimaced nervously, unsure of what to expect next. 'You do play cribbage, do you not, madam?'

Countless pots of tea had been drunk, and games of cribbage won and lost. The women took it in turns to keep Rebecca hydrated and cool down her fevered body. Miriam asked Geraldine what devilry could have caused Rebecca to be in such a lethargic state, and so quickly too. Geraldine leaned over and pulled open one of Rebecca's eyes. The pupil had almost disappeared. 'I would hazard a guess at large doses of laudanum delivered over a very short space of time, possibly combined with some other drug, but I cannot be sure. It is most fortunate that she purged when she did, otherwise I would fear for her heart, young as she is.' Miriam felt like taking issue with the word 'fortunate' as most of the puke went over her, but she realised what Geraldine was saying was the truth. Whatever the child had been given that dreadful night needed to work its way out of her body. Until then there was no way of really knowing if she was unscathed. Miriam debated whether to tell Rebecca what had happened to her, finally confiding her fears to Geraldine. The bookseller's response was short and valid. 'Say nothing. Rebecca's own mind will give her access to what she needs to know, and anything else is of no value. If she does remember it all, then it is for us to help her deal with it in the best possible manner.' Miriam felt curiously warmed when her new friend said 'us'. It felt good to be able to share these dark times with one who would neither judge, comment or gossip. With that thought uppermost in mind, she slumped down into the comfort of the bedroom chair. As the first fingers of light crawled across the rooftops of London she fell deeply asleep.

CHAPTER 22

WHEN REBECCA WOKE, she was confused. She reached to her feet to find they had been covered in a mustard poultice. The smell repelled her. More to the point, what was Geraldine doing in her bedroom? It was definitely her, large as life, arms folded, hair loose, sleeping peacefully in the basket chair by her window. She tried to speak, but her throat felt parched and raw. She reached out to her nightstand, and promptly knocked over the carafe, both waking Geraldine and awakening a sudden memory of glass breaking. Lots of glass, everywhere... but before she could pull the memory closer, Miriam entered the room carrying a tray, and the delicious smell of hot buttered teacakes pushed any other thoughts from Rebecca's mind. She was hungry. Hungry and thirsty, and she was both delighted and bemused to discover that Miriam and Geraldine seemed to be firm friends and were fussing around her quietly as she drank the proffered tea. She wolfed down the teacakes gratefully, then, before she had a chance to ask any of the many questions which were circling around her mind, she fell into a deep and natural sleep for the first time in days.

More time had passed since her adventure at the Egyptian

House than she had realised. What she thought had been one day had actually been five. Weakly, she propped herself up with her bed pillows and tried to marshal her thoughts. Rebecca could clearly remember arriving at the house in Piccadilly, transcribing the Hebrew text and then consuming the sherry and madeleines. After that her recollection was sketchy, and she became unclear on what were memories and what were dreams. Dog-headed men and flying women populated the London streets which turned into rivers of blood. During the past five days and nights her mind had been colonised with the most bizarre of images and strangest of sensations. She reached down to touch the dressing on her thigh, and the activation of the pain brought parts of these visions into sharper focus. Feeling overwhelmed by the effort, she leaned her body back into the pillows. It was all so confusing.

On the afternoon of the sixth day, Rebecca woke feeling more alert, more connected. Her aunt was fitfully dozing in the wicker chair by the window. Rebecca tried to sit up in bed, and exhausted herself from the effort. It was true that although her body was still lethargic, her mind was now racing. How had her aunt known she was in danger? She still had a blank about the events in the temple room, but moments were beginning to crystallise in her mind's eye. Above all, what had happened, and how had she been injured?

Miriam stirred at the sound of Rebecca's movements. She looked lovingly over at her niece, and then leaned over her as if to kiss her, but instead raised her spectacles and stared deeply and intently into each of her niece's eyes. 'Excellent. It's good to see your eyes looking normal.' 'Normal' in this instance meant that Rebecca had lost the pinprick pupils which had marked her drugged state. To be accurate, her eyes were bloodshot right through and very teary, but to Miriam they indicated that her niece was coming back to them. She sat on the bed and stroked the counterpane absently. 'I know you have questions, but before you ask, I have a confession that I want to make. Since you have been here, you have never been alone on the streets of London.' Rebecca stared intently at Miriam. 'In all that time, either Aisha or Karim has been close by as your shadow. I'm sorry that I didn't tell you before, but you perhaps would have thought the worse of me for insisting you were not unaccompanied. There are some very strange people out there on the streets, and I wanted to ensure that you did not come to any harm.' Rebecca smiled. There were some very strange people in this house, let alone out there on the street, she thought to herself. Strange isn't necessarily harmful. She brought her attention back to Miriam's words as her aunt continued. 'On the night of... well,' Miriam swallowed, unsure of the words to use to describe the night of Rebecca's rescue, 'On that dreadful night, Karim and Aisha arrived at the Egyptian House before you. They have a particular talent for making themselves invisible.' Rebecca was curious now. The Indian twins were, she thought, extremely distinctive, especially when dressed in their robes. How would it be possible for them to disappear? It was a question which Miriam avoided gracefully, going on to tell her that Aisha positioned herself in a place where she could observe the movement around the Egyptian House, and Karim was on the building itself. 'On the building, not in?' Yes. Miriam continued. On the building. It seemed that both Aisha and Karim were highly skilled in *walking the leads* – using the rooftops as a different way of navigating London. It appeared that Karim had, some years before, befriended one of the boys of Covent Garden who slept in the tiny round structures at the top of the building. He had taught Karim how to use the roofs as a street, and how to avoid harm from the gangs who roamed them. 'Yes. I know. Extraordinary, isn't it?' said Miriam in response to the look of incredulity on Rebecca's face. 'However, this is not the time for such a diversion. To resume, Aisha watched over you as you were left alone in the library, and realised that something was very wrong with you once you had drunk from the decanter.' However, when she saw you were unconscious, and watched the women start to disrobe you, she immediately came for me.' So that was how Miriam had known she was in danger. A part of Rebecca's mind rebelled against the knowledge that all this time her freedom in the streets of London had not been as complete as she had imagined. No matter. This was not the occasion to take offence. Miriam only had her best interests at heart, she felt sure of that now. 'Now then, my dear. Tell me what you remember.'

Dusk had fallen, and Rebecca was now asleep, exhausted by her efforts in trying to remember what had happened to her in the Egyptian House. Miriam silently watched the eyes of her recumbent niece moving rapidly from side to side. Occasionally Rebecca's body twitched and her lips moved as if in silent prayer. Miriam quietly closed the door of the bedroom, and made her way to the comfort of the kitchen. She needed food, and she needed a space to think in complete silence.

The routine of the household now revolved around Rebecca. The weekly circles had decamped temporarily to the colonel's house, and Miriam had not attended. Every day the colonel had come to visit her to distract her with news from the circle or gossip from the participants. Even Clarissa made the journey to visit the sickroom. She was hysterically distressed to see Rebecca in her weakened state, so much so that Miriam thought it better if she did not come again.

There had been no further news about the inhabitants of the Egyptian House. The colonel had discovered all parties to that dreadful evening had decamped to Hawsley's country house in Norfolk. It may as well have been the moon, he commented wryly, so far removed from them were the Hawsleys and the Osbornes now. Miriam prayed for normality to return and for Rebecca to just come back to her. She felt sure that if her memory returned fully, then she could start to recover. She was convinced of it, unlike Geraldine, who debated with her the importance of leaving some doors of Rebecca's mind firmly closed.

As her time in her sickroom moved into its second week, Miriam tentatively brought to her niece's bedroom the book, and some papers. Rebecca recognised them immediately as the pages on which she had transcribed the Hebrew from the margins of the book, and the slim volume as that from which she had copied them. It appeared that Karim had learnt more skills than just walking the leads from the Covent Garden boys, as in the chaos of the rescue he had 'retrieved' these documents from the library. Rebecca was starting to view the Indian twins with new eyes, and a dawning, albeit dubious, respect for their abilities. She leaned back in the chair and closed her eyes, her fingers still tracing the outline of the book in her hands. Her eyes moved rapidly beneath their closed lids.

Miriam and Geraldine watched over her. Geraldine had been firmly against taking the papers to Rebecca as she feared it might act as a prompt to memory, and she felt it was too soon. Personally, she believed the old leather book to be a fake – a good one to be sure, but a recent one certainly. There were a number of them about lately, in fact someone had come into the bookshop and offered her one for sale, so she recognised the style. There were too many nouveau-esoteric seekers who believed that they could learn all there was to know about arcane magic from one, special book, and were prepared to pay handsomely for a short cut. The pitch was always the same – only a select few to whom the wisdom would be revealed. One book that only they were able to understand and decipher. Poppycock. There were plenty of predators around to give those Emperors of Mysticism a new set of clothes. The more the knowledge cost, the more these dupes would be prepared to pay to get sight of it, and the less scrutiny they chose to put to it. More Fool than Magician. It was ever thus. For herself, she wasn't about to pander to those shallow people, and she had seen many of them off out of Atlantis with a flea in their ear. True seekers of knowledge were prepared to study, and to work hard. With that thought, a tiny alarm momentarily went off in her mind, and as she tried to trace the source of it, it vanished.

For the present, Geraldine held her counsel on the authenticity, or not, of the volume. Knowing that Rebecca had been attacked was bad enough, to discover that the reason for it was all a sham would, she felt, have been too much for Miriam's already guilt-laden mind. As she so often did, the bookseller chose silence.

Miriam, however, felt that seeing the book might help settle her niece's troubled mind, so she had overruled her friend's counsel. Rebecca's eyes were still firmly shut, the two elder women waiting silently before her. Suddenly Rebecca's eyes flew open. She looked up at Miriam and Geraldine, looked down at the papers, and began to scream. The fragments of memory now cascaded around her and shattered her fragile mind. The sound which emanated from her was a howl of pure animal anguish, and seemed to come from a place much older and darker than the frame which contained it. The cry penetrated the fabric of the whole household, ripping it open, and they all came running.

CHAPTER 23

THIS TIME THERE was no rescue. The prison was in Rebecca's mind, and no amount of soothing embraces and calming words seemed to penetrate its walls. Eventually when the screams turned to sobs and she could cry no more, she slumped into her chair. Her eyes were open but unseeing, her mouth agape. Now it was Miriam who broke down, her sobs silent and wracking. She was afraid, now. Afraid that her determination to be right had caused this. Afraid for Rebecca. Afraid because she no longer knew what to do, and she knew the clock had started ticking for Rebecca on the day Miriam had written to her father informing him that Rebecca had been taken ill. She was rudely roused by Geraldine's words. 'Miriam. Pull yourself together, woman. You are of no use to her in this state.' She reacted as if she had been slapped in the face. How dare this woman talk to me in this way, and in my house too? 'Please leave, madam. You offend me with your tone and your words. Good day to you, Mrs Beskin.' She pulled herself upright, haughtily, as Geraldine turned away from her and silently collected her belongings, leaving without another word. Closing the door of the bedroom carefully behind her, she allowed the smallest of smiles to play around the corner of her lips. Geraldine's work was done for now. Besides, her time would be better served investigating the source of the nagging feeling she had earlier. It was relevant. It was important too. She just felt it in her bowels, and when she had these intuitions there was nothing else she could possibly do but to follow her gut where it led her.

Miriam, in the meanwhile, had been propelled rapidly from helplessness to action. Once she was sure that Rebecca was settled in her bed, and with Aisha tasked to watch over her, she ventured out of the house in Gower Street for the first time since the rescue. She took a hansom to the home of Colonel Burbridge. She needed to find out what, if anything, had been reported to the police about the event, and to talk to him about what could be done to help Rebecca. Thinking about Geraldine's words had really upset her, and, at the same time, drove her determination to prove that she was very much in control of her emotions, thank you very much madam.

The colonel had not yet arrived back from his luncheon at his club, so she was invited to wait in the library. Miriam had never had the opportunity to look closely at the room, and she took this chance. It was a typically masculine room, with some souvenirs of the colonel's military postings. The books were classics, with a smattering of Spiritualist volumes in a section which looked better kept and more accessible than the shelves. It suddenly struck her that the colonel was probably lonely. He did not have any kith or kin as far as she knew, certainly there were none that he had ever mentioned. Walking around the back of his desk she saw the volume which was currently occupying his attention, and noticed that as a bookmark he was using the handkerchief which she had used to wrap his pistol. She smiled, and, hearing the sound of his arrival, rapidly relocated herself to a corner of the room where, when he entered, she was earnestly inspecting a volume of Cicero.

Since she had seen him last, the colonel had put his Masonic network to good use. He had discovered that not only had Osborne lost his forefinger, 'I told you so!' but that the household had concocted a very different version of events than actually occurred. According to Lord Hawsley, 'a group of vagabonds' and street Arabs had broken into the house, and Osborne had discharged a pistol at the group, only for it to misfire. He claimed that the injury was self-inflicted, and that not one of the inhabitants of the house got a good look at the intruders, so wouldn't be able to identify them even if they were caught. The Hawsleys has subsequently closed up the London house, and had decamped to their Norfolk country home with the Osbornes. As far as the police were concerned, the matter was now concluded, if not completely, at least to the satisfaction of the apparently injured parties. As she listened to the results of his intelligence gathering, relief began to flood through her. At least Rebecca would not have to be subjected to an interview, and it seemed that, publicly at least, the matter was at an end.

The colonel listened silently as Miriam told him about the state Rebecca was in. He displayed no curiosity as to who the female companion to her sleepless nights had been. His suggestion was, as she would have expected, stunningly practical. The Mesmeric Hospital. It was close by in Weymouth Street. He would send a letter with his batman post-haste requesting advice. In a moment of unexpected emotion, Miriam hugged him, and left for Gower Street. When his servant appeared for his instructions some minutes later, Colonel Burbridge was still standing in the same spot Miriam had left him, stroking his beard and smiling contentedly.

When Miriam returned to Gower Street she was informed by an

agitated Aisha that Rebecca had a visitor. Anna Coren had arrived. The letter which Miriam had sent to Ramsgate informing Rebecca's father about her illness had been received the previous morning and Anna Coren had taken the next available train to London to be by her stepdaughter's side. With Aisha unable to prevent her from doing otherwise, she had immediately gone up to Rebecca's bedroom. Miriam raced up the stairs, disturbed beyond belief. This is not what she needed. If Rebecca told Anna Coren what had happened to her, the consequences were unimaginable.

Some hours later, Miriam and Anna Coren were to be found in the drawing room, partaking of a surprisingly formal tea. Miriam enquired as to how Anna's journey had been, and Anna asked how long Rebecca had been suffering from a fever. Miriam kept her responses short and to the point. If she didn't precisely lie, she was judicious in her choice of words. She had no way of knowing what exchange Anna and Rebecca had had before she arrived home, and she did not want to bring the adventure in the Egyptian House into the conversation if Rebecca hadn't already brought it up. The conversation, therefore, remained stilted and awkward. When asked directly, Miriam affirmed that a physician had been sent for, although she did not actually specify what sort of doctor. She settled her mind to this Jesuitical statement by reminding herself that a doctor was going to come from the Mesmeric Hospital at the request of the colonel. She only hoped that Anna Coren would leave soon. Her anxiety must have shown on her face as Anna began placating her by telling her how pleased Rebecca's father had been at the care she had taken of his daughter, judging from the contented letters which she had been sending home to Ramsgate. Miriam smiled, and tried to push the dialogue along into a different direction. 'How is your brother, Isaac? Is he well?' The conversation moved more freely, as Anna told of Isaac's unexpected promotion and furthermore how delighted he was that Rebecca's father had agreed to his proposal of marriage. Anna talked of his attributes with the affection of an older sister, and went on to say that he was currently away from London, in Norfolk in fact, on important business for his employer. Otherwise, she felt sure, he would have certainly been to visit Rebecca by now. The conversation had come full circle, and Miriam's anxiety escalated once more. Her search for a different topic was broken gratefully when Aisha knocked on the drawing room door, announcing that Rebecca was awake and asking for food. Miriam jumped up from her seat, issuing instructions for a nourishing boiled egg to be prepared, and turned to Anna. 'I do not want to keep you from catching the train back to Ramsgate. I will inform you directly of any change to Rebecca's condition.' Anna Coren was no fool. She could tell that Miriam wanted her out of the house. 'Not at all. I will be staying in London for a few days. I will come up with you to say goodbye to Rebecca, and will return tomorrow.' Miriam politely showed her guest out into the hallway and followed her up the stairs. The temptation to trip her up on the way was surprisingly strong.

Her fears, however, were blissfully unfounded. Rebecca was sitting up in bed, her hands outside of the counterpane. She was pale but no longer perspiring, and her pupils looked normal. Her long, loose hair was plastered to her forehead, but she did look more like her old self. It seemed that the fever had broken. Anna Coren sat with Rebecca, stroking her unmoving hand, until food arrived.

Later that afternoon, a knock at the door heralded the arrival of two tall, bespectacled gentlemen. Anna Coren had long since left, promising to return and sit with Rebecca tomorrow. Miriam gratefully let them in and, as each took turns to examine Rebecca, she sat with the other answering their questions about her niece's general health. She chatted amiably over tea as each asked her interesting questions about Spiritualism and her niece's beliefs and habits, even discussing the benefits of vegetarianism. She felt calmed with the knowledge that the doctors from the Mesmeric Hospital were taking a thoroughly holistic approach to Rebecca's care, not just focusing on the physical symptoms, but concerned with her mental and spiritual wellbeing as well. An hour passed and, after checking that Rebecca was sleeping peacefully, she retired to her sitting room to take stock of the events of the day. It wasn't many minutes before her meditations turned to a gentle snore.

Aisha's insistent knocking at the door of the sitting room had not produced any response. Miriam was fast asleep in the chair. She was suddenly awakened by Aisha standing over her, gently shaking her shoulder. 'Madam – please come. You must come with me now.' Miriam's heart began to race. 'Rebecca?' she said, suddenly afraid. 'No madam. There are two gentlemen at the door. They say they are from the Mesmeric Hospital...'

CHAPTER 24

AFTER INSISTING ON seeing proof that the bemused gentlemen in her hallway were actually doctors from the Mesmeric Hospital as they actually claimed to be, Miriam finally relented and allowed them in to see Rebecca. This time she stayed in the room with them, arms folded, lips pursed. She was very disturbed. If the other men who had declared themselves to be doctors were not, in fact, doctors, who or what were they? She reviewed her conversations with each of her earlier visitors, and realised that at no point had they actually said that they were from the Mesmeric Hospital. Yes, they had claimed to be doctors, but from where, she wondered, and how had they come to be paying a visit to Rebecca? The only possible answer was that Anna Coren had arranged for them to come. She would have to wait until tomorrow when Anna came back to the house to find out. In the meanwhile, she was becoming progressively more agitated.

The doctors from the Mesmeric Hospital had been very kind, and were gentle with both Rebecca and Miriam. They asked what treatments she had already undergone, and who had treated her. Miriam told them about Geraldine Beskin, and all her ministrations.

They approved, both of the treatment and of Geraldine. It appeared she had a reputation as a healer, and had been invited to work with the Mesmeric Hospital, but had refused, stating she was a 'purveyor of knowledge', nothing more. Miriam felt her ears burning with shame as she realised that she had also been taught a lesson by Geraldine, one which, to be fair, galvanised her into action. Obviously that was the intention, and it had worked. She would seek out her friend and apologise. This was not the time for pettiness, and right now she deeply felt in need of allies. Without being able to put her finger on why, she felt as if enemies were closing in, and her fear for Rebecca escalated to a new level.

Once the consultation was over and Rebecca had once more been made comfortable in her bed, Miriam did something which she had not done for a long time. Taking the key to her bureau from within the faux-book where she kept it hidden, she opened the largest drawer and pulled out from beneath her writing paper a rarely used planchette. Carefully she screwed the wheels onto the heart-shaped device, and inserted the pencil as per the instructions, placing a sheet of paper beneath it. She knew that this tool usually required more than one person, but right now she didn't care. Right now she wanted guidance, and really didn't know where to turn to, other than seek it from the other side. Setting it up so she could comfortably rest her hand on the device, she closed her eyes, and waited. And waited. And waited. Finally, tedium overcame her, and she fell asleep.

Planchette forgotten, she woke to the sound of the gentle voice of Aisha, announcing that food had been prepared for her, and was now ready in the kitchen. Miriam smiled. She had not instructed anything of the kind, but her quiet retainer had taken matters into her own hands. Right now she found herself sitting in the warm and comfortable kitchen, eating nourishing pea soup. Miriam soaked up the precious moments of peace. Before her was a pile of periodicals and from it she selected the most recent edition of The Spiritualist, and began to read. A happy hour passed in perusal of reports of lectures, debates and letters from individuals telling of their amazing experiences of Spirit manifestation. Miriam missed the solace of the evenings in circle. She wondered how different it would be for her now she had received her answer. Would she still enjoy the séances as much? She didn't know the answer to that. However, she did feel better. Now full, warm and content, she made her way back to Rebecca's room.

Peering through the door, she saw that Rebecca appeared to be sleeping. She tiptoed into the room to take the seat by the window and begin her vigil, when Rebecca spoke to her. 'I am awake, Aunt Miriam. I can assure you that I am feeling much better and would dearly love to see other walls than these of my sickroom soon. I know that I have been suffering from a fever, and that it has created some visions. Nightmarish, awful dreams too, but I feel that this is over now.' Miriam scrutinised her face carefully, taking particular notice of her pupils, which appeared to have returned to normal. 'Honestly. I do feel fine now.' Miriam sat on the bed and pushed a stray strand of hair from Rebecca's face. She smiled gently. 'If you sleep well tonight, and eat well tomorrow, mark you, I will consider that an outing may be in order.'

Rebecca reached out to her aunt and squeezed her hand. She was still pale and drawn, but she seemed to be fine. Geraldine was right all along. The young do have a remarkable capacity for recovery. Perhaps Rebecca had closed and locked the doors to the memories of recent events, and possibly, no, certainly, it would be for the best if she had. She left her niece sleeping, and retired to her own room for the first time since the rescue. In those hypnogogic moments between waking and sleeping she found herself thinking of a way in which she could help Rebecca. When the answer floated towards her, she grasped it and put it in her pocket, the better to reach for it in the morning when she woke. Then, and all through the night, she slept the deep, peaceful sleep of the righteous.

Miriam arrived for breakfast later than usual, having woken and immediately taken action on her idea from the previous evening. Letters had left the house, and Miriam felt both relief and a satisfaction as a result. Rebecca was not only awake when Miriam came down for breakfast, she was seated at the drawing room table. True, she still looked pale, and her clothes seemed looser than before but she was upright, dressed and, apparently, hungry. Miriam resolved that an excursion could be arranged, and she felt sure that it would speed her recovery. A nagging thought passed through her mind – Anna Coren had not returned to the house since she had seen Rebecca was ill. Finally, as there had been no further contact from them, Miriam pushed her anxieties about the identity of her visitors to one side. Hopefully her letter to Anna Coren would be received in time for her to join them in their planned excursion.

It had taken Miriam some time to think of a suitable diversion for Rebecca. It needed to be something which was not too taxing physically, so no wandering around parks or museums. It would have to be something which was sufficiently entertaining to take the child's mind away from the darkness and move her over into a positive state of mind. This, she felt sure, would ensure that the doors Rebecca had closed would remain securely sealed. The idea had come to her when she looked at the page which had been beneath the planchette after her recent experimentation. It had been a sign – of sorts. Miriam had drawn circle after circle on the page. There were no words of great wisdom imparted, but when she held the page in her hand and thought about what she could see, the only thing which came into her mind was the three rings of the circus. So it was, on the third day after Rebecca had risen from her bed, both she and her aunt were collected by Colonel Burbridge in his private carriage. They were to attend a performance at Lord George's Circus in Westminster Bridge Road. 'Of course, he is no more a lord than I am,' their host genially informed them as they left Gower Street. 'Sporting a title is good for business, you see!' Rebecca watched silently as they progressed through the streets. The smog had lessened and the streets started to react to the presence of spring. Flower sellers, costermongers, knife grinders, all loudly touting for business from the general population of London hungry for colour and relief from the darkness of winter. In spite of herself, Rebecca shivered. Miriam noticed and fussed around her, bringing the shawl they had chosen together in Burlington Arcade closer to her niece's throat. Rebecca allowed these tender ministrations listlessly. Miriam and the colonel exchanged glances, and both began to speak at once, Miriam commenting on the street scene outside, and the colonel describing the wonderful spectacle which awaited them. Both stopped speaking, then started again at the same time. Rebecca laughed at their discomfort, and they gratefully joined in with her amusement at their expense.

By the time they had reached Westminster Bridge, Rebecca was becoming excited. She had heard of the Water Carnival from Clarissa. She missed her friend, and had no recollection of Clarissa's visit during her fever. In fact, Rebecca remembered very little. Days or was it weeks had passed since she had visited the house in Piccadilly. The fuzziness of her memories and the awful nature of the feverish visions and dreams would have troubled her if she had enough energy to pay attention. For now, she preferred to hold onto the reality of the moment. Disembarking from the carriage outside Lambeth Palace, the trio joined the happy crowds walking to Astley's Amphitheatre. Once inside, Rebecca became aware of the brightness of the colours therein. Garish lemon-yellow paintwork and gilding predominated in the auditorium. Shown into a private box which was lined with crimson hangings, Rebecca took a seat, her legs shaking from the small exertion, and focused her attention on the fabric. She noticed that the low lighting was a blessing, as, rather than being magnificent and sumptuous, they were somewhat threadbare and ragged. The sight depressed her more than she could understand. In an attempt to lift her spirits, she moved her attention to Miriam and the colonel. He was keeping her occupied by pointing out various people in the audience below them. Miriam seemed to be flushed and happy, occasionally tapping the colonel on his arm and indicating towards something she wanted him to explain. Rebecca realised with a start that her aunt was flirting. Her emotions were mixed. Part of her was pleased at the thought that Miriam may finally find some well-deserved happiness, or at least a good companion with whom to share her life, while at the same time she was saddened to feel that this part of her life was moving away. She would have to return to Ramsgate, she would have to marry Isaac. Her fever had created blank spaces in her memory but she hadn't forgotten what had gone before. She found herself sighing deeply. Miriam looked over at her, and drew her into their conversation. She joined in willingly, now wanting to soak in every experience she could.

The performance was engaging. Horsemen (and women),

carriages, and even a water battle. The audience was transported to other lands and exciting adventures. Rebecca found herself inexorably drawn into the spectacle. Time passed by all too quickly and she was completely absorbed, her worries momentarily forgotten. The colonel pulled out his pocket watch and made a sign that they should start making their way out of the auditorium so as to avoid the crush, but Rebecca didn't want to miss a thing. Indulgently, he offered to leave them in their seats and ensure that their carriage would be brought as close as possible so Rebecca would not need to walk far.

When the last of the performers had left the stage, and the auditorium began to empty, Rebecca and Miriam made their way down the stairs to the ground level. Tired but happy, she leaned on her aunt's arm as they walked out into Westminster Bridge Road. Neither of them could see the carriage. 'We had better wait here. He will find us,' Miriam assured her. Suddenly, she heard a female voice, calling out her name. Anna Coren was waving her handkerchief to her. Rebecca waved back and Anna Coren stepped forward and kissed her niece, moving Miriam aside to do so. Rebecca looked into Anna Coren's eyes and started to speak. Before she could utter a sound Rebecca felt a tobacco-soaked hand cover her mouth, and she was lifted off her feet and bundled into a waiting carriage, her Chinese shawl dropping onto the pavement. Frantically she pushed against the carriage door but her captors, who she now realised were women, forced her back down onto the seat inside. Rebecca could only watch in horror as her aunt began to scream and tried to run after the carriage. The last view she glimpsed from the window as the carriage pulled away was one of Anna Coren's hand, unmoving, and still holding the white kerchief.

CHAPTER 25

IF SHE HAD not been mad before committal to the tender ministrations of the Middlesex County Asylum, her time spent there would doubtless ensure that she ended up that way. The building itself was large and austere, providing shelter for some two thousand souls, and although Rebecca had no idea of its size or shape, she could feel the overwhelming fear and despair emanating from each one of the inhabitants.

Her first few weeks had been spent inside the confines of one of the women's wards. There were fifty beds in this cramped space. Each space held a narrow, coffin-like, metal bedstead. Each bed had a meagre, mould-cold covering. Beneath each was located one (often stinking) slop bucket. Beside it, one chair for the inhabitant of the bed to occupy during the day. Rebecca preferred to seek out a corner of the room where she would sit in complete stillness, her back pressed against the coldness of the walls. Somehow, being here connected her to her mother, she could not recall why right now, but it didn't matter. Memories of her seemed to come easily here. It was a small, cold comfort but she wrapped it around her gratefully. She knew that she was not insane, and she tucked this knowledge away fiercely. She hid it from sight of all around her in case it was snatched away.

The sight of Anna Coren that day outside Astley's Amphitheatre had firmly convinced her that there was something else at stake here, and it was about more than her sanity. She could only think that it was an attempt to break her will. Thankfully her secret ability had not deserted her and now she utilised it to its full here inside the asylum. She would float peacefully out of her body, able to look back on it still sitting on the floor in the corner with her arms wrapped tightly around her knees. She spent long periods of time in the landscape of her mind. Here she would spend her long days in taming the wilderness which she found there. The landscape was a neglected wilderness but she had time now, and would make it beautiful again. Each day she would clear or prune or plant so that new growth could occur. She built herself a home for her sanity to live in, and decorated the rooms with elegant rugs, books and music. She wasn't really existing in a filthy asylum any more, she now lived in a country manor, a place where she was in control of all around her. Here she was the Lady of the Manor. As long as she could preserve this landscape she could stay sane, separate and disconnected from what passed for reality around her. Reverend John Hopps' words about the nature of reality and perception floated into her consciousness and she felt a little less alone. All she had to do now was survive until Miriam found her, sorted out the misunderstanding, and then she could leave.

How long she had been incarcerated here she wasn't sure. She was losing all track of time. It felt like years, but it could not have been more than a few days? Or had it? The screams and banging from other inmates kept her awake through the night from the first, and she had lost the will to eat. Eventually she would only drink her medicine, and that was only when cajoled to do so. The drink, at first anyway, helped her to sleep. Slowly the walls between realities broke down, and she found herself at war. The Angel had found his way into her beautiful landscape. He arrived on horseback at the head of an invading army. On his cloak was an emblem – the same design as she wore around her own neck. Rebecca was more afraid than she had ever been before. Her garden was trampled by the pounding hooves of the horses. The doors of her country sanctuary were blown open, one by one. In the end, the nightmare of the asylum around her became nothing to the hell she was enduring in her mind. The Angel was moving from room to room, seeking her out. He was ever present now, both in the asylum and in her visions. Silent, cloaked, faceless, waiting. Dog-headed men and flying harpies superimposed themselves on the bodies of other inmates. No-one but her seemed to be able to see them.

When it had started, the visions were confined to her dreams, so she fought desperately to stay awake. To calm her terror, more and more of the liquid medicine was given to her and finally she spent her days and nights in a hypnogogic state of half-wakefulness, half-sleep, where the drugs forced the edges of differing realities to flow into one another. Her sanity receded ever further into the house she had built to protect it. Finally, with nowhere else to hide, crouched down in fear it rocked away in a corner of the cellar of her destroyed sanctuary as the terrifying figures searched through the ruined building for her. She knew that this was the last refuge. After this her sanity would have nowhere else to hide. She knew that if the Angel Azriel discovered her hiding place now, she would be lost forever.

Miriam had stood rooted to the spot in terror as she watched Rebecca being manhandled by those dreadful women into the waiting carriage on that terrible day in London. She had cried out for the police and, a few moments later, the colonel arrived with an officer of the law in his wake. He had seen the whole event, and had dragooned a loitering policeman. He insisted that the constable inform the authorities immediately that a young woman had been kidnapped off the streets of London, in daylight. The officer lifted his whistle to his lips to summon help, when the imperious drawl of a male voice instructed him to desist, and, opening his coat, withdrew a large, folded sheet which he handed to the officer to read. Raising a handkerchief to his face to delicately mop his upper lip, the figure turned to Miriam. 'Madam, you must stand aside. Rebecca – my fiancée – is being taken to a place where she can be cared for.' It was Isaac. Miriam began to protest furiously. Isaac raised his hand for her silence. 'She has been seen and certified by two different physicians and they have each deemed her to be insane. This action is for her own good.' He turned to Anna Coren. 'Sister, we must leave. We have a prior engagement and it would not do for us to be late.' With this he took Anna Coren's elbow and guided her through the crowd to the pavement's edge, and a waiting carriage. 'You bitch!' Miriam shrieked at Anna Coren who was just about to step into the carriage. Anna turned back with an agonised expression before Isaac gestured impatiently to her from the depths of the carriage, and she climbed in after her brother, the door slamming noisily behind them. At that moment, Miriam broke down into tears. There in the street, in public, she cried. Blind, desperate tears. Her fears *had* foundation. She had been right to be afraid. The men who had talked their way into Gower Street to visit Rebecca had, without a doubt now, been mad-doctors. They were there to interview Rebecca and decide whether she needed to be incarcerated. That was why they had gone into the room singly. That was why they had been so curious about Spiritualism. She had heard about the trials and tribulations of Georgina Weldon who had been snatched from her home and locked up in an asylum for her beliefs. Who in the Spiritualist world had not? But for this appalling thing to happen to Rebecca, it was so wrong on so many levels. She needed to talk to someone who understood – she needed to talk to Geraldine. There had to be a way of helping Rebecca. Poor, terrified Rebecca. The thought of her vulnerable niece gave her strength, and galvanised her once more into action.

In the carriage on their way to Museum Street and Geraldine, she explained to the colonel what she intended to do. She was going to get Rebecca out of there – wherever *there* was – and get her to safety. The colonel smiled. 'You are a good woman to have close by in adversity, Miriam. I would want you on my side in any battle.' In spite of the situation, Miriam found herself returning his smile. As the carriage made its way across Waterloo Bridge, she stared out at the busy Thames with its traffic of cargo vessels. She realised that the colonel had been talking to her, so she brought her attention back to him. In order to do so she squirreled an idea into the back of her mind and let it rest safely there. She watched as the colonel impatiently tapped a document on his knee. She realised that it was the self-same paper which Isaac had handed to the policeman earlier. Miriam knew better than to ask how the colonel had managed to get the officer to hand the writ over to him. She was beginning to learn that the signet ring he always wore with such pride and which bore the square and the compass gave him authority, or at least access in the most unexpected ways. She stared down at the symbol of his Freemasonry. Noticing this, he twisted the ring affectionately.

'I wear it with the legs of the compass pointing towards me to remember my obligations.' Miriam cocked her head in a movement that suddenly reminded her of her niece. 'In this instance I choose to obey a summons in response to my duty to a neighbour.' Miriam didn't quite understand the meaning of his words, but what she did recognise was the fact that he was prepared to help her, and if that meant utilising all means at their combined disposal, so be it. Without another word, two heads now leaned in close together over the contents of the paper as the carriage crossed the water and made its way to the sanctuary of Atlantis.

Geraldine welcomed them into her home above the shop. It was accessed by a small staircase neatly hidden behind a bookcase. It was compact but comfortably appointed with books, a good fire, and a few very strange objects which Miriam allowed her eyes to skim past. She chose not to look closely at them for now, for fear of staring. Having heard tales of her visits from Rebecca who had never progressed beyond the shop itself, she recognised that she should consider herself honoured to be in Geraldine's home. The colonel behaved with utmost gallantry towards his hostess, regardless of the oddity of his situation, and Miriam found herself warming to this bluff man. He had a kind and generous heart and was here for her in her need. She allowed him to tell the sorry tale of Rebecca's abduction, only interjecting when necessary. Geraldine narrowed her eyes when Isaac's name was mentioned, but she said nothing.

The document which had been handed to the police officer was now dissected in detail. It was an authority to restrain Rebecca and signed by the two doctors who had visited Gower Street. The diagnosis was hysteria, and she had been taken to Middlesex County Asylum for 'her own safety'. The doctors had been consulted by Anna and Isaac Coren with the specific and written approval of Rebecca's father. Isaac had signed the order. No wonder the policeman didn't want anything to do with it and had handed it over so readily. There was no abduction. This was a legal process and, said the colonel, the most appropriate way to deal with this was through the due process of the law. He would hire a professional to take up the cause, and 'cost be damned!'. Miriam and Geraldine were reunited in their friendship with a conspiratorial glace. Whatever the colonel was thinking of doing, they already had other ideas. Encouraged to make haste by the ladies, he left them together in Atlantis for the legal peaks of the Inns of Court, there to seek out an understanding barrister.

Miriam had enough sense to realise that making an apology to Geraldine was no longer necessary. Both had only one objective: to find the fastest way to ensure Rebecca's release from the asylum. Geraldine summoned the ever vigilant Jonathon to carry a missive to Mrs Weldon in Tavistock Square. 'You should find her in. At this hour she is schooling her musical orphans. Just follow the noise. Knock hard – and if she doesn't answer, be sure to stay there until she hears you.' Geraldine began searching her bookshelves and pulled out a volume, *The History of my Orphanage, or The Outpourings of an Alleged Lunatic and How I Escaped the Mad Doctors*. 'This is her book. Please, take it. The more information we have, the more effective we can be.' Miriam had read it already, but in the spirit of friendship rekindled she put the book into her bag. What she had learned about asylums from her own reading of that volume only increased her fears. She must get Rebecca out, and quickly. The colonel meant well, but the due process of the law would take time, time that Miriam knew Rebecca's fractured sanity did not have. Besides, she was not a legal guardian and, she felt sure, would not make the best witness for her niece's sanity as she was a Spiritualist. For some people that alone was sufficient grounds for her own incarceration in an asylum. Besides, if Rebecca had spoken about the night at the Egyptian House she may be lost to her forever. Who would listen to a single young woman, against the weight of the British Establishment in the form of Lord and Lady Hawsley? Rebecca would be declared irredeemably insane and remain incarcerated for life. Miriam felt physically sick at the thought. She would *not* let this happen. Not while she drew breath.

CHAPTER 26

T HE MAD-DOCTORS HAD been right, in this instance at least. Georgina Weldon was *quite* insane. That was Miriam's opinion at least. Geraldine's hand-delivered letter to the inhabitant of Tavistock House had produced a verbal response which Jonathon had delivered on his return. 'Come immediately!' Miriam did just that. Surprisingly, Geraldine did not accompany her, pleading a prior engagement, and suggested that they should reconvene as planned the following morning at the house in Gower Street.

The mansion in Tavistock Square where Georgina Weldon lived was a conservatoire, orphanage and home. Filled with children running and yelling, the noise was spectacular. 'All rescued from the street. My musical darlings!' Georgina exclaimed, attempting to sweep into her arms a passing child, who ducked easily to evade her embrace. It was the smell, however, which caused Miriam the most distress. She quickly realised there were also four-legged inhabitants of the building, having trodden in a (thankfully desiccated) portion of shit which was on the drawing room carpet. The smell of dog excrement assailed her nostrils, distracting her from Georgina's constant stream of invective about doctors, asylum keepers, the legal profession and numerous individuals whom she believed had wronged her in some way, shape or form. Miriam found her utterly exhausting. She had come for help as Georgina had campaigned vigorously for a change in the law as a result of her experiences, but Miriam soon began to realise that she would gain little of practical help from Georgina. Miriam was now convinced that, as awful as Georgina Weldon's experiences in the asylum had obviously been, she was definitely *off with the fairies*.

Desperate to get away, and try as she might, she was unable to get a word in edgeways to make her escape. Fortunately help came from the unexpected quarter of a monkey, which had positioned itself atop a bookcase in the drawing room and was now tearing up and throwing sheet music in the direction of his mistress. Miriam made her exit, as Georgina climbed onto a chair to retrieve the chattering creature. 'I am, as you can see, far too busy to help you. Go and see Louisa Lowe. Lunacy Law Reform Association. Berners Street. Do not mention my name. It may prejudice your suit.' With this extraordinary pronouncement she grabbed the angry monkey by his foot, whereupon it promptly bit her.

Mrs Louisa Lowe was an altogether different individual. Matronly, calm and measured, she listened to Miriam's account while asking questions and making copious notes in a large ledger identical to many on the bookshelves surrounding her. When Miriam had finished, Mrs Lowe put down her pen delicately, closed her book, and then looked Miriam in the eye. 'Hopeless I'm afraid. If the consultation took place as you described, on the instructions of an individual authorised by law to do so, you have very little chance of gaining your niece's release on the basis of false imprisonment – the only way for her to walk free quickly. The best possible course of action for you now is to arrange for her to be transferred from the public asylum where she is currently kept, to a private institution – one more suited to a refined individual such as she, where she can be reassessed. Then when she demonstrates herself to be sound in mind by her behaviour, she can be released either fully or into the care of her family.' The stout figure leaned back in her chair, which responded by creaking disconcertingly. 'Mark my words, madam – it will cost you. Private asylums are expensive. Part of my campaigning is against those doctors who certify their inmates and also own the private institutions where they put them. This is an abuse and a direct conflict of interests. These individuals want their patients to stay sick – of course they do – because it lines their pockets. At least now asylum owners can no longer sign the petition themselves, but they have friends who will. Friends who are remunerated financially for their work. So shocking it is to me that in this day and age a woman can be taken off the streets from the love of her nearest and dearest and incarcerated in hell on earth for no real reason or actual benefit to themselves. If there is *anything* I can do to help, I will. Be assured I will think about the case of your niece, and I will show you how to find out a way for you to visit her, if possible. You will need to seek permission, of course.' Miriam didn't know how to respond to this, and had not even considered the possibility of seeing Rebecca and leaving the asylum without her. Having heard Louisa out, she recognised that the process would be slower than she would have wished. Miriam therefore needed to take a modicum of hope with her, and leave that, at the very least, with her niece. She sighed. She would have to find some hope herself first.

The colonel visited Isaac at his offices in Piccadilly to request permission for their visit to Rebecca. As he had been the one who had signed the papers incarcerating her, this meant he would from then on be responsible for vetting any visits to the asylum. Miriam could not bring herself to ask him in person. She feared what she would say – or do – to Isaac if she saw him now. The request was grudgingly granted, and the colonel chose to spare Miriam his experience and observations of the man. He felt nothing more or less than absolute contempt for Isaac. All he could bring himself to say to Miriam was: 'He is no gentleman, m'dear. No gentleman at all.'

Miriam and the colonel travelled to Hanwell together the following morning. The journey to the Middlesex County Asylum took the best part of a day. Rising before the sun, they took the colonel's carriage to Mansion House station, where they joined the Windsor train, before alighting at Hanwell and Elthorne station and completing their journey by a waiting hansom cab. 'Asylum, right mister?' said the cabbie, touching his cap lazily. The occupants of the vehicle nodded silently. It was evident that the asylum was the only possible place which anyone might be visiting out here in this godforsaken landscape. Even the birds seemed silent out here. Miriam shivered. She had brought with her Rebecca's shawl, a basket of food, and some books. She clutched at the handle of the basket spasmodically, trying desperately to calm herself. It would not do for her to be agitated when seeing Rebecca. She wanted to be able to offer support and hope, even though right now she felt herself in need of the former, and sadly lacking in the latter. The intense cold, and her fear, was penetrating her frame, and she started to shiver. The colonel reached across and, without a word, cradled her in his arms protectively. Miriam allowed herself to rest there for a few moments, before pushing him away gently.

The Middlesex County Asylum was huge and intimidating. The first thing which Miriam noticed was the sounds. Low moans and rhythmic knockings, punctuated by an inhuman yelp and, on one occasion, a scream. As they were led through seemingly endless corridors, their guide behaved as if they were on a tour of Belvoir Castle and not an asylum. He pointed out the chapel, the common room and various architectural features of the building as they made their way to the women's quarters. Miriam's shivering had not abated. It was as if the chill in the building had penetrated right through into her bones. She could feel her heart racing and had a strong desire to run as fast and as far away from this place as possible. She could not begin to imagine what effect it was having on poor, sensitive Rebecca. She pulled her thoughts together, stilled her shaking by a conscious effort of will, and followed their guide to the door of Rebecca's room.

It was all she could do not to cry out. The figure seated on the solitary chair was a ghost of her niece. Smaller, thinner, with deep, dark rings around her eyes, she looked as if she were halfway to death. Miriam calmed herself and made her way to the figure in the chair, holding the basket of gifts before her almost like a protective shield. Rebecca did not stir, and it was only when Miriam looked into her eyes she saw her pupils were dilated. She was unresponsive and seemed completely unaware of their presence in the room. Rebecca had been drugged. She reached out for her wrist to feel a pulse, then recoiled in horror as she saw bright red, unhealed wheals there. 'I *demand* an explanation for this – why has she been restrained in this terrible manner, and why has she been drugged so heavily? I insist that you summon the chief physician

– *immediately!*' The pock-faced young man with them took a step back from Miriam as she blasted this command in his direction. '*Immediately, mind!*'

'Can't do that, missus. He don't leaves his chambers until after lunch. He would 'ave my head, he would, if I was to disturb 'im at his luncheon.'

Miriam brushed him aside as she strode from the room. 'In which case, this mountain will find her own way to Mohammed…' She marched off down the corridor, ploughing past the attendant with the colonel bobbing behind in her wake.

Huge though the building was, it wasn't too difficult to find the private quarters of the senior staff, as the improvement in looks, decorations and cleanliness of the hallways acted like a thread back into the Minotaur's lair. Indeed, Miriam felt as if her quest to free Rebecca were starting to take on mythic proportions, so all-consuming was it for her now. Arriving at the door bearing a brass plate inscribed 'Medical Superintendent', and beneath it the name Dr H. Rayner, MD, CH., she knocked with one hand and turned the handle to enter the room simultaneously, to be greeted by the sight of a rotund and bearded man with a napkin clipped neatly into the top of his waistcoat. The remains of a lamb chop still in hand, he gaped open-mouthed at the sight of this Valkyrie who had just strode into his chamber. He leaned back on his chair to pull on the rope which was obviously designed to bring servants running. The colonel, who was by now in the doorway, said quietly, 'I strongly suggest that you delay your alarm for the moment, sir. Wait until you have heard what we have to say.'

Having seen the proffered hand of the colonel and succumbing to the social norm of shaking it, he begged a moment to adjust his dress (as he was still wearing his bib), and became nothing less than cordial towards them. Inviting both to sit down, he summoned an assistant to bring Rebecca's file to him, and after offering sherry (which they refused) to his guests, spent some minutes reading the – as far as Miriam could tell from trying to read upside down – meagre contents, he dropped the file casually beside the remains of his lunch. 'All proper procedures were observed in both the instigation and execution of the order to commit your niece, madam. She is here for her own good, and at the request of her father.' Miriam remonstrated furiously. 'If she is here for her own good that would imply treatment. What treatment, pray, involves restraint and being drugged into oblivion?' Dr Rayner leaned over his desk and laced his pudgy hands together, before bringing his full attention on Miriam, as if he had not seen her properly before. 'Sadly, madam, when she came to us she was in the throes of hysterical apoplexy, delusional and quite disturbed. She needed to be restrained for her own safety. The drug she is currently taking, antimony, is a tried and tested treatment for her condition.'

'What condition, specifically?' Miriam responded tartly. He casually flipped open the file and quoted from it. 'The patient displays classic symptoms of the hysteric. Visions, erratic behaviour, delirium. Be assured, madam, she is insane.' Miriam was on the point of leaning over the desk and reaching for a convenient steak knife from the doctor's luncheon to plunge into his heart, when the colonel, in a moment of exceptional mind reading, took her hand and spoke directly to Dr Rayner. 'I understand what you are saying, Doctor, but Miss Zimmerman is a refined and cultured individual. Conditions such as these are not conducive for one of her class. She needs her own room, fresh air and good food, as well as more appropriate companionship and stimulation.'

Miriam's heart was racing with anxiety, and the pain in her

chest which she was usually able to ignore caused her to wince. Her breath felt short and painful. Dr Rayner noticed her distress, and called for a glass of water. 'Madam. Forgive me. I can see that this dreadful situation is causing you some disturbance and I will do what I can to see how this situation can be ameliorated. Perhaps, if there is a place available, Miss Zimmerman would benefit from the surroundings of Lawn House – a private institution. I will contact the chief medical man there myself. I am sure something can be arranged.'

The colonel looked over at Miriam reassuringly, and the pain gripping her heart subsided. She could, at the very least, leave this dreadful place if not with hope, at least with a little more faith that Rebecca would be out of there soon.

CHAPTER 27

Lawn house was close in proximity to the Middlesex County Asylum, but a world away in its execution. Centred around a well-proportioned building, it had a pleasant garden and small lake. The main building, however, was secured with locks on all the doors and windows. It may look like a country home, but it was still a place of incarceration. The inhabitants, or 'guests' as its proprietor, Dr Maudsley, preferred to call them, were only six in number. All were gentlewomen whose illnesses were caused by their sensitive nature, continued their guide, Lawn House's visiting physician. Unlike the conditions of the lower-order females, he continued, whose ailments were due to overwork. As Miriam and the colonel walked around the silent house their guide, Dr Williamson, explained to them that Rebecca would be directly under the care of Dr Henry Maudsley himself. Miriam sincerely doubted that, but she held her tongue, smiling gently instead. It was vital that Rebecca be moved, and as soon as possible. On her last visit her niece lay in bed. She was dirty, catatonic, and her eyes were wide open and unresponsive. She was also painfully thin. Miriam had to get her out of there, and soon.

Two weeks had passed since she had seen Rebecca in that pitiful state, and both colonel and aunt had been very busy. Colonel Burbridge had been occupied with his (as yet unsuccessful) attempts to persuade a barrister to represent Rebecca's case, and Miriam busy with information gathering. In her heart of hearts she felt the colonel's activity was pointless, but she appreciated his efforts, and at least it kept him occupied while she attempted to put together a plan. On her return to London she had met Louisa Lowe once again. Louisa, she knew, had in the past been one of the so-called guests at Lawn House herself. 'Pestilential place. Cold. Food awful. No medical staff to speak of, and Maudsley was never to be seen. Of course not. He was far too busy with his lucrative London clients.' She paused for breath before continuing her tirade. 'Lawn House is nothing more than a holding-pen for his milk-cows, and an expensive one at that.' What Miriam did surreptitiously obtain from Louisa, however, was a fairly detailed description of the routine at the private asylum. Now she and the colonel were walking around the building, she added to this knowledge by mentally mapping the layout of its internal space, such as it was.

The colonel was, by tacit consent, acting as intermediary between Miriam and the rest of Rebecca's family. Both he and Miriam had decided it best to deal with Rebecca's father direct, and appeal to his snobbery to have her moved to Lawn House. It would be Rebecca's money, after all, which would be used to fund her stay there. Miriam felt he would be unlikely to refuse when informed that Rebecca was cheek by jowl with the lower orders. Whatever he felt about his daughter, he would not allow his own standing to be tainted by such association. Miriam was correct, and within the month a place became available and instructions were made for Rebecca to be transferred to Lawn House. Every time she thought about Rebecca in that dreadful county asylum she felt physically ill. Hopefully soon it would be over, she thought. Please, please may this nightmare end soon.

It took another month for the appropriate paperwork (and money) to change hands, and Rebecca was to be welcomed to her new home. Dr Maudsley himself had arrived to escort his new 'guest' to Lawn House. Rebecca passively allowed herself to be walked along the corridors of the Middlesex on Miriam's arm and out into the courtyard where the carriage was waiting. On seeing the carriage, she became progressively more distressed. 'It's perfectly safe, my dear. I will be coming with you. There is nothing to fear here.' Miriam assured her. But there was. Rebecca could see the Angel quite clearly, seated beside the coachman. She turned away and started to run blindly across the grounds.

Some hours later, and Rebecca had been safely delivered to her new room in Lawn House. She had been bathed and her hair was still damp from being washed. She was dressed in the new clothes which Miriam had brought for her. They hung loosely on her thin body, but for all of that she looked considerably better. 'I'm sorry to have troubled you, Aunt Miriam,' she said, evenly, in the voice of a child. Miriam found herself unable to speak, so choked was she with emotion. 'None of this is your doing. None of it – and I am the one who is sorry I did not protect you and prevent this dreadful thing from happening.' Rebecca raised her hand slightly from her lap to stem the flow of anguish from her aunt. 'I told Anna Coren. She asked me about that night and so I told her what had happened to me in the Egyptian House. I don't think she believed me.' She shifted stiffly in her seat, as if her body had aged years not months since then. 'Then I told the doctors the same. For this they imprisoned me in my mind.' Miriam was not quite sure what Rebecca meant, but she continued to listen intently. Rebecca opened her mouth to continue, but her eyes betrayed her, and pupils dilating, she drifted away from the surroundings of Lawn House and into her own place of safety. No further sound could be drawn from her. Miriam stayed with her until night fell, gently stroking her hand, but Rebecca had gone. The Chinese shawl which the colonel had retrieved from where it fell in the street Miriam now wrapped around her niece's shoulders. She prayed its texture would anchor her mind to happier memories from their outing in the Burlington Arcade. She could do no more for now.

Some days were better than others, and Rebecca progressively found herself spending more time in Lawn House and less in the country mansion of her mind which she had built as a place of safety – as an asylum. The Angel Azriel and his avenging army had retreated from the light which Miriam had shone into her life. Now, when she went there it was to do repairs, to plant new growth in the gardens, and to seal up all the gaps where the darkness had got in. She breathed deeply. I have made it safe again, she thought to herself. The Angel hadn't appeared to her for some weeks. Now she was beginning to feel safe enough to allow her mind to spend more time in the reality surrounding her, and she was pleased to find that things had been provided to occupy her. Here she had her books and her paints, and now that she was getting stronger she was able to walk in the garden. She would have preferred to walk anywhere else as, in the height of summer as it now was, the stench of ordure coming from the pond was almost overwhelming. Far from being a beautiful clear stretch of water to sit by, it was a disgusting, shit-infested pool. Fortunately, her room was at the back of the house. She pitied those guests whose rooms overlooked the pond as they were unable to ever open their windows for fear of letting in the disgusting stink.

Days were followed by weeks, and Rebecca was now into her second month at Lawn House. Miriam has been her only visitor. As time moved forward and Rebecca slowly recovered her senses, she realised that since her incarceration she had not only had no other visitors, but there had not even been any correspondence from her friends. She hadn't expected any from her family, but she was sad to register that there had not even been a letter from Clarissa. Perhaps Rebecca had misunderstood the nature of their friendship. Perhaps she was just too busy with her studies. Perhaps she didn't even know the situation. Either way, she felt her connections with London and her life there slipping from her grasp, or, to be truthful, she was letting them go. There would be no point now. Especially when she thought of the different imprisonment which her future would contain. Ramsgate, Isaac, children certainly, and the stultifyingly narrow confines of her father's religious convictions and social aspirations. She felt herself withdrawing into her mind and checking the locks on the main-doors. Perhaps it wasn't too awful here after all.

In fact, there had been another visitor to Rebecca while she was at Lawn House, but this was no social call. A week before she had been sitting in her room, an unopened book on her lap, and Dr Williamson knocked and invited himself in. Rebecca remained seated. She found that since she had been brought here, her capacity to either sit or stand virtually motionless had grown. She liked to be still. There were even times when she was still enough to devote her consciousness to its effect on others. It secretly pleased her to notice that this stillness had an unnerving effect on her keeper/companion

Mrs Hew, so much so that she had begun to absent herself when Rebecca became statue-like. Rebecca was pleased. She had found a way of creating privacy. A small success, but progress nonetheless. So it was on the morning of the unexpected visitor.

When Dr Williamson walked into the room, he smiled at Rebecca and patiently explained the presence of another man. Tall, thin and smelling faintly of tobacco, his first words seemed harsh, even if his movements did not. Rebecca still hadn't moved. As Dr Williamson wandered over to Rebecca's window, where he stood for the duration of the interview, the stranger pulled up a chair close to Rebecca, and, without asking permission, tried to pull the book from her lap. Without meaning to she grabbed onto it, tightly, and pulled it close to her chest. The stranger leaned back in his chair and smiled. 'So, m'dear. What do you think of Mr Darwin?' Rebecca stroked the cover of Samuel's precious gift, and began to speak. At first her voice was little more than a whisper, it had been so long since she had engaged in a conversation, but little by little her interlocutor drew her out.

After the men had left her, her awakening curiosity caused Rebecca to wonder what the visit had been about. The smell of tobacco floated in the atmosphere like a question mark, until dispelled by the returning presence of Mrs Hew. Tobacco was replaced with the smell of sweat and wine, and with it Rebecca sank back into motionlessness.

The following morning, she decided to walk outside and try to clear some of the fog from her mind. Soon tired, she sat down on the bench at the far end of the garden, and looked back on the house. Since her arrival she had taken no more of the medicine which she had been given at the County Asylum and she did have more and more times when she felt connected to the world, rather than out of her mind. She was starting to feel better. If only she didn't have to be watched all day, every day, she knew that her recovery would accelerate. The worst part of this constant companionship was the fact that the woman assigned as her keeper was truly unpleasant. Not that Dr Maudsley would like to hear her called that. He preferred the term 'companion'. Although why anyone would want a low creature such as Mrs Hew as a companion was beyond her. Shadowed by day, and locked in her room with her by night, this was the constant reminder which demonstrated that Rebecca was indeed a prisoner. The woman was fat, barely literate, and had a substantial moustache. Further she frequently smelled of cheap wine, and as a result of her drinking snored like a pig. Rebecca did not get much sleep, and when she did, visions of the Egyptian House kept floating across the gallery of her mind. Although quieter than her last place of incarceration, she had little peace here, and she desperately wanted some so she could concentrate and recall a fact which she knew was very important, but it just kept slipping out of her grasp. It was something to do with Isaac, but for the life of her she could not remember what it was. Leaving the relative peace of the garden bench, she began to walk back towards Lawn House, and the loud trump of a fart announced Mrs Hew had risen to follow her.

CHAPTER 28

IT WAS IRONIC to Miriam that the one individual who could have offered some genuinely practical advice was the one person she could not really ask – and that was the colonel. If she had let him know of her intention she knew that he would immediately veto her decision on the grounds of it being dangerous, illegal and doomed to failure. Not that it would have stopped her from doing it, mind you, but Miriam was aware that the colonel had both obligations and connections through his Freemasonry and if he knew of her plan to liberate Rebecca from Lawn House he would, she felt sure, have been duty bound to try to stop her. Miriam was now on a mission and she wasn't about to allow anything to deflect her. After all, she thought to herself, she had engineered a rescue of her niece before, and she would do so again. She felt her shoulders slumping as she thought of that time. Pull yourself together, woman. This time the outcome would be different. Of course it would take much more planning than freeing her from those despicable people in the Egyptian House, but piece by piece it was all starting to fall into place.

As it turned out, the seeds of the idea had already planted themselves after their first visit to Lawn House. On the train back into London, Miriam had pretended to be dozing to avoid conversation with the colonel, allowing her to concentrate on her idea to get Rebecca away from the asylum. She had no faith that Isaac, Anna Coren, or indeed Rebecca's father had much intention of fighting her corner. Indeed, she now had no doubts that it would be up to her – and her alone – to get Rebecca out of this abysmal situation before the poor child became drug-addled or lost her mind to the sheer awfulness of the state in which she found herself.

Once home in Gower Street, Rebecca's bedroom became the centre of operations for Miriam's plan to liberate her. It felt right, somehow, and also meant that any casual visitor to the house would get no idea that anything was going on. The regular séances continued at the colonel's house, and she preferred it that way. She could continue with a semblance of normality by attending, but without the added stress of anyone in her house inadvertently finding out what she was doing. At first, it was just her alone; planning, scheming. She had drawn out a plan of the interior of Lawn House from her visits there, and then mapped out the regular routine of the place from her own observation and the conversations with Louisa Lowe. Initially, she had no idea of what she would do with Rebecca once she had freed her. She soon came to the realisation that she would have to take others into her confidence if she was going to make this rescue work. There was no other choice. She needed to talk to Geraldine. Geraldine had access to different people, and skills. She would be able to think of something. If not, at least she would be a sounding-board for Miriam's ideas, and an honest one at that.

On arriving in Museum Street later that day, she found the Atlantis Bookshop closed. Disappointed, she looked around for a doorbell for Geraldine's home, but there was none to be found.

Turning to leave, she heard the sound of the window sash above opening, and Geraldine's head appeared. 'Can't talk now. Imperative that I see you. Meet me at eight this evening in the Deveraux Arms.' With that the head withdrew and the window was slammed firmly shut. Miriam walked away with a rueful smile on her face. There would have been a time, she mused, not so long ago, when I would have been offended to be spoken to in such a manner in the street, and absolutely *no* way I would have gone into a public house alone (or under any circumstances for that matter). I am a different woman since Rebecca came into my life, different and happier too. As her thoughts moved to her niece, her resolve to see this through hardened. She slowed down her pace for a moment, aware of a wave of discomfort surging through her body. When this is all over I will go with Rebecca to a spa, perhaps in the Alps. She smiled and continued her walk home. Yes. We will do that together when this is all over.

That evening, Miriam found herself outside the Royal Court of Justice. She was lost. As far as she knew, Deveraux Court, where the inn was located, was around here somewhere. She was starting to attract attention and didn't want to hang around on the corner of the street for too long. Suddenly a little hand closed itself around hers. Alarmed, she tried to pull away. It was Aisha. Karim stood close behind her, casually leaning against the building, smoking. Both were dressed in ragged street clothes and blended into their surroundings with ease. The darkness of their skin had been masked with a grubby hand. She was ready to admonish her servants for following her when she realised that they were only trying to protect her. They were there to do the right thing. As they always did the right thing with her. After all, she had kept their secret, and they were now keeping hers.

She allowed herself to be led across the road and down a dark alleyway. Suddenly the atmosphere seemed much less friendly and much more claustrophobic. These weren't the broad and well-lit London streets which Miriam was used to. These were more like the stews of old. These streets hadn't changed their lines since the great fire of London. She looked around her, cautiously. There were lots of people milling all around her, both adults and children. Some watched her progress with little curiosity, others seemed to stare openly. Miriam was now glad of her dark cloak and simple clothing. She felt Aisha tug at her cloak. The Deveraux Arms loomed large and black on the corner, and Karim pushed open the door to the saloon bar before Miriam had a chance to think about whether she wanted to enter or not. She followed him into the smoky darkness.

Miriam waited anxiously by the doorway while Karim boldly called over the barkeeper and beckoned him down to his height, whereupon he whispered in his ear. The barman stared over at Miriam, and indicated upwards with a gesture of his head, before walking away to attend to the demands for more porter from of an already drunk customer. Miriam was amazed to see this drunkard appeared to be a clerk of the court, but before the shock had time to register on her face, Aisha was pulling Miriam forward and past the bar, shadowing Karim who was already halfway up a flight of stairs hidden there. Miriam followed him, no longer afraid as coming from the room above she could hear the voice of her good friend Geraldine, the redoubtable Mrs Beskin.

Two hours had passed since she had ascended the stair, and Miriam had been given the rare chance to listen to a lecture as good (if not better) as any she had heard at the Swedenborg Centre. She estimated that the upstairs room held around fifty people, men and women, although there seemed to be more women than men as far as she could tell. Geraldine had indicated to a seat at the back of the room, which Miriam took with alacrity. Aisha remained seated beside her, and Karim seemed to have made himself comfortable in the bar below, only returning upstairs to bring two mugs of small beer, one for Miriam, one for Aisha. The lecture was by Geraldine herself and was on matters metaphysical. She found it both beautiful and challenging. If she had understood Geraldine correctly, the world she recognised, believed in and interacted with was about to be turned on its head. This was a time of social and spiritual revolution – of sedition even – a time when each individual was being asked to question the norms of reality and make up their minds for themselves. She felt excited and afraid, but one thing was for sure, she was now in absolutely no doubt that this was the right place to get the help which she so desperately sought for Rebecca. Watching Geraldine as she took questions from her audience, her respect for her new friend grew, especially when she saw how she was treated by others. As the room began to empty, Miriam found herself becoming strangely shy in front of her friend. She had been brought up to put too much store in breeding and money, and now she felt utterly embarrassed at her own past behaviour and beliefs.

Finally, the room was almost cleared and there were only a few people left in the room, Aisha, Karim and Miriam, Geraldine and the ever present Jonathon, and, unnoticed, a miserable Clarissa. She had only met Rebecca's young friend once before, when she had come to the house when Rebecca was ill, but she would not have recognised her as the same girl. She looked utterly defeated, anxious and, to be frank, somewhat dirty. Instinctively, everyone looked towards Geraldine to take the lead. She slowly stretched her neck, and when she had finished, she pointed to Clarissa. 'Sit down, girl. Tell Miriam everything.'

When Clarissa had finished her sorry tale of deception and grubby dealings, she sagged like a rag-doll and burst into hysterical tears. 'Enough.' Geraldine silenced her and she receded into snivelling sobs. 'Your self-pity does you no good here. This is a place for restitution. What you have done has caused untold damage, and it is for Miriam to decide how best you will make good.' Miriam stared at Clarissa. She couldn't bring herself to speak.

CHAPTER 29

IT WAS SOME hours later when Miriam was finally able to express her feelings about what she had heard. After Clarissa's confession, Geraldine had dismissed the despairing girl and the remaining party had repaired to Geraldine's sanctuary above the bookshop. Aisha and Karim had made themselves invisible, Jonathon was in the kitchen making tea, and Geraldine began to toast teacakes on the open fire of her cosy sitting room. 'What is done is done. What matters now is what can be done. Do you agree?' Miriam nodded imperceptibly. After Clarissa's admission, so many of the missing pieces had fallen into place. The whole sorry tale began when Isaac had approached Clarissa to spy on her friend, and to report back to him in exchange for a regular payment. This she did, including Rebecca's private outpourings to her friends about the Angel. Isaac, it transpired, was in the employ of Osborne, and he fed everything he had heard back to his master. Miriam was still confused. This explained how those despicable people had known about Rebecca's Angel, but surely her fiancé wouldn't want to see her come to harm – would he?

Butter was wiped from mouths, and tea consumed in quantity

before either woman spoke again. It was Geraldine who broke the silence. 'It seems that Mr Coren has a nasty little habit. One which, if it became public, would ruin his career in banking forever. He is an opium addict, my dear, and addicts think of no-one other than themselves. Have you ever noticed his odd manners? Always dabbing away at his upper lip? Poor eye contact? Loud and obnoxious or falling asleep? Rebecca did!' Miriam remained silent. There was no point in asking Geraldine whether she had verified this claim. She was learning that the knowledge contained in this bookshop stretched far beyond its walls and the books within it. Miriam was still not convinced. 'So you are saying that Isaac agreed to marry Rebecca to ensure that whatever happened in the Egyptian House would not become a public scandal?'

'I believe so.' Geraldine looked up at Miriam to gauge her response to this. She continued. 'I believe that his lord and master knows about his habit, and has given him some role within the business where he can do no real damage until he leaves for Ramsgate. All this to ensure his compliance with their plans, and to silence Rebecca. They have been seeking someone to complete their absurd ritual for some time. Believe me when I say I know this as fact. The last girl they identified as "suitable" was only eleven.' Miriam looked up in horror. 'How did no-one do anything to stop them?'

'Miriam. My dear woman. You are very naïve. This is London. The clap is rife. Poor mothers will sell you their daughters if the price is high enough. There are enough wealthy men out there who are terrified of catching a disease but not strong enough to keep their todger in their trousers. A virgin is considered a healthy option. Besides, whether they wanted a girl for sex or not, you can buy a child – human life is cheap.' Miriam found herself retching at the distress of it all, recalling Rebecca's tale of her visit to the stews of Shoreditch. Geraldine paused to give her friend time to digest. 'It was only after visiting Rebecca in her sick-room that Clarissa came to me with her confession and I did some more digging about our friends at the Egyptian House. That's when Isaac's habit came to light.' Miriam desperately wanted to cry, to run away from this knowledge, but she could not. She had to be strong for Rebecca.

She pulled her thoughts to the present, and looked across at Geraldine. 'It's all so wrong. So wrong.' Her chest felt tight and she paused to catch her breath. 'Right now there is only one child I can think about – and that's Rebecca. How do I get her out?' Geraldine reached over and touched her hand. 'We will. We will... and I have had an idea.' If anyone from the building opposite had looked through the window into that upstairs room they would have seen two middle-aged women seemingly engaged in innocent but intense conversation. However, if they could have heard the words spoken they would have realised that these women were warriors. Warriors planning a campaign, and both – if either of them would have cared to admit it – feeling energised and alive.

Two days had since passed, and Clarissa had now been forgiven by Miriam for her part in Rebecca's ordeal. Seeing Clarissa's obvious distress, it was clear to her that Rebecca's friend had no idea of the implications of her actions, and her strained financial situation had helped her to mask any concerns of that kind which she may have had. Clarissa was not a bad person, but her poverty had loosened the connections to her moral compass. It was clear that she cared for Rebecca, and had never intended for any harm to come to her. No-one else needed to punish her as it was obvious that she was full of self-loathing for her actions. Besides, it was Clarissa who had come up with the strategy by which they could release Rebecca. To make it work, the plan would need more people involved (itself a risk), but the idea itself was beautiful in its simplicity. Once Rebecca was out, it would be up to Miriam to get her away from England and to a place of safety. While Miriam wrote countless letters and set events into motion to ensure her safe arrival at the destination, Geraldine and Clarissa smoothed out the plan itself, even visiting Hanwell to peek into the gardens of Lawn House itself. Nothing could be left to chance. They would have only one shot at this, and all three women had their own reasons for needing to make it work. Miriam for salvation, Clarissa for redemption, and Geraldine for her reputation (although she wouldn't have admitted this to anyone other than herself).

Two weeks flew by since the plan itself was set in motion. In that period Miriam had visited Rebecca once more and her resolve to make this work was unshaken, if anything it had grown stronger. She calmed her mind with the knowledge that next time she would see her niece properly it would be when she was safely installed in Paris. A suitable time would have elapsed by then, and no-one would be suspicious at her sudden desire for continental travel. On the train to Hanwell, Miriam caught herself repeatedly clenching and unclenching the handle of her basket to try to still the thoughts in her mind. Colonel Burbridge looked up at her over his newspaper, but said nothing. Miriam tried to calm her thoughts and still her body. It wasn't easy. She took a deep breath and sank back into her seat, allowing her eyes to skim past the view from the window. At first, identical grubby back-gardens and seemingly endless rows of houses punctuated the journey, followed by the building sites and then when they almost reached their destination came fields. It wouldn't be long, she thought, before every field by a railway line would be filled with these mean dwellings. Miriam shook herself from her snobbery. Who am I to judge? Why shouldn't everyone be able to have a nice, safe home with a garden? Somewhere for their children to play and be educated. Safe from those who use children for their own sordid purposes. Miriam's love of London was sinking under the dirt she was uncovering. Perhaps a move to the country would be good for her too? She could care for Rebecca and pay attention to her own health which, she acknowledged, was suffering. For now, her focus was on the short term. Get Rebecca away from the asylum and safe. After that, she would take stock.

The morning had finally arrived. Geraldine had advised Miriam against telling Rebecca what was going to happen. This time, Miriam listened to her advice. She recognised that it was hard enough for her to remain calm, let alone to expect Rebecca to be able to keep a secret of this magnitude. On that day she was due to visit Rebecca. All parties agreed that it was best if Miriam go about her business as normal, this leaving the actual rescue to others. It also established a perfect alibi should anyone suspect her involvement. Miriam dressed with care, and made a special effort to chat to the colonel on the journey. She was growing fond of this bluff, lonely man. He had a good heart and was kind. He had accompanied her on every visit, and remained calm and positive about Rebecca. She was coming to depend on him, and she wasn't sure how this knowledge made her feel. Happier certainly. More vulnerable, definitely. She was now coming round to the idea of exploring this unusual relationship, wherever it might lead. She touched his sleeve affectionately, causing him to smile gently. 'Almost there.' He responded, looking out of the train window. 'Yes.' She replied with a small smile of her own. 'Almost there.'

That day itself had started, as it always did at Lawn House, with a light breakfast of toast and porridge, both of which were cold by the time they reached her. Rebecca ate alone in her room. She had little appetite, but at least was now able to make herself eat. The Angel had not appeared in her surroundings since she had arrived at Lawn House, which was no small relief to her, and she could no longer sense his presence in her safe place. For the first time in months she felt calm and connected with her surroundings. Her senses felt alive, or at least as if they were coming back to life. If only the first sense to awaken hadn't been that of smell. The odours emanating from Mrs Hew had got much worse recently, and now Rebecca had tuned into them she found it hard to tune them out. For all of that, she felt better in herself. It was going to be a good day. She would see Miriam later on and she looked forward to talking to her and showing that her mind was clearing. She was coming back.

Rebecca recognised that she was recovering. She was more aware of her situation than before. She recognised that she was in an institution, and felt herself becoming strangely accommodated to it. At least while she was here she didn't have to think about her future. She didn't have to think about a wedding and a return to Ramsgate as Isaac's bride. The fact that he hadn't been to see her had been no surprise, nor her father or indeed Anna Coren. Although she recognised that this should have bothered her – after all they were her nearest and therefore, supposedly, dearest people – their absence reassured rather than disappointed. Nothing had changed with them. As long as Rebecca was in an asylum she was safe from their plans for her. She realised that she wasn't alone in using this place as a refuge. A few days earlier she had overheard a conversation in the library between two of her fellow inmates (or guests as the proprietor preferred to call them). These two refined and, seemingly, sane women were discussing a book which they were both reading. There was nothing at all in their behaviour to indicate that they were insane. Perhaps the crazy people were on the outside, and only the rational were being kept here for their own safety. Rebecca smiled inwardly. She felt her hunger for knowledge and information rising as she listened in on their conversation and knew this was a turning point. She would ask Miriam for more books, and use her time at Lawn House to educate herself. Thoughts about an education and then memories of her studious friend saddened her momentarily. Rebecca made her way from the enticement of conversation and back to her room. It would have been nice if Clarissa had written, she thought. Surely she must have known that Rebecca was ill. She walked back up the grand staircase towards her room. Maybe Clarissa, like many other people, didn't know what to say or do. Perhaps Rebecca had frightened her away. She pushed open the door to her room and, there, was a figure in her room. Standing with her back to the window, legs splayed and arms akimbo and silhouetted in the sunlight, was Clarissa, grinning wildly.

CHAPTER 30

REBECCA RUSHED TOWARDS her friend and opened her mouth to speak, but Clarissa raised her finger to her lips urgently. 'Hush, my dearest friend.' Silently she indicated to Rebecca to close the door. 'We don't have much time. I will explain as we set to it.' Rebecca stared at her friend as if she were the one who should be in an asylum. 'Trust me,' Clarissa said, urgently, as she started to unbutton her dress. 'We have to change clothes. We're getting you out of here.'

It didn't take long for the women to exchange dresses, and for Clarissa to rearrange Rebecca's hair into a reasonable facsimile of her own messy style. 'It will have to do.' Clarissa gently took her friend's hand and walked her to the bed where they sat together side by side as Clarissa explained the plan. All the while, she tenderly stroked Rebecca's hand. 'Please forgive me. It is partly my fault that you have suffered like this.' Rebecca put her remaining hand over that of her friend. 'I don't understand what you are talking about, but of course I forgive you, Clarissa. I would forgive you anything for the danger in which you are putting yourself for me today.' The chimes of the grandfather clock in the library began signifying the arrival of the hour. Clarissa pulled her hands away and walked back over to window. 'We don't have much time. It's about to begin.'

She ran back over to the bed and lightly kissed Rebecca on the head. '*Guarda la luna* – look at the moon.' She raised the sash window, pointed, and pushed a large potted aspidistra out onto the window-ledge. The light in the room began to dim, and Rebecca watched as the sun began to fade as the moon made its way across the face of the sun. Clarissa draped Rebecca's distinctive shawl over her hair, turned to her friend, smiled and nodded. Then she slowly pushed the plant off its ledge, and climbed out after it.

Rebecca did as she had been instructed, and hid herself in her wardrobe. Clarissa, from her perch outside the window, began to scream loudly to attract as much attention as possible. The eclipse would not last long, but its shadows obscured Clarissa's face sufficiently for the people below to believe it was Rebecca out there on the window-ledge. Her hearing was heightened now as she crouched in the darkness of the wardrobe. She heard Clarissa jump back into the room, run across the floor and down the stairs out of the main door towards the neighing of a horse which was waiting there. The eclipse had obviously unnerved it, and as soon as their charge was aboard, cantered off into the distance, the sound of Clarissa's voice declaring her freedom would leave no-one in any doubt that this was an escape in progress. It took some while before the sounds subsided, and when they did, Rebecca peeked out of a crack in the wardrobe. Normality had returned to the skies, and she crept cautiously out from her hiding space.

Heart pounding furiously, and now wrapped in Clarissa's cloak, she made her way down the silent staircase and into the hallway. She could see the back of Dr Maudsley himself in the main doorway issuing orders to various lackeys to make chase. Rebecca turned away from him and headed off to the servant's door, through which she passed and, going down the stairs and through the kitchen, she paused only to throw the bolt of the pantry door open, there to reveal the bound, gagged and still stupefied form of Mrs Hew. Clarissa had dispatched the keeper by her own greed, and would argue later that anything that had happened to her as a result was an appropriate punishment for theft. Her accomplices had arranged for a bottle of porter to be delivered to Rebecca as a gift, trusting full well that it wouldn't arrive at its destination and that Mrs Hew would help herself. Unfortunately for the thief, it had been spiked with laudanum, rendering her inert. The hefty frame of the companion was then easily overpowered and she had been locked away in the pantry until the time when it wore off.

Rebecca reached the exit from the kitchen to the outside courtyard. Suddenly afraid to leave the relative safety of the house, she paused momentarily. A grunt from Mrs Hew who was now waking spurred her to turn the handle and make her break for freedom. It was as Clarissa had promised. Waiting for her outside was a horse and delivery cart, a workman at the reins, and a woman by his side. Humble, obscure, and no-one would look twice. On hearing the door open, the man jumped down from his seat and came towards Rebecca. 'Now then, miss. Let me help you up.' Placing his hands on her waist, he easily lifted her up to the seat, and jumped up after her. Now sandwiched between the couple, Rebecca kept her head down and the hood of her cloak up. With a lurch, the cart began to pull away from Lawn House, around the side of the building and towards the main gate. The gardens were still full of people. Through the corner of her eye, Rebecca saw someone handing her shawl to Maudsley. Suddenly, the cart stopped. A man stood before them barring their exit. He walked up to the driver and started firing questions at him. 'Had he seen anyone around the building? Had he heard anything unusual?' The carter answered monosyllabically. Rebecca was terrified now that their interlocutor would want her to remove her hood, but she was spared that with the arrival of a hackney carriage unable to enter until they had left. The horse and cart moved slowly through the gates, and Rebecca caught sight of the inhabitants of the carriage. It was all she could do not to cry out as she saw Miriam and her companion seated within. A female hand gently rested itself on her shoulder and eased Rebecca back into her seat. The delivery cart continued on its slow journey with a more valuable cargo aboard than anyone had realised.

No-one spoke until they had left Hanwell far behind them. The village itself was awash with news of the 'escaped lunatic', and she watched as well-dressed women were stopped in the street by villagers and questioned as to who they were. Rebecca looked down at her own clothing. The dress which she had changed into was shabby even by Clarissa's standards, its colours obscured and paled by countless washes and numerous repairs. No-one questioned them again, even though the cart itself stopped on two occasions so the driver could pick up cargo. The second time this happened, she allowed herself to steal a glance at her companion. Even before she looked, she felt sure that she knew this woman. It was Cook's sister, Hilda. She was now plump and pregnant, and her face glowed with healthy colour. Hilda squeezed her hand happily, and Rebecca somehow knew that everything was going to be fine.

The sun was now starting to sink, and the moon was clearly visible in the dusky sky. All three had travelled in companionable silence. It was the gentle voice of William, Hilda's husband, who broke it. He eased the horse forward unhurriedly along the dusty lane. 'We will start looking for a nice dry hayrick to sleep in soon. Don't you worry, miss. You will sleep like one of God's own creatures in there. Warm it is, and safe. No-one will think of looking for you there.' He was right. Not only would no-one think of looking for her there, but even if they found her, she suspected that they wouldn't even see her. Some years later, Geraldine made a comment about this which would always stay with her. 'The rich travel in straight lines, Rebecca. They journey along railways and roads. They move from place to place as quickly as they can. It is because of this you always know how to find them, and to spot them when you do. The poor don't do this. They move at a much more natural rhythm and pace. The poor travel in circles. Some of these circles are very small, just home to work, work to village, village to home. Even when these circles and the lines intersect they do so on different levels. They move amongst one another without taint. The poor remain invisible to the rich and the rich are not much noticed by the poor. Both seem to prefer it this way. It is a co-existence which has lasted for as long as civilisation. It is changing, mark you, but slowly, slowly.'

So it was that Rebecca found herself that night in a field, ensconced high in a hayrick. William had been right. It was warm. She pulled her cloak around her and listened to the rustling of the hay. On the other side of the haystack her rescuers slept peacefully. She could sense their love for one another, and fervently hoped that one day she would be able to thank them for the risk they had just taken for her. As they bedded down for the night, she had tried to say as much to Hilda, but the words just wouldn't come. She turned now and looked up at the sky. It was beautiful. Beautiful in a way she couldn't describe. The stars seemed close enough to touch. She watched as a shooting star passed close to the horizon. Settling down to watch this incredible show of nature, she momentarily closed her eyes. Sleep overcame her immediately. Deep, peaceful and dreamless sleep. In this sleep, Rebecca finally began to step back into her true self and allowed it space and time to heal, here beneath the stars.

The journey to the Waltons' home at Bosmere Lock took the best part of the next day. By the time they arrived at the lock-keeper's cottage it was late afternoon. Rebecca remained outside the house while William tended to the horse and Hilda carried in the goods which had been collected on the back of the cart. Rebecca offered to help, but Hilda refused. Pregnant though she was, she remained strong and had no intention of allowing 'their guest' to be put to work. Any awkwardness which there had been between Hilda and Rebecca had been left on the road to Stowmarket. Hilda was no longer 'Cook's sister', but Mrs Walton, and even that formality was now gone as she entreated Rebecca to call her Christine. Rebecca mused that she could not have chosen a name more designed to lose her Jewishness than this one. 'Christine Walton I am now, and will be until the day I die,' she declared, '...and my Billie, he can do anything he puts his hand to.' Pride shone from her eyes. Rebecca realised that Hilda was a name from her past – a person who didn't exist anymore. Here in the countryside she had been able to recreate herself as a new person. Rebecca liked that idea, and an admiration for her new friend's spirit had developed as she sat by her side on the road to their home. William Walton held a responsible position here as lock-keeper and maintenance man at the new mill close by. Hilda (it would take time before she called her Christine) obviously adored him, and from the way Rebecca watched him as he gently watched over her, they would make good parents to their unborn offspring. Rebecca was no fool, she realised that their life wasn't idyllic, as the callouses on their hands showed, but there was love in this house, and for this she felt the unmistakable twinge of envy. She pulled away from this feeling as Christine called to her to come into the house and eat. Rebecca smiled genuinely for the first time in an age. For now, she was content to take pleasure in each moment as it came to her. From the smells emanating from the tiny kitchen she was in for a treat, and her stomach rumbled appreciatively. Yes, she thought to herself. Life can be good. No. Right now, life *is* good. She sat down to eat with her hosts, and allowed the minutiae of their conversation and their love for each other to spill over her and cover her like a blanket.

CHAPTER 31

Rebecca stayed at Bosmere Lock for a month. In that time, she walked along the tow-path and ate simple, home-cooked meals. She went to bed with the sun's departure and woke to its return. There was no gas here and candles were a precious commodity so she spared her hosts additional expense and gave them their privacy by retiring to her room early each evening. It was obvious that they were happy to have her there, but even more apparent that they had no need of anyone else except each other. Each day, unasked, Rebecca helped Christine around the home. She even worked in their cottage garden, weeding and planting and tying up beans. The physical labour gave her pleasure and she grew stronger. Each day her mind felt clearer, and her body began to fully belong to her once more. She was getting better.

Not once in those weeks did she ask the Waltons what would happen to her next. It was evident that she couldn't stay there, but part of her didn't want to know. Eventually she asked William. He responded to her question. 'We wait, miss. We wait. When Mistress Beskin sends word that it is safe, then we will take you to her. She will know when the time is right. She always does.' His pronouncement was the longest speech she had heard from him in the whole of her time at Bosmere Lock. With that said he retreated into his usual silence.

As it turned out, she didn't have long to wait. A few days later, and carrying a fully laden basket, she returned from a walk along the riverbank. She had been collecting comfrey for Christine to make into fertiliser for the cottage garden when she saw the familiar shape of her friend in an animated conversation with Christine. They were seated close to one another on the bench outside the lock-keeper's cottage. As she got closer she could hear them discussing the relative merits of different herbs and methods of preparation. Christine talked of preparations for her lying-in. Rebecca looked at her and realised with a jolt that it wouldn't be long now before she gave birth. Suddenly she was overcome with a faintness as the memory of her mother's death in childbed flooded her mind. Her legs buckled beneath her and she found herself on her knees.

Now seated at the scrubbed kitchen table with a cup of sweetened tea between her hands she felt embarrassed at her sudden weakness. Geraldine looked intently at her from the other end of the table. 'I see that you are much better, but not yet fully recovered. It will take time, you know.' She smiled broadly. 'Such excitement. I expect you want to know how Clarissa's escape went.' Rebecca found herself grinning in anticipation of the tale. Clarissa's theatrics had been a resounding success. From the moment she had appeared out on the window-ledge of Lawn House in the gloom of the eclipse the observers had believed it was Rebecca. When she had subsequently mounted the waiting horse and galloped her way out of the main gate, conveniently dropping Rebecca's shawl along the way, no-one was in any doubt of what they thought they had seen. Rebecca had escaped from Lawn House. Added to this, a torn ferry timetable had been discovered in her room. This had been conveniently marked with the times for crossings from Harwich over to Holland. Dr Henry Maudsley himself had said it would be useless to attempt pursuit now. He declared Rebecca could be anywhere in Europe by now. By the evening the chase had been called off, and the story of the escaped lunatic was soon adapted into the stuff of local legend.

Rebecca couldn't help thinking that this all sounded like something out of one of Aunt Miriam's Railway Books. Glancing over at Geraldine, she noticed a wry smile on her face. That was enough. Both women burst out laughing. The thought of a gangly Clarissa on horseback was enough to keep them giggling for a long time after. 'I didn't know she could even ride a horse!'

'She can't!' replied Geraldine. 'That's why it was so hysterical!'

That evening, William Walton took Geraldine by cart back to the village, from whence she could continue her journey back to London. Rebecca watched them until they disappeared off the tow-path and out onto the main road. She listened until she could hear the hooves no longer, and even then was reluctant to go back into the low-ceilinged cottage. She wanted air to breathe, and with which she could take in all Geraldine had told her. Her friend had brought more than information; she had left with her the means for the next stage of her journey. Wrapped in her newly returned Chinese shawl, and with a purse of money in her pocket, Rebecca felt more secure than she had for a while. On her lap was her passport, a single, folded sheet of paper with which she could travel abroad. It was not the first time she had left England, but her travels before had been when she was a child voyaging to her mother's homeland – Germany. The memories of this came in the form of smells. Food, sea air and a particularly fragrant tobacco. This time would be different. She would be travelling alone. There would be no-one to protect her, and she would be going not to Germany, but to France. Thankfully she could speak (or at least make herself understood) in the language. She looked down at the passport on her lap. Could this be the passport to freedom? Perhaps there would now be some way for her to change the direction of her life. Was it inevitable for her to return to England after this flight abroad, she wondered? As she mused on the possibilities of her future life, she heard a sharp cry from within the house. It had started. The baby was on its way.

If she had been unwilling before, Rebecca was now certain that it was time for her to leave the shelter of this family. The child – a girl – was loud and healthy, and the mother soon back on her feet and working around the house. Rebecca tried to give them some of the money which was now weighing down her purse but the family would have none of it. She could feel the family closing in around the child and she knew that she didn't belong here. The cottage was small enough before the arrival of the child, but now she really was in the way. William and Christine continued to be kindness itself, but could see the relief on both their faces when Rebecca announced that she was leaving soon. This was not her world either, but she would never forget their kindness and would find a way, if she could, to repay their generosity one day. On the last evening of her sojourn she sat with William outside of the cottage as Christine tended to the baby upstairs. 'Life is what you make it, miss. I know you are afraid, but there is nothing to be scared of if you have a plan.' Methodically he cut a chunk of tobacco and tamped it down into his pipe, using it to outline his dream for the future. 'One day I will plant a wood, tree by tree. Well, *we* will, the missus and I will do it together. William Walton's Wood I shall call it, and my grandchildren will be able to shelter beneath its tall trees and remember me. He bowed his head, lighting the pipe and taking a long, slow pull on the tobacco. That's my plan.' He turned to Rebecca. 'What's yours?'

Two surprisingly frenetic days had passed since that conversation, and Rebecca was now on deck of the tidy ship carrying its boisterous human cargo from Harwich to Boulogne. Her ticket included the fare by train to Paris, where, on arrival, she was to wait at the station. To be collected like a parcel. That was the plan – at least that was as far as she was able to look into the future. William Walton did have a point. She didn't have a plan. Until now she had allowed others to direct her course. This was understandable, but she realised that soon enough she would have to, indeed want to, make some decisions for herself. The difficulty was that she didn't actually know what her situation was right now. Was she a fugitive? Certainly. Would someone come looking for her abroad? Possibly. What, if anything, was going to happen about her marriage to Isaac? In response to this thought she fervently prayed that her recent interlude in an asylum had put paid to any desire Isaac might have to still marry her. She needed to know where she stood before she could decide upon a course of action. One thing was for certain, she really missed Miriam. Some small part of her hoped that her aunt would be waiting for her in Paris. She smiled at the thought and turned her face towards the coast of France, taking the sea air deep into her lungs.

Miriam had not seen Rebecca on the cart. She was leaning forward in her seat and watching the chaos of people running around outside Lawn House. When the carriage came to a halt outside of the main entrance she saw the figure of Dr Henry Maudsley, tall and distinctive, with Rebecca's shawl in his hand, trailing it down the stone steps. Miriam rushed towards him and grabbed the shawl from him, clutching it to her. He reached out as if to touch her shoulder, but she pulled herself away and into the waiting arms of the colonel, hiding her face in his chest. She could feel the low rumble of his voice as he then calmly asked the doctor to explain this extraordinary situation.

On conclusion of this dialogue there was nothing else to do except return to London. Unusually, the colonel seated himself deliberately next to Miriam, rather than opposite her as was his usual habit on the train. He took her hand and Miriam looked up at him cautiously. He was smiling. Miriam was livid. 'How can you possibly smile at a time like this? My poor niece...' she tried to maintain her feigned anger, but the words which he next spoke stopped her in her tracks. 'Where is your basket?' Miriam looked around her confused. 'You know, my dear, the basket which you always carry when we visit Rebecca. The basket in which you bring sweetmeats and books with which to tempt her back to health.' Miriam felt her face suffuse with confusion. 'You didn't bring it because you knew that she wouldn't be there, didn't you? I know you have engineered this, and I know why you didn't tell me about it,' he raised his hand to stop her as she tried to interject with a denial. '...and I understand your reasons. However, in the spirit of our continuing friendship I beg you to tell me all now.' So she did. She told him how Clarissa had originally come up with the idea of using the cover of the eclipse to pretend to be Rebecca. Miriam had thought of leaving the red herring of a ferry timetable and also engaging the help of 'below stairs' to spirit Rebecca away and keep her safe. Rebecca had no idea of it, but she was loved. It seemed that most everyone she had encountered had been willing to help.

The next stage was down to Miriam alone. Calmly she explained her plans for Rebecca once she had been safely conveyed to Paris. Miriam would join her there in due course, and Rebecca's future would become clear to her. 'I want to give her choice, freedom to make her own decisions. You do understand, do you not?' The colonel smiled slowly, gently grasped both of Miriam's hands and took a deep breath. 'Miriam Blumenkranz, will you do me the honour of becoming my wife?'

CHAPTER 32

Paris gare du Nord was huge, noisy and full of activity. People of all shapes and kinds were densely packed around her. It was a sea of movement. Rebecca had never been in a crowd of such energy before. She was not, however, in the least bit afraid. Taking a moment to evaluate her feelings, this realisation surprised her. After all, she had no idea who was going to collect her, nor indeed where she would be going next, but she was happy to climb up on a pile of trunks, there to sit and wait patiently. On her lap she held a small bundle with her book and a change of undergarments made by Christine's sister and given to her as a departure gift when she left the shelter of the Waltons' home. So Cook had stayed true to her sister and found a way to keep in touch. This pleased Rebecca a lot. Connections. As she adjusted her position to get more comfortable it occurred to her that there were more people than she had imagined who had been complicit in her delivery from the asylum. These were people who cared enough about her as a person to keep a secret. She readjusted her package and bundled this awareness up with its contents and pulled it closer to her body. It made her feel just a little more secure.

As the hands of the clock moved slowly towards the second hour of her wait, she climbed down from her perch. Her body (and more specifically her behind) was starting to become numb with the cold and inactivity. She began to stamp her feet to get the circulation back. Far from feeling anxious, she felt oddly liberated by this experience. It was the first time in her life she had been truly alone in a public place. No-one around her (as far as she was aware) knew who she was or what she was doing, or even cared. There were no thoughts of the Angel appearing in this place teeming with life and activity, and she knew that she would stay grounded and connected to her surroundings as her mind needed to stay on high alert. She felt alive, and realised she was smiling.

The gentle voice came from behind her, and from a place in her past. She spun around to seek its owner and found herself face to face with Samuel. He grinned and grasped her shoulders in greeting, keeping himself at arm's length as he did so. 'Well, well, well. If it isn't the fugitive Mademoiselle Zimmerman.' He turned and took her hand. 'Hold tight, Rebecca. I don't want to lose you again.' The young couple fought their way through the surging tide of people, eventually reaching the shore of relative tranquillity which was the pavement outside the station. Soon they were ensconced in an omnibus, slowly making its way across the city.

Samuel had not spoken since greeting Rebecca. Sitting next to him on the omnibus, she stole a glance at his profile. He did not turn, but continued to look ahead of him. He looked very different from when she had last seen him. His peyot were gone. Without the curls his face looked younger. He was no longer wearing his skull cap, and the uniform of black was also gone. He was wearing a jacket of dusty green, a simple shirt and cravat, and dark brown trousers. His clothing looked worn but well cared for, the cuffs of his shirt appearing from the sleeves of his jacket had been repaired, but with attention. As she allowed her eyes to move over his form, she remembered him as he was, and was pleased with the changes she saw in him. Without turning to look at her, he spoke, and she could see the shape of a smile creeping around his features. 'It seems you are still as inquisitive as ever. Good. I am glad to note it. In this city you will find much to keep your attention occupied.' He certainly spoke like the Samuel she remembered, even if he didn't look like him. She felt her body relax in response to this unexpected reunion. Aware of the subtle change in her, he turned and took her hand once more. This time he squeezed it affectionately and they dropped back into companionable silence for the rest of the journey.

Samuel's home was to be found in a tiny attic squashed beneath the eaves of a ramshackle building in the centre of Le Marais. His living space was broken into areas by the addition of curtains. One around a bed and a washstand, the other curtained off an area which she could not see, and the rest of the space held a chair, three upended crates which served the multiple uses of table and seats when required. Two others had been put to use as storage areas, one containing meagre utensils for eating, and the other containing books. The floors were bare and unpainted. On the wall was the only source of colour or decoration: the painting which his friend Vincent had given to him back in Ramsgate. Rebecca walked over to it, and in the process bumped her head on the sloping roof. Pretending that he hadn't noticed, Samuel came and stood next to her. Standing side by side looking at the painting, they allowed the view from their shared past to neutralise any awkwardness that there may have otherwise been between them. It was Samuel who broke the silence. 'You will be staying here for now. I know it is not what you are used to, but being summer you will find it sufficiently warm. Above all it is safe.' Rebecca found herself glancing at the single bed. 'I will be staying with a friend of mine. I won't be far away, in fact if you sneeze I will be able to hear you. I will be in the atelier next door.'

Later that day, now fed and sufficiently tired to watch the world as it passed before her on the street, Rebecca found herself seated outside a bistro with Samuel and a group of his friends. Most were male and appeared young. Many were artists (or at least self-proclaimed artists, Samuel whispered), and all were at this moment in various stages of intoxication. Samuel watched his friends indulgently. His glass contained water. 'As the elder here I feel it is my responsibility to remain sober and care for my less capable fellows,' he declared to the table. 'Prick,' someone muttered, but in a voice not without affection. Other epithets followed, which Samuel allowed to drift over him tolerantly. The rapidity of the conversation soon outstripped Rebecca's linguistic ability, and her schoolgirl French faltered in the bog of their countless colloquialisms. Samuel noted her frustration. 'It will come. At first you recognise little, then progressively you understand more and more. You will find that there will be times when you have achieved this fluency,' he continued, stretching and lifting his face to the afternoon sunlight, 'that you wish that you could go back to your innocent state. Sometimes understanding more of what is being said makes you aware of the fact that your friends really are quite idiotic.' Across the table, the youngest and smallest of the companions caught Samuel's eye, smiling broadly. Samuel ignored him and turned to Rebecca. 'Conversely, there are those who will surprise you.' He glanced up at the young man who was still watching Samuel. 'Especially when you discover that they speak excellent English.' He broke the mood and stood up suddenly. 'Come, Rebecca. Let us leave these sots to their debauchery and take a walk in the fresh air.'

It took a further ten minutes of discussion, debate and more ribbing for Samuel and Rebecca to take their leave of their lunch companions. By now, Rebecca understood that Samuel had found a group to which he could belong. It was certainly eclectic, probably highly dysfunctional, but a kind of family nonetheless. As she walked beside him through the park she started to re-evaluate this strange and no longer solitary figure. In the time since she had seen him he had transformed himself into someone new. He even walked differently. He seemed taller and his limp less pronounced. He had changed himself. Not unlike Christine Walton. She, however, had changed her name and moved away from all she had known to be with someone she loved. Samuel's journey had been different, and Rebecca was not sure whether his journey was about the process of moving away from an old self, or travelling towards a new one. Not that it mattered to her. He was Samuel. Her Samuel. With him she felt safe.

The days in Paris settled into a routine. In the asylum she had learned stillness, and this ability continued as now she spent much of her time in Samuel's room, initially only leaving to eat (usually in cheap bistros) and visit the privy. Samuel brought her water for washing, and took away her linen to be cleaned. She asked no questions of him, preferring to feed herself on his book collection before seeking any nourishment outside of that small space. Just as her body repaired during her stay with the Waltons, so her mind was healing itself in this garret beneath the Parisian stars. As the world busied itself in the streets beneath her, Rebecca slowly found herself treading the path from knowledge, through study, and ultimately back to more questions.

Two weeks had now passed since her arrival in France, and an unspoken question was now answered. While Rebecca occupied his room, Samuel was living and sleeping in the atelier of his young friend, the one Rebecca had noticed smiling at him on her first foray into Paris. Patrice was not an artist but an aspiring writer. The next day after her arrival, this young man engineered himself a seat beside her at lunch. The same group was congregated outside the same restaurant, and it seemed to Rebecca that the same debate as the day before was still continuing. As she tried to tune into the conversation he began to chat to her. He spoke English in an idiosyncratic manner, but well enough for her to understand his questions. His command of English rapidly deteriorated and soon mixed in with French as he warmed to his favourite subject, Samuel. Samuel himself watched this exchange with the indulgence of a father watching a child. Patrice wanted to know everything Rebecca could tell him about Samuel 'before'.

It seemed as if Samuel had indeed left his past behind when he had made his way to Paris. Patrice had threads of information which he had previously dragged from Samuel, but not enough to spin the cloth of his friend's history. Rebecca feigned an inability to comprehend Patrice. She was sure that if Samuel had not opened the book of his past to his companions already then it was not for her to rifle through its pages. She contented herself (and pacified Patrice) by telling him how much Samuel meant to her, and how he had the place of a beloved elder brother in her heart. Patrice sighed contentedly, leaned back expansively in his chair, and raised his glass of pastis to Samuel. For the briefest of moments, their eyes locked, and Rebecca saw in that glance an intensity which she had only seen once before. She understood now. Samuel and Patrice were lovers. She looked around the table. Although there were women with this group, they were not part of the group, more like an audience for the main players. These girls were the models who posed for the artists. They were very young, vivacious and loud, and it was obvious to Rebecca that these women were not of the same social background as the men. They were hangers-on. Here for the food and the wine, preferring to have a conversation among themselves and rarely, if ever, participating in that of the men. Rebecca realised this was another layer of humanity. They were decoration. Unacknowledged, interchangeable but somehow necessary to the scene before her. Even though it seemed to her that the artists and writers had little money, they were still better off than the average person inhabiting this quartier. Rebecca watched, observed, and finally registered what was before her eyes. This wasn't a collection of individuals, but a group of couples. All of them men. She had entered an alien world. Her feelings of not belonging once more forced their way to the surface as if desperate for air.

CHAPTER 33

Miriam was, for the first time in her life, speechless. For all her fear of what Colonel Burbridge might say to her when he discovered that she had not only lied to him, but gone against his advice and furthermore, planned and executed Rebecca's liberation from the asylum, she had never imagined his response would be to propose marriage to her. He smiled indulgently at her look of amazement, compounding her rising irritation. Finally, she found her voice. 'You knew all along?' Still holding her hand, he squeezed it gently. 'Not at first, and not all of it, to be sure, but yes. I did have more than an inkling that you were planning something.' Her irritation subsided, and in its place she felt shame. 'I shouldn't have lied to you, but...' The colonel released her hand and lifted it gently to his lips for her silence. 'Enough. Let us put that part of our story to bed, and acknowledge that you had your reasons for not telling me. Not least of which was the fact that you knew if I was aware of your plans I would have been obliged to try to stop you.' Miriam composed herself and relaxed her shoulders which had been stiff with anxiety. She scrutinised her companion carefully and allowed the tiniest of smiles to creep around her lips.

By mutual consent, they continued their journey back into London talking trivialities, reserving the telling of the tale for the evening. Colonel Burbridge had, like the good organiser he was, already booked them a table for two at the Café-Royal that evening. 'A yarn such as yours deserves the accompaniment of good surroundings, food and wine, don't you think, m'dear?' Miriam concurred with a nod, and began to stare out of the window at the endless suburban gardens, her smiling face reflected back at her through the window of the carriage.

Later that evening, dressed to the nines in her best gown and jewellery, Miriam told her companion everything. The formality and beauty of the surroundings of the Grill Room in the Café-Royal was a bizarre backdrop to the intense conversation which was now taking place. Anyone looking at them would have assumed they were a married middle-aged couple celebrating some event, rather than an anarchic plotter and her confidant. Miriam's eyes sparkled in the reflection of the chandeliers, and the light was kind here. Catching sight of herself in the many mirrors, she realised that she looked young and animated, and felt alive. Reaching the conclusion of her recitation of events, she put down her champagne glass and sat back in her chair to compose herself. The colonel was a very good listener. He had only interjected when he wanted clarification, and at no time did he imply that she had been wrong, or could have managed the events differently. He leaned forward for his own glass, and in doing so brought his face close to hers. Quietly he spoke. '... And what about the future?' Miriam was slightly bemused. She had already told him what her plans were to secure Rebecca's future. Seeing her expression, he continued. 'Not Rebecca. Us.'

Miriam fell back unceremoniously onto the bed and rubbed her ribs ruefully. Aisha had unburdened her of her corset and she was now able to breathe properly. Breathe, and think. It was now many hours since her conversation with the colonel and she was readying herself for bed on what had been – without a shadow of a doubt – one of the most intense and exciting days which she had ever experienced. Not only had Rebecca been successfully liberated from the asylum, but Miriam was also standing on the threshold of a new life. She had been offered, and accepted, a new life for herself as the colonel's wife. They had parted earlier at the doorstep of Gower Street, with the colonel gallantly escorting her from the carriage to her own front door and kissing her fingertips gently. Aisha opened the door wide and her eyes even wider as she witnessed this exchange of affection. Since then, Miriam had not spoken a word to her, and she was worried. Change was not always welcome. Aisha retreated into the back of the house to impart this information to Karim. Neither slept well that night.

In the morning, Miriam woke to the sight of her silent servant waiting in the doorway of her bedroom. 'Come here, Aisha.' Miriam sat up in bed and ushered the silent girl to the bedside. She looked at her expression. 'There is nothing to fear. In fact,' she followed, throwing back the covers and padding barefoot over to the window, 'I have something to tell you. Both of you. I will take my breakfast in the kitchen, and would like you and Karim to join me there. We have much to discuss.' Suddenly noticing her cold feet, Miriam thought of her cosy slippers and a possible retreat to her bed, only to change her mind at the last moment. '*Carpe diem*! Seize the day, my child. It is time to start living.'

It was just as well that the majority of the below-stairs contingent were not in London for that week, having been sent to the coast as an unexpected treat by Miriam. She had thought it best for them to be absent while Rebecca was being spirited out of the asylum. Her original idea had been to bring her back to Gower Street, but as Geraldine had pointed out it would be the first place which anyone would look for her. It also followed, she reasoned, that Miriam should have an alibi for Rebecca's deliverance from Lawn House so that no-one (should they decide to investigate) would be able to suggest that she was involved. So, when Miriam made her way down to the kitchen it was through a silent house. The echo of her own footsteps made her realise just how large it was. She would not regret leaving it. Now that Rebecca was no longer returning, there would be no reason for her to stay here. She would sell, and move into the colonel's neat home. She paused for a moment outside the kitchen door. Perhaps she could use the money to buy a cottage in the country – or even by the coast, somewhere they could visit on weekends to get out of the smog of London. She smiled. Life had taken an unexpected turn, and she was ready to embrace a new way of being. First, she thought, walking barefoot into the kitchen and seeing her loyal servants waiting there for her, there are some important matters to conclude in this one.

The conversation had gone well, and Miriam was happy with the outcome. She assured Aisha and Karim that on her marriage to the colonel (she really would have to get used to the idea of calling him Hugo) they would be free, and with sufficient finances so that they would not have to work in service again. She would provide them with a roof above their heads, and monetary backing for them to set up in business. Miriam had no concern that they would not succeed in their enterprise. She knew them to be both competent, capable and sensible individuals. Actually, Miriam was rather excited on their behalf. This conversation was not one which she would be sharing with the colonel. She reflected ruefully that she would probably always call him this. Why not? It was not the name that mattered but the delivery and she now addressed him with affection rather than formality. She shook this thought from her head to concentrate on the matter in hand. Her soon to be ex-servants would be setting up their own private detecting agency. As they talked and presented their ideas to her, it transpired this notion had come about when they had done some 'private work' for Charles Frederick Field, an ex-Scotland Yard detective-turned-freelancer after his retirement from the police force. Miriam chose to ignore the implications of this statement and remember that their skills had been invaluable to both her and to Rebecca.

Continuing with their recitation, the pair revealed that not only did they have a talent for this kind of work, but also a phenomenal network of connections, both in London and the provinces. Miriam recognised it as an excellent idea, and within the week she had taken an annual lease on suitable premises (to wit; one tiny room to operate as an office), and made an arrangement with her bank for stipendiary payments to be made to Aisha and Karim for the period of one year. She reasoned that if they were unable to make a success of the enterprise within this time, further money spent would be money wasted. This office was, by a strange coincidence, in the same building where she had visited Louisa Lowe what felt like a lifetime ago.

So it was, when she went with them to take possession of the property, she noticed that a sheet of brown paper had been tacked to the wall by the door to the office. Karim bowed formally, and invited Miriam to officially open their new premises by removing the paper. Miriam laughed at their serious faces. 'I should have worn my best hat if I had known that I was to be launching an enterprise!'

She tugged at the paper, to find a newly installed brass nameplate. Capitalised and in bold lettering it declared, 'Reith Investigative Services'. Beneath the title were the words 'Confidentiality assured.' Ceremonially, Miriam handed over the key to Aisha, with which the petite woman opened the door to her new life. They would work for her for one more month then their life in business would begin. She prayed that it would be a success. No, actually, that was not how she felt. She *knew* they would make it work.

Installed in the client's chair, Miriam looked at the room. It smelled of fresh paint. Along with the chair on which she sat, there was also another opposite, and behind it a battered but immaculately clean bookshelf with a tiny glass vase on top, the only sign of individuality in the room. She remembered giving it to Aisha some years before as she had not particularly liked it, and now Miriam felt guilty at the pride with which the recipient now displayed it. She pulled herself back to the present moment. She thought of the similar space inhabited by Louisa Lowe, and the authority bestowed by a piece of furniture which was significant in its absence in this room. 'You must have a desk. Absolutely essential to the proceeding, I think. Allow me to gift you one.' Karim bowed again and thanked her once more. Both he and Aisha seemed suddenly taller, and more mature. Miriam sighed inwardly. Life was changing around her, regardless of her wishes. It was time to move with the tide. As she left the pair to the excitement of their new enterprise, she touched the nameplate. Reith, from wreath, translation of Blumenkranz. They had named their business after her.

CHAPTER 34

S PRING WAS AROUND her, and Rebecca grew progressively stronger and more adventurous. She began to explore Le Marais on foot, and then began travelling alone on the omnibus, something she had never done, and would never have considered in London. There were moments amidst the sea of faces out on the streets when she imagined she caught glimpses of Aisha or Karim. Of course she was mistaken, but she felt strangely comforted. Instead of looking for the Angel her eyes were seeking out kinder shadows.

As she journeyed she drank in the sights and sounds and all the new and tantalising smells around her. Paris was so different from London. For a start, her senses were acutely aware of her foreignness. Everything around her was different. The language, the people, the culture. She noticed with a surprise that this did not bother her at all. Far from it, she relished this freedom it gave her. Far from being disturbed by the fact that she was unknown to others, she allowed this fact to give her space in her mind to consider recreating the self which she inhabited. Perhaps here in Paris she could make a new start, like Samuel. Perhaps this was the city where she could study. Perhaps she could find a home here, a community, and people to love her. Perhaps.

The omnibus stopped in the crush of humanity around Quay d'Orsay. Rebecca's ears had been the first of her senses to attune to her surroundings, and she was now able to understand most of the conversation taking place on the bus around her as people complained about the mess made by Eiffel's ridiculous tower. 'When would this eyesore be demolished?' someone grumbled, and others joined in the diatribe. Rebecca decided to jump down from the slow-moving bus and complete her journey on foot.

Her first visit to the tower had been with Samuel and his friends on one of their rare forays beyond Le Marais. They had been loud and, as often was the case, drunk, but by the time they had travelled up the legs of the structure and then on to the viewing platforms most were silenced by the view. 'I signed the petition, you know.' One of the more louche of the group, a painter known by all as Père, leaned back onto the guardrail with the view behind him. He looked up at the rest of the tower looming above him. 'I was wrong. An engineer can create a thing of beauty – it's not just artists.' Samuel's young friend Patrice took Père by the shoulders and turned him around to the majestic view of Paris spread below. 'There,' he pointed. 'There is our inspiration. His inspiration. The glories of Paris. Close enough to touch, but far enough away so you don't see the shit all over it.' Père retorted: 'It would seem some of us lack inspiration, at least for our art. When was the last time you actually wrote anything yourself?' Patrice was not deterred by Père's sarcasm. 'My words are here, and here.' He pointed to his head and to his heart, looking at Samuel as he did. Words of this kind were frequently exchanged among the group, and Rebecca soon learned that they were the glue that held them together. No matter how harsh or seemingly judgemental the words sounded, they came from the mouths of friends.

This time around she was alone, and would not be venturing up the structure. She came to walk in the Champs de Mars, and to better take in the incredible edifice in her own company. Reading the boards around the foot of the building, she noticed Eiffel himself had compared his tower to the pyramids of Egypt. Her mind slipped away and grabbed a handful of darkness at the association. She walked away. Her heart had started to race and her thoughts chased after it. She needed a place to sit quietly and pick at a memory which was poking its way through like a thorn beneath her skin.

More than an hour had passed, and she was still sitting silently on the park bench. Lunchtime had arrived and with it the park had emptied itself into the local cafés and restaurants. Rebecca was not hungry for food, but for details. She closed her eyes and allowed herself to wade through the pain and find what it was she sought. It was not a vision, but a series of sounds. Through the fog of her memory came the words which had been hissed into her ear by Osborne in the room atop the Egyptian House, 'Don't worry, my dear, you will not be ruined. Isaac will still take you. We have an – arrangement.'

Isaac was not happy. Right now he wanted nothing more than to lie down comfortably in the Chinaman's parlour with a pipe or two. One short journey down to the docks and he would be again transported into the arms of his love. He would have to postpone that pleasure. For now, he was forced to endure the tedium of a lecture from his employer, that insufferable bore Osborne and his inseparable brother-in-law Lord Hawsley. Isaac let their words wash over him silently, until he realised that they had stopped talking and were staring at him angrily. 'Listen well, you drug-addled little prick.' Isaac started at such unexpected language from the usually implacable lord. Hawsley turned away furiously in an attempt to contain his anger, allowing Osborne to finish his sentence for him. 'Find the girl, Coren.' He spat out Isaac's name. 'Find her and make sure she goes back where she belongs, in the asylum, and that she stays there. The longer she is free, the more likely she is to remain so, and that wouldn't be good for me – or for you.' Here he jabbed a finger on Isaac's chest, pushing him back into the chair as he did. Osborne turned his back, his shoulders visibly stiff with anger. 'Leave now. Succeed in this and you will maintain your position within my organisation. Fail and I will ensure that any damage I suffer will be inflicted on you tenfold.' Osborne silently indicated towards the door with a tilt of his head, and Isaac bowed deeply towards his back, repeating the movement to an unmoving Hawsley. As the door of the townhouse was closed behind him he ran down the steps of the building and raised his hand to hail a passing hansom cab. 'Limehouse, and post-haste, man!' He sank back into the carriage seat and smiled. The arms of his beloved opium were waiting patiently to gather him up and release him from all his cares.

Isaac was not the only member of his family who was unhappy that morning. In her Ramsgate drawing room, Anna Coren was pacing the floor weeping silently. The relationship with her husband had worsened rapidly when Rebecca had become ill, and virtually disintegrated when she had been spirited away from the asylum. Far from not caring, Jeremiah Zimmerman indeed cared about the situation. In fact, he cared very deeply indeed. Perhaps his concern about the situation was for reasons that were more to do with him and his standing in society than his daughter's distress, but nevertheless he wanted this situation to be quickly resolved. Determined to lay blame somewhere, it fell squarely on the shoulders of his wife. She, after all, had encouraged him to allow Rebecca to visit her aunt. Had this not taken place, Rebecca would still be fine. He was sure of it. Naturally taciturn, Jeremiah was now virtually mute. Mealtimes were tortured events and when he did deign to come to her bed at night he did so without speaking. Servants tiptoed silently around the house as if someone had died. Anna tried everything to draw him out from his silence but nothing was working. There was only one thing which would, and that was the safe return of Rebecca to the family. Anna wiped the tears from her face, returned to her dressing room, and pulled out her writing materials. It was time to make peace with Miriam.

Rebecca made her way back to Le Marais in a dream, back up the stairs to the safety of Samuel's room, and back onto the single chair where she gently seated herself, as if afraid to disturb the air. Samuel found her still in this position by the open window. She was in semi-darkness. Samuel was carrying his own candle with which he lit hers. Her face glowed yellow in its light, and her eyes shone brightly. She looked up into Samuel's face. 'The memories are coming back to me, Samuel, and I no longer know what is real.' She hid her face with her hands, and slowly began to rock back and forth on the chair. Samuel stood behind her, resting his palms gently onto her shoulders. He allowed her to let these emotions flow out of her, through his hands and into himself. In turn his eyes filled with tears, and he wept for her without sound.

Patrice and Samuel stood by the foot of Rebecca's bed, and watched her sleep. When she was too exhausted to stay awake, it was they who guided her to the bed and lay the coverlet over her. The Chinese shawl was draped over the bedpost, a splash of colour in this monochrome space apart from Vincent's painting. Patrice leaned his head onto Samuel's shoulder as he slipped his hand comfortingly into that of his lover. 'What to do, what to do with her?' he crooned gently. 'Samuel, it is time to talk to Père. His brother will help her I am sure of it.' Samuel pulled away from Patrice angrily. 'I have no desire to put her in the hands of those foul Alienists.' He spat out the last word disparagingly. 'Remember, my love, they would have you and me imprisoned in a heartbeat for what we are, for what we do. That after dissecting every aspect of our selves for their scientific papers. No. There must be another alternative. I need to think.' He faced Patrice. 'Alone.' Patrice pulled on his jacket and left the room without a word. Samuel allowed his shoulders to sag. Sometimes he felt ancient, as old as the stones. Patrice was his first lover and he marvelled at the way he was able to lose himself in the moment of passion, but his youthful enthusiasm and naivety were starting to grate. It was time, perhaps, for him to move on from this nursery of desire (fascinating though it had been), and find a different life. Again. Perhaps he was doomed to be the Wandering Jew after all. Rebecca stirred in her sleep, and Samuel smiled. The small figure lying there was more to him than a pupil, more than a friend. He loved her and he would do anything in his power to protect her from more harm, even if that harm came from within herself. Perhaps Patrice was right. He would make peace with him later. For now, he could only watch over his charge, a guardian angel who no longer believed in a deity.

CHAPTER 35

PÈRE AND HIS brother Cornelius were identical twins. The first time Samuel had seen this confusing vision he was silently reading at the usual table where the group would meet for lunch. He remembered being unnerved by the likeness, feeling that he himself was the stranger, not this newcomer. It was when Cornelius Mercier had looked up at Samuel that he realised this was not his friend. It was a doppelganger of the most insidious kind. The disgust and sadness he found in Cornelius's eyes as he stared at Samuel transformed the features of this bearded stranger. Rather than the loving and open expression of his friend, Samuel realised that he was looking into the face of an enemy – someone who hated him on sight and had already judged him to be both amoral and stupid. Samuel's pride quickly disabused him of the latter opinion, but he felt that this only served to make Cornelius despise him all the more.

When Samuel was first introduced to the group, Cornelius would occasionally join them for their lunchtime debates over a pastis. He was an academic, and he specialised in illnesses of the mind. Samuel soon came to believe that Cornelius's visits were more like archaeological digs as he questioned his fellow diners on their loves and lives. Samuel did not trust him and did not like him, so when Patrice suggested they go to talk to him about Rebecca he was angry and rejected the idea without consideration. When they did talk to Père he countered Samuel's objections calmly and logically. 'Come with me to see my brother at work. Talk to him, then make up your own mind.' Later in the week he found himself in the company of Père making their way to the thirteenth arrondissement. Père gently explained that his brother was a physician of the mind, and not at all the judgemental creature Samuel believed him to be. Père smiled. 'Cornelius sometimes lacks social grace. To him we are all creatures to be studied – and understood.' He went on, 'My brother wants to heal mental pain just as the classic doctor heals physical pain.' Père stopped in his tracks in the street as if to emphasise his words, allowing irritated Parisians to push past him as he ignored their curses of annoyance. 'Cornelius prefers to believe my pederasty is a mental illness, rather than feel a moral viciousness in my desire for other men.' He smiled ruefully. 'He means well, Samuel, truly he does. He wants to cure me – to make me normal.' He linked arms with Samuel and continued walking. He walked deliberately slowly as if wanting to antagonise the people trying to reach their destinations on time that morning. 'Who in their right mind wants to be cured of love? Perhaps he is correct, in some ways being in love is a form of insanity. Any kind of love. It is not me who is insane, but society itself which is sick to label me in this way.' Père squeezed Samuel's arm affectionately. 'Love, eh? One does not choose its object.' Samuel said nothing, knowing that Père was referring to Patrice. Wild, young and adorable Patrice who could not resist the lure of a boy with a pretty smile. Samuel was no fool. He knew that most nights Patrice crept out of the bed which they now shared. He remained philosophical. For now, he would take such comfort as he could from the fact that at least Patrice still slept with him. For now, at least, both would pretend that their affair was still alive.

The hospital where Cornelius worked was enormous, and not at all what Samuel had expected. It was more like a small town. He greeted them both at the main entrance. He was courteous and, to Samuel's surprise, smiled at them both. 'Please, do come this way. I have a surprise for you. Charcot, my mentor, is giving a public lecture this morning. I want you both to hear him speak.' He led them through a maze of corridors and into a lecture hall. It was packed and noisy. The wooden benches made the clattering of the audience echo loudly and it felt more like a place of entertainment than an academic space. Samuel felt his heart quicken. He missed the communication of intellect. Regardless of his initial reasons for being here, he recognised that there was a part of him which hadn't been fed for a long time. Perhaps he would find nourishment here.

Jean-Martin Charcot was both popular with his students, as evidenced from the cheer which emanated from them when he arrived, and the packed lecture theatre which contained as eclectic a mix of individuals as Samuel had seen in any Parisian street. Eclectic – but exclusively male. Patrice would like it here, but for very different reasons. Dragging his thoughts away from his errant lover he pulled them onto the speaker himself. Charcot was heavy browed, white haired, and authoritarian in both his delivery and manner. Samuel did not warm to him, but when he began to speak it was obvious that his strong views were well considered and, as he continued, offered a glimmer of hope for Rebecca. A neurologist, Charcot used hypnosis with his hysterical patients to enter their minds and free them of their demons. In short he spoke of case after case of women whom he had cured in this way. From the corner of his eye, Samuel caught sight of Père from his seat beside him smiling gently. No. He was wrong. It wasn't Père. It was Cornelius, and he turned the smile on Samuel. He leaned in to him and whispered, 'Would you like an introduction?' In spite of himself, Samuel returned the smile and nodded, suddenly shy.

Père pleaded a prior engagement, and left them immediately after the talk, kissing his brother affectionately on both cheeks. Cornelius straightened his waistcoat in a curiously nervous movement, and ushered Samuel to follow him further into the hospital. Instructed to wait in the corridor, Samuel felt a sudden urge to smoke. This was something he had done only once before in his life, in the moments after he had first made love to a man. It was not a romantic encounter, little more than an urgent fumbling beneath the arches of Waterloo Bridge not long after he had left Ramsgate and arrived in London. His lover had been a smoker, and in those post-coital moments this nameless man had offered Samuel a cigarette, which he had accepted with shaking hands. The smell was distinctive. He now knew it to be Turkish Latakia, presently fashionable in France, especially with women. It was strong and aromatic. He could smell that same aroma now and the memories it conjured disturbed him. He brought his attention back to the present and sat down on a bench to wait. He watched the busy life of the hospital around him and tried to compose himself. He continued to wait. Then wait some more.

From the chiming of the church bells outside, Samuel could tell at least an hour had passed. Bored and now feeling that Cornelius had either forgotten him or was taking him for a fool, he began to make his way back down the corridor. The stiffness of waiting had made his limp more pronounced. Just as he was about to turn the corner of the corridor he heard Cornelius calling to him. He waited, watching Père's double push his way through the crowded corridor.

'Samuel, forgive me. I was called to an urgent situation. I had no way to get word back to you. Please. Allow me to buy you lunch and after that I will take you to your rendezvous with Charcot.' He looked so anxious that Samuel couldn't find it in him to turn him down. He nodded his agreement, and in a curiously expectant silence they made their way out into the street and followed the crowds decanting themselves into one of the many bistros nearby.

Lunch was prolonged and stimulating. Samuel found himself engaged in an academic debate the like of which he had not experienced since his rabbinical training. In spite of himself he was warming to Cornelius. He recognised a fellow intellectual and found himself starting to open up about his own history. Their table was outside of the bistro, and Samuel could feel the warmth of the afternoon sun on his face. He shielded his eyes as Cornelius continued his barrage of questions. 'I fear I will give you no more material for your papers, Cornelius. I have no desire to end up as a case history.' Cornelius leaned his elbow onto the table, suspending his coffee cup before his mouth. He looked deeply into Samuel's eyes. 'It is I who should fear you, Samuel. Not the other way around.' Suddenly downing his drink, he rose from the table and summoned the passing waiter for the bill. The moment, whatever that had been, had passed.

Charcot's office was as Samuel would expect of such a man, large and impressive, but it was to a simple ante-chamber beyond to which they were escorted. This room, unlike the other, was made for work not show. Here books were piled randomly around the floor, papers were strewn around the shelves, and, as Samuel looked more closely, the remnants of a meal had joined them – and none too recently judging from the smell. Charcot himself was on his knees in the corner, apparently attempting to entice a cat from behind a bookcase. On registering he had visitors, he stood, stiffly, with a lamb bone still in his hand. Samuel couldn't help himself, perhaps it had been the lunchtime wine which had emboldened him, but he found himself saying, 'A Pascal offering, I presume?' Charcot looked at the lamb bone in his hand as if surprised to find it there. He placed it gently on the seat of a chair, and, wiping his hand carefully, extended it to Samuel. He smiled, and looked over at Cornelius. 'A new student, perhaps, Monsieur Mercier?' Cornelius smiled in response but said nothing.

Jean-Martin Charcot was already a famous man. He was also stubborn, opinionated – one could not doubt his conviction. After listening to Rebecca's history in silence, he stood and walked over to the window. 'Her case interests me, and I am therefore prepared to see her as a patient. On condition, that is, that her family give permission – of course. To do otherwise would not be acceptable. I will leave the details to you. Good day.' Any questions which Samuel had would not be answered today. As they rose to leave, a group of students made their way into the room, scrambling for seats at their tutorial with the great man. As Cornelius and Samuel left the main office, they heard a yelp of surprise and both looked at each other, laughter in their eyes. 'Someone found the lamb bone...' They didn't speak again, parting in silence. Samuel had a lot to think about and consider. First and foremost, he needed to talk to Rebecca.

As he made his way back to Le Marais, he wryly admitted to himself that he had enjoyed his day. Cornelius had proved to be a good companion, and the academic environment had stimulated him. Perhaps it was time to move on from Le Marais. Perhaps. The walk up the stairs to the room which he shared with Patrice was slow. His leg ached and he felt old. As he reached the room he was greeted by his lover who was completely naked and unembarrassed. Patrice threw the coverlet to one side and patted the bed beside him, grinning. Samuel returned a smile and allowed himself to be undressed, falling submissively into his lover's arms. He would take his pleasure gratefully. Afterwards he lay beside a sleeping Patrice, aware that this act of love would probably be – if not the last – one of the last. He rolled over in his lover's arms and allowed his tears to flow. Patrice did not wake.

CHAPTER 36

Rebecca was terrified at the thought of her family finding out where she was. She argued that Samuel had no idea of what she had been through, and that he was still clinging onto the image of her father as an upright and moral man. Perhaps this was still true, she relented, but he had agreed to her incarceration. He had allowed Isaac to sign her into that dreadful asylum. He had not tried to help or communicate with her in any way while she was there. As far as Rebecca was concerned, if it hadn't been his choice then he was being controlled by the Coren siblings and that was just as bad. There was no way she was going to permit Samuel to contact them. Without approval from a family member, treatment with Charcot would therefore not be an option. Stubbornly Rebecca set her mouth into a thin line, and folded her arms. To her mind, the dialogue was now over. In spite of the seriousness of the situation, Samuel found himself smiling. In many ways Rebecca was still a child, and he recognised that pose from the nursery in Ramsgate.

Calmly, he continued with his rational argument. 'Rebecca, if you do this, you will be able to return to your home, your family.' Her face became even more stone-like. 'For what? To marry a man

I despise? A man who was prepared to sell my body to his masters to use as a whore – just to benefit his career? No. I cannot and will not return to England for this.' Rebecca's frame sagged. 'Samuel, I want to study. I want to use my brain. There is so much I have to learn, and if I go back there I will *die*.' Dramatic though her words were, her delivery of them was calm, and Samuel understood their meaning. He stared out of the garret window, in an unconscious echo of the scene when they were last together in Ramsgate. Turning back to face her, he caught sight of Vincent's painting, talisman-like in its position above the head of the bedstead. He spoke slowly. 'There is *one* avenue which we haven't considered – what about getting permission from Miriam? After all, she is a member of your family.' Rebecca began to smile. 'Strictly speaking she isn't your guardian, but Charcot did not specify.' He looked at Rebecca and tried to stay serious. Rebecca jumped from her chair and hugged him, an act which took Samuel by surprise. 'Samuel, how very Jesuitical your thinking has become – and you an ex-rabbi!'

Later that evening, having written to Miriam, Samuel contemplated the silence of the room in which he stood. Almost identical to his own, but lacking books or anywhere else to sit apart from the bed, he looked around at the barrenness of space which he now shared with his lover. It was nothing more than a place to couple, not a space to live and thrive. The bed may as well have been a coffin. He was alone, again. Patrice had made up some feeble excuse for the third night in a row to go out without him. Samuel knew he would return late, smelling of cheap wine and sex. As before, Samuel would pretend not to wake when his lover climbed back into their bed. He allowed the tears to roll down his cheeks unchecked this time. The room grew dark around him, and Paris put on her cloak of mystery and roamed the streets looking for entertainment. He did not belong here. What was he, anyway? An ex-rabbi? Not even that, an ex-student rabbi. He had no role, no anchor, no path. He could, if he wished, walk out into the streets right now, find a bridge and find oblivion in the Seine. Put an end to this miserable existence. Even as he thought this, he knew that he would not do it. Rebecca. She cared for him, and he loved her unconditionally. Ironic. A woman. Yes. Love is never clear-cut. He rose stiffly, suddenly aware of the darkness. Perhaps he would leave now and find a bridge, but not to jump. There he would find others like him with whom he could find comfort. Even as he thought this he let the idea go. It wasn't what he really wanted. He wanted – no *needed* –stimulation of a different kind. The encounter with Cornelius had stirred him, reminded him of his intellect, his capabilities and his love of education. Perhaps, just perhaps, he could become a student, or even a teacher once more. Perhaps. He realised all he wanted to do right now was to talk to Cornelius. He had found the lunch conversation stimulating, and the man both personable and confusing. He undressed and climbed into bed, laughing wryly to himself. 'If I continue like this I will probably find myself being written up by him as one of his case studies. Pederast. Thirty years old. Jew. Male. English.' As Samuel listed out his own vital statistics he felt loneliness crawl through his body like the cold. Statistics for a tombstone. He turned to the wall and lay there with his eyes open to the darkness waiting for Patrice to return and for dawn or his heart to break. He prayed that sleep would claim him first.

Miriam responded to Samuel's missive with uncharacteristic efficiency. She had included in her letter a separate note to Dr

Charcot giving him the authority to treat her niece, and empowering Samuel to give instructions as to her care should it be deemed necessary. That day, Samuel took himself to the hospital with no other plan than to find Cornelius and have him take the note from Miriam to Charcot. The problem was it was a huge place, and even though there was a reception of sorts, there was no way of knowing where Cornelius might be on any given day. So Samuel waited in the entranceway, reasoning that at some point he would have to come through there, even if it was only to go out for his lunch. He had a long wait, and when Samuel eventually caught sight of him at the end of one of the long corridors he had to run after him to catch him up. He called out his name. Cornelius looked through the crowded corridor in confusion, and with apparent irritation. Samuel blushed unconsciously as he ran towards him. His gait was awkward, and his leg was painful. Reaching Cornelius he almost fell, but Cornelius caught him. 'Are you okay?' Samuel pushed him away, his heart racing. 'Of course I am.' The irritation was contagious. He tried to compose himself and responded stiffly, pulling Miriam's note from his pocket. 'I have the permission for Charcot. Please can you take it to him?' Cornelius gently guided him to a bench in the corridor, took the letter and seated himself close to Samuel. Samuel could feel the pressure of Cornelius's leg on his and a nerve suddenly responded, sending a tremor of movement coursing down to his foot which tapped rapidly on the tiled floor, echoing loudly in the suddenly empty corridor. Apparently absorbed in reading the letter, Cornelius seemed not to notice, and as quickly as it had started, the tremor subsided. Samuel forced himself to be still, and waited patiently for this curious man to finish reading. It was true; Cornelius was a curious man, at least to Samuel. He had had time to think about him, and he had had plenty of time on his hands since their encounter. Since Samuel had written to Miriam there had been more nights alone than spent with Patrice, and last night his lover had forgone the niceties and hadn't returned at all. Not waiting for the scene which would obviously ensue, Samuel moved back into his own room. He would sleep on the floor. Rebecca, at least, valued his company.

Cornelius touched Samuel on the knee, bringing his attention back to the present. 'Seriously, Samuel, are you well? Père has told me about Patrice. Perhaps I can help you with your living arrangements.' Samuel stared at his companion wordlessly. 'If Dr Charcot takes Rebecca on as a patient, there is a possibility that she can be housed nearby. Not in the hospital, of course, but within a family environment where she will be free to come and go. It will be easier for her to attend her appointments this way. I will see what I can do.' His hand still rested on Samuel's knee, and the pressure increased as Cornelius used it to push himself off the seat. He smiled, tapped the letter before putting it in his breast pocket, and disappeared into the once more crowded corridor. Samuel didn't move for some time, confused by the feelings which now wrapped around him.

Rebecca was in high spirits. She had used the few sous she had left to buy bread, wine and cheese and she had arranged this meal with a tiny dish of salt on the tea-chest table with the care of an artist arranging a still life. Her Chinese shawl had been put into service as a table cloth and she obsessively smoothed out a tiny wrinkle in it as she waited for dusk and Samuel to return and light the candle to mark Shabbat. It was Friday night, and the last night she was to sleep here. She felt the need of this ritual meal to mark the passing of one phase of life to another. Her possessions had been neatly arranged by the bed, ready to be bundled up in her shawl the next day. She had already visited her new quarters, and the family with whom she was to live seemed simple but kind. She smiled at the thoughts which were running through her head. Perhaps, just perhaps, it would be alright. Perhaps, if she could only persuade the doctors of her sanity, she would be allowed to make her own choices. She had learnt from Père that women were now accepted at the University of Paris. With this glowing ember she lit a fire in her heart and fanned it with the oxygen of hope. A dream had been forming itself into an idea and then into a plan. William Walton would have approved. It was a dream that she hadn't been able to articulate before, but now she would at least try. She wanted to train as a doctor. If she could do this it would enable her to be free from her past, and free to help others do the same. Perhaps, just perhaps. Hearing Samuel's uneven footsteps mounting the stairs she sighed and jumped up to greet his return with the eagerness of a lover. The evening itself was spent in stimulating discussion and debate as the unlikely pair shared the light of the candle and their last meal alone together. As he reviewed these events and readied himself for sleep later that night, Samuel smiled. 'Love has many faces.' He mused, and at that moment the face which peered around a corridor in his mind was that of Cornelius.

CHAPTER 37

NLIKE ANY PATIENT Charcot could recall, this particular specimen
had spent time reading his own academic papers. Initially he
found this flattering, but soon found it interfered with the flow of
her treatment as she constantly questioned his actions. Furthermore,
as this was a teaching environment, his students were present. The
great man had no objection to debate, in fact he welcomed it, but
between student and tutor, not doctor and patient. His view of
women's 'opinions' was based on his own expectations, and he was
not happy to find that Rebecca was confounding all of them. Not
only had she read the papers but in some instances she appeared
to have a better grasp of their meaning than some of his lazy male
students. In response, he took to holding his sessions with her
tête-à-tête. His argument (mainly to himself) was that he would
be better able to study her without the distraction of an audience.
When Charcot was being honest with himself he began to look
forward to these in-camera sessions, which would have troubled
him had he cared to analyse this aspect of his own behaviour. His
vanity, however, prevailed, and he decided to invite Cornelius along
as amanuensis to make notes of this remarkable dialogue and to

compile the appropriate reports so he himself could concentrate on his treatment.

Time and care had been taken to prepare as full a case history as possible before he had even met Rebecca. He preferred to work this way as meeting the patient could, he believed, compromise his initial assessment. He had therefore left this information gathering to Cornelius who had conscientiously interviewed the patient and now had to hand a dossier from her time in the asylum. In addition to this, he spent time with Samuel – quite a lot of time. Ostensibly this was in order to understand the influences of her upbringing and family life. Samuel's companions soon started to spend their lunchtimes teasing him mercilessly about his developing relationship with Père's twin. In truth it was preferable to them dissecting the details of Patrice's new life. Samuel's lover had left the quartier without a word and was now installed as a companion to a wealthy and much older man. All Samuel has caught of the gossip was that this swanky apartment was close to the Champs-Élysées. This proximity prompted one of the group to comment bitchily that the rich man had better put good locks on his doors, otherwise Patrice would soon be out at night there 'shopping' for the many men he could find in the bushes along its length. Samuel pretended not to hear, and allowed the tide of teasing to drift on to their speculation about his long lunches with Cornelius. Closing his ears to the sound around him, he finally allowed himself to admit it. He liked Cornelius. In truth, he liked him very much. He looked over at Père as he mused. 'Père is the artist, Cornelius the scientist. They look identical from the outside but their inner selves are very different.' Hearing his own name spoken, he tried to pay attention to the conversation around him, but throughout the lunch his thoughts kept swinging back to Cornelius. Eventually he stopped the pendulum. 'Enough. I am obsessing like a love-struck youth. My interest in Cornelius is purely for his intellectual stimulation.' Even as he said these words to himself, he knew that this wasn't true. He feared this obsession would not end at all well.

By the time of Rebecca's third week of sessions at the hospital, Charcot had begun to forget he was working with a woman patient, and a hysteric at that. Her ability to debate clearly and logically, her study of, and subsequent insightful dissection of his written work was stimulating. She appeared to him to be as sane as, if not more so than the majority of his students. It was time, he felt, to push her. This morning was to be different. Instead of the intimacy of his study they were to work in a lecture hall. Not only were there other students present when Rebecca arrived for her session, but she had been provided with a chaise longue on which to recline, not the usual chair. Charcot quietly instructed her to lie down. She was not completely unprepared for this element as he had discussed the possibility of using hypnosis with her before. He had even asked her permission. Rebecca recognised that this was in itself unusual; however, she entered the auditorium not without some fear. She realised that it was whatever happened in this session and not those which had gone before that would be critical to his deeming her sane. Rebecca lay down carefully, pulling her Chinese shawl around her shoulders as if to stem the uncontrollable shivering which had just started. The shawl was becoming talismanic in its ability to calm her, and she straightened its tassels nervously. Rebecca took a deep breath and made a conscious effort to calm her nerves by looking over at Samuel who was seated alone on the first row of benches, his eyes level with hers. He had persuaded Cornelius to allow him to attend this session. Samuel knew that this was important and wanted to be there to support Rebecca. Cornelius himself stood casually by the door, neither student nor participant, somewhere between the two. In his left palm he supported a large ledger into which he was now writing. Samuel looked across and caught sight of Rebecca's shaking, and found himself shivering in response. He tried to catch her eye but she seemed to be miles away already. This did not feel good.

At first, Charcot spoke to his audience explaining the hypnotic process and the rationale for using it with hysterics. 'Only women, of course...' Here he turned back to Rebecca who viewed him passively. 'Only women suffer from hysteria. They are not to blame for this; it is their physical differences – their wandering womb – which makes them prone to this illness. It is a similar enfeeblement of their intellect which means they can be hypnotised.' Rebecca stiffened at this lecture. Charcot was speaking to his audience as if she herself had no more feelings than a cadaver waiting be dissected. She waited for her turn, and tried to still the shaking of her body. When he finally turned to her, it was with a gentleness in his voice. 'Close your eyes, Rebecca. Close your eyes. You will trust me.' She complied with the first part, but her rational mind screamed out that 'trust' had to be earned, not demanded in such a way. His voice started to flow about her, as if it came from many different places. She felt her body become limp and lethargic, as if she had been given the sweetest, most gentle of drugs. She breathed heavily. If she slipped from her body now into death she knew that there would be nothing to fear. Charcot's voice seemed to come from a distance now. He was directing her to go back in time, to the time when she first saw the Angel. Suddenly her body stiffened, but, unable to move, she found herself trapped within the memory of her mother's death. Charcot asked her questions, so many questions she couldn't remember all of his words, but she could hear herself responding. Finally, she began to cry. Deep, painful, fractured sobs. Tears of grief and loneliness. Tears of confusion and fear. Then, too suddenly, too forcefully, she was brought back to the room where she opened her eyes to view the sea of male eyes watching her. She sought the comfort of Samuel's familiar face, but there, seated next to him was another which she knew so well. Her father.

The lecture hall was now emptied of students, and all that remained were the main players. Charcot, Cornelius, Samuel – all were grouped together by the doorway. Rebecca was still seated on the chaise, but her father was now beside her. Silently he took her hand, and she was shocked to see the tears coursing down his face. 'Will you ever forgive me?' he said, quietly. 'I cannot bear to lose you again, my dearest daughter. I lost your darling mother because of my needs, and fear through my coldness I have lost Zachary also. You are not the only one to feel alone.'

With her hand she gently turned his face towards hers and wiped his tears away as if he were the child and she the parent. She took his hands in hers but didn't respond to his words. Father and daughter sat together holding hands in silence as the room emptied around them. Eventually the sound of Samuel's uneven footsteps disturbed their reverie. 'We have been invited to join the great doctor himself for lunch.' He tried to lighten the mood as he continued. 'I, for one, could do with a good meal. Do say you will come.'

It turned out to be the right thing to do. Seated around a lunch table in the busy restaurant allowed Rebecca's father to explain how he had found out where she was, and also for Rebecca to open up to him about her dreams and plans. Somehow, the presence of Charcot and Cornelius made both father and daughter select their words with care, while Samuel's grace and peacefulness created an atmosphere of safety and security – a bridge from the present to the past – which otherwise would not have been there. Rebecca began to relax, especially when it came to light that her whereabouts had not been betrayed by intent but by accident. When Cornelius had requested Rebecca's case history from the asylum it had been in the belief that her father had known, and was comfortable with her treatment taking place here in Paris. He apologised to Rebecca, and she in turn apologised to Charcot for her disingenuity in having Miriam write the letter giving 'permission to treat'. He accepted her apology with a wave of his fork as he focused intently on digesting both his food and the conversation between father and daughter.

Rebecca suddenly felt a pang of homesickness, though not at the thought of Ramsgate. She really missed Miriam and her life in London. 'Please tell me, Father, how is Miriam, is she well? Can she come to visit me? Do say you will allow her to come. Please?' Eagerly she waited for her father's response, but it did not come. Silence crept around the table as three separate conversations came to a halt and all turned to Jeremiah Zimmerman.

He took his daughter's hand and looked tenderly into her eyes. 'Rebecca. I am so sorry that I am the one who will bring tears to your eyes so soon, my dear. Your Aunt Miriam is dead.'

CHAPTER 38

REBECCA COULD NOT find the right words, or in truth, any words. Miriam's letters to her since she had arrived in Paris had been full of joy and excitement. In the last one she had talked of her forthcoming wedding to Colonel Burbridge and her excited news that they intended to use their honeymoon to experience the Grand Tour of Europe. She wrote that they would conclude their trip in Paris, with the colonel returning to London after a few days so that Miriam and Rebecca could have lots of time alone together. Rebecca had been sorry that she wouldn't see her aunt's wedding, but it was true that she could not have been happier for her. Miriam hardly attended the Spiritualist Circle any more. As she put it in her last letter to Rebecca: *It was time now to spend my time on this earth communing with the living, not communicating with the dead.* All that excitement, all that joy. Now she was dead. Rebecca found it hard to believe, and she couldn't help but feel angry. She put her emotions in a box and forced the lid closed until she had the time to examine its contents properly.

Her father was staying at the home of a business colleague. This man himself was not in Paris currently, but had offered his house and servants for Jeremiah to stay there rather than him staying at a hotel. When her father had asked her to move temporarily into the house for the duration of his stay, Rebecca's first inclination was to refuse but he had been so crestfallen, and the house was so large and empty that she didn't have the heart to say no. The treatment with Charcot was temporarily suspended, and father and daughter spent their days experiencing Paris as tourists. Museums, galleries, concerts and the inevitable trip to the viewing platform of the Eiffel Tower. It had been the longest time she had ever spent in her father's company. He had changed. Something or someone had changed him and as far as Rebecca was concerned it was a change for the better. He seemed younger and more alive. As they walked around the parks of the capital he told her stories about Alma, her mother. He spoke about how much he missed her and how much Rebecca resembled her mother. He admitted that this was one of the reasons why he didn't want her around. He didn't want a reminder of his own foolishness. 'There are days when I no longer know who I am, because who I am supposed to be is not someone I recognise any longer.' Rebecca listened. Somewhere in the back of her mind she registered that when Jeremiah relived his wife's death through Rebecca's eyes when she was under hypnosis, it had unlocked something which had been buried deep. He could now talk, and talk he did. He seemed to want forgiveness. Perhaps he was starting to acknowledge his needs had played a part in Alma's early death. Rebecca was neither able nor willing to be the one to provide this absolution. For now, she let him talk. The more he talked, the more she realised it was all about him. She realised that his love for Alma and need for his children were all about his requirements: what he felt, what he wanted, what he needed. He hadn't asked Rebecca about her feelings on watching her mother die, or what had been the effects of growing up without a mother or indeed having a new mother foisted onto her without the least discussion. The change in her father – if indeed there was a change – was only superficial, and she feared that it would not last. The previous night as she lay awake in a huge bed in the almost empty townhouse she realised that this time alone with her father was her opportunity to make a bid for freedom. It may be her only opportunity before Jeremiah's mind closed again around the conventions of his position and he would not be able to hear her voice any more. Rebecca wanted to make plans, and now was the time to initiate changes in her own life. Miriam's death had taught her this much at least. Don't wait. Take control of your life, make the changes happen, and live. Who knows, it may not work out but at least she would be able to say that she had tried.

Rebecca bided her time until the last day of her father's stay. Both were, in truth, exhausted of walking around the city and had enough of its sights. Instead, they found themselves resting in the walled garden of the house, enjoying a simple outdoor lunch of bread, cheese and fruit. Jeremiah raised his face to the sunlight and he looked younger and more relaxed than she could remember him. When they had both finished eating, the surly servant removed the food from the table and left them in private. On the table a single goblet remained and a wine bottle chilling in a metal cooler filled with water. Rebecca stared at the condensation running down the neck of the bottle, her train of thought broken when her father lifted out the bottle to replenish his glass. At no point had he offered her any and this had irritated her. She had grown accustomed to *un petit verre de vin* with her lunch. No matter. This was not the time to allow her emotions to get the better of her. Quietly, she broke her father's reverie with a touch of her hand. He turned to her, smiling. 'What is it, little one?' Rebecca calmly and methodically set out the plans for her future to Jeremiah. It did not go as well as she had hoped. In fact, it had not gone well at all.

Later that evening she found herself back in the safety of her lodging house. The family had all seemed pleased to have her back. Cynically she recognised that they needed the money which she provided, but even so, she was pleased with their welcoming reaction, especially when the youngest boy raised up his arms for her to lift him into an embrace. She pulled the child to her, aware of his smell and the strength in his small frame. She thought of Zachary and held back the sob which threatened to escape from her throat. In the privacy of her small but clean room she undressed and curled up under the scratchy covers. Jeremiah had left Paris and returned to England, but she could still hear his voice, feel his anger and sense his determination that any plans which she might have would have to be forgotten. The conversation ended abruptly when he told her that her insane notions showed that her mind was still unbalanced; she was obviously still disturbed and needed more treatment. They had not parted amicably. The next day she woke to an empty house. Her father had instructed the servants to arrange for her to be collected and returned to her lodgings. He did not say goodbye.

Rebecca realised that the anger which had been bubbling up inside her was still there. There was only one person she trusted to share these thoughts with, and that was Samuel. She navigated her way to Le Marais in time for lunch to find the usual – but somewhat diminished – crowd at their regular table. Samuel was not to be seen. She was greeted with great enthusiasm, and expansively invited to sit, eat, drink, talk. Judging from the level of noise, more than the usual amount of alcohol had been consumed already. It seemed that Père had sold a painting and the group seemed fully intent on drinking all his profit. Not that he seemed to mind. Rebecca made her way over to his seat where he pulled her onto his knee and hugged her happily. 'So pleased to see you, child. We thought you had deserted the reprobates for respectable society!' In response, she asked about Samuel. 'Ha! He is another one. We have hardly seen him since Cornelius used his mesmerism to entice him away from us.' Rebecca stared at him quizzically. 'He spends more time with the words of the dead in the library than the songs of the living out here on the street.' He stretched out his arm expansively as if to take in the whole scene before him. The conversation took Rebecca down numerous dead ends before she extracted the information about Samuel's whereabouts. Even then she was dissuaded from leaving and spent a pleasant few hours with the group while they ate, drank and argued and generally wasted the afternoon.

She would not have been able to find Samuel any earlier, anyway. Her afternoon's diversion meant time passed quickly until early evening, when, according to Père, she would find Samuel at home. As they dispersed, she made her way up to his lodging where, until recently, she had lived while he slept with Patrice. Samuel's friends had filled her in on the gaps in her knowledge, so she now knew about Patrice's new situation. She sat on the bed and waited for her friend. As she picked up one of his books from the floor at the bedside, she realised that, like her father, she had been very self-centred – especially with regard to Samuel. She knew he was some form of distant relation, but that was all. He no longer worked for her family, in fact there was no real reason other than his own kindness for him to help her now. Her assumption that he would be there for her was just that, an assumption, based on a relationship which no longer existed. She knew little of his history, or his life, except that his inclination to love men rather than women put him outside of society. He was an outsider just like her. If she chose to be a woman who wanted the right to live her own life under her own terms she would stay outside the reach of polite society. It was no wonder she felt insane sometimes. It all felt like a game – and not one which applied the same rules to all the players. Absently, she riffled through the pages of the book in her hand. She had a choice. She could go back to England, marry a man who did not love her and abide by the rules of a religion which meant nothing to her. She would live a lie and produce children and then the whole charade would start again. She would rather die a quick death through her choice than a slow one moment by moment. If she chose to die now, would the Angel come for her? Since she had encountered Charcot and had been reading, reading, reading about the mind she had begun to formulate her own theory about the Angel. This vision – and she now believed it to be a vision – was of her creation. Perhaps it was her own way of escaping the narrow parameters of her life. After all, her time in the asylum had released her (at least for now) from the threat of a loveless marriage. Perhaps this was the reason why she hadn't seen the apparition since she had come to France. She wanted so desperately to have an explanation to give to Charcot so he could certify her sane. Perhaps, just perhaps, her father would then be prepared to reconsider his rejection of her plans.

She heard Samuel's tired footsteps climbing the stairs. It was time to be kind to her friend, to give something back to him for his kindness. All she had to offer right now was kindness in return. As he walked in, she hugged him enthusiastically, not letting go until the stiffness of his body lessened and he put his arms around her in response. As he pulled away he reached into his pocket and handed her the contents. It was a letter. From Miriam.

CHAPTER 39

REBECCA TURNED THE envelope over in her hands and looked at Samuel who was now sitting on the upturned crate. Beckoning her over to him, he signalled for her to open the letter. On the envelope was her name, neatly written in a lurid purple ink and underlined. She could just picture Miriam at her bureau, completing her correspondence. Always she underlined the name, always she used her ruler as a guide. It was this detail from her memory that opened the box of her feelings and she started to sob, messy, angry tears. Samuel watched her as they fell, dropping down onto the envelope and smearing the ink. He silently opened the book on his lap and quietly waited for the emotion to subside. Still clutching the unopened letter, she finally spoke. 'I can't believe she is dead, Samuel. It seems so unfair. Just when she had taken her chance to be happy. It makes me angry. She was a good and kind woman, so why did she have to die now?'

Samuel turned to look at her, his mien every inch the rabbi he no longer was. '*Emunah*, Rebecca. Emunah. When you possess a faith that transcends all reason and can accept this as truth you can live your life in peace.' Even as he spoke these words, it was evident that he no longer believed what he was saying. He sighed. 'I'm sorry, Rebecca. I have no answers any more, only questions, and the more I ask of Elohim the less I believe in his existence – except as a shadow of the goodness which lies at the heart of all of us. All the rest are stories. Stories told to make sense of the world, stories told to quieten a child, stories told to construct a society. Just stories. Other religions and other cultures have their own. Who is to say what is right?' He stretched out his weak leg and massaged his calf methodically. 'There is no religion I know of on this earth that accepts a man such as myself. My love for other men places me beyond the comfort of religion and into a place where death is the only end. Here in Paris I have met many others who live life for every moment in excess; eating, drinking, debauching and all because the present moment is the only gift which society will allow them. At any instant I could be imprisoned or worse.' Rebecca remained statue-like as Samuel exposed his inner self to her for scrutiny and judgement. He stood abruptly, testing his leg, and uncovering an earthenware flask and two cups from beneath the upturned crate on which he sat, he filled the cups from the flask and handed one to Rebecca. He smiled, ruefully. 'Now read.'

The contents of the envelope were only two pages long. In the envelope was one crisp five-pound note (a veritable fortune!) folded into a card which said, 'Go shopping, my dear!' The letter itself was neatly written at first, but as Miriam became more excited the words began to crab across the page as if in a hurry to reach the end of each line. It was both practical and emotional. It spelled out Miriam's awareness of the brevity of life, and how she intended to live every moment to the full from the moment that Rebecca had freed her from her guilt about betraying her marriage vows. This newfound zest included accepting the colonel's proposal of marriage, travelling abroad, finding a place to live in Italy and inviting Rebecca to come and live with them as exiles away from, as she put it, '…the tedium and narrow minds of Anglo-Saxon pedantry.' Rebecca found herself smiling in spite of the sadness. Miriam's enthusiasm was, as ever, infectious. She turned over the page and read through to the end, and then read it again, then once more until she had fully absorbed the impact of its contents. The last line read: 'Therefore, and with the full support of Hugo, and having no children of my own – I intend to leave everything I own to you.'

Stunned into silence by what she had read, she reached out for the cup of wine, surprised to find it empty. She had been unconsciously sipping its contents along with the contents of the letter and the combination of both left her lightheaded. 'I think we should eat something, don't you?' Samuel's words penetrated Rebecca's head full of thoughts, and they descended into the evening streets to find a bistro. It was time to digest the contents of the letter, but not on an empty stomach.

Half a chicken, more wine and a coffee later, Samuel walked Rebecca back to her lodgings. It was a long walk and it was late, but no-one paid any interest to this man and woman arm in arm as they meandered along the Paris streets, talking animatedly. They looked to all the world like lovers. In another world they might have been. Rebecca pulled herself closer to his body and realised how much she cared for this man and how much he returned this love through his understanding and protection of her. She wanted him to be always a part of her life.

The next morning she rose early, or at least she tried to. When she lifted her head it felt as if it had grown to three times the size and weight. She promptly threw up. In the throes of her very first hangover she believed, genuinely, that she was going to die. With a hint of humour in her voice, her landlady politely explained to her the reality of her situation, and Rebecca resigned herself to a morning in bed, feeling as if the world had just spat her out. She reached under the pillow for Miriam's letter and read its contents again. They had not changed. She had left all that she owned to Rebecca. Rebecca was now financially independent. That is, she would be if she could prove her sanity. Her long walk with Samuel last night had resulted in a conversation, and the realisation that her father knew nothing of this bequest. She finally had to accept that the inheritance could not be claimed until she was deemed to be sane. Maddening.

She pulled out her copy of *On the Origin of Species* and hid the envelope between its pages. Thinking properly would have to wait for tomorrow. When she had her head back. A head which was the right size and weight. A grudging respect for her Le Marais companions and their lunchtime drinking bouts swam into her thoughts, before they sank down into a sea of alcohol-induced exhaustion. She dozed for the rest of the day, cared for by an indulgent landlady who believed what she saw as the first signs of a love affair between Rebecca and the young pale man who had carried her upstairs. She had been young herself once, before the children. She smiled indulgently down at Rebecca. Better that she gets some happiness now, while she is still young. Leaving her charge sleeping peacefully, she retreated to her own domain of the kitchen, and began to address the mountain of linen piled up on the floor.

Charcot was in a quandary. He was both delighted that his hypnotic treatment had already effected such a remarkable improvement in the patient, while at the same time he was unhappy as to the depth of this transformation. It had all seemed to happen so suddenly. Rebecca had presented herself for her subsequent session as a model of decorum and social respectability. Neatly dressed, speaking in submissive and demure tones, she was a picture-perfect lady. Too perfect for his liking. He tried to goad her, to cajole her into debate, but she wouldn't be drawn. After she had left he found himself scratching his head at this change, but he was even more intrigued at his own reaction to this change. If he was to be completely honest with himself he actually preferred her as she was before – feisty, contradictory and vibrant. Whoever she seemed to be now that she was cured was a pale reflection of her troubled self. Charcot moved away from the window where he had stood and watched her neat figure merge with the rest of humanity in the Paris street below and seated himself in the outer office. Pulling out an empty form, he began to fill in the gaps. Name: Rebecca Zimmerman. Date of birth, and so on and so on as he progressed through the bureaucratic process of discharging his patient and certifying her sane.

His task completed, Charcot blotted the ink carefully and leaned back in his chair. He could relax now, his reputation as a miracle worker undiminished. Even so he was troubled as he tried in vain to swat away the irritating fly of doubt which was even now trying to escape from his head. Opening a drawer in his bureau he carefully placed the certificate therein and locked it with a key which he kept on his watch chain. Pulling out a fresh sheet of paper he started to write. *Dear Mr Zimmerman, I write to you in the capacity as physician to your daughter Rebecca...*

When the letter was completed, he left it in the tray for Cornelius to address and send. For now, the certificate would stay locked in his drawer.

Obviously, Cornelius should not have told Samuel who then told Rebecca. Obviously the letter's contents should have stayed confidential. Obviously. However, Cornelius argued with himself, it was for the greater good that the patient was made aware and could then act accordingly. In his more pensive moments (of which there were many with regard to Samuel), he had to admit to himself that his judgement was not exactly clouded. Tinted perhaps, coloured, but not clouded. He would focus his attention back on his work. There was much to do and he had allowed himself to be sidetracked. His own cases waited for him, unread and neglected. These people needed his help. He brushed his hair back with both hands and sighed. It was time to get back to work.

With no idea as to what the future would hold for either of them, Samuel and Rebecca set about spending a sizeable chunk of Miriam's gift to immerse themselves in Paris and all it had to offer. Rebecca declared that the money was to be spent. Samuel reasoned that this was a fortune which would have secured rent on the garret for at least a year – and probably all the food too. Rebecca countered that these few weeks would most certainly be her last chance for freedom before father arranged for her to be somehow transported back to Ramsgate. Samuel did not have the heart to argue with her, and so he threw himself wholeheartedly into his role of guide and companion.

Both wanted to free themselves from thinking of the future. That meant for now at least there would be boat trips down the Seine, visits to the Louvre, mornings arm in arm trawling through the flea markets to buy books, afternoons spent shopping around the Champs-Elysée to buy fine new clothes for them both to wear at the concerts they would attend in the evenings and wonderful days of eating out without worrying about the cost. All this activity meant that neither needed to think further than they wished to. Whenever Rebecca retreated to her thoughts, Samuel would follow her right in and distract her, and she did the same for him. To the outside world of observing Parisians, only the image of young love, perfectly matched, could be seen as Rebecca and Samuel consumed all that Paris had to offer them.

CHAPTER 40

Soon enough, the inevitable letter arrived from Jeremiah, care of Dr Charcot himself. Cornelius passed the message through his brother, Père, that Rebecca was to present herself in Charcot's office to learn of its contents from him directly. Samuel offered to go with her but she refused. He could wait for her in the café opposite the gates of the hospital and she would meet him there after the meeting. She dressed carefully in the sombre clothes which she had worn before her windfall from Miriam. No point in drawing attention to herself in any way, she thought, morosely. Samuel arrived early and escorted her the short distance from her lodgings in silence.

After retreating to the café he seated himself at the window where he could watch the entrance to the hospital with ease. Turning to the waiter, he ordered a café crème, and as he did he saw Cornelius standing at the bar sipping delicately on a café noir. Cornelius stared back in silence. Using the glass of coffee to indicate to the seat opposite Samuel, he raised his eyebrows, quizzically. Samuel nodded imperceptibly, and Cornelius slipped into the seat. The silence stretched between the two of them, a chord of unspoken communication waiting to move into another key. Both raised their cups simultaneously, and broke into broad smiles. The silence continued, but this time its music was harmonious. By tacit agreement all talk was suspended until Rebecca appeared beneath the portico of the hospital.

Lunch completed, and the men waited for Rebecca to tell them her news. When she exited the hospital it was with a smile on her face, and neither Cornelius nor Samuel could contain their curiosity. 'I'm not saying another word until I have eaten! I'm ravenous!' Even though they did not know the contents of her news, they at least caught its tenor and lunch was a happy affair, with Rebecca asking Cornelius lots of questions about what he had been doing since he had last seen them. Samuel listened intently. It was as if Rebecca had known what he himself had wanted to ask, but he felt curiously shy. Cornelius settled happily into a recitation about his last few weeks. It seemed that not only had he been working hard with his own patients, but he had been also burning the midnight oil in preparation for submission of his doctoral thesis. Samuel found himself relaxing with every word that Cornelius uttered. Truth be told, Samuel had been afraid that Cornelius had been going out of his way to avoid him. Now he knew that this was not the case he could breathe again, and mentally berated himself for his feelings. 'Why on earth would this man want to avoid me? I have given him no reason to. None at all. Perhaps we could be friends after all.' He found himself focusing intently on Cornelius's hands as he spoke. At the same time another part of his mind imagined those hands touching his face. Suddenly Cornelius laughed and gently punched his shoulder. 'Samuel, where are you? You seem to be miles away.' A blush flew to Samuel's cheek. He blocked Cornelius out of his mind and drew his chair closer to the table, planting both elbows on the table to better direct his focus away from him and onto Rebecca. 'So, my secretive student. What news?'

When Rebecca had walked into Charcot's rooms she was directed to take a seat opposite him in the grand outer office. As far as she was concerned that was not a good sign. She sat meekly, waiting for him to speak. Rebecca had no intention of making this an easy conversation for him. What made it even harder was having to pretend that she didn't know about his letter to her father. She waited. The picture of passive womanhood.

'So. How have you been, my dear?' Charcot spoke gently. Rebecca replied conventionally, keeping her gaze firmly on the rug beneath her shoes. She noticed how scuffed and sad they looked. She sighed, but did not look up. He spoke again. This time the calm authority in his voice compelled her to listen – and she was grateful that she did. Methodically and reasonably he explained about why he had sent a letter to her father, and then outlined the response he received. What Cornelius had not known was that Dr Charcot had recommended to Jeremiah Zimmerman that Rebecca should take a rest-cure in Austria, in the world-famous Mayr Clinic there. He had made it clear that under no circumstances should she return to England until her treatment had been completed to the satisfaction of his medical colleagues there and, once suitably rested and recovered, she was to return to Paris for a final examination by Charcot himself. At this point, he pulled from his waistcoat pocket a key and rapped the surface of his desk with it. 'When these formalities are completed, I will release the contents of this drawer to you. Be assured of this, Rebecca, I know that you are sane. What you need now is rest – rest, and time.' Concluding with this oblique pronouncement he then walked around the imposing table which had been separating them. He stood directly in front of

Rebecca now. She rose and looked him straight in the eye, genuine delight shining from hers. She hugged him briefly and tightly before running out of the room. Charcot grinned at the diminutive figure as she slammed the door behind her. 'Women!' he smiled. 'Wonderful creatures, all!'

Jeremiah Zimmerman was a man of his word. When Dr Charcot had written explaining why Rebecca would benefit from the rest-cure he released funds from her trust to pay for the visit. It was expensive, but reassuringly so. Jeremiah had been persuaded that the mental aberration which Rebecca had experienced had almost certainly been a direct result of her 'refined nature'. If Jeremiah had realised that he was being manipulated by his snobbery, he chose not to regard it. As far as he was concerned, once his daughter had been to Austria she would be fit to be returned to society in Ramsgate. Of course, the subject of her marriage would be reintroduced, but not, this time, to Isaac. He had done some investigation of his own into Anna Coren's brother. Although he would never express those feelings directly to his wife, he believed she had tried to dupe him into marrying his daughter to her brother. He knew that it was only his perceptiveness which had prevented that tragedy from occurring. After all, who wanted a drug-addled son-in-law? True to form, Jeremiah did not see the danger from his daughter's personal perspective, only from his own professional and social standing. Dr Charcot knew the type well. By appealing to Jeremiah's snobbery and not to his love of his daughter he managed the situation perfectly. Rebecca would have time and space to recover both in mind and body, and when she returned to Paris would be in charge of her own destiny. With a certificate of sanity in her possession she could not be forced to do anything. Charcot reflected. Now women are accepted in the university here, why not Rebecca? Perhaps when she returned to the city he would discuss the possibilities with her then. He smiled to himself. If a patient of mine had thought in such a manner, I would have told him that he was attempting to engineer a way of seeing his beloved again. He picked up the notes on his desk, and replaced them almost immediately. I am in no mood for work, he mused, and left his office for the solace of the crowded Paris streets.

It had not taken long for the train to carry Rebecca to Austria. The journey had been uneventful, and the scenery was beautiful. She felt happy and alive. Samuel had seen her off at the station with a picnic from their favourite bistro, and she settled back into the first-class carriage to enjoy the freedom of movement. She would miss Samuel's company, but not too desperately. She knew that when she returned to Paris he would be waiting for her, and the next chapter of her life would most certainly include him in it. She had insisted on leaving the remains of Miriam's money with him so he could move out of the garret and into better accommodation. On their last night together they had talked of the future and dreams of study. Samuel talked of becoming a teacher, and Rebecca shared with him her dream of studying medicine. True to the Samuel she had grown to love, he did his best to dissuade her, and then applauded her rational arguments. 'You will make a good physician, Rebecca. Just the right combination of knowledge and arrogance!' She laughed uproariously at his calm insults, and threw herself into his arms. 'I will be back soon, Samuel. Life is wonderful, and I want to share my joy with you.' He extracted himself from her embrace and held her at arm's length as if to study her better. 'I am happy for you, my dear, but I do not expect to share in your largess. Miriam left the legacy to open up opportunities for you, not for you to start collecting lame ducks.' Rebecca pulled her shawl around her tightly as if to hold the memories of Miriam closer to her. 'You are my rock, Samuel, and I love you dearly. I would not have survived these times without you.'

Later that evening when Rebecca had gone to her lodgings to pack for her journey, Samuel reflected on the vagaries of life. He did not doubt Rebecca's affection for him. Nor was there any doubt about his love for her. It was, however, and always would be, a platonic one. How much simpler life could be if only he was normal. He stopped that thought in its tracks. 'Normal. No. I am normal. I am just a different kind of normal. I am a good man with a good heart. The only difference between me and those whom society accepts is the object of my desire.' He sighed. It would help if he hadn't become infatuated by a 'normal' man. Cornelius. Always Cornelius. Always intruding into his thoughts. Always on his mind. He shook his head. 'No. It is time to stop this foolishness and start making plans.' With this thought, and for the first time he could recall, Samuel was looking forward to the future, if not with joy, then at least with a sense of direction.

CHAPTER 41

THE MAYR CLINIC was smaller than she had imagined. Considering its international reputation, she would have thought it to be grander somehow. The complex comprised a number of smallish wooden buildings with a larger stone structure located between the chalets and the lake. In some ways it felt like precisely what it was, an alpine village. However, unlike those ramshackle towns clinging to the landscape of the surrounding areas, there was a high perimeter fence around this one and the buildings themselves were arranged for ease of access to one another, not to a village green. There were no shops or public buildings to speak of, and it was extremely quiet. On her first day of orientation this is what she noticed above anything else. It was virtually silent apart from the sounds of the surrounding landscape. That and the fact that there were no children. For some reason she felt a gloom descending on her which her guide failed to alleviate.

When she had arrived at the clinic, she had been met at the gate by a white-clad employee. From a distance this man had appeared to be extremely tall, but it was only when he escorted her to her lodgings that she realised he wasn't tall at all, just very thin. Thin and pale. She soon realised that they were all like that, employees, assistants and doctors alike. All thin and pale, their movements slow and measured, as if the life within them had been dimmed. It took her a few days to be able to differentiate the different levels of functionaries here. The differences were subtle, but visible to those who chose to look properly. The collars on the uniforms of the cleaners, cooks and menial staff were plain and round, those of the medical assistants such as the masseurs were upright and stiffened, while those of the medical staff had proper collars with white piping around them. She herself, like all the guests, was given white, loose clothing to wear. Theirs were differentiated with a delicate checked thread which ran through the fabric. So at a distance you could not tell who you were looking at. Her guide had carefully explained to her that this visual removal of external trappings was to create a more egalitarian group. This was symbolic of the clinic's creator to encourage a space in which the inhabitants could free themselves from the more obvious social constraints of their outside lives. Rebecca very much doubted it. If the other guests were anything like her, it just made them pay more attention to the subtleties to be able to position themselves within this hierarchy of ghosts.

For the first few days, Rebecca was busy. A visit to the physician to identify her specific needs and tailor her treatment. It wouldn't be arduous, explained the gentle-faced doctor. Stimulation such as reading or corresponding with the outside world was prohibited, as was coffee and alcohol. Being found with either in your possession would result in expulsion from the clinic. 'Walking in the hills, swimming in the lake, massages and a frugal diet will be the order of the day. Routine. Hay baths. Bed rest.' He walked around his room as he was speaking, caressing the specimen bottles located all around the shelves of the consulting room. 'As you recover, the exercise programme will be increased. The most important element of this treatment is that you rest, rest, rest. At the Mayr this is our, and your, priority. Of course if you do not like the constraints of the diet you are free to take one of the bicycles which you will find by the main door and cycle into the nearest village. It is twenty kilometres away. We feel that if you are sufficiently recovered to do this, then you are well on your way to being cured!' Rebecca smiled wryly. She had become rather fond of French cuisine (as her abortive attempt to fight her way into her corset to fit into her travelling clothes had proved), and the thought of restricted meals did not fill her with great joy, especially when she realised that restricted really did mean restricted. Three times a day she and the other ten guests, entered the dining room overlooking the lake, and each sat in glorious isolation at their own, beautifully laid table. Elegant cutlery, beautiful china, and fresh cut flowers adorned each linen cloth. However, the food itself was, well, non-existent, really. Her first meal had been a shock, the second had been confusing, and on the arrival of the third meal when she had been served the identical fare of a cup of herbal tea and an extremely hard spelt biscuit she had called the waiter to fetch one of the medical staff to her immediately. She felt her cheeks burning as the guests on other tables either ignored her, or stared openly, chewing their biscuits like cows chewing cud. Mesmerised by this activity, she failed to register the appearance of the doctor at her table. She opened her mouth to speak, only for him to raise his finger to his lips and with his other hand he pointed to a small piece of paper on her table which she hadn't noticed before. He indicated for her to read it. It was in German, but she read it easily enough. As she did she could hear accompanying sounds of her stomach growling and the large, and now in her mind, ominous clock ticking away on the wall behind her. It was a list of rules for the dining room, which read:

1. *Absolutely no talking. Speech will interrupt the flow of digestive juices and will be counter-productive to your treatment.*
2. *Each mouthful of tea is to be introduced into the mouth with the teaspoon provided. The mouthful is to be then held in the mouth to allow the flavours to be fully appreciated before swallowing.*
3. *The spelt biscuit is to be broken up into sections and pieces no larger than the thumbnail is to be introduced into the mouth. This piece is to be chewed no less than FORTY times. Failure to do so will interrupt the flow of digestive juices and will be counter-productive to your treatment.*

The list continued. Rebecca reluctantly looked up at the doctor, who was now smiling benevolently down at her. He bowed, and made his way around the remaining tables, bestowing smiles or frowns as he observed the behaviour of those seated there. Rebecca rested her elbows on the table and pushed her palms into her forehead. 'This is going to be harder than I thought.' She sighed, and dejectedly picked up her teaspoon, catching the eye of a woman nearby. Rebecca essayed a smile. The woman frowned, and continued to chew furiously. It was going to be a long and tedious stay.

After a week of lean pickings, walks in the foothills and *endless* hay baths, reluctantly she had to admit she had started to relax into the routine. Not exactly enjoy it, but she was at least becoming accustomed. The hay baths themselves consisted of taking an afternoon nap in the hayloft of a nearby barn, and being covered in hay until only her head was visible until a bell was rung, signalling the end of the treatment. The first time she had a hay bath her feelings varied between irritated, itchy and baffled, but as she lay there, memories of the night on the road to Bosmere Lock and freedom from the asylum flooded her mind. She dozed peacefully, and when she woke felt happy and energised. Each treatment involved another dream, and as the days went by Rebecca began to find a peace in her mind, the like of which she had not experienced before. It had now been three weeks and last evening she had even managed to coax a smile from the doctor on duty at supper with her proficiency in chewing slowly. She had been the last to leave the table, and bizarrely, she had felt – if not full exactly – at least satisfied. It was obvious that she was growing stronger, fitter and, thanks to the diet, losing some of the weight which she had put on in Paris. It was true that when she had first arrived, she would lie in bed and feel a momentary panic at the thought of returning to Ramsgate. Almost immediately her consciousness would then remind her of Miriam's gift, and her fear subsided. During the last few mornings there had hardly been any anxiety at all, and this morning the emotion had changed into one of excitement. Most important of all, there had been no sight of, hint of, or feeling of the Angel. It was as if he had ceased to exist in her life. Perhaps he had. Perhaps she was cured of this illness, this vision, and she would be finally free.

Rebecca now found herself looking towards the future and not back to the past. She would honour Miriam's gift to her by following her dreams to become a doctor. Smiling at the thought, she washed, dressed and made her way contentedly to the dining room. At this time in the morning it was usually deserted, but as she entered she saw a new guest had arrived. Small, dark and unusually voluptuous, she saw a girl of her own age. This figure stood immobile and in silence by the window looking out at the lake. From the doorway, Rebecca took a moment to study her as she would a painting. In profile she had strong features, unusually so, and her hair was long, black and looped in a loose plait on one shoulder. Without understanding where this knowledge came from, Rebecca could sense she was different. The girl stooped badly, and Rebecca realised that she was actually not so small after all, she just carried herself this way, as if trying to make herself small and invisible. She knew how this felt. The desire to disappear. The mark of the outsider. The waitress arrived in the room and the moment of stillness was broken. The figure at the window turned, and as she did she looked straight towards Rebecca. Slowly, she stretched out her hand and turned her palm upwards, staring at it as if she had never seen it before. Rebecca watched fascinated, as a livid scar across the palm flashed into her view. Her hand turned again and just as suddenly the scar was gone. Other guests began to appear at their tables, and the moment of understanding had passed.

Rebecca tried to focus her attention on the insipid green colour of her tea, staring at it and lifting the tepid liquid teaspoon by teaspoon to her lips. Her heart was racing and she could not concentrate. She felt a powerful connection with this unknown and unnamed girl, and she knew that it would be a long time until she could feel peaceful again.

CHAPTER 42

THAT DAY HAD been a particularly full one and Rebecca was grateful for the distraction it afforded her. After breakfast she had the third of her weekly consultations with the medical director of the clinic. He checked her reflexes and her pulse, her weight and her strength. He said little, but seemed pleased with her progress which he recorded meticulously in her case notes. He appeared to be a kind and mild individual, as pale and thin as all the others at the clinic. Rebecca had been amazed to discover that he was in his seventies. He had smiled at her reaction. 'Yes, my dear, it is both achievable and desirable to maintain good health into old age. In fact, I myself fully expect to live to see one hundred summers.' All of this information was imparted in heavily accented English. When he discovered that Rebecca could speak German he switched to his native language, and, as he did, she noticed his manner changed also. He became much more brusque, more pared down in his speech and much more practical. She smiled as she noticed these changes. Rebecca soon regretted this lack of attention as he took her smile for agreement to his words and, as a result of this, she found herself moved on from her gentle regimen of hay baths and massage to a much more active one of hiking and swimming in the lake. As she left the consulting room she was aware of the smallest smirk on the doctor's lips. It had served her right. She would make sure she paid much more attention in future.

As day moved towards evening, Rebecca walked down to the jetty which projected out into the lake. She lowered herself down onto the slatted boardwalk and peeled off her stockings. Angling her body so she could just about dip one toe into the water, she lowered her foot into the liquid. Immediately she pulled it out again. The water was freezing. The thought of lowering her whole body into its darkness and swimming in there sent a shiver through her whole body. Too late, she mused, miserably, it's my own fault. I should have been listening to the doctor properly. 'It's really not that bad you know, once you get in there.' The speaker lowered themselves onto the boardwalk next to Rebecca. 'The best way is to jump in. If you try to lower yourself into the water you will never do it. Once you are in, you are in. Do you know what I mean?' The girl dangled her own feet into the water, then pulled up her skirts. Rebecca could see knees and the edges of a pair of red garters which had until recently held up the stockings which were now balled up in the girl's hand. Rebecca didn't speak. 'This isn't my first time here.' The figure shifted as if to make herself more comfortable. 'This is the third time I have been sent here.' Rebecca still had not spoken. Intuitively she knew that this was the time for her to fulfil the role of listener.

From that moment, Rebecca and Sofia had been inseparable. Other than the times when they were having treatments, they spent every waking moment together. Rebecca had been right. Sofia was an outsider. Over the first four days, Sofia had poured out her life story to her new friend, and it was unlike anything that Rebecca had heard before. Sofia was an orphan, or at least as far as the authorities were concerned. As the newfound friends had walked in the woods together, Sofia had poured out her history. She had been born in Vienna, but raised in Budapest. Her mother had been from a wealthy, respected family. Sofia's eyes misted over. She had also been beautiful. Each evening Sofia and Rebecca would meet at the jetty, and she would continue her story. On the third evening, Sofia pulled a photograph from her pocket. 'My darling mama,' she said simply, and Rebecca found herself holding an image of a dead woman, seated by a baby basket, her hand draped into the crib. Repelled, Rebecca forced herself to look at the image. 'She died soon after I was born. That's me in the crib,' Sofia pointed to a blurry figure bundled in lace. Rebecca turned again to the *memento mori*. Eyes had been painted onto the dead lids of the woman, and her lips were parted. Lines of pain were etched into the forehead. These were the only traces of life in this figure, and they did not point to a life of ease. Sofia took the image carefully from Rebecca's hands, and cradled it gently before wrapping it in a lace-edged handkerchief and replacing it in her pocket and looked out over the lake. 'It is all I have of her, apart from my memories of her love.' Rebecca reached over and squeezed her friend's hand. When she tried to pull away, Sofia drew her hand back. They held hands in silence as the sun disappeared behind the mountains.

Each day, a little more of Sofia's story seeped out, and each day, without realising it, Rebecca lost a little of herself in the story. By the time her next weekly visit to the doctor had come around, she found herself defending her new friendship from the scrutiny of medicine. 'You are here to heal yourself, Rebecca,' Doctor Stroh sighed gently, folding his arms. 'It is not unusual for situations of this type to develop. You are a young woman who has experienced trauma and you are vulnerable. Above all, it is time for you to have children and your natural instincts to nurture are burgeoning – hence your desire to protect others. I have seen this many, many times before. Young women forging strong emotional attachments with one another and vowing eternal loyalty.' He lifted Rebecca's hand to take her pulse, giving her a momentary flashback of Isaac. The memory caused her to shudder. He noticed, but did not comment. For once, Rebecca did not argue. Her feelings about Sofia were too mixed up right now. She needed time alone.

Time alone was not something which Sofia was going to allow her. She followed Rebecca around the compound like a lost duckling. When Rebecca lay in bed at night she had to admit that this admiration and adoration had its charms, and she decided to ignore the doctor and throw herself into this developing friendship. Why shouldn't she? There was nothing wrong in it. In the moments when she was being honest with herself she also recognised a resentment at the doctor's words. As if being a mother was the only conclusion for a woman. As if, without a child, she was incomplete in some way. What did he know of women? She stirred fitfully in the warmth of her room, her conviction to train as a doctor strengthening each time she revisited her conversation with Doctor Stroh.

Sofia and Rebecca had walked for the entire morning, and were now high up in the foothills around the lake. Both now lay flat on their backs, watching the wispy clouds drift by above them. Without turning, Sofia reached out for Rebecca's hand. 'When my mother died,' she began, as if no time at all had passed since she had put away the *memento mori*, 'I was cared for by the nuns. I use the term "cared for" loosely, for as a bastard child in the convent there was little by the way of nurturing.' She let go of Rebecca's hand and turned onto her front, pushing herself awkwardly up onto her elbows. As she turned, the scarred palm of her right hand was momentarily visible. Sofia noticed Rebecca's look, and then held her hand in front of her face as she had done on the first day they had met. 'This happened when I was around nine. I don't remember much about it. I was told that I had tripped in the kitchen and had grabbed a carving knife as I fell.' She drew closer to Rebecca, letting her hair form a curtain between their faces. Sofia continued to speak, but this time in more of a whisper than a voice, as if sharing a secret. 'Three weeks later he came to collect me. I was to become his ward. The nuns fussed around me, telling me how fortunate I was for a man of his standing to honour me in this way. I have lived with him ever since. He clothed me, educated me, shaped me into the woman you see before you. I *hate* him with every fibre of my being.'

Drops of spittle fell on Rebecca's face as Sofia spat out her final sentence. Repelled, she spun her body away to break the intimacy between them. Both women sat up – and Rebecca found her heart racing as if she had been running. She knew that she shouldn't ask the question, but she found it irresistible. 'Why? Why do you hate him so if he saved you?' Sofia drew up her knees to her chest and wrapped her arms around them. Her hair was like a half-closed curtain around her face, making her seem much younger and even more vulnerable than ever. The figure shuddered and then looked directly at Rebecca. 'My mother was a beautiful woman. She came from a bourgeois family. Not old money, to be sure, but respectable. They did everything correctly. Mother was an only child, and her parents only wanted the best for her. When Mother started to sleepwalk they did what was expected of them. They took her to see a doctor, an Alienist who specialist in disorders of this kind, and like the gentle, naïve people they were, they had no idea what was happening until it was too late. He gave her drugs supposedly to cure her, but she quickly became addicted. He used her when she was at her most vulnerable. He used her and when she became pregnant with his child he denied having had intimacy with her.

'Her parents tried to force her to go to another city, give birth and hand me over to the nuns for adoption, returning at a suitable time so no-one would guess what had happened. She wouldn't do it; she wouldn't give me up. Stupidly, she believed that he loved her and would come to his senses and marry her, but this did not happen, and without her supply of drugs she had to find another way of getting them. She became a streetwalker. Am Strich. The lowest of the low. Most shameful of all, she did this on the streets of Vienna. In her own city. In the place where she had been born, had travelled in carriages and attended balls. She became a prostitute.'

Rebecca moved over to her friend and gently cradled her in her arms. Sofia did not move. She shuddered and carried on. 'My mother's parents were more concerned with their own reputation than their daughter's life. She died out there on the streets. They could have taken me in but instead they left me with the nuns. All I took in there was the photograph. My darling mother. Foolish, foolish, foolish mother. That is why I hate him so. This man, this oh so good and upright man who took me in is the reason my mother's family threw her out. The reason my mother killed herself. The reason I exist. He raped my mother and left her to become less than dirt on the street'. Rebecca rocked her as Sofia clung to her, Sofia sobbing soundlessly.

CHAPTER 43

REBECCA'S EMOTIONS WERE in turmoil. Sofia's presence at the Mayr had changed everything. It was no longer the peaceful place it had been, but she acknowledged that she didn't care. For the first time in her life she had someone to look after. Sofia became her shadow, and they started to spend as much time together as they could. Doctor Stroh knew – how could he not? – but in Rebecca's next session he appeared indulgent. All her vital signs indicated that she was recovering her strength and her vitality, so much so that for the first time he spoke with her about the future. 'So, my dear. Soon you will leave the Mayr and return to your home.' Unconsciously gripping her chair, she responded. 'Back to Paris, yes.'

'Of course,' he replied, shuffling the pages of her case notes. 'To Paris. To my good friend Dr Charcot.' He smiled widely this time. 'Dear Jean-Martin. We studied together. Does he still keep cats?' A smile came to Rebecca's lips as she remembered Samuel's tale of him trying to coax a feline with a lamb bone.

If Rebecca had taken time to assess her feelings she would have had to acknowledge that she was in no great hurry to leave the clinic. Her friendship with Sofia had fallen into a comfortable routine, and she found herself imagining ways in which this could be prolonged somehow. Part of her mind knew that this wasn't to be, but she allowed herself the indulgence of imagination. Her final week at the Mayr had come, and Sofia clung to her more than before.

Sofia had been waiting for her outside of the door to the consulting room. She had an impish look on her face. Rebecca tilted her head, quizzically, and Sofia opened her palm to reveal an opaque blue glass marble in her hand. She placed it in Rebecca's hand. 'A present for you.' Incomprehension suffusing Rebecca's face, she stared at it silently. 'Listen,' Sofia whispered, 'take it to the nurse this afternoon and say you found it in your stool this morning.' Rebecca shuddered. One of the more unusual treatments at the clinic had been the daily doses of Epsom salts which had confined her to prolonged admiration of the porcelain glories of her bathroom for the first week of her visit. That noxious liquid accompanied with seemingly endless glasses of warm lemon water was meant to cleanse her internally. Sofia giggled at her confusion. If you do this, you will get a surprise – I promise you.' This sentence was delivered in a curious sing-song way, like a little girl with a secret. Sofia ran away, leaving Rebecca turning over the child's toy in her hand.

She did as she was told, and presented the marble to the nurse, dropping it as instructed into the proffered metal kidney bowl with a loud clang. The nurse had greeted this 'gift' with a thin-lipped smile, and had escorted Rebecca to the door without another word. I have absolutely no idea what that was all about, Rebecca thought to herself, and put it out of her mind until later that day, when all became clear. She had dressed for dinner as usual and at 6 pm precisely waited patiently at her table for her tea and spelt biscuit. As all of the tables were arranged in such a way that the guests could enjoy the view and not be distracted by one another, she could only see Sofia's back. However, knowing her friend as she did now she could tell that Sofia was alert to her arrival. She sighed. One thing she wouldn't miss was the food – or to be more precise – the lack of it. *Oh, what I wouldn't give for a boiled egg right now.* She almost laughed out loud. Such was the strength of her imagination that her stomach rumbled noisily and she could almost believe she could smell boiled eggs. Actually she could, and so it seemed could everyone else in the room, as suddenly all of the guests turned towards the door to the kitchen. The waiter, followed by Dr Stroh, appeared through its doors. The former carried a large platter, covered with a metal cloche. They walked towards Rebecca's table, all eyes in the room following the procession. Standing before her, the doctor smiled and lifted the cloche with a flourish. Nestling beneath its lid was a boiled egg. Beautiful in its isolation, and perfectly white. The fellow guests gasped as this prize was deposited on Rebecca's plate. Dr Stroh leaned down to her and whispered in her ear. 'Well done, my dear. Enjoy your reward.'

Rebecca had taken her time to eat each extraordinary mouthful. This was better than anything she had ever eaten before, ever. Even with every eye in the room still on her, she consumed the egg in complete absorption, and when she had finished it she was full. Unbelievable. A tiny egg, but a taste she would remember forever. Eventually this gourmet experience was over, and she left the room, slowly savouring the last taste through the envy of her fellow guests.

It was some hours later, and Sofia and Rebecca had escaped their rooms and slipped out of the clinic to be by the edge of the lake.

The sun was low in the sky, and insects dipped and dived over the surface of the water. Both girls were barefooted and dressed in their night-shifts. Sofia now allowed herself to laugh uproariously at Rebecca's face at dinner. She did not seem to tire of repeating how funny she had found it all. 'How did you know?' Rebecca asked.

'I have been here before, remember. The first time I came a man passed a small stone, and he got an egg too! I thought if you can pass a stone, why not a marble – after all, lots of children swallow them. I thought it was worth a try so my darling Rebecca could eat!' Both girls laughed happily and Sofia suddenly rose. She lifted her shift to reveal her naked body and dived noiselessly into the lake. Rebecca waited anxiously for her to come up for air. When she did, Sofia's long, loose hair was slick around her head and pooled around her in the water. 'Join me. It's *so* wonderful.' Rebecca wasn't a confident swimmer, nor was she sure that she would like the temperature of the lake, but she felt it hard to refuse. She lifted off her nightdress awkwardly, folding it carefully on the jetty, and started to climb down the steps into the water. Sofia swam towards her. 'No. My friend, you must jump in. Jump in or you will never do it.' Rebecca jumped.

As the sun rose on the next morning, Rebecca heard the click of her door lock as Sofia let herself out of Rebecca's room and made her way back to her own room. She pretended to be still sleeping. Her heart was pounding. She needed to think but too many emotions were crowding her mind. She felt confused, exhilarated, tainted, strange. She had too many emotions in her head to know where to begin. What she did not feel was happy – and with this thought she decided to take to her bed for the day. When the doctor arrived to see how she was feeling she pleaded a stomach-ache – probably as a result of eating the egg. Dr Stroh sat on her bed and placed his large, damp hand on her forehead. In English he said, 'You are probably correct, my dear. Indulgence is the root of so many of our ailments. Just when you were making such wonderful progress as well.' Giving her permission to stay in her room for the day, he left her, switching to German for his last words as he closed the door behind her. 'It is not just food that can poison a body, Rebecca.' He looked at her closely before leaving her in peace. 'Some friendships can be both addictive and poisonous. Rest – and think, child.'

Once alone, she tried to do just that. The events of last evening had been both shocking and confusing. She tried to retrace the timeline without emotion. It was difficult. Last night she jumped off the jetty steps and the shock of the cold water had hit her body, taking her breath away. From that moment her world changed. Rebecca found herself under the surface of the lake, looking at a submerged and naked Sofia. Her hair was a waving halo of strands pulled and pushed by the currents. She looked like a water nymph. Beautiful and strange. Rebecca stayed there as long as her lungs could bear, and when both came up for air they could hear the sound of voices. Sofia pulled her underneath the jetty so they could not be seen, clamping a hand over her mouth to stop her friend from making a sound. Someone was walking onto the jetty. Another voice called from the distance and the footsteps receded. In silence both women trod water in the shadows beneath. Sofia released the grip on Rebecca's mouth and moved her hand around to the nape of her neck. Looking deep into her eyes, she pulled Rebecca's face towards hers, and kissed her on the lips. Gently at first, and then with passion. Rebecca froze, and then started to shake uncontrollably. The coldness of the water had penetrated her limbs and she felt its pull. She began to feel fear. Fear that she would die out here in the lake. In silence, Sofia half-dragged, half-carried her onto the jetty, tugging her nightdress over her damp body. Miraculously they were not seen re-entering the house. In Rebecca's room Sofia took a towel and dried her, rubbing her skin hard to bring warmth. Eventually the shivering subsided, and the girls lay together side by side on the bed. Rebecca wanted to be alone, but the water nymph clung to her. Sofia's hand reached across her body and traced the outline of Rebecca's collarbone with her fingers, then dropped her hand lower to her breast. She stopped, and looked into Rebecca's eyes. Rebecca hadn't moved, didn't speak, frozen once more. Sofia stroked the nipple with the back of her fingers, then gently squeezed it between finger and thumb. Rebecca stiffened, her heart racing, her breathing growing faster and more shallow. Still she did not react. Sofia raised herself up and straddled Rebecca, still squeezing – harder now. Prone and frozen, Rebecca opened her mouth to speak, but Sofia leaned down and closed off the sound with a kiss. Like the night-hag Sofia rode her now, smiling triumphantly, moving her other hand down her body where it finally came to rest between her legs. Rebecca felt herself jolt with pleasure. She reached up to pull Sofia towards her, and the women lost themselves in each other and the darkness of the night.

CHAPTER 44

R EBECCA HAD NOT been totally naïve about sex before her encounter with Sofia. She had heard her Parisian companions speak of their exploits in – to her mind – far too much detail. She had heard the rattle of iron bedsteads and the grunt of their inhabitants as she lay awake in Samuel's garret in Paris. She had felt the emotions of love and romance through her aunt's collection of railway novels, but none of these things had prepared her for her experience with Sofia. The events of the night had been intense and intimate in a way which she could not have predicted. Once the act itself had been over, and she lay cocooned in the pleasurable warmth of her responses, she found herself talking. She told Sofia everything (well, almost everything) about herself. Sofia listened intently. Rebecca spoke of Isaac, about the night at the Egyptian House, about the asylum. Once the floodgates were open she poured out her connection with the Angel and how desperately she wanted to be free of him. Sofia soaked up her lover's knowledge silently, allowing Rebecca to unburden herself of emotions that she did not know she even harboured.

Rebecca spent the following morning avoiding her friend. It was not too arduous as her routine of exercise, treatments and massage kept her occupied. As she was nearing the end of her programme the regime also included an education. The Mayr Clinic was notable for its efficiency and determination that the changes made within its walls would be lifelong. It was more than a treatment; it included a prescription for health. As the weeks had gone past, she had become more aware of her fellow guests and realised that they fell into two categories – those like herself who were there because their systems had broken down, and those who were proactive about their health. These were the regulars. Mostly German or Austrian, they were older than Rebecca had first realised. Their adherence to the Mayr principles of exercise, frugality and self-medication produced positive results, at least as far as their physical wellbeing was concerned. Rebecca noticed that, although they all seemed fit and well, generally they didn't seem to be all that happy, in fact quite the reverse for some of them. There was a joylessness about their demeanour and a ghost-like pallor which disturbed Rebecca more than she cared to admit. Furthermore, it made her even more acutely aware of her encounter with Sofia. Sofia was strange and erratic, childlike sometimes, but she was – most definitely – alive. Her vibrancy and joy of all things about her made her both appealing to be around and quickly exhausting. That afternoon, Rebecca sought her out and threw herself into Sofia's arms. Until she left the clinic, Rebecca thought to herself, she would devote herself and her time to her friend, believing that when she left for her new life she would take her memories with her, but nothing more.

Sofia, however, had a different idea. 'Come with me to Budapest.' At first, Rebecca was intrigued by the suggestion, then horrified, but once she had disentangled Sofia's strange and twisted endpoint from the suggestion she realised that there was some merit in the idea. If nothing else, it would give her more time to think about her plans for the future. 'You can be treated by my father. He will help you release your demons – free yourself from the Angel.' Rebecca was dumbstruck. Why would Sofia want her to be anywhere near the man she hated so much? Sofia responded, reasonably. 'He is a very well respected Alienist. His papers are widely read and he is famous for his treatments.' She continued, 'If you elect to see him as a patient you are proving to everyone that you are well enough to recognise that you *had* a problem, and you are choosing to ensure that it will never return. You can return to Paris with a letter from him to Dr Charcot. Charcot can claim your diagnosis and the start of your recovery, and the great Professor Farkas can claim a victory for the benefits of Alienism in helping you maintain these improvements. What do you think?' Rebecca was about to respond in the affirmative, when Sofia's thought process disappeared down a dark passage. 'Besides, you could marry him and then can call the Angel to come and kill him. You will get all his possessions and then we can be together forever.' Sofia delivered this outrageous monologue in the same voice as the reasoned argument which came before it. Sofia looked at her from beneath hooded eyes and then smiled at the look of horror on Rebecca's features. She leaned onto her friend's shoulder submissively. 'Joke, Rebecca, I'm only joking!' Rebecca wished she could have been sure of this, but she let the cloud of doubt drift out of her mind. One thing was for sure, she was glad she had held back on saying anything about Miriam, or the inheritance. There was, however, an advantage to be had so she decided to write to Charcot and ask his opinion on her continuing her treatment in Budapest. If he agreed to it she would go to Hungary with Sofia. If not, she would have a perfect excuse to sever her ties with Sofia at the end of her time in the Mayr. She chewed nervously at her thumbnail, something she had not done for some time. She would let Charcot decide.

From that moment on, Sofia was the perfect friend. She listened to Rebecca's plans, talked of trifles, went walking and swimming in companionable silence with her. There was no more discussion of the Angel either. Only on one more occasion did Sofia try to kiss her, but Rebecca pulled away, making it abundantly clear there would be no repetition of the events of that night. Afterwards Rebecca had been afraid that Sofia would cry or make a scene, but she did not. She had drawn back like the tide and gave Rebecca enough space to breathe again. Perhaps, thought Rebecca, there would be room for Sofia in her future. Perhaps they could write to one another. Perhaps she could find a way to be generous to her friend once she herself was safe. All of these notions floated through Rebecca's mind but she chose not to vocalise them. She was learning once again to separate herself from her surroundings, but now she felt she was in control of this experience. It was becoming a choice as it had been before. Before she had become ill.

It was true. After her experiences with Charcot she now had a new vocabulary. One which allowed her to express her relationship with the Angel in terms of science. She could now contextualise the visions and her illness without the cloud of emotion. The hypnotism had removed it from her mind. Time spent with an Alienist talking through the whys and wherefores of how her illness came to manifest itself in this way would help her, she believed. As it turned out, so did Dr Charcot, whose letter – affirming her idea as a good one – arrived, care of the Mayr Clinic, just a week after she had sent hers to him in Paris. At the same time, he wrote one letter to Professor Farkas himself, proposing Rebecca become a patient and another to Rebecca's father clearing the path for his approval. She showed Sofia Charcot's letter from Paris and allowed herself to be enfolded in an enthusiastic embrace. 'We will have more time together.' Sofia cried. 'I am so happy. It will be for the best. You will see.' Rebecca's disquiet faded in the light of her friend's undiluted pleasure at the news.

Sofia returned to Hungary first. Excited to be able to make preparations, she demanded a token of friendship to take with her while they were separated. She asked for the locket containing the hair of Rebecca's mother. Rebecca was not happy and her first inclination was to refuse, but Sofia wheedled and wore her down, promising faithfully that she would return the token when they were reunited in Budapest. Rebecca eventually complied, but not without trepidation. She watched Sofia put the necklace around her own throat and tuck it away beneath her dress. She touched it happily. 'It will rest close to my heart until I can hold you again!' She seemed so happy that Rebecca responded to her smile. 'Yes. Until then.' Sofia was so often like a child, and Rebecca found her emotions being drawn into this simple and innocent exchange. It brought so much joy to Sofia. What harm could it possibly do?

It was all arranged. Rebecca was to be a guest in the professor's home. Of course, this would mean payment, and her father released the funds grudgingly. A brief, unemotional note from him stated his acceptance of the arrangement and that he would expect Rebecca to stay for a period of two weeks only, after which she should make her way back to Paris for Dr Charcot's final assessment before returning directly home to Ramsgate. It was obvious from the way he addressed her that Jeremiah Zimmerman had not discovered anything about Miriam's bequest. Rebecca had absolutely no inclination to tell him. At least until she had been declared sane and claimed her inheritance. Then and only then would she tell him that she had no intention of returning to Ramsgate and that she would instead be staying in Paris to train as a doctor. Then and only then would she seek out her brother Zachary and give him the (now large) pile of letters which she had written to him since she had escaped from the asylum. Unable to send them for fear of betraying her location to anyone, she had kept them all, leaving the bulk with Samuel for safe keeping. One day he would have them and know that she hadn't deserted him and that she loved him still. Even if he didn't want to know her now, she wanted him to understand what had happened. She smiled to herself. Perhaps he dreams of becoming a rabbi? Perhaps he wants to escape too? She paused. Is that what the Angel was to her, an escape? Was it a way of claiming some unique supernatural power because she had no natural power on this earth of her own? Too many questions bounced around her head. She would store them away. She would wait until her sessions with the Alienist. There, at least, would be a space where she could safely ask them, and finally be able to take control of her life.

Without the distraction provided by Sofia, her last week at the Mayr proved to be peaceful. She slept deeply and well, and no longer experienced hunger after she had chewed endlessly on her spelt biscuit. She felt lighter in her mind and fitter in her body. It was time for her psyche to heal. Yes, she thought to herself. Sometimes things do happen for a reason. Meeting Sofia was a good thing, she told herself. But somewhere, deep in a dark corner of her consciousness, the doubts still lingered.

CHAPTER 45

THE JOURNEY TO Budapest proved to be exciting but uneventful. Rebecca left the Mayr early in the morning, and was pleasantly surprised to find several of the clinic staff waiting outside in the courtyard to say goodbye. She exchanged handshakes and bows with some, and surprised herself by hugging the nurse to whom she had presented her marble some weeks earlier. As her starched surgical apron crackled on their embrace, the nurse leaned into Rebecca and whispered in her ear. 'I am no fool, you know.' She pulled back and smiled at Rebecca who found herself blushing deeply. Before she could respond, the good doctor himself was standing before her. He took her hand and kissed it, bowing deeply as he did so. 'Remember, child. Health is wealth. Health is wealth. Make sure you protect it from now on.' Rebecca smiled and promised that she would continue with the principles she had learnt from him. He smiled gently. 'See that you do and all will be well!'

Once safely inside the carriage she waved back at the ghostly group disappearing into the early morning mist. All things considered, the experience hadn't been too bad, she thought to herself. I expect I could keep it up. All the while another part of her brain was busy planning her next meal. Real food. Real food with meat in it. Real food with meat in it and a glass of good wine... She began to salivate and realised she was grinning. In this moment, in this carriage, on her way to a new place and experience she realised something that she hadn't felt for a long while – if ever. She was content. She was neither looking forward nor back, but she was engaged with the moment. Was this happiness? Perhaps, perhaps not, but it certainly was contentment and she was happy to settle for that right now. She made herself comfortable in the carriage and allowed the gentle swaying to lull her into an early morning doze.

She woke when the carriage arrived in Velden am Wörther See and deposited her at the train station. The Mayr network extended out here and she was greeted, then accompanied onto her train, by an unknown staff member with the pallor and set jaw she had learned to recognise as an adherent of the faith of 'many chews'. By now her stomach was growling loudly, demanding to ingest the originators of the beautiful smells which were now assailing her nostrils. Fresh bread, coffee, jams and fruits were all presented beautifully in the railway café, but she was forced to sit passively outside this palace of delights and just stare longingly. Her companion admonished her in heavily accented English, reminding her of her new commitments to frugality and self-denial. Rebecca remained silent. She was afraid that if she opened her mouth drool would flow out of it, she was so very hungry. Her companion reminded her with a thin smile that there would be no food available in the train either. Sadistic, really.

The train journey was itself peaceful, and she distracted herself with the views from the window. Small, neat alpine houses and a lush landscape with grazing goats gave way to more rustic cabin-like structures and rough-looking cattle. Sporadically she dozed, and each time she awakened, the countryside had grown wilder and more alien to her eyes. Finally, after many hours travelling, she stepped down from the train, stiff and now too tired for hunger. The sun was starting to set over the river before her. Slowly, she walked to the quayside where she was to take the overnight ferry down to Budapest. The tributary was dark and wide, and the sounds of lapping water and activity, accompanied by the smells of the waterside, reminded her momentarily of Ramsgate Harbour. Cautiously, she stepped out onto the walkway which led her onto the large, low vessel which would carry her to Hungary. Almost aboard, she reached out towards the handrail and as she did a rough male hand met hers, ready to steady her final step onto the deck. She felt an unexpected shiver of pleasure as this large hand encircled her tiny one. The sailor then touched his cap and smiled at her cheekily as she blushed in the semi-darkness before being guided by the purser to her cabin. No words had been exchanged at all but a frisson of excitement lingered on her palm. She took stock of her small cabin and caught sight of herself in the mirror. She looked well. Young and healthy – and, yes, perhaps even attractive. Her blush returned and she combed her hair self-consciously before twisting it into a loose loop as Sofia had taught her. Before taking to her bunk, she ventured out onto the deck. She breathed in deeply, taking in the freshness of the air. Figures were moving on the level above her speaking in low, foreign tones. She registered the confidence emanating from those men. Men comfortable in their element. She leaned her elbows onto the rail and rubbed her eyes with her palms. It had been a long day – and tomorrow she would wake in Budapest. Another stage in her journey to reclaiming her sanity. Another step towards freedom. She yawned. Her bunk beckoned. The moment her head reached the hard pillow she was asleep and dreaming of the future.

She woke the next morning to a pale yellow light streaming through her porthole. Feeling refreshed from her sleep, she was ready for the day to start. As she rose and looked out onto the river she could see a town in the distance shimmering on the edge of the water. Keen to see as much as possible, she dressed and packed her travelling bag, hauling it onto her bed so as to waste no time when the ferry docked. The moment Rebecca opened her cabin door she could smell the tantalising aroma of cooking. Following the sound of voices and the smell of food –which was by now irresistible – she headed onto the top deck, where she found a small gathering of sailors squatting around a makeshift wood-stove. They looked up at her, and one stood and came towards her. It was the man who had helped her onto the boat the previous night. He smiled broadly, and began to speak to her, but she did not understand a single word. He mimed the action of eating, and rubbed his stomach, pointing at her as he did. Unable to respond with words, she nodded, and once again he took her hand and led her towards the group of men. Reaching over to the fire, he picked out a wooden stick on which an unidentifiable meat and strange, red vegetables had been skewered. He handed it to her, and returned to the group of men, who began to laugh. Rebecca felt no fear, only hunger, and she walked away from the group towards the edge of the deck where she then lowered herself down onto the wooden boards and allowed her legs to dangle over the water. The meat juices were escaping, and she cupped her hand to prevent them from dripping onto her dress. She sighed contentedly, and began to eat – slowly – savouring each pungent mouthful. The sun was rising and the gentle breeze carried from the shore the strains of strangely harsh violin music. She finished her food, and the temptation to suck the stick was strong, but she resisted. As far as she was concerned it was the best meal she had ever eaten. You could keep the fancy restaurants of London, with their polite formality, glittering chandeliers and exquisite bone china. Here, on this ferry, all alone and eating who knows what, Rebecca was beginning to learn what it meant to be happy. She threw the skewer into the river, and a contented burp escaped her. The men around the cooking fire cheered appreciatively, and Rebecca smiled at them gratefully. Home is where the hearth is, she mused, not the heart. She made a silent vow to herself that some time in her future she would devote herself to learning how to cook, a skill which had eluded her until now. From homemade fare, her thoughts moved naturally to Miriam and her vegetarian stew. Preparing food is definitely a way of showing love, I am sure of it, she thought to herself. It is generous and wants nothing in return, other than for it not to be wasted on someone who doesn't want it. Without intending to, her thoughts then segued into images of Sofia. Sofia wanted love like a starving man craves food. Sofia, however, seemed never to be satisfied. She needed a constant and conspicuous supply. Rebecca pushed their solitary intimate encounter onto a rickety shelf at the back of her mind labelled 'experiment', and tried to leave it there. It wasn't easy. She shifted uncomfortably. Rebecca had never met anyone like Sofia before. At first she had found it flattering to be the focus of such intense attention from another individual, but very soon she had found it cloying. Rebecca instinctively realised that love had to be mutually desired for it to work, otherwise it would end up making one or both parties miserable. The loud clang of the ship's bell brought her out of her reverie and the sound of raised voices heralded that the ferry would be soon arriving at its next destination of Budapest. She turned to thank the sailor for his kindness, but they had all dispersed to their work, leaving no trace of their existence.

Rebecca returned to her cabin and collected her bag. She then positioned herself at the prow of the ship where she could lean into the wind and best enjoy the view of the magnificent and ancient cities of Buda and Pest as they came into sight on either side of the Danube. The ferry first approached a large island, and she could see what looked like an ancient fortress clinging to the hillside. As they passed the island only then did she appreciate the full width of the river. It must have been half a mile across. The boat soon passed beneath a majestic and modern bridge and she could see others spanning the river beyond it, at least one still incomplete. It was a beautiful and unexpectedly large city, and had both the feel of age and modernity as she glimpsed building work going on around the quayside. In fact, the more she focused on the details around her, the more like a gigantic building site it became. She noticed what looked like elegant apartment buildings being constructed close to the waterside, and felt – before she could hear – the noise of this alien city as it rose to greet her.

As the ferry eased itself onto the quay, Rebecca picked out the small figure of Sofia on the crowded shore waving her handkerchief and smiling broadly at her. Rebecca was touched by her friend's enthusiastic embrace, and by the tears in her eyes. 'I didn't believe you would come!' Sofia cried. 'Now you are here everything is going to be wonderful. I just know it!' Sofia tucked Rebecca's arm in hers, and manoeuvred her through the crowded quayside. They made slow progress as it was full of people and produce, some arriving, others leaving. Rebecca turned back to the boat and caught a glimpse of the sailors working in rhythm to lift cargo on and off the ferry. Sofia followed her gaze. 'Come on, my darling, let me take you away from these dreadful people.' Rebecca shivered. Why do people who claim to love you assume they know what you are thinking?

CHAPTER 46

THE WOMEN RODE through the streets of Budapest in a carriage-for-hire similar in shape to the hansom cabs of London, but more ornate. Rebecca sat on the edge of her seat, eagerly scanning the streets and buildings around them. It was a hectic city, but less crowded than London. It was also hot. Surprisingly so. For some reason, Rebecca had not been expecting this. She had not associated cities with heat. Sofia laughed as she helped Rebecca pull off her jacket. 'We are on the edge of two worlds, here in Budapest. The Orient and the Occident. Christianity meets Islam in architecture, art, music, cuisine and inevitably in business. It makes for a fascinating mix. When I first came here it was a shock. It confused me and I craved the order of my homeland. My childhood was spent in the convent in Vienna – as you know – and coming to this city had its own challenges for me. Everything seemed different – the language, the culture, the expectations. However, I got used to it quickly. My father made sure of that, and now it is my home and I love it.'

With her head gently tilted, Rebecca listened intently as Sofia spoke of the man she called Papa. It was almost as if this woman had forgotten that she had shared the story of her mother's rape and her abandonment by him. To anyone listening to Sofia you would think that she was the model of a dutiful daughter to a perfect and diligent parent. Rebecca's anxieties bubbled to the surface once more. She sincerely hoped that she was doing the right thing by being here. The carriage slowed, and Sofia smiled. 'We are nearly home. You will like it here, I know. The professor has helped many, many people who were sick in their minds, and I know Papa will be able to help you as he helped them, my darling.' Rebecca made a conscious effort to deposit her anxieties on the pavement, as the door to 21 Baross Utca was opened from within and a pretty maid bobbed a curtsey to them both. Sofia ran inside and over to the sweeping staircase which drew the eyes upwards towards a lightwell. 'She is here, she is finally here. I told you she would come!' There was no response to her call. Rebecca stood on the threshold nervously and waited with her heavy travelling bag beside her. The maid within remained statue-like, holding the imposing door open but made no move to help her with her luggage. Picking up her bag with both hands, Rebecca carried it over the doorstep and stood there clutching it to her body. Laden, she waited for someone to relieve her of her burden.

A week had quickly passed since the ferry had brought her to Budapest. Her host, Professor Farkas, was not at home, being deeply involved in a medical conference which was taking place in Vienna. This left the two young women to enjoy some time of freedom which they used up in sightseeing around the city. A day was spent on Margaret Island where they swam and walked together. Visits were made to various museums and a glorious afternoon was squandered relaxing in the volcanic spa of the elegant Gellert Hotel. Most wonderful of all, Rebecca sampled the delights of Hungarian cuisine. After the spartan fare at the Mayr Clinic, she gorged herself. The food was rich, spicy and resplendently full of meat and she discovered flavours she never knew existed. She consumed Hortabágyi palacsinta – a meat-filled pancake, paprikás csirke – chicken and dumplings in a paprika sauce, and töltött káposzta – cabbage stuffed with minced meat – all dishes as unusual to pronounce as they were to her taste buds. She insisted on Sofia asking the restaurants for their recipes, and marvelled at the fluency with which her friend spoke Hungarian. Spending these few days with her in her home city Rebecca began to wonder if she was being too judgemental, too harsh about Sofia. Her friend was being the perfect hostess and Rebecca was grateful for the lengths to which Sofia went in demonstrating her friendship. One note jarred, however. Sofia was still wearing her mother's mourning locket, and when Rebecca asked her to return it Sofia's hand flew to her throat and enfolded the necklace. She begged to be able to wear it until Rebecca left them, and her pleading was so pitiful that Rebecca relented. She really wanted the locket back, but decided that it would not be too great a hardship to wait until she left Budapest. After all, Sofia was her friend and she did not want to hurt her feelings.

There had been no repeat of Sofia's advances to Rebecca, for which she was grateful. In fact, as time went on she found it harder to reconcile the events of that night with this friendship. Shelving the memory securely away she put it down to experimentation by them both, and nothing more. With this memory safely moved from the rickety shelf and into a high cupboard at the back of her mind she now allowed herself to fully participate in this newly developing relationship. In her own home, Sofia seemed to be less needy and more secure. Rebecca felt altogether more comfortable with this version of her, and they settled down into a routine of sharing in a way she imagined that sisters would. They shared their clothes, books, knowledge and dreams. Rebecca let slip her desire to become a doctor but still did not lower her guard enough to share knowledge about Miriam's legacy. Sofia talked of her dreams to marry and have many children. Rebecca was curious enough to ask why this was, and Sofia spoke of her desire to give a child what she herself had not experienced, a home life with two parents. Rebecca listened but did not interrupt, and couldn't help feeling that this mawkish speech had been culled from the pages of a railway novel. Sofia's dreams seemed so conventional, so bourgeois that they did not even qualify to Rebecca as proper dreams. In Rebecca's view, all Sofia had to do was allow the tide to flow and time to move for Sofia to become the conventional wife and mother she dreamed of becoming. Sofia noticed her friend's silence, and spoke as if reading her thoughts. 'Who will have me, Rebecca? I have no money, no family and I am a bastard. Any man who loved me for myself would have to be a curious individual, one with no regard for society or its conventions.' Shocked by her own thoughtlessness, Rebecca tried to make light of it all by remarking that any man who would want to marry her would have to be very unusual too. Sofia joined in her game. 'Perhaps you *can* marry Papa and become my mother and then I will have a proper family at last!' Rebecca joined in the laughter to cover her discomfort, but couldn't help allowing the worm of doubt to eat its way back into her thoughts. Sofia was like a child in so many ways. There were times when she opened her mouth and words fell out regardless of any consideration, and yet she could be both kind and attentive. Rebecca recognised this through the clarity of her own improving state of mind. There was a time when she would have been unable to process Sofia's oddness, such was the strength of the strangeness within her own mind. She felt calmer now, more self-contained. There had been no appearances of the Angel for some time, and the longer this period lasted, the more secure she felt. It was time, she was sure. Time to understand her illness and to move forward into a new life. A new life in Paris. At this thought she smiled and Sofia returned the smile. In that moment, Rebecca had a revelation that Sofia's issues were her own responsibility and she could not – and would not – allow herself to be drawn into her friend's strange reality. She was here to deal with her own. It was time, as Shakespeare had said, to understand that 'self-love was no vile a sin as self-neglecting'. It was time to allow herself to look back so she could move forward. With these musings, the sombre chimes of the gong in the hallway invited both women downstairs to dine.

By the date that Professor Zoltan Farkas was due to arrive back in Budapest, Rebecca was more than ready to leave it. Sofia's newly revealed normality slowly drifted into oddness and Sofia had become progressively more cloying. Soon she started following Rebecca around the house and demanding to know what she was thinking. Sofia was also becoming sulky and argumentative, so much so that Rebecca began to lock herself in her room to get some peace. Her agitation suppressed her ability to float out of her body and escape into the space around her. She was locked in the cage of her own body with her thoughts, forcing her to consider her situation and how she had got into it. She decided to write down her worries as a way of putting them in order and to prepare for her session with the Alienist. Among the many conversations with Sofia, Rebecca had been able to question her on how the professor worked. It seemed that his process concentrated on the past and how one's understanding of it could influence the present. He worked by studying his patients' dreams, and encouraged them to talk about anything that they felt was relevant, without censorship or guidance. He then somehow drew together this information to help them to an understanding of themselves. With this mechanism they could create a pathway to free themselves of their fears and anxieties. Rebecca wrote as much as she could about her memories of childhood. She wrote about her mother and father and the deaths of her siblings. She wrote of her love and fears for Zachary, her brother. Writing of the past held few fears for her. However, she made a conscious choice to censor her dreams for the future and her plans for how she would make this future real. Even as she wrote down these thoughts, she realised that she wasn't being truly honest. She was writing a novel for an audience – a version of the 'truth' with which the professor could work, so he could ratify Charcot's conclusions and she would be certified as sane. Nothing more or less than a plea for sanity. No mention of the Angel. Rebecca instinctively knew that this would muddy the waters. Furthermore, her scientific mind recoiled at the apparent spuriousness of analysing dreams and thoughts. It could be nothing more than opinion, surely? Considering this, she decided to take time and care with her writing to mould the opinion of the professor. She would present as a willing but pliable patient, open to his suggestions, and ready to be healed by his powerful words. She put down her pen and paper as Sofia escalated her frantic banging on the bedroom door. Rebecca relented, and unlocked it only to find Sofia slumped against the door, sobbing desperately. She knelt down and put her arms around her friend to comfort her, but Sofia pulled away from her embrace. 'Never lock your door again, Rebecca. Please. Never lock me out again. I can't bear it. Just let me sit at your bedside. I will be quiet. I promise. I just want to be with you. To look at you. Please. Please.' Rebecca did not speak. This time Sofia allowed herself to be embraced. She rocked silently back and forth, her features stiff and eyes glazed. Rebecca tried not to shudder, instead pulling her friend closer to her. 'Of course, Sofia. I promise.'

CHAPTER 47

PROFESSOR FARKAS WAS small and round. He was not at all the imposing and dominating figure that Rebecca had imagined from her conversations with Sofia. His hair was wild and liberally sprinkled with white, and it framed a face which had unusually milky eyes. His fleshy lips were topped with a luxuriant moustache which he pulled at with his bottom teeth when he was engrossed. There was a prominent scar across his nose. 'An unfortunate encounter with a rich woman's lap-dog,' he explained when he noticed Rebecca staring at it the first time they met. Rebecca was embarrassed, but he quickly dispelled her discomfort. 'To be observant is an excellent quality, my dear. I, myself, take pride in noticing details. It is a significant aspect of what I do and how I work.' He expanded on his subject. 'Most people do not pay attention to those around them at all. They are far too busy worrying about what others might think of them.' He laughed. 'The truth is that the majority of humankind do not use their senses effectively at all. They see only what they want to see, hear only what it suits them to hear, and feel what they choose to feel. Modern society has become locked in a mass hallucination which allows it to exist. Without this we would all be walking around naked, gratifying our desires at will.' Rebecca was speechless at these pronouncements, and, suspending judgement for now, she found herself open to listening to this diminutive figure speaking German with a peculiar accent and strange idioms.

With Professor Farkas installed in the house, it sprang to life. Not only did he arrive but with him came his (as yet unseen) assistant, Stefan. He also brought an energy with which the household seemed to connect. Servants cleaned with more rigour, the maid who answered the door was more polite and helpful, the food served at mealtimes was prepared with more care. Sofia was the only exception to this galvanising effect. She seemed to have aged and could be seen dragging herself around the house unwillingly. She even stopped her obsessive shadowing of Rebecca and two days after the arrival of the Alienist she virtually disappeared from sight, claiming illness.

When Rebecca went to her room to see how she was, Sofia was to be found in bed with the coverlet over her. There was not a crease or fold in it, and her arms were rigid above the covers, like a doll. The curtains had been closed and the room smelled musty. When Rebecca tried to talk to her, Sofia turned her face away and refused to respond. Concerned at her friend's behaviour, she sought out Professor Farkas for help. She had yet to have a proper conversation with him since he had come home, preferring to keep out of the way until the upheaval of his arrival settled down. When she told him about Sofia, his response to the news confused her. 'We will start our sessions this afternoon. Come to my room at 3 pm.'

She did as she was instructed, surprising herself at her own willingness to comply and her decision not to question him about Sofia, but, as she reminded herself, she had one aim here. She needed to stay focused on her objective. Once Professor Farkas had ratified Charcot's opinion of her sanity, Rebecca promised herself that she would allow no man, for that matter, no-*one* to ever be able to control her again.

The Alienist's consulting room was on the second floor of the house and occupied the entire front of the building. It was a well-proportioned room with two bay windows overlooking the street and a pair of elegant chandeliers framed by each window. Professor Farkas opened the door and stood silently by as she walked into the room. She walked around the space inspecting the bookshelves, the mahogany single-legged table with its mass of papers and finally running her hand across the rough texture of the loosely draped Turkish rug which covered a large chaise longue close to the bookcase.

He did not invite her to sit down, so she stood silently waiting for him to speak. He walked over to the furthest window and looked out of it. With his back to her he spoke quietly. 'What do you see in this room? Tell me what you observe.' Unmoving, Rebecca described what she had seen. He continued to study the streetscape. 'That is what you saw. Yes. But what did you observe?' Rebecca walked over to the chaise longue and seated herself stiffly on the edge of the seat. 'I see a room which has been staged. I see an occupant who wants to be thought of as a busy intellectual, hence the mess of papers and the laden bookshelves. I see furniture positioned to create an unequal relationship between the patient and the Alienist. I see what you want me to see.' Rebecca watched as Professor Farkas moved his hands behind his back and held them there, left wrist in right hand. He remained silent. 'I see a right-handed man who enjoys playing games, but I do not yet see to what end.' At this he turned to face her, eyes narrowed, but the faintest of smiles appeared around the corner of his lips, and his head bent in an almost imperceptible bow. Rebecca knew she was being mocked, but she chose not to react. Silence is my ally in this room, she mused. I will act and react. I will be what he wants me to be, and in doing this I will be free.

Professor Farkas moved towards her and seated himself in an imposing leather chair. It was positioned squarely in front of a window, discouraging the occupant of the chaise longue from looking at the Alienist. In fact, as Rebecca became more familiar with the contents of the consulting room she realised that her first observation was an astute one. Wherever the professor positioned himself, it was to maintain ascendancy over anyone else present. If she tried to look at him, she either had to squint into the sunlight or contort herself in such a way as to be uncomfortable. Wherever he stood or sat she was unable to see his features properly. It is hard to read what you cannot see, and as a result of this arrangement the sessions which took place in there gradually became more confessional. It started to feel as if she was the only person in the room, and any interjections from the Alienist were questions from her own self.

Thereafter, each morning at eleven she presented herself at the door of the consulting room. The routine was always the same. He opened the door in silence, she walked around the room then seated herself on the chaise longue. He began by standing at the window before positioning himself neatly on the leather armchair. On the second week of this he began asking about her past. Rebecca paused momentarily before offering him her carefully constructed writing to read. He waved it away dismissively. 'I already know its contents. It is a nothing. I am still waiting for you to tell me the truth.' Rebecca drew back as if she had been slapped. 'How could you know?' She had been so careful in the sessions before not to ask questions. He leaned forward in his chair so she could see his face. Silently he scrutinised her features and then slumped back into the chair, allowing the sunlight from the window to turn his face into a shadow once more. He removed an invisible speck from the crease of his trousers and sighed slowly. He did not reply to her question, but instead he said, 'Allow your attention to be drawn by one object in this room. I want you to describe it in detail. Tell me all about it.'

Rebecca drew herself up and stretched her neck. She was stiff from holding herself so still. She lay back on the chaise longue and looked up at the ceiling. Above her she could see one of the chandeliers. She scrutinised it. It had six arms and was made of some type of reddish-gold metal. Each arm ended with a candle. She looked at it more closely. Each of the candles was held in place by a winged figure. Angels. Adult figures, beautifully cast, and each different. At the centre of the chandelier was another, larger angel which appeared to be holding the whole piece in place. She felt her heart pounding her ribs hard and fast. She closed her eyes, breathed deeply and then slowly, quietly she told him everything about the Angel. About Azriel. Uncensored and unemotionally she talked of her connection to the Angel of Death.

The session had ended oddly. Professor Farkas gently shook her shoulder and she looked around, momentarily confused. It seemed that she had slept. Darkness was arriving in the sky outside, and a gas lamp had been lit and placed on the table beside the Alienist. Professor Farkas smiled at her, mildly. He leaned towards her, speaking conspiratorially. 'Congratulations, my dear. Tonight, I think we will dine out. I expect that you would enjoy that, yes? Of course, for propriety I am sure that Sofia and my ever-hungry assistant Stefan will be delighted to join us.'

Later that evening Rebecca found herself being helped out of a carriage by a newly gallant Professor Farkas who had invited her, just for this evening, to call him Zoltan. He led her by the hand, up the steps of a white-stoned and beautifully lit building on the edge of a park. Like much of Budapest this area seemed to be full of half-completed buildings, but at night all Rebecca could see were the lights surrounding the doorway and the elegantly dressed individuals who were leisurely making their way into the restaurant. It seemed that Professor Farkas was well known by both the customers and the proprietor, as the party was ceremoniously shown to one of the tables which stood on a raised platform at the back of the restaurant. The professor seated Sofia then Rebecca allowed the Alienist to seat her. As he eased her chair under the table he leaned in and whispered to her. 'Here we can watch the world.' He smiled, and she smiled back despite her discomfort at the oddness of this situation. What he said was true. There were only five tables in this semicircle and anyone seated here could watch the occupants of the tables below. The arrangement bestowed an immediate feeling of superiority on those who dined here. Rebecca looked around the elevated section to the other tables. All of them were occupied, and each by two people. They were replicas of one another. A dark, often portly, older man seated with a young, pallid woman. She caught the eye of one of the women who smiled back at her with her mouth only, before leaning into her companion to rest her hand possessively on his. He in turn took no notice as he was leaning away from her and chatting to one of the men seated at a different table.

Rebecca moved her attention back to her host and watched as he smiled expansively to greet an imposing figure bounding up the stairs holding out both his hands. Zoltan rose in greeting and the men embraced and kissed one another on the cheeks before noisily calling each other's name by way of greeting. Zoltan turned to Rebecca. 'Where are my manners, my dear? This is Gregor, the owner of this temple to gastronomy!' Gregor bowed deeply and raised Rebecca's hand to kiss it. In broken English, he spoke to her 'Wampetich Restaurant welcomes you! It will be our task to fill all of your senses with much delight!' Zoltan slapped him on the back as he bowed, and Rebecca saw a momentary look of hate cloud Gregor's face. He soon disguised it and by the time he stood upright the host's smile was fixed in place and he clapped his hands loudly. On this cue, three violinists burst into the restaurant below from the doorway of the kitchen and began to play wild and exuberant gypsy music.

Rebecca's senses were overwhelmed. The music, the food, the spectacle of the other customers and the dance of waiters as they made their way among the tables was stunning. It reminded her of the theatre. No. It *was* a theatre. Each person here knew their role and the part they were expected to play. It was a strange revelation. She realised that the only reason she could see through this was because she did not have a role, or at least a designated script to which she could adhere. Once again she felt like a ghost, but this time it was liberating. She settled into the part of observer and took in the spectacle around her.

When the first four courses (and the accompanying wines) had been delivered, consumed and appreciated, the tableware disappeared as did the musicians. The whole room became more peaceful and contemplative as the wine and the food began to take their soporific effect. Gentle murmuring and a background hum of conversation replaced the sound of clinking glasses and raucous violins. Sofia chose this moment to rise from the table and loudly declare, 'I cannot stand this any longer. Am leaving *now.*' The room went silent. Rebecca was stunned. This outburst had seemed to come from nowhere. Sofia flounced down the stairs. Zoltan sighed as he delicately wiped the corners of his moustache with a napkin. 'I am sorry, my dear. I must attend to the fractious one.' A ripple of coarse laughter followed him as he made his way down the stairs and around the tables, ending in a buzz of conversation as the hive-mind in the dining room passed its knowledge across from one table to the other.

CHAPTER 48

REBECCA SHIFTED UNCOMFORTABLY in her chair, unsure of what to do. As awkward as she found this situation, it was nothing in comparison to her companion. She had been left at the table with Stefan, a man to whom she had not, until this moment, spoken. Tall, pale and with dark long hair, Zoltan's assistant had returned to the household with his master but had been kept in a constant state of movement as he ferried heavy books and papers up to the consulting room. In fact, Rebecca had barely had an opportunity to study him properly even though they had sat opposite each other for the whole evening. He seemed taciturn and on edge as if unused to sitting still. She had hardly heard him speak, and when he did respond to a question from Zoltan it was in Hungarian so Rebecca had concluded that they would not be able to communicate anyway. She decided that he would not have much to say to her even if he could bring himself to speak (which he probably couldn't). Now she watched as his face coloured and he seemed to be struggling with all kinds of conflicting emotions. At one point, he moved to the edge of his seat as if ready to spring up and follow the others out of the restaurant.

Rebecca was mellowed by the wine and decided it was not for her to initiate anything. Amused rather than annoyed, she waited to see how her companion would manage the pantomime of getting her to accompany him. His next action surprised her; in fact the rest of the evening turned out to be a revelation, and a very pleasant one at that. Stefan was not Hungarian, he was French. Instead of hurrying them out to follow their hosts, he asked her if she would mind if he came to sit next to her. He explained that he had a slight hearing difficulty in one ear (the result of a shooting accident) and struggled with conversations when there was a lot of noise. The rest of the evening was spent in rapid and easy discussion between the two of them as they talked of Paris, of study and of books. The owner Gregor arrived soon after and assured them that the bill was covered as his personal gift to the good Professor Farkas, and, of course, the pair were free to stay and enjoy the evening as long as they wished. Puddings were brought, more wine consumed, and Rebecca and Stefan began to talk freely like old friends. She told him of Samuel, and how much she missed him, and laughed as he feigned an arrow being plunged into his heart. Rebecca was not about to explain the reality of that particular relationship, but his pantomime of being the rejected lover flattered (and amused) her. She told Stefan of her time with Charcot and – thanks to the lubricating effect of the wine – revealed her own dreams to study medicine. He spoke of his studies under Professor Farkas. It soon became clear that Stefan was passionate about his subject, and happy to debate the intricacies of its construction. 'It will be five more years of study for me, and then I will be able to begin in practice. I want to help people. I want to help them to build a better society. A place where each man respects other men, and poverty and abuse is consigned to history. I want to live in a world where

I am free to have an opinion and express a view which is not of the norm.' As he spoke he crooked one arm over the back of his dining chair. In the other hand he held a lustrous glass of Tokay. 'Is it too much to ask, do you think, Rebecca? Too much to expect of people?' Rebecca leaned forward and picked up her own glass of the sweet honey-wine. She looked at the golden liquid. 'When will it be a world where a man respects a woman? Where the sex with which you were born is no longer a disability?' Stefan put down his glass and looked straight into her eyes. 'It takes an education to understand the truth of what you say, Rebecca. Education not just for the rich but for all.'

It was late, and there were no carriages waiting outside the restaurant to take them home. 'Don't worry. We can walk to the other side of the park. It is perfectly safe. From there we can take an omnibus.' They walked briskly, the cold now setting in. Stefan took off his jacket and placed it around her. Rebecca tried to shrug it off, but he rested his hand on her shoulders gently. 'Please. Professor Farkas would not forgive me if you caught a chill. Neither would I.' He followed this remark with a surprisingly impish grin. The expression took years from his face and she realised that without the rings of fatigue around his eyes and the stoop from constantly carrying heavy books, he could look quite attractive. In a certain light that is, and, she laughed to herself, a copious quantity of wine. Rebecca suddenly wondered whether she should be concerned. After all, this man was a virtual stranger to her and they were walking through the park in the dark. In the dimness around her she could see loving couples strolling slowly, arm in arm. Stefan made no attempt to take her arm, for which she was grateful. He seemed happy to walk beside her keeping up a running commentary about his opinions, books he had read and the wonderful libraries in the city. Rebecca studied him unobserved. Men have no shame about expressing their thoughts, she noticed. Truly, communication between the sexes would be much smoother if men just shut up once in a while. She smiled at her own judgemental attitude, and Stefan noticed and stopped walking. 'Forgive me. I don't get much chance, none at all really, to talk like this. So freely, I mean, and to someone who is intelligent.' Rebecca broadened her smile to a genuine one, but did not reply. Perhaps this one had more insight than most. Perhaps. She thought of the young man who had taken it upon himself to be her guide at the Swedenborg Centre what felt like a lifetime ago, and then the touch of the sailor's hand on the boat to Budapest. This was different. There was no spark of attraction here. Instead, there was an intellectual connection. She shelved that thought for further consideration some other time.

The rest of the journey back to the house in Baross Utca passed in silence. Tiredness (and the effects of alcohol) had taken their toll on Rebecca and the gentle sway of the horse-drawn omnibus had lulled her into sleep. She awoke with a start to find her mouth slack and her head resting on Stefan's shoulder. 'Nearly there,' he said casually, as if he hadn't noticed. She had snored, she was sure of it, but was grateful for her companion's discretion. She slipped off his jacket and insisted he put it back on despite his protestations. It would not do to arrive back at the house with her wearing it, and as they approached the building she became progressively more anxious as to what she would find there. Perhaps they should not have stayed in the restaurant? Perhaps Sofia was ill? Perhaps Professor Farkas would be angry? She set aside her fears as Stefan held her back from walking up the steps to the main entrance of the house. 'This way,' he said, pointing down the steps to the servant's entrance. Rebecca followed him, surprisingly grateful that she would not have to encounter anyone from the household that evening. Later in her room, she undressed and climbed into bed as quickly as she could. What a strange evening. Strange but pleasant for all the oddest of reasons ... before she could pursue that thought any further she was soundly asleep.

Breakfast the next morning was a peculiar meal. Not the food or the setting, but Sofia. She was as ebullient and playful as Rebecca had ever seen her. When Rebecca arrived in the breakfast room Zoltan was seated at the dining table with a napkin spread widely across his protruding stomach, and an even wider smile on his face. Sofia was at the buffet selecting the smallest and sweetest grapes, which she then carried over to Zoltan and proceeded to pop them into his mouth one by one. As Rebecca walked into the room she was momentarily transfixed by this sight. Zoltan looked up at her just as Sofia tried to push another into his mouth and caught her hand and kissed the inside of her wrist before pushing it away playfully. 'Enough, child. I am not your pet cuckoo!' Sofia laughed merrily at this, and danced over to Rebecca, holding the grapes close up to her face. 'These are not for you, no, no, no. Not for you, Rebecca, not for you!'

Zoltan motioned Rebecca to take a seat and then silently poured her a black Turkish coffee. It was small, thick and grainy and she had not liked the taste of it at all to begin with. Surprisingly, this morning she found it much more palatable. Perhaps it was after all that rich food last night. On that topic, no mention was made of the events of the previous evening, and Rebecca was happy to leave it that way. Sofia ostentatiously made her leave of the room and the rest of breakfast was spent in silence. It wasn't companionable, but Sofia's absence made her feel less uneasy. She would have been happy to make conversation but as soon as Sofia left, Zoltan picked up a newspaper and created a wall between them – suddenly reminding her of her father. It would seem the convivial atmosphere she had witnessed between father and daughter in this house did not include her.

She spent the rest of the morning in her room, reading alone, or at least trying to read. She felt very unsettled. There were currents and undercurrents in this household which had little or nothing to do with her and which she did not understand. This lack of comprehension bothered her. Sofia's volatility was unnerving, Zoltan seemed remote and Stefan had once more disappeared into the background of the household. She allowed her attention to move onto the assistant. Her feelings about this young man were ambivalent. He was both reserved and talkative, and this combination made it difficult to know how to connect with him. He was not a servant, but neither was he a member of the household. Just like Samuel back at home in Ramsgate, Stefan didn't really fit anywhere. She had wanted to talk more to him about his studies. Furthermore, she would have liked to alleviate the nagging feeling that she hadn't made the best of impressions with regard to her intellect last night, as she had drunk quite a bit of wine... The only way she could dispel this vague feeling of discomfort would be to see him again soon and judge, from his response to her, whether she had made an idiot of herself or not. Over and above these feelings, Rebecca just wanted to talk to someone. Anyone. Leaving her bedroom, she made her way down the stairs to the consulting room. The door was open but the only occupant was a maid reaching to sweep away the cobwebs from the top of the over-mantle mirror with a feather duster. The servant turned and glared at Rebecca, arms akimbo, and Rebecca quickly changed her mind about intruding into the room to find a book. She would have to seek some other way to take her mind away from the household and its oddities.

She found herself wandering around the house aimlessly before returning to her room, where she allowed her thoughts to gnaw away at her peace of mind. Eventually she lay on her bed and tried to float out of her body as she had done so many times before. The chimes of the house clock told her that more than an hour had passed while she tried, and still nothing happened. She turned onto her side and, seeing Samuel's book lying there, she reached out and touched its cover. Comforted by the memories it brought to her she sat up in bed and determined to put her thoughts in order. Writing tools and paper had been provided to her, and setting to her task with a determination not to waste this precious time she began to put down her thoughts and feelings. These would be for her eyes only, she decided, and poured out her uncensored emotions onto the blank pages. Feelings about Sofia, thoughts about Stefan and Samuel, ideas about the future. Perhaps not completely uncensored, as even now she kept the knowledge about her inheritance to herself, reasoning (not unreasonably) that it was not relevant to these musings. The more she wrote down, the more she could see her true self escaping the walls of her time in the asylum and finally stepping through the door, released into the sunlight of the future. Inky-fingered and exhausted from her efforts, she folded the pages and carefully hid them away between the leaves of Samuel's book and returned it to her nightstand. She stroked its cover lovingly. Right now, it felt like her only connection to reality and the one person she knew she could truly rely on to support her. Curling up in the bed she closed her eyes and slept without dreaming.

The gentlest of knocking on her door woke her, and the darkening room told her that she had been asleep for some hours. She watched groggily as the doorknob turned and Sofia's face peered into the room. 'Wake up, sleepyhead! Papa has something special to show you!' She grinned and bounded into the room before shaking Rebecca's shoulder urgently. 'It's so exciting! I can't tell you what it is, you must come and see for yourself!'

CHAPTER 49

Rising awkwardly from the bed, Rebecca tried to smooth down her wrinkled dress before catching sight of her haystack hair in the bedroom mirror. A vain attempt to create some semblance of order ensued, but Sofia was already pulling her away from the mirror and out of the room. Giving into her friend's excitement, she allowed herself to be led down the main staircase of the house, and from there along a narrow corridor to the back of the building. For a moment, she thought they were going down to the kitchens, but next to the door of the backstairs world of the servants she noticed another, less obvious doorway. This one was little more than a gap in the design of the wallpaper, but a door nonetheless. There was no handle, but Rebecca noticed a keyhole which was carefully cut into the centre of a rose design, making it hard to see. Sofia grinned. 'Isn't this wonderful! A secret door to a special place!' Rebecca's senses were now fully awake, and Sofia's boundless enthusiasm was starting to get on her nerves. 'What is this place?'

'Why, it is Papa's workshop, of course! I begged and begged for him to show you, and now he has. She clapped her hands coquettishly. 'Generous Papa! Kind Papa!'

Workshop? What sort of workshop? Rebecca mused, but before she could pursue this thought any further, Zoltan's footsteps could be heard coming down the main staircase. Rebecca noticed that for a portly man he was light on his feet. She found herself staring down at his footwear when he appeared at the foot of the stairs. His feet were small and shod in highly polished shoes like a toy soldier. The absurdity of her thoughts made her grin. She couldn't help herself. As a result, when Zoltan reached the women they were both wreathed in smiles. He responded expansively and leaned between them to reach for the key and opened the door. 'Ladies, your smiles of greeting delight me. I will reward you presently.'

Rebecca laughed inwardly. People are so vain, so self-centred, she thought, and men the most of all. They are perfectly happy to attribute any pleasure you display to them or their actions. She squirreled this nut of information away to feed on later and followed her host through the secret door and down a narrow flight of stairs. It was unlit, and she stepped carefully, unlike Sofia who ran down the stairs with ease born of familiarity. This was a place she obviously knew well.

The room they entered was large and low-ceilinged. The only lighting appeared to come from oil lamps around the walls and on various surfaces. Rebecca estimated the room was around half of the footprint of the house itself. Above her she could hear the muffled sound of servants moving around what she soon realised was the kitchen. She was in some sort of cellar which had been fitted out as a mechanical workshop. One of the walls was covered with racks containing all manner of tools and metal parts. There were cogs and pinwheels, ratchets and springs. In front of it was a workbench with a work-in-progress laid out. On the opposite wall was a similar arrangement, but instead of tools she could see rattan containers beneath the bench with fabrics in them. She also noticed what looked like feathers and fine leather sheets. A box describing its contents as a 'modern miracle by Kodak' sat unopened on the floor. Everything was tidy and ordered, in its place. Even the projects which were being worked on were neatly arranged. Rebecca was baffled. She had never seen anything like this before and, for now, she was speechless. Zoltan appeared before her and studied her features closely. 'No?' he stated, questioningly. 'You do not know what it is that I make here?' He smiled broadly. 'I will leave you in the dark no longer.' He walked to the far side of the room where he threw open a pair of unseen double-doors. He turned to face them, his arms stretched out theatrically. 'I bid you welcome to my palace of the impossible!'

In the pools of lamp-light, Rebecca saw what looked like twelve covered chests, six on either side of a wide walkway. She stepped into the room and stood before the first one on the right, and waited. It was obvious to Rebecca that Zoltan wanted to show her these objects one by one, but when he pulled away the first cover she took a step back, unsure of what she was looking at. It resembled a roughly carved wooden statue of a prone man, with a fierce animal sitting on his chest, teeth bared and bloody. Suddenly Rebecca's eyes were covered by Sofia's soft hands. 'You mustn't see just yet. Wait!' Unconsciously Rebecca's shoulders sagged in irritation at Sofia's immaturity, but she stood patiently nevertheless as her ears tuned into a familiar sound. Someone had begun to wind up a clock. A large clock...

Her eyes were freed from Sofia's hands, and she looked again at the wooden figure before her. Not a carving, but an automaton. She had seen one last Christmas, a winter scene in the atrium at Fortnum and Masons. She had been unable to get close to it because of the crowds, but she was fascinated. The movements of this automaton were much less benign. The wooden tiger bowed its head and opened its jaw around the neck of the recumbent figure. Rigid legs and arms clacked up and down as the animal repeated its attack. Zoltan stood by this mechanism. 'This is the first I saw – and bought. I brought it home and took it to pieces to understand how it worked. Then I began making my own.' He indicated the covered plinths. 'One by one, my creations. My creations and my relaxation.' With this he turned to Sofia. 'Now, my sweet one. I want you to go to the kitchens and have the cook make preparations for my favourite goulash this evening. Make sure that everything is precisely as I like it.' He raised her hand and kissed the tips of Sofia's fingers just as Rebecca had seen her father do with Anna Coren. It was a moment of intimacy that she wished she had not seen. Her observation was required, she realised, as Zoltan looked straight into Rebecca's eyes as he did this. Sofia too was looking at Rebecca. Once again she was being forced to be the observer to a scene she did not understand, and she fought to hide an involuntary shudder.

Sofia broke the spell and walked languidly to the stairs leading out of the workshop. 'You promise that you won't be too long, will you Papa? Promise?' A childish, wheedling pitch moved into her voice, and the shudder which had been suppressed burst its way through Rebecca's shoulders. Thankfully, there was no-one to see it. Both Sofia and Zoltan had their backs to her now, the latter as he started to uncover the next plinth then released the mechanism with which it burst into life.

Later that evening as Rebecca lay in her room awaiting the summons for dinner, she replayed the events of the afternoon in her mind. She had already believed that there were undercurrents running through this household, and now she knew it was true.

She was, if anything, more confused. Information, she recognised, did not necessarily lead to clarification, and the only way for her to shed light on these facts was to lay them out separately and see which fitted together. One thing was for certain, lies and deception were at the centre of her confusion.

When Sofia had left the workshop, Zoltan focused on his automata. Lifting cover after cover on progressively more sophisticated creations, his monologue focused on the mechanical nuances and intricacies of these objects. As he showed Rebecca increasingly more complex and ambitious mechanisms, he talked of understanding their complexities, of the act of deconstructing and comprehending the role of each of the parts, of the act of repair. He spoke of the difficulties involved in a decision to replace broken parts with new ones of his own construction, and finally the reconstruction of the whole. Rebecca realised, progressively, that she was not only being shown his diversion but Zoltan was using the automata as a vehicle to explain his work. He made the process seem so mechanistic, as if there was no difference between a human and these clockwork facsimiles of life.

Zoltan did not seem to acknowledge Rebecca's feelings as she watched and listened. She was starting to feel cold, and the shudder which had started as an emotional reaction was now settling into her body as she shivered from the cheerless basement workshop. Zoltan did not seem to register this, as he continued to show her the automata, covering each carefully as he finished its demonstration. Each automaton was not only more sophisticated in design, but they were becoming progressively more humanesque. There was a figure of a boy playing a keyboard, another with a female performer on a unicycle, yet another with two figures dancing, their wooden legs swinging uncontrolledly as the mechanism spun them around, this way and the other. Not all the figures were made of wood, some of them had facial features made from fine leather. These contained glass eyeballs with blinking eyes which clicked and clacked as they opened and closed. Rebecca was starting to feel nauseous. She wanted to go back upstairs, to the daylight and normality of street level. She couldn't help it, but she just wanted to leave this place. As if reading her mind, Zoltan turned to her. 'Come. Let us return to the workshop. We can sit by the fire and warm our bones together.' Closing the double-doors to the room of automata, Zoltan motioned for Rebecca to occupy the worn, leather chair close to the stove. Zoltan dragged a stool from the workbench and perched on it, looking down on Rebecca. He pressed his hands into his thighs and started to speak, quietly. 'Sofia's mother was a – how to put this delicately – troubled woman. She suffered from delusions and sought out dangerous experiences. She took risks, and the form which they took for her were sexual. Her family eventually threw her out of the house, hoping this shock would bring her to her senses, but it did not. When I began to treat her she was already a kept woman. Yes, Rebecca, just like those pretty creatures which you saw dining at the Wampetich last night. The excitement was not sufficient for her, and she grew bored and restless and began to play with drugs. Her lover was not a man to tolerate weaknesses and when he found out what she was doing she found herself once more without a roof. By then, the drugs had spoiled her looks and she was a hopeless addict. So she became a streetwalker to survive. Sofia was born at that time. Born in a convent near Vienna and left there by her mother. I only discovered this when Sofia's grandparents died. They knew about Sofia, but had kept this a secret out of shame. They made no provision for this bastard girl and did not want to know of her existence. It was I who took Sofia from the convent. I *chose* to make her my ward. I *chose* to educate her and clothe and feed her. I *chose* this.' He paused. 'Whatever you have been told, I want you to know this.' He leaned over her and looked her straight in the eye, 'Know that Sofia suffers from the same condition as her mother. The same. I try my best with her but this illness is, I fear, beyond even my capabilities.' He lowered himself from the high stool, replacing it neatly beneath the workbench. 'It is the cross I bear.' He moved the stool slightly to the left, aligning it with the others. 'With all of my many skills, I cannot help those who are closest to me. It is the curse of my profession.'

Helping Rebecca raise herself from the low chair, he ushered her out of the room. It was only then she remembered that he had shown her all except one of the automata. In a veiled attempt to normalise the conversation, she asked him about it. Zoltan smiled, and sucked at his moustache, reflectively. 'Ah, my latest creation. Maybe one day you will see her.'

The rest of the day passed by normally enough, or what passed as normal in this odd household. Rebecca took herself off to bed early, tired from the late night before and from trying to make sense of what she had learned. This was a household full of secrets, that much she did know. She climbed into bed gratefully and fell into a dreamless sleep.

Across the road the motionless, cloaked figure watched the house as Rebecca's light was extinguished. Watching, and waiting. Patiently waiting.

CHAPTER 50

I N THE WEEKS since Rebecca had left Paris for the Mayr Clinic, Samuel had moved through many different emotions, but in general the progression of his feelings was downhill. He had started with emptiness, stepped neatly into grief, swum through into sadness then sunk deep into loneliness. Finally, he had settled himself into a regular routine consisting of boredom and anxiety. The boredom came from wondering how to fill his days (and nights), and the anxiety was about what the future might hold for him. He felt lost, and all the more so as he feared losing Rebecca to the wealth she was about to inherit. At best, it would change little, at worst he would lose her altogether. His fears oscillated between the two polarities and he was unable to allow the mechanism to wind down.

While Rebecca had been in Paris he had a purpose in life. She had given him a focus and a reason for getting up each day. When, he wondered, had his sense of self become so diminished, so invisible that he needed another person around to create an existence? When Rebecca had left, there was still the shadow of structure as she had left him the remainder of Miriam's cash and instructed that he find them somewhere better to live. Somewhere with two bedrooms and a space in which they could live and cook together and yet with enough room for them to lead their lives separately. Samuel had found the ideal place surprisingly quickly. Strangely, it was Cornelius who had suggested it to him. Salpêtrière Hospital, where he worked, owned a number of buildings nearby into which, one day, it hoped to grow. The buildings were old, and in some cases decrepit, but the hospital management reasoned it would be better to rent them out than have them colonised by ex-soldiers, prostitutes and other random flotsam which had drifted to the capital looking to better their lives.

For the meantime, the powers that be rented them out to students and suchlike. They installed the luxuries of running water and even water-closets for the inhabitants, reasoning that with such hygienic additions the tenants would be kept relatively free from the sicknesses which periodically swept the city. Cornelius obtained an introductory letter to the buildings' manager from Dr Charcot, and then boldly introduced Samuel as Rebecca's cousin, 'Well, you are related, aren't you?' He smiled expansively, and offered to take him to the marketplaces where one could rent or buy cheap furniture for his new home. Samuel was uncomfortable under this onslaught of kindness, and found himself trying to refuse Cornelius's help. His motives for doing so were mixed, to say the least. First of all, he did not want to feel obligated to Cornelius. Second (and more significantly), he did genuinely enjoy this man's company and was afraid that if he spent any more time by his side, he would be likely to make a fool of himself at some point. This he was most afraid of. He wanted Cornelius to like him, it is true, but most of all he wanted to earn his respect, and, sadly, in his current situation he saw no way of doing this. Days spent in the hospital library reading the books which he found there did little to assuage his intellectual thirst either. The fact that his ticket had been given to him by Cornelius also made him feel further diminished in his friend's view. Samuel needed, at the very least, to find a way of supporting himself financially.

Each time he encountered Cornelius now he found him friendly, affable even, and his constant enquiries for news of Rebecca's stay in the Mayr gave them enough of a topic to maintain a conversation of sorts. However, the encounters had not progressed beyond these social niceties and petered out into awkward silences, or so it seemed to Samuel. He reasoned that if he had an employment of some kind, a purpose, then perhaps he could converse with Cornelius as, if not an equal, at least a fellow traveller on the road to knowledge. The trouble (and the truth) was that Samuel really did not know what he wanted to study. His skills in the Torah and rabbinical doctrine would not serve him here. His interests in science seemed nothing more than the unstructured dabblings of a dilettante compared to the application and discipline of someone like Cornelius. He felt too old and wise to become a student, and yet too young and ignorant to become a teacher. He needed focus, and without Rebecca he had no-one with whom he could talk freely about these ideas for his future. Perhaps he was being ridiculous not to take up Cornelius's offer of a visit to the furniture markets. They could share a meal together. Perhaps with the neutralising effects of food on the table, Samuel could speak more freely. Thinking about it, there was more than enough money for him to be able to offer to pay for a lunch a-deux by way of thanks and he reasoned that this was a legitimate use of Rebecca's funds as he would be saving them money. Ever the Jew, he thought ruefully. Not that he dressed like one any more, or even behaved like one, but he still carried the stigma of his heritage. Part of the reason for his depression this morning had been the sight of the small but lurid posters which had appeared overnight on the walls of the arrondissement. Rabid, racist and transparently anti-Semitic, the posters advertised a candidate in the local election. It was a rallying cry of hate, blaming Jews for every social, moral and political malaise of the Republic. 'Voters! The Jews stand tall because we are on our knees! It is time to rise up! Judaism is the true enemy!' it screamed.

Nothing has changed, nothing at all, Samuel mused despondently. The Jew will always be a scapegoat. Always be blamed no matter what. Always pushed over the edge when times get tough for others. Tolerance requires stability – he understood that as a fact. Stability and, equally important, education. Pulling his jacket around him he stared at the poster with its crudely drawn caricature of a snivelling Jew. Perhaps this loathsome ideology was something for him to work against, something to give him a focus. The drops of rain which had begun to fall now came down harder and faster. Raising his jacket collar to protect his neck from the raindrops he began to run in the direction of the hospital. It was still early, not even light yet. If he was lucky he could find Cornelius in Charcot's office at the Salpêtrière. If not, he would wait. He smiled despite the deluge. One thing which had not left him was his patience. He would wait. Cornelius was not to be found. So, still soaked from the rain, Samuel found a wall in the hospital corridor on which to lean and felt his clothes steaming on him as he silently watched the activity all around. Yes, he smiled to himself. He could wait.

It was just as well that Samuel had patience, as it was some hours later when Cornelius finally appeared. Samuel almost missed him as tiredness was starting to overcome him and his eyes had closed. He opened them with a start, to see the round and benevolent face of Cornelius smiling at him. 'You look all done in, old man. Come into the office and take a seat. I just need to collect something and then we can get out of this place of sickness. I will buy you a coffee.' Turning from his occupations, he stopped momentarily and looked back at Samuel. '...and a croissant. It is already 10 am and I have not yet broken my fast. It would be good to have company.' Samuel nodded slowly, torn between a moment of irritation that Cornelius would assume he was waiting for him, and a stronger wave of gratitude that he was being so kind. Acts of kindness were rare in Samuel's life, and, although it pained him to do so, he wrapped himself around this one gratefully.

Breakfast in the nearby café brought back memories. Earlier that year, Rebecca and he had waited there before first visiting Charcot. It was now winter and the windows were clouded by the damp and thirsty people within keen for the attention of the waiting staff. Obviously known, Cornelius had been able to use rudimentary sign language from the back of the crowd to order coffee and croissants for them both, and they soon found themselves crammed against a wall with little more than a shelf to act as their table. Samuel did not mind, and Cornelius, for all his peaceful attitudes, seemed to be very much at home in the crowd. The proximity (and noise) of the other people forced them to stand close together to be heard. It was a strange seclusion, Samuel mused. The intimacy of crowds. Each person was so tightly packed by their neighbour that they turned off any curiosity about them. Being so snugly wedged together seemed also to change the rules of physical contact. It meant that Samuel was close enough to Cornelius to feel his hand brush past when he picked up his coffee cup. Samuel laughed out loud despite the oddness of the moment. 'What is it?' Cornelius asked, putting down his empty cup and dabbing any stray drops of coffee with a neatly pressed and folded handkerchief. 'Everything. Something. Nothing.' Cornelius leaned in towards him as if to catch the words better. 'Sorry, old man. I didn't get all of that.' He rested his hand gently on Samuel's forearm, but didn't speak for a moment. 'I need to get back to the hospital. Will you walk with me?'

Out in the rain-washed streets the men walked leisurely and in silence back towards the hospital. As they reached the main door, Samuel asked Cornelius if he would take him to the furniture market one day when he had time. 'Certainly. Certainly! I would be delighted to help you furnish the boudoir of our dear Rebecca. You must miss her, Samuel. I certainly do.' Arranging a rendezvous for the following Saturday, Samuel left Cornelius to return to his work. He couldn't help it, but the way in which Cornelius had mentioned Rebecca's name had broken the spell of intimacy which Samuel had felt so strongly in the café earlier. Samuel shivered. He needed to get out of his damp clothes. He wanted to find a book in which to immerse his thoughts, but he knew that there was little which had the power to hold his attention once the face of Cornelius floated into his mind. Enough. He admonished himself. He was not a child, he was a man, and men don't think this way. Oh, but they do, he rejoindered miserably. They do.

With no desire to return to his lodgings, he changed direction and headed back to, and then past, the hospital, to the space which was to become his and Rebecca's home, for a while at least. As he walked up the steps of the building, he could hear the guard within singing an old campaigning song. It was a song of loss and death and did little to dispel the mood which had been threatening to settle itself around Samuel's shoulders, but he had shrugged it off by the time he reached the upper floors, and his resolve had returned. Opening the door to the apartment he took stock of the space and began to plan the layout. He smiled. It was a project, of sorts. He grinned to himself. He was creating a nest. He was making a safe space into which he would welcome Rebecca when she returned from her ordeal. Like a mistress waiting for her soldier-lover to return from the wars, as in the song sung by the guard in the vestibule below.

Samuel walked through the rooms slowly and methodically, pacing the space. It was larger than he had first envisaged. What he needed was to draw up a plan. His smile widened. If anyone needed to draw up a plan, it was certainly him. He left the building for the library. In it he would find writing materials, and warmth in which to sit and write. Most of all, he would find the company of others. Even if he did not speak to them, he wanted – no needed – to be around others. It was strange to admit to, but for the first time in his life he felt the weight of his loneliness.

CHAPTER 51

S AMUEL WAS TO meet Cornelius at the hospital. As he walked along the corridor toward Charcot's office he couldn't help but feel nervous. He decided to chalk his anxiety down to the number of times when he had accompanied Rebecca here for her sessions, and the many hours through which he had sat on the hard bench outside the consulting room, straining to hear the words spoken therein. He found himself slowing down as he approached the room, realising that he was early and not wishing for this fact to make him appear eager. He smoothed down the front of his shirt which had been washed and carefully stretched flat so it looked as good as new. Until the new apartment was furnished, he was living in Rebecca's old room where the landlady had cheerfully assumed he was mooning over his absent lover. After all, she had seen him carry Rebecca up the stairs after their celebratory evening. It was true to a certain extent. He *had* moved into the room by the hospital to be closer to his lover, even if that lover was only a figment of his imagination and had no idea of the feelings which Samuel harboured for him. As he neared Charcot's room he could hear Cornelius's voice and felt his heart begin to beat faster in response.

Samuel was starting to regret his decision to take up Cornelius's offer of a trip to the furniture market. Perhaps he could just turn around now, quietly walk away and go home. Cornelius could think him rude or that he had just forgotten. Anything would be better than embarrassing himself in front of this man.

Almost at the doorway, he turned back, his shoe squealing in protest on the polished floor. Cornelius's head immediately appeared in the doorway. 'Ah, excellent my friend. You have arrived at last.' He put his hand on Samuel's shoulder and squeezed it vigorously. 'Please do come in, I need an arbitrator.' With this, he guided Samuel into the room where Charcot was sitting at his desk, papers in hand. Samuel hovered close to the doorway, and tried to appear nonchalant by leaning against the wall. From this vantage point he watched Cornelius debate with his mentor. Samuel was pleased that he had the wall to stabilise himself, as he could feel tremors of anxiety beginning to pulse through his body. There was no doubt in his mind that he was attracted to Cornelius, and as he stood and watched, these feelings – rather than subsiding – increased. When animated, as he was now, Cornelius lost much of the awkwardness which Samuel had first mistaken for aloofness, and although Samuel had no idea of the subject of their debate, he could appreciate the facility with which Cornelius debated his point. He looked over at Charcot, and was disconcerted to see the doctor staring back at him, smiling gently. He pushed aside the papers which Cornelius was currently waving at him, signalling that he had heard enough. Not taking his eyes from Samuel, he stood and stretched out his hand to him, forcing Samuel to relinquish the safety of the wall. They shook hands, and Charcot placed his other hand over Samuel's in a surprisingly affectionate gesture. He motioned for Samuel to sit. 'So, my friend. How fares the lovely Rebecca? Do you have news?'

Feeling he was now on safer ground, Samuel kept his focus firmly on Charcot as they chatted amiably about the letters which Samuel had received from her. As far as he knew, Samuel continued, she was settling into her sessions with Professor Farkas. What he did not mention was Rebecca's disquiet about Sofia, and discomfort at the conflicting accounts of life within the household. Samuel decided it better not to allude to anything which could disturb Rebecca's chances of gaining a clean bill of health. The truth of the matter was that he was none too happy about her going to Hungary, but he would share his concerns with Cornelius later. A safe topic. He would stick to talking about Rebecca. Yes. That would be safer.

His resolution lasted for little more than an hour, for as soon as Cornelius and he left the confines of the hospital, both began to speak simultaneously and at great speed, laughing spontaneously at the effect. It later occurred to Samuel that Cornelius had been nervous, but he hadn't registered this through his own fear of making a fool of himself. As it turned out both men found plenty to talk about and their conversations ranged widely, especially after the lubricating effects of lunchtime liquor loosened their lips. After a long (and substantial) meal they headed off towards the depths of the flea market, a phenomenon which Samuel had heard of but not personally experienced. First of all, the sheer size and complexity of the stalls and shops stunned him, and then the way in which business was transacted. It was like the images of Turkish bazaars, of which he had seen in books, but considerably more raucous (and less romantic). It came as a surprise that not only was Cornelius comfortable in this environment, but he seemed to know many of the stall-holders. Noticing Samuel's discomfort as he asked the owner to uncover a chaise longue which was almost submerged beneath a sea of rugs, Cornelius laughed and took

Samuel's arm. 'Doctors are always welcome in a place like this, even a doctor of the mind such as me. I count myself fortunate in that I have been able to help people, and in turn,' he panted, pulling aside rugs to help the stall-holder reveal the small but elegant piece of furniture beneath it, 'they are willing to help me. Aren't you, Armand? For example, what pittance will you accept for this piece of junk? Perhaps you should pay me to take it off your hands?' He smiled widely at the stall-holder who, rather than being offended, responded with a toothless grin and the game of barter commenced. Samuel watched his companion in admiration as he bargained for the piece which Samuel knew Rebecca would adore. As a result of today's events he was swiftly becoming aware that some of his preconceptions about this man were based on Père, Cornelius's twin brother. They were not the same man, and the more Samuel studied Cornelius, the more differences he could discern. Cornelius had a frown line deeply etched on his brow, whereas Père's brow was smooth. It was obvious to Samuel, as he started to enjoy the bargaining as a piece of street theatre, that Cornelius had lived a different life from his brother and these differences told on their faces, and in their bodies too. Damn it, Samuel said to himself. It didn't take me long for my thoughts to wander onto his body. He smiled ruefully. A man can dream, can't he? Surely there can be no harm in that?

Cornelius guided Samuel away from the stall with the shouts of its owner following them. 'You bastard, you are trying to ruin me. I have my pride, you know. Take your ridiculous offer and stick it up your arse.' Samuel stiffened nervously at the aggressive tone, and once again Cornelius took his arm, this time leaving it there. He leaned in towards Samuel's ear and spoke in a conspiratorial tone. 'Don't worry about Armand. That is all for show so his neighbours think he is a hard man to bargain with. The chaise is Rebecca's and he will deliver it to the apartment. We can pay him then.' Samuel felt his body respond, not to the kindness, but to the use of the word 'we'. He needed to sober up or he might do something to ruin this burgeoning friendship. Suddenly he realised how much he wanted Cornelius as a friend, and holding onto this, and to his friend's arm, they made their way together deeper into the flea market.

The desire for sobriety was not to be fulfilled any time soon, as Samuel found himself willingly bludgeoned into a bar on the periphery of the market. It was below stairs, dark and noisy, and even though it was early evening it was packed – not only with men. Samuel found an alcove with a tiny ledge which served as seat and table, and installed himself, while Cornelius fought his way to the bar. Samuel waited patiently until he saw two raised arms weaving their way through the crowd, one holding two rough goblets, one clutching a jug. 'I think I lost half of it on the way!' Cornelius laughed, filling the goblets deftly and stashing the cider jug away beneath their seat before depositing himself awkwardly at Samuel's side. He sighed, turned to Samuel, and raised his goblet. 'To life!' Samuel responded as the goblets clinked together. 'To life.'

Three more jugs were interspersed with heated debate, until Samuel found himself yawning. 'Where are my manners, my friend?' Cornelius jumped to his feet, with what Samuel felt was an unnatural level of energy for a man who had just consumed a considerable amount of alcohol. Taking Samuel's hand, he pulled him off the seat. 'Come! Fresh air and fresh food!' We shall dine at my expense this evening. I have an appetite!' As they made their way out of the bar, Samuel was trying to protest, especially as it seemed far too early to dine, but on reaching the street level he saw the scene outside was not as he had left it when they had entered the bar. For a start the road was now empty: no people, no stalls and, most of all, night had already fallen. He found himself staring up at the stars. He had never noticed them in Paris before. Perhaps he should look up more often. He smiled gently at the thought. They must have been in the bar for hours and yet time had flown by in the company of this man. Cornelius broke into his reverie, linking their arms and gently guiding him down the cobbled street.

Once inside the restaurant, Samuel was grateful to sit down. He had walked a lot and his leg was starting to stiffen. His embarrassment at his gait had lessened in opposition to the amount of alcohol he had consumed, but now that seemed to be wearing off and his discomfort with his physical disability was mounting. Cornelius watched him silently, increasing Samuel's discomfort. They ordered food, and the convivium which they had shared in the crowded bar seemed to have dissipated. Perhaps it was the alcohol which depressed the mood. Perhaps it was the fact that Cornelius had picked up on Samuel's feelings and was drawing himself away. Perhaps it was Samuel's own fear of sharing too much about himself that caused the change in the atmosphere, but it was definitely there. The meal passed pleasantly enough with both men commenting on the food and chatting about Rebecca. Neutral ground. Safe ground. Common ground. Dull.

The meal ended with Cornelius paying and, Samuel noted, leaving a generous tip for the waiter. Samuel felt this action highlighted the difference between them. There were so many things which Cornelius could take for granted, but not he. Samuel would be grateful for the time which he had spent with him, but would not seek out Cornelius's company again. It would be too awkward.

The night had turned cold, and it was late. Both headed off in the same direction, silently, but no longer uncomfortably so. It was as if perimeters had been established and that would be enough for now. Suddenly it started to rain – heavy, wind-propelled, painful drops. Both men started to run and Cornelius signalled towards the shelter of a shop doorway. Cramped together once again and already soaked, both began laughing as if the rain had re-energised the alcohol in their systems. Cornelius moved closer to Samuel, then suddenly swore. 'Those bastards! When will the people learn that this is *not* the way. Hate is not the way!' Samuel turned to see what Cornelius was looking at, only to catch sight of a small hand-bill posted to the wall. It was another of those repellent political posters, from a candidate in the local elections whose slogan vilified the Jew in the most vile and disgusting terms, blaming them for everything from unemployment to inflation and more. The cartoon Jew with his bloodstained mouth straddled the world like a monster. Before Samuel could react, Cornelius had torn it from the wall and was ripping it apart. Samuel could not speak, his breath still in short ragged bursts after his exertions. Tears and rain mixed on Cornelius's face, and Samuel reached out to wipe them away. Both men moved closer, unspeaking, then leaned closer still. The embrace was inevitable. Hidden by the wall of water each man surrendered himself to the moment.

CHAPTER 52

Looking back on it, neither Samuel nor Cornelius could remember who had first suggested that they move into the apartment together. There would be no doubt that Rebecca would live with them in the new accommodation too, of course she would. Cornelius reasoned that it was the only logical option as the location was perfect for his work at the hospital, and his income could be used for the benefit of the entire household. Samuel had decided against telling Cornelius about Rebecca's inheritance. It was her secret and she could tell him herself soon enough when she returned to Paris.

Borrowing a handcart from Armand, the furniture seller, on the promise that they would soon buy more, they moved Cornelius's furniture, books and clothes from his lodging room. That room was crammed, but when the contents had been decanted into their new space they looked forlorn. There was little by way of comfort except one bed, and that creaked noisily when they were making love. Cornelius teased Samuel mercilessly at his fear that someone might hear them. 'This is Paris, my friend! The sound of lovemaking is always present – day or night!'

Samuel was overjoyed and overwhelmed at the development. Cornelius was more sanguine. The night they first spent together, he swore, was one which he would never forget as long as he lived. A picnic of cold meats, bread and wine turned into an exploration of each other's bodies, endless butterfly kisses and luxurious lovemaking. Afterwards they lay together, bodies pressed close for warmth and in affection. Then they talked, and talked, and talked, until dawn intruded through their curtainless windows. Samuel was close to tears that night. He felt raw and vulnerable – and alive. Never had he felt so alive, and never had the fear of loss been so vivid to him. It was this fear that turned their nocturnal discussion to the poster which Cornelius had torn from the wall that night when they first kissed.

The spectre of hatred of the Jews was never far from Samuel's mind. Ever the outsider because of his Jewishness, he knew that it was compounded by being a foreigner. Add that to his pederasty and if it was known on the streets, he knew his life would not be worth living. Cornelius listened intently, and, waiting for the outpouring of years of rejection to end, cupped Samuel's face in his hands and spoke with a quiet intensity. 'Fear is their weapon, my dearest love. If you give in to fear, then those who would harm you are ever present. They need to do nothing as you yourself moderate your behaviour, your language, your choices based on what might happen if they discover your secrets. They – the haters – have no power unless you give it to them.' Samuel pulled himself upright in the bed and tried to plump up a meagre pillow. Cornelius would never know what it meant to grow up in fear – powerless and friendless and so subject to the whims of a society which didn't care for the outsider. Even as Cornelius reasoned that this fear was unfounded, Samuel knew better, and a realisation of the naivety of his lover made him fear for him. For them. For there now was a 'them'. Samuel and Cornelius. Paramours. He terminated his lover's philosophical peregrinations with a kiss, and soon there was no need for more words.

A routine of sorts quickly developed. Cornelius went out to work, and Samuel began to clean, paint and decorate their new home. A table and chairs at which they could dine, and would act as a desk for Cornelius's work, was bought and laboriously carried up the stairs. The building attendant helped them carry it and shared a few words of conversation and a mug of cider by way of thanks. Henceforth he smiled in greeting whenever they came home, touching his cap in acknowledgement. Samuel began cooking, buying food at the local market daily. When Cornelius objected to this self-imposed servitude, he argued that, as he could not contribute with finances, he could at least contribute through his actions. Besides, he argued, he was saving money and that was no bad thing. Both men would spend every moment possible in each other's company, and Cornelius took to returning home even at lunchtime. Samuel's fears of loss began to subside and there were moments when he found himself standing still to take stock of his situation. He had found love, and it was reciprocated. In one of the frequent post-lovemaking tête-à-têtes he asked Cornelius when he had first known that he was 'not as other men'. Cornelius smiled sadly. 'I knew, just as Père knew, from the beginning. There was never any doubt for either of us that we were different. At first, we had believed it to be part of being twins, and, knowing no others like us, just thought it was another oddity about us. One day, when we were – I don't know – no more than six or seven,

Père told our cousin, and she told father. Father beat him so badly that he couldn't walk. I, to my eternal shame, said nothing, and from that day our progenitor favoured me over Père. I could have anything I wanted. I said nothing but shared everything I had and everything I later earned from that day with Père. I owe him that much. I still do.' Samuel silently stroked his lover's hair as he continued. 'His name is Pierre, in case you wondered. I call him Père because he is the elder of the pair of us, and when our father died he became the head of our family. He stayed in Toulon and nursed our mother through cancer. It was horrific but it meant I could continue my studies here and be able to earn for both of us. He joined me here in Paris when she died. That was four years ago. I can begrudge him nothing, although I would prefer if he did not drink quite so much. I fear he has a death wish.' 'He lives for the moment.' Samuel responded, quietly. He was aware, perhaps more than Cornelius, that when you were already thought of as criminal for loving another man, there were many who would choose to live their lives recklessly. Why not? Society had already ostracised them. For Samuel, rather than this being liberating, he found it oppressive. He didn't want to spend every evening expectantly in a bar and every morning puking in remorse. He wanted stability and normality, or at least the semblance of it. They talked of Rebecca, and Samuel teased Cornelius when he confessed that he had thought his lover's interest was in Rebecca. 'Jealous, my darling Samuel? Of a woman? Whatever next!' Play fights led inevitably to sex as both men exposed their histories and their hearts to one another. The outside world and its opinions had ceased to exist, at least in those moments.

However, this was not to last. Nothing does, Samuel thought ruefully. He had enjoyed the secret nature of their liaison and, when

Cornelius returned one evening with the news that he had met his brother Père for lunch, a pang of regret crossed his mind. Cornelius spotted it and smiled gently. 'It is only fair that I let my brother know of my joy. I want to spread the happiness not contain it. All the old crowd want to see us for an evening back in Le Marais. We will be teased, dreadful jokes will be made, and then we can come home.' Here he smiled and swept his hand around the sparsely furnished room, clasping Samuel's hand with the other. 'Our home!'

The evening was just as Cornelius had predicted. Some pretended to be shocked, while others claimed that they had known all along that this would happen, in fact they were surprised it hadn't started *long* ago. All in all, it wasn't as bad as Samuel had feared. It was pleasant to see some of his old friends again, and there were new faces in the crowd. Their announcement was not to be the only news that evening, as Père revealed that he, himself, had something to tell the company. 'It is with the greatest regret,' he started, much to Cornelius's consternation, 'that my work has been recognised as worthy of the name "masterpiece" and Durand-Ruel himself has demanded, nay, begged me to allow him to sell my work in his gallery.' Amidst the flippant smokescreen of Père's tone, the words which he spoke meant Père's life was about to undergo a seismic change. The noise levels had increased in the bar, and in silent agreement Cornelius and Samuel decided to slip away while the group were distracted by Père's momentous news. Samuel had been grateful for anything which took the focus of attention from them, but didn't understand what all the commotion was about. Taking his lover's arm, Samuel asked Cornelius to explain why everyone was so excited about Père's announcement.

It seemed that there were two art dealers in Paris (at least two whose patronage really mattered to the artists), Paul Durand-Ruel and his fierce rival Georges Petit. If an artist was represented by either man it meant commercial success. As much as the artists would joke that this was the ruin of a man's art, most, if not all of them, secretly craved this honour. It was all very well to say that money corrupted an artist, but starving was no great pleasure and the cold of the Parisian winter bit very hard when you had to choose between food and warmth. 'What Père hasn't made common knowledge yet is that his negotiations with Durand-Ruel are much further advanced than he admits. His work has already been taken to the gallery, and he is moving out of Paris.' Samuel's face betrayed his surprise. 'I will tell you why ... because of his drinking. Durand-Ruel has insisted that he leaves for the Côte d'Azur within the month. Why all the way to the south of France?' Cornelius continued. 'There are already other artists there – starting some sort of colony no doubt – enjoying the inspiration of the light. Most importantly, Père will be away from the negative influences of some of his artist friends who put the "piss" into artist and do more drinking than painting. Durand-Ruel is no more a fool than he is he a philanthropist, the weather is such that the painting season is much longer than it would be in Paris, so he will get more work out of him. No fool at all.' Samuel took this all in silently. Life was indeed changing.

They continued their walk home through the dark Paris streets and talked, arm in arm, oblivious to the cold and to the small group of men who appeared as if from nowhere. Samuel registered them first, and knew what was about to happen. He tugged at Cornelius's sleeve. 'We need to run. Now.' His words fell on stony ground as Cornelius turned to the group. 'Gentlemen. How can I help you?'

Momentarily the group stopped, and one of them spoke. 'Move aside, monsieur. We have no truck with you. It's the Jew we want.' A stone flew towards them, hitting Samuel on the ear. He could feel the blood trickling down his neck. Cornelius turned to him and spoke. 'Run. Don't turn back.' Frozen by fear, Samuel stared at his lover. 'Run!' Cornelius ordered. So he ran.

CHAPTER 53

THEY HAD ALMOST made it home. Only two more streets and they would have been safely ensconced in their bed. Samuel ran blindly towards the doorway of the apartment block, yelling at the top of his voice for help. The door was wide open, and within the dismal entrance-hall four men and one dog hunched around a brazier. 'Please. Help. Cornelius…' Everything seemed to happen at once from that moment. The men running into the street towards the sound of the shouting, a neighbour appearing with a cloth to staunch Samuel's wound, the dog barking furiously soon to be joined by others, lights appearing in apartment buildings and people leaning out to identify the source of the commotion. Disorientated by alcohol and fear, Samuel tried to stagger back into the street, only to be pushed aside at the doorway by two men carrying Cornelius's body. Dropping him to the floor, they ran once more into the streets, following the frantic yapping of the dog. Cornelius wasn't moving. Samuel, half-blinded by his own blood, fell to his lover's side, desperate to see. Once again he was pushed aside, this time more gently. The neighbour now leaned over him and checked his wound, then turned her attention to Cornelius. 'He is breathing. I don't know how bad his injuries are, but I have seen worse sights at work.' It was only now that Samuel looked properly at the woman. Dressed in a distinctive work pinafore he could see she was a nurse. 'Tell me what to do,' he said weakly. 'Well, we should really get him to the hospital,' she said and began to examine Cornelius, 'but I have a feeling that he would rather not have this happen.' She stood upright, hands on hips. 'We need to get him upstairs and into bed. She looked down at Samuel critically. You must help me carry him. I can't do it alone.'

Later – much later – Samuel would laugh about how they had taken Cornelius up three flights of stairs. Partly dragged, partly carried, and when Cornelius regained consciousness, partly supported. Most of the carrying had been done by Valerie, who would forever be called their guardian angel. Small and fiery, she seemed to have the constitution and strength of an ox. As the days went by and Cornelius recovered, it was the daily visits from Valerie which made it bearable. Once she had cleaned him up, she diagnosed that Cornelius had been fortunate enough to escape with only three broken ribs and a cut across his cheek. The day after the incident she carried a letter to the hospital, from him, addressed to Charcot, explaining that he had 'taken a tumble in the street'. Less than an hour after sending it, Charcot himself appeared at the door to the apartment. He stepped inside and grasped Samuel affectionately by both shoulders. 'So, where is my patient?' It was only then that Samuel noticed he was carrying his medical bag. Leading the doctor to the bedroom, he watched miserably as Charcot entered their private space and closed the door behind him, leaving Samuel staring wretchedly at the closed door. He felt useless and, worse still, vulnerable. Charcot was no fool and it would not take much observation of the bedroom to see that both men shared one bed. He wandered around the apartment, picking up books randomly and putting them back down again. If Charcot chose to act on his observations then, at best, Cornelius would be out of a job and, at worst, they could both find themselves imprisoned. Samuel found himself looking around the apartment again, now with the eyes of someone assessing what to take with him this time when flight was necessary. Vincent's picture hung on the wall between two windows in the sitting room. He would probably have to leave it and just take clothing and the small purse of coins which comprised the remains of Miriam's money. Would Rebecca understand? He knew she would accept his flight from Paris, but whether she would accept its necessity he found himself doubting. She had never experienced the irrational hatred directed towards the Jew. Not a human, a caricature figure of hate at whose feet all blame could be lain. In this at least, she had been sheltered. His perambulations around the apartment had brought him back to the bedroom, where he leaned his forehead on the cold surface of the door. It was his fault that Cornelius had been beaten.

Two days after the attack, Samuel limped slowly downstairs in search of the porter. Standing in the entranceway he could see that the brazier had burnt out, and he found himself staring at the scorched ceiling above. A muscular man appeared at his side and stretched out his hand. 'Monsieur. Enchanté.' Samuel started, and then shook the proffered hand gratefully. He could feel the marks of hard work on its roughened surface, and the obvious signs of new bruises on its knuckles. 'Un verre, monsieur? A glass of wine to take away the chill of the morning?' Although Samuel was no good at drinking in the morning, and the chipped cup in which the wine was being poured was obviously less than clean, he placed his gratitude for this man above his fastidiousness and they raised the cups and drank together. For a moment, both sat in silence contemplating the cold brazier. 'Those bastards won't bother you again, monsieur. They are nothing more than street thugs. The bastard politicians employ them to put fear into people so they will vote them into office. Bastards. Politicians never do anything for anyone except their bastard selves.' He spat into the brazier angrily. 'You have both been decent to me. Why should I hate you for your crazy religion? Why should I care what you do in bed?' He laughed loudly. 'You don't ask me, monsieur, and I won't ask you!' His loud laugh turned into a harsh cough which he shrugged off when Samuel suggested that he see a doctor. 'I would rather have that pretty nurse who lives here come and visit me. She could warm my bed any day of the week!' He spat a bloody gob into the brazier and wiped his mouth with the back of his sleeve. 'Paris is large and she is cruel, but there are good people here. We are not powerful or rich, but kindness is our currency. Liberty, equality and fraternity are all very well, but kindness binds us all.' With this curiously poetic pronouncement he patted Samuel on the back and left for the street. Samuel watched the porter walk along the pavement and disappear around the corner. It was a while before Samuel moved away from the cold brazier and made his way slowly back to the apartment.

News travels fast, especially in a city like Paris, and before another day had passed, Père and his cronies appeared at the apartment. Turning the whole visit into a party, they came laden down with a picnic of bread, wine, cheese and all manner of tasty sweets. They swarmed up to the apartment, and then, once they had heard the story of the rescue, back down again to the porter to leave their thanks (and a bottle of red wine) with him. Samuel couldn't help it, but he felt somewhat embarrassed by his friends' flamboyant behaviour; however, the porter seemed to be unimpressed by their noise – unlike the wine, with which he was very impressed indeed. 'So he should be,' laughed Père. 'Only the best for my brother's saviour!' Cornelius was still in his bed, and now had the benefit of medication generously prescribed by Charcot. He was still groggy but able to share in the party atmosphere. Samuel found himself hovering around the edges, uncomfortable with the sight of this unruly group in their bedroom. He had a sudden urge to throw out the guests, wanting just for a moment to turn back the clock to the time before anyone knew they were together. He was conflicted. He realised his dilemma was in wanting both to be left alone and to have public acceptance. Cornelius watched him and caught his eye, and it was as if they were the only ones in the room. He reached out to Samuel, and signalled for him to sit on the bed where he held onto his lover's hand. Publicly. Samuel felt himself blushing, but no-one else seemed to notice. Here, in this moment, in this room, he felt loved and accepted. Cornelius clasped his hand, and for the briefest moment Samuel allowed himself to let go of the past and the future and just live in the moment. Content for the first time in his life.

Cornelius' recovery was slow, but it marked a phase shift in their relationship. Samuel cared for him tenderly, and was almost regretful when Charcot indicated that soon Cornelius would be well enough to return to his post. Whilst his lover was ill, Samuel could lavish him with care and spend every waking moment in his company. He feared that when Cornelius was back at the hospital this closeness would end. He knew he was being selfish, and he admitted his feelings to Cornelius who laughed loudly, then quickly stopped as the pain in his ribs reminded him to stay still. 'My dear man, we will never part. My wish is for God to grant me the pleasure to grow old and to die in your arms.' Samuel felt tears prickling his eyes. 'Hand me my jacket.' Cornelius fumbled though its pockets before awkwardly pulling out a watch chain. Attached to the fob was a simple gold band inset with a smooth ruby. He placed it in Samuel's palm. 'It was my mother's – our mother's should I say – and now it is yours.' Samuel closed his hand on the ring. Even as his mind told him that he should refuse the gift, his heart said otherwise and he placed it on his little finger. It was tight even there, but he knew that over the years it would become a part of his hand. They embraced clumsily. Samuel held Cornelius gently for fear of hurting him and they stayed entwined until they slept. No words were needed now.

Less than an hour could have passed, but when the loud sound of someone knocking on their door started, it had already grown dark outside. The first of Samuel's senses to wake was his fear – fear that somehow the thugs had found them and had returned to finish what they had started in the street, but Cornelius quickly reassured him. 'It will be Armand – the street trader. I forgot all about it. Remember him? The one from whom we bought Rebecca's daybed. Père saw him and told him what had happened to me, so he said he would bring the daybed over himself sometime this week.' Clearly, when Samuel opened the door it was he who was waiting there, leaning on the doorframe and panting for a drink. This sight was not, however, what Samuel was focusing on. Behind the man, seated on the waiting daybed, was a small, neat couple. On seeing Samuel, the man rose and walked towards him, bowing politely. To Samuel's surprise he spoke in English. 'Mr Samuel, sir. It is a pleasure to meet you at last. Miss Rebecca spoke of you often.'

The daybed delivered, the trader was then dispatched with alacrity, a liberal tip and a flask of cider for his pains. Samuel and Cornelius now found themselves seated opposite the strange couple, holding their visiting card which read 'Reith Investigative Services'. Clearly and simply they explained who they were, and why they had tracked Samuel down. More importantly, they explained why it was critical that he leave Paris with them. Rebecca was in danger and she did not even know it yet. Samuel was torn, he did not want to leave Cornelius. His lover made it all so simple. 'I am coming with you,' Cornelius said. 'If Rebecca needs a knight in shining armour then two are surely better than one.' Bags rapidly packed, and the doorman entrusted with a letter to Charcot, the curious quartet made their way to the station, and onto the first train out of Paris.

Later that evening, Armand the street trader found an ear into which he poured the events of his afternoon. The more words flowed from his mouth, the more wine was poured into it.

CHAPTER 54

L ARGE AS IT had seemed when she first arrived in Budapest, Rebecca felt the house in Baross Utca closing in on her. It was as if the conversation in the workshop had never taken place. In the ensuing weeks which had passed since that time, Zoltan had not referred to it, and there was no way for Rebecca to bring it up again. It seemed to her as if the house itself had turned its back on her and was keeping secrets, some below stairs, some above. It was starting to become all so exhausting. She felt herself become progressively more withdrawn and unhappy. The sessions with the Alienist had, as a result, been strained and unsatisfying. Rebecca began to sleep badly and found herself becoming short-tempered and tearful. For all of this, she was unable to pinpoint the exact source of her misery. The truth of it was she was able, but unwilling. To be in a household where one individual's version of reality was so at odds with the other exhausted her. The dynamic which played out between Zoltan and Sofia did not fit with either party's portrayal of reality. 'She is either his unacknowledged child and he is the villain of the piece, as Sofia would have me believe, or she is insane, as he would have me think. Or perhaps the truth is both, or neither.'

The constant round of speculation dragged at Rebecca's spirit and she became listless and fretful. She neither slept well, nor did she eat much. Unlike Sofia, who, Rebecca had noticed, was starting to get stout. Her rational clothing had concealed her widening girth for a while, but even that was beginning to look tight. No matter. She looked happy and free from care, something for which Rebecca envied her.

Another week passed with the same dull routine, and Rebecca's visits to the Alienist's consulting room had become the focal point of her day. Finally, she broke through the silence, and her own rule not to ask the question to which she so badly wanted an answer. 'The Angel. You have said nothing since I told you about the Angel. I want to know. I need to know. Am I insane?'

From his seat in the shadow Zoltan responded. 'For an individual to get help they must acknowledge that they have a problem. Do you, Rebecca? Do you acknowledge this?' Rebecca started to shiver. She realised that her answer could condemn her to the asylum, but there was no going back. 'No. I do not believe I have a problem.' She paused, her breath coming short and hard. 'I believe that I had a problem, but not any more.' She tried to find his eyes in the shadow of his face but he receded further into the shade. 'Go on...' She drew in a deep, ragged breath before continuing. 'I believed the Angel was real,' she licked her dry lips before continuing, 'but a reality which I created.'

'And now? What do you believe *now*.' He leaned in closer. She responded with a whisper. 'Now,' she faltered. 'Now I believe in a different reality.'

To her utter shame and surprise, Rebecca felt herself begin to sob. Deep, painful, rattling sobs came from within her, and kept coming. All the while Zoltan remained motionless in the shadow as Rebecca threw herself down on the chaise longue and sobbed into its cushions. The cloched clock on the mantelpiece ticked and chimed, and still she cried. The Alienist did not speak, but watched her impassively. As Rebecca became more aware of herself and the sobs began to subside into deep, tiring breaths, she caught sight of him watching her. Observing her. Monitoring her. Their eyes met, but he made no move to comfort her, or even to acknowledge the state she was in. Like one of the stone angels from Ramsgate cemetery, he gazed down on her humanity impassively.

Eventually, and to her amazement, after this raw display of emotion she slept. The roughness of the rug which covered the consulting room couch scratched at her cheek and she woke in confusion at the sensation. Looking up, Professor Farkas was still watching her. Her first thought was an odd one. She observed how curious it was that here in this room she could not call him Zoltan, even in her mind. In here he is a different creature altogether, almost as if the person is absent and only the most necessary of mechanisms remain. She sat up stiffly, and tried to repair some of the damage to her dignity. She knew that this could be no more than a token gesture, as her face was peppered with the indentations of the rug on which she had slept.

A gentle tap on the door broke into the silence. A maid walked timidly in, carrying a tray with a pot of coffee and one tiny glass. Wordlessly, she arranged them on the table next to the Alienist and left the room. Slowly and ritualistically, he poured the coffee into the glass and held a sugar cube above the dense liquid, allowing it to leach the contents before releasing it. He repeated the action three more times before drinking the syrupy contents in one draught. It was as if Rebecca had ceased to exist, so absorbed was he in the activity.

Eventually the Alienist leaned back in his chair and began to speak. 'Your problem is, and always has been, evident to me, Miss Zimmerman. You are the Angel, at least in as far as you are its creator and it exists because of you. Without you it ceases to exist. It is quite simple, no?'

Rebecca chose silence. It was not as if she had anything to contribute and it was obvious that she was not expected to talk. This was the time for her to listen, and she did, as if her life depended on it. At first, Professor Farkas spoke to her as if she was a child, using simple concepts, easy words, but as he continued and warmed to his theme, it became more like an academic lecture. On and on he talked, and carried on speaking until the clock had chimed the quarter hour, then the half, then the quarter hour again. A full hour passed by and still he continued. This was a man who loved the sound of his own voice and his own opinions. A man who loved himself sincerely and without the need for any external validation. A narcissist of the highest order.

On and on he talked. He spoke of the inner story, of repression of the self, and of the fundamental drive for a woman to have a child. He spoke of female libido and original sin, of the essential requirement for a woman to be guided by a strong and positive male influence. He droned on about man's superior intellect and the neurosis created when a woman attempts to emulate this male drive. He pontificated, preached, lectured, instructed until finally he had strung together his words into threads that bound Rebecca helplessly. Finally, he stared directly into her eyes. 'So, you understand, yes?'

'No.' She sighed in exhaustion. 'No. I do not understand what you have said to me.'

He watched her intently, and suddenly it came to her. The long and intense monologue to which he had subjected her was not meant to educate her. It was designed to demonstrate to Rebecca the superiority of the Alienist, and the power which he held over her. The realisation came that if she questioned him she would be lost. It was time for her to play a part. The part of the submissive, weak and feeble-minded woman. She had to submit to win. 'Help me,' she cried weakly, 'Please, Professor, only you can save my mind. I beg you!' As the words spilled out of her mouth it was all she could do to swallow the bile which followed them. She threw herself down onto the daybed, hiding her face as she felt him swell in triumph. She acted her part well. He was not such a good actor, or at least did not seem to think any dissemblance was necessary now. His voice became triumphant. 'It is over, child. You are cured. Your foolish delusion of being able to summon an Angel is now at an end. It was nothing more than a metaphor for your inappropriate and unnatural desires to be more like a man. You are not special, you are just a woman, and as such you now realise your place in society. You will soon marry and raise children. The folly is over.' Rebecca seethed with fury, but she remained motionless on the couch, her face hidden. She could feel him triumphantly standing over her as she lay there, but still she did not move. Momentarily, Miriam and Geraldine, Clarissa, and Mrs Burton all came into her mind. What would they say to such misogyny? The Alienist would probably be dead on the street outside having been cheerfully defenestrated by furious women if they were here now, or at least hung out of a window until he cried for his mother. Thoughts of these women gave Rebecca the courage she craved. She recognised that she was doing what she had to do, however humiliating it felt. It was a means to an end. She needed to stroke this male ego sufficiently for him to give her a clean bill of mental health and then she was out of there. Away from Professor Farkas, away from Sofia, away from this house with its automata and secrets. Free to start her life.

She sighed dramatically and raised herself up from the daybed. 'Yes. I understand. Thank you, Professor. Thank you. You have used your wonderful skills to heal me and I am grateful.' She walked slowly towards the door as if unsteady, keeping her head bowed low and turned away from him so he could not see her face. Leaving the room, she turned just enough to catch a glimpse of his exultant features. She had done enough. Rebecca was to have her absolution. She was sure of it now.

She crept quietly along the corridor to her room, trying hard to compose her own features as she fought the conflicting sensations of anger and a recognition of the absurdity of the situation which threated to spill over into a fit of hysterical laugher. Seeing Sofia in the corridor, her features settled into an impassive mask and she stopped to ask again for the locket. Now she was leaving she was determined to take it back. 'Sofia,' Rebecca began softly, 'I see you are not wearing my mother's locket any longer.' At this Sofia's hand played around the lace of her collar. She kept her tone even. 'I really miss it. It would please me very much if I could have it back.' Sofia moved close to her and whispered in her ear. 'Me lost it. Gone. Bad Sofia. So sad.' She pulled away and, allowing her head to drop to one side, she pulled a clownish sad face. Rebecca froze, tears sprang to her eyes at not only the news, but the way in which it had been delivered. The expression on Sofia's face changed suddenly. Her eyes narrowed calculatingly before a slow smile made its way across her lips. She twirled around and threw her arms in the air, dancing away from a shocked Rebecca. For what felt like an eternity she stood stock still before making her way stiffly back to her bedroom. She felt as if she had aged twenty years in the space of a few moments.

CHAPTER 55

THE NEXT MORNING, Rebecca went downstairs to her solitary breakfast to find a formal note on her plate telling her Professor Farkas had been called away and would not return for ten days. She could feel her anger rising that he had left without acknowledging the completion of her treatment, effectively trapping her here until his return. Once again the house had closed its doors on her and left Rebecca wandering its corridors feeling shut out and isolated. Sofia's escalating erratic behaviour made her own return to Paris and normality feel even more urgent, and Rebecca found herself wryly remembering her time at the Mayr Clinic when Dr Stroh's words had warned her about the toxicity of some relationships. She hadn't listened then, but she had now learned. The loss of her mother's locket burned her cheeks with a furious determination not to soften her feelings towards Sofia again. She would try to avoid all contact with her. It shouldn't be too difficult as she seemed to have retreated to her bedroom. Good. Rebecca hoped she stayed there.

Pulling her thoughts together and her mind to practicalities, she determined that she wasn't going to waste her time here until the Alienist returned. She would set about some serious reading and try to make some preparations for an application to medical school on her return to Paris. She knew that there was a selection of suitably absorbing books in the consulting room, and, folding the note in two, she headed back upstairs to the Alienist's room to look for them. Her ingress was frustrated by a locked door. Angrily she kicked out at it, only to realise that there was someone moving about inside the room. As she reached for the handle again the door was pulled open by Stefan. He looked surprised to see her, and she detected an air of disturbance about him. His hair stood curiously on end as if he had been running his hands through them. She breathed deeply in a vain effort to calm her escalating heartbeat. It was true that they hadn't spoken to (or even seen) each other since that evening at the restaurant, and his discomfiture was possibly due to the fact that he had been avoiding her, but she had the feeling that there was more to it. Nor could she think of a logical reason why she found her heart racing. Suddenly she was curious. Why should he not be in his employer's consulting room… but then what reason could he have for locking the door?

As if in response to her unspoken question, Stefan said, 'While Professor Farkas is away I am taking the opportunity to organise his papers. He does leave things in such a mess.' Rebecca stepped into the room and looked around. Throughout her sessions she had become very familiar with the minutiae of this room. It didn't look any different from how it had always looked, except for one area of shelves which was now emptied. The books were piled randomly on the floor. Whatever he was doing could be none of her business, she decided, so she selected two large volumes from the desk. 'I will take these to my room,' she explained. 'I will, of course, return them,' she continued unnecessarily. As she walked away, she couldn't resist making a comment to Stefan. 'You had better put things back in the right order. He will notice if you don't.' Suddenly Stefan looked panicked, and Rebecca took pity on him. 'I can help you, if you like. I know where everything lives.' She watched his shoulders drop as the tension left him. 'Thank you. It is kind of you.'

Promising to return after breakfast the next day, she made her way back to her bedroom. Passing Sofia's bedroom, she heard a retching sound from within. 'Attention seeking. That's all it is. She is trying to play games and I am not going to allow myself to fall for them again.' Nonetheless, Rebecca tiptoed past so she wouldn't be heard. She didn't feel good about ignoring the sound, but was determined that she would not be manipulated by this woman again. On reaching the safety of her room she closed the door quietly behind her. This time she locked it too. This is a house of secrets, she mused. I, too, must protect mine. Holding the books close to her body, she carried them over to the bed where the rest of the cold day was spent wrapped in the covers of the one, and immersed in the covers of the other.

True to her word, Rebecca arrived at the consulting room the following morning. The door was both unlocked and open, and Stefan was clearly visible inside having returned the books to the shelves. He turned to greet her. 'Good morning! Thank you for coming, but as you can see I have no need of your help.' He moved aside to show Rebecca the shelf. She walked towards it. 'Yes,' she said slowly. 'You have returned them, but they are not in the correct order.' He frowned, and pushed his hands through his hair. 'They are alphabetical, as are the others,' he retorted. 'I concur, but this shelf was not in alphabetical order. These books were in the order of their publication dates. I remarked on this discrepancy the first time I came in here, and Professor Farkas explained that it was essential for this to be the case, as he needed to have the most up to date information to hand and this was the easiest way to achieve it.' Stefan stared at the identically bound volumes in irritation. 'Here. Allow me.' Rebecca moved books forward and backward until the order was re-established. 'Now if you align the spines with the front of the shelves they will be back as they were.' Stefan stared at her as if he had not seen her before. 'Observation is a wonderful quality. Most people look but do not see.' Rebecca realised this was a paraphrase of the words of Professor Farkas, and found herself disliking Stefan for using them. 'Do not patronise me, please. I have a brain in my head.' Stefan stepped back as if shocked. 'I am so sorry. Please forgive me. I only meant...'

'What? What did you mean? Oh! How clever of the little woman. She can sort things into order. What other little tricks can she perform?' Rebecca's anger at her treatment by the Alienist was pouring itself like a toxic oil onto the man before her, who was now holding his hands in front of him as if to stem the tide of her words. 'Please, I am sorry! You don't understand.' As she turned to storm out of the room, she watched his hand reach out to her face. Tears had escaped her eyes and he touched the wetness on her cheek with surprise. He spoke as if he was alone. 'Back in France in my home village, a young girl believed she saw tears of blood pouring from the eyes of the Virgin Mary. No-one questioned her belief.' He withdrew his hand. 'Now it is a place of pilgrimage. Even if she did lie, it makes no difference now. Sick are healed and local merchants grow rich – so all is well, no?' He sighed and continued slowly. 'Some of us are cursed with the necessity of maintaining our beliefs – oftentimes long after we have lost our faith.' Rebecca stared at him in incomprehension. 'Forgive me. I have important decisions to make,' he said, turning his back on her and starting to straighten the books along the edge of the shelf. Rebecca turned and left the room. More secrets. More confusion. She mused. I must get out of this place and soon.

That night Rebecca replayed the moments with Stefan. Her response to his touch was not like that of the sailor's rough hand, nor (although she had tried to obliterate it from her memory) that of Sofia's penetrating fingers, but it was a different sensation. It was both sorrowful and strong. It was a feeling that she realised she would like to explore again. It did not make sense to her. This was no great sweeping passion like that described in books, but something much more subtle. More nuanced. She turned over in bed. Right now, she did not have the inclination to analyse herself. Frankly she'd had quite enough of analysis and had moved from doubt through to curiosity, onto compliance via confabulation and then back to doubt. Unsure whether her experience with the Alienist had truly benefitted her mental state, she was more convinced than ever that all that mattered now was to present the right 'face' to the world in order for it to present as few objections as possible to her following her dream of training to become a doctor. Actor first, then doctor. She smiled to herself. We are all actors, dissemblers. It just took me a while to learn this. Her final thought, before sleep took her, was that she was getting rather good at acting. It became easier once you recognised your objective. She slept well that night.

The 'important decisions' were not alluded to again, and nor did Stefan try to touch her.

The days which followed settled into a pattern. Each morning she would go to the consulting room after breakfast. She rationalised that it was because she could read undisturbed there, but in her more honest moments she admitted to herself that she looked forward to Stefan's company. He was intelligent, ready to debate and happy to challenge her. He seemed to enjoy these encounters too. Their mornings passed in companionable discussions, and the days soon flew past.

Professor Farkas' return to Budapest was heralded by shrieks of delight which could be heard throughout the house. 'Papa is home! Darling Papa!' Rebecca leaned over the balustrade of the first floor landing to watch Sofia throw herself into the Professor's arms as he walked into the vestibule. While allowing himself to be embraced by Sofia, he looked up at Rebecca and their eyes locked. She made herself perform a small curtsey before pulling away from the scene below. Rebecca could maintain her act as the meek woman for a little longer until she left this place forever. She wasn't, however, prepared to wait too much longer.

That afternoon, after having dressed herself carefully and modestly, she walked slowly towards the door of the Alienist's consulting room. It was closed. She raised her hand to knock but held back at the sounds she could hear coming from within. It was Sofia's voice giggling and whispering, and she suddenly felt a pang of jealousy which momentarily froze her. Was Stefan inside? Was this the reason he had taken to locking the door, to keep his assignations with Sofia private? She could hear a male voice now, and couldn't help herself. Despite her fear of what she might see in there, or even that she might be caught, suddenly her need to know took hold of her. She bent down and pressed her eye to the keyhole to try to see what was happening. From it she could see the Alienist's chair. The occupant was obscured by the figure of a woman. It was Sofia. Rooted to the spot, Rebecca watched as she raised her skirts and started to straddle the chair. Suddenly the male figure reached forward and pulled at her loose loop of hair, turning her face roughly towards the door and then pulling her down until she was kneeling before him. He had not spoken. Sofia was kneeling now, and Rebecca watched as the Alienist pushed Sofia's head down towards his erect penis, staring directly at the door as Sofia started to gag. Rebecca could watch no more. She felt her gorge rise, and began to retch, echoing the sounds made by Sofia. She ran for the safety of her room. From the other side of the door, the Alienist's eyes narrowed as the light reappeared around the keyhole. They slid out of focus and he smiled tightly, his pleasure heightening in the knowledge that he had been watched.

CHAPTER 56

REBECCA MADE IT back to her room before spewing copiously into her piss-pot. Thankfully it was empty, but the faint whiff of urine emanating from it caused her to retch again until there was nothing left inside her. Shaking and perspiring she threw herself down on the bed, remaining motionless until the churning sensations in her stomach had subsided. The churning in her mind did not settle so simply. If only she could reject the memories of what she had just seen in the same way as her body had rejected food. An hour or more passed before she pulled herself upright and splashed her face with the contents of the ewer from which she had washed that morning. Still shaken, she went back to the bed and pulled the coverlet over her. Emotional exhaustion overcame her, and she slept.

To her surprise when she woke she felt better. Her mind had continued to process what she had seen, and in the interim period had come up with a strategy to deal with it. It was neither sophisticated nor complicated. She would pack her bag and leave, whether the Alienist would discharge her or not. He couldn't hold her here. After all she came voluntarily so she could leave the same way. She would explain to Charcot (somehow) why she had left, and that was all there was to be said. It would have been better to wait on the quay – all day if she had to – for a ferry to take her away from the city than to spend another night under this roof. It wasn't much of a plan but it was all she had. Pulling her possessions from drawers where they had lain so neatly, she dragged her carpet bag from under the bed and began to fill it. Once full, she took Samuel's book, which had lain at her bedside for so long now, and wrapped it in Miriam's scarf. Touching its softness, she drew strength from the contact, and taking one last look at herself in the mirror she left her room, and headed towards her final confrontation with the Alienist. Rebecca was not about to run away, but would face Professor Farkas and then leave this house with her head held high.

It was not however to be, as the moment she opened the door, she was presented with Sofia's back. Facing the wall, she appeared to be straightening a picture which hung in the corridor. 'I want to show you something.' Sofia spoke softly, turning to face Rebecca, tears glistening in her eyes. 'I know you must hate me but please just do this one last thing for me.' Rebecca was unwilling, but realised that compliance would be quicker (and hopefully less dramatic) than refusal. As if she had seen a ghost, Sofia turned from Rebecca and ran back to her room and slammed the door behind her. Rebecca had had enough of Sofia's madness. It was too exhausting. She turned around to see Professor Farkas watching the scene silently. He turned and walked slowly down the stairs. Rebecca followed him silently as he motioned her into the consulting room. He indicated towards the daybed for her to sit down. She ignored his suggestion and chose instead to sit at the table. It was all she could do not to grip the wooden arms of her seat, but instead she moved her body into stillness, as she had before in the asylum. It calmed her, and she raised her head to look directly at him.

He began speaking. His voice was neither low nor apologetic, but had the didactic tone which she associated with his pronouncements. 'Solipsistic Sofia. Within her world only Sofia exists, and those of us around her are actors in her play. Solipsistic Sofia. It flows off the tongue, don't you think?' He had remained standing and did not look at her once. As he spoke he began to prowl around the room, touching books, shifting papers around the desk. He slowly moved behind her but she would not turn. She would not give him the satisfaction. Her heart pounded. She felt his hand stroke her shoulder, then move her hair aside, leaning in to brush the nape of her neck with his lips. She flinched but did not move. Some animalistic instinct told her it would be safer for her this way.

'Neurasthenia, hysteria, delusions.' He walked around Rebecca until he stood before her. He paused and rocked on his heels, hands clasped behind his back. 'One could study the child Sofia for a lifetime and still not uncover all the layers to her illnesses. She is fascinating. Here I have a unique opportunity to conduct a study in madness. Yes. A unique specimen indeed. In and amongst all of these fascinating traits, she is still a child and, with that, has a capacity to grow and develop, Rebecca. A child of thirteen years and possessing of more than rudimentary intelligence. Yes. Very intelligent. Precocious one might say. It is a shame that her intelligence is focused around manipulating others. She utilises her sexuality for attention and gain, to draw all of us into her orbit.' He bent forward until his face was only inches from Rebecca's. 'You see, my dear. I know about your encounter with Sofia. Not only did she confess all to me, but I have seen your scribblings. All of them. The games which you tried to play with me by rehearsing your speeches. I saw through them all. Above all, you are sick,

Rebecca. Sick like Sofia. Kraft-Ebbing summarises your cerebral neurosis perfectly. Your sexual deviance is an illness and one which we have not even *begun* to uncover.' He reached out to stroke her cheek. 'You are going nowhere.'

Rebecca's body reacted to his caress as if she had been touched with fire. She sprang to her feet, knocking the chair on which she sat to the ground. She stood face to face with him, shaking with fury. 'You bastard. You manipulating, evil bastard.' He responded with the faintest of smiles and one word. 'Nowhere.'

Rebecca ran. It was all she could do to stop herself from screaming out loud. Screaming in anger, screaming in frustration, screaming in pain. She held in the sound and balled it up inside her to drive her away from this place. Blindly she ran from the room and crashed into Stefan. He reached out and caught her by the arm. 'How can you work for such a man? How could you stay here?' Stefan opened his mouth to speak but it was the harsh voice of Professor Farkas that Rebecca heard next, summoning his assistant into the consulting room. Stefan's body sagged visibly at the sound. Rebecca pulled her arm free of his grip. 'Go. Your master's voice demands your obedience.' For one moment, their eyes locked – his pleading, hers burning. Slowly Stefan backed away from her, disappearing quietly into the consulting room and closing the door silently behind him.

Rebecca's heart was pounding violently. She could hear its thudding in her ears, feel the taste of blood in her mouth and the combination threatened to overcome her. She knew that at any moment now she would faint. Her knees began to buckle beneath her, and before she could allow herself the grateful release of oblivion, Sofia's voice broke into her consciousness. She felt herself being gently guided back up the stairs and towards her room.

Some hours must have passed before Rebecca woke on her bed. Her first thought was that she had experienced a vivid nightmare, but opening her eyes and seeing Sofia seated silently by her bed, Rebecca quickly realised it had all been real. 'How are you feeling now?' Sofia whispered. Rebecca pulled herself upright and sat on the edge of the bed. 'I have not the faintest idea.' Despite the events of the day, Rebecca's first emotion was that of gratitude towards Sofia for taking care of her. 'There are no clear-cut lines any more,' she mused, and allowed Sofia to stroke a strand of sleep-dampened hair from her face. 'Do you feel strong enough to come with me now? I have something I want you to see. I ran away because I saw Zoltan. I didn't want him to know where I was taking you.' More secrets. More confusion, Rebecca thought. She sighed and nodded her agreement. Wordlessly, Sofia led her from her bedroom and down the stairs. On each landing, Sofia stopped and checked around her. It seemed as if the house was empty. Arriving on the ground floor, Rebecca thought that they were leaving the house, but Sofia turned once more towards the back of the house, and the invisible door.

Even though the stairwell was lit, the walk down the steps to the basement workshop was gloomier than the first time she had descended into the depths of the house. Passing by the first level of the kitchen, Rebecca could smell food and her body responded with nausea rather than hunger. She swallowed her disgust and continued to follow the figure of Sofia as she passed down into the level of Zoltan's workshop. Without the burning stove, it was icy cold down here. Her fear accelerated her breath and she watched as the cold air appeared in clouds before her mouth. Sofia passed through the workshop and into the room with its covered automata. Rebecca could not help it now, the shudders which had started as a response to the cold had now penetrated her mind. She was shaking uncontrollably, and, as she walked through the pathway between the lumpy automata covered in their shrouds, fear started to grip her. Sofia had not turned once, and continued to walk silently towards the last automaton, the one which Zoltan had not uncovered. Finally reaching her destination, Sofia turned and stood by the covered mound. Fixing her eyes on Rebecca, Sofia pulled the cover away.

The uncovered rectangle was a crude mechanism of cogs and wheels encased in a bare cage of metal. Staring out from the edge was a life-size head. A woman's head. Her head. It was crude but obviously meant to look like Rebecca. The hair was dressed the same as hers, the shape of the ears like hers, a mole high on her cheek like hers, the hairline high and distinctive, like hers. Each of the separate elements was fashioned to resemble her. All those hours in the consulting room had given Zoltan time to observe and study her in detail. It was, however, not the face which appalled her most, but the realisation that around the throat of this abomination was her mother's locket.

CHAPTER 57

CALMLY, FAR MORE calmly than she could have believed, Rebecca unhooked the chain from which the locket hung around the neck of the automaton and placed it in her pocket. Sofia watched her in silence. 'You see now, don't you? I was not enough for him. He had to have you as well.' She reached down to a switch at the base of the creation and turned to watch the wheels as they grated slowly into life. The sound was loud and utterly inhuman. Rebecca could not take her eyes away from the dreadful face trapped in its cage. The eyes blinked, and the mouth slowly opened, then closed, then opened again. The lips drew themselves together and the eyes closed as the horror blew sightless kisses again and again. It took less than a second for Rebecca to realise the purpose of this motion. Positioned perfectly at groin height, the head could be made to suck endlessly. Efficiently. Dispassionately. A machine to satisfy the lust of a man. She watched as the mechanism speeded up, before finally ending with the head slack mouthed and eyes partially closed. A parody of satisfaction.

Rebecca took the anger inside her. She might need it later, but not now. Right now, all she needed to do was get out of this loathsome house. As she turned to leave, Sofia caught her arm. 'Please. You must take me with you. Please!' In that moment, she threw herself into Rebecca's arms and Rebecca could now feel her altered form. Sofia was pregnant. That explained the listlessness, the morning sickness, the mood swings. He had made this child pregnant. 'He wants to send me away. I know this. I have been listening. He will send me away and force me to give up my child, just as he forced my mother.' Rebecca had no more time for Sofia's ever more convoluted and changing stories, but the shape of her friend's tiny body deformed by the child she was carrying was no delusion. 'Please don't leave me here. I cannot bear it any longer. I want to go home, home to the convent. They will help me.' Sofia fell to her knees before Rebecca and pulled at her gown. 'If you leave me I will die here, I just know it.'

More roughly than she meant to, Rebecca hauled Sofia to her feet. 'Go. Pack a bag. I will meet you in the park across the street in thirty minutes. If you are not there then I will leave without you.'

The heralding of the quarter-hour on the church chimes announced that Sofia had run out of time. Rebecca picked up her carpet bag, and, pulling Miriam's shawl around her shoulders, began to walk to the end of the street, towards the main road where the closest carriage stand could be found. Turning around once more before she disappeared from the street, she saw Sofia running down the steps of the house. Her hair hung loose and wild around her reddened features and she dragged the same travelling bag which Rebecca had seen before at the Mayr. Her anxious wait in the park had convinced her that taking Sofia along was not a good idea, but in truth, Rebecca could think of no other way of getting out of the house without detection. She was sure that if she had said no to Sofia, then she was more than capable of raising the alarm and ensuring that Rebecca could not make her escape. Now safely in the carriage, Sofia dragged on Rebecca's elbow until her arm was around Sofia's shoulders. She then rested her head on Rebecca's breast and sighed contentedly. Sofia seemed tiny now, and Rebecca was angry at being forced into the role of protector. Forced? In truth, no-one had forced her, but Rebecca couldn't help feeling that she was still being manipulated. She stared down at the top of Sofia's head. Not, perhaps, by this poor, disturbed creature but by the 'good Professor Farkas'. She stroked Sofia's hair absently. Taking a deep breath and eager to put as much space between her and the house in Baross Utca, she used her sparse knowledge of Hungarian to urge the coachman to more speed, all the while praying that the daily ferry had not yet left the quayside.

They were in luck, arriving just as the shipboard bells had begun to sound the imminent departure. It warned all those on board who did not wish to make the journey to now return to the shore. Rebecca and Sofia fought their way along the gangway as the tide of well-wishers poured off the ship, almost pushing them back to shore. Forcing their way finally onto the deck, they made their way to the purser's office. All Rebecca wanted to do now was find a cabin and sleep before the memories of the day overwhelmed her. Behind her, ropes keeping the ferry still were being thrown from the shore and the ferry began to drift away from the dock, as two figures raced up the now empty gangway before being finally lifted onto the deck. It would seem she was not the only one who was determined not to miss this particular ferry. As the sailors sprung into activity and the gangplank was withdrawn, one old hand looked back towards the quayside. A cloaked figure stared out towards the ferry, motionless in the swell of people surrounding him. The sailor spat noisily into the river and crossed himself, closing his eyes for a moment in silent prayer. When he opened them again the figure had disappeared. He wasn't afraid of the figure, not he, but no mariner wishes to see Death's messenger at the start of a voyage.

Safely installed in a cabin, Rebecca stood with her back to the porthole and watched Sofia sleep. Now she knew that Sofia was a child, her caprices and tantrums made sense. What she didn't know was what would happen to her next. Could she return her to the convent in Vienna? One thing for certain was that Rebecca could not, and would not, take her back to Paris. That much she knew. Sofia's problems, and how she would manage to disentangle herself from them, was not what Rebecca wanted to be thinking about. Even though she tried not to, the revolting thought that Zoltan Farkas had created a sex automaton with her features, kept rearing its head in her mind, and she needed to deal with it, or at least to shelve it somewhere so she could maintain a clear head. Head. Oh, that disgusting head! Rebecca found herself swallowing down the bile which was rising in her throat, and the motion of the boat wasn't helping one bit. She needed some air.

Closing the door quietly behind her, Rebecca made her way up and onto the top deck. Evening was drawing in, and the landscape was bathed in a rosy glow. Budapest had long since disappeared around a bend of the Danube, and Rebecca drew in deep breaths, allowing her eyes to defocus and enjoy the play of the colourful light as it touched the ripples of water. She leaned over the railing, then, gripping the handrail, she allowed the weight of her body to hang off her arms. Standing straight now, she stretched her arms out above her head. She yawned widely. It felt good to move. Her entire body felt constricted as if it had been held in stasis for weeks. She permitted herself to feel the tiredness that had threatened to overcome her for days now, and knew that she should make her way back to the cabin, but she hung onto this moment of solitude. Once again she appreciated the joy of being alone. Unbidden, Stefan's face came into her mind, and she shook her head as if to shake her feelings free from their moorings. It was better to be alone, she mused, than to be with someone who did not understand you. Much better. Samuel's voice came to her, and a momentary vision appeared of the two of them arm in arm as they walked back from their drunken revel in Paris. She felt as if she had lived a lifetime since then. One thing was for sure, she would not be going back to Ramsgate any time soon, if at all. With Miriam's inheritance, she would be free to study and to live her life as she wished. Samuel would be part of that future, she knew. Rebecca smiled to herself. Perhaps she wasn't completely alone after all.

She turned away from the setting sun to head back to her cabin and any thoughts of sleep were obliterated by the sight which greeted her. She must be dreaming. A man and woman, neat and small, were advancing towards her smiling shyly but ever more broadly. For one fleeting moment Rebecca remembered the story of the Doppelgänger, as before her were two faces which she knew very well, but they were not the same. Not the same at all. At all. Gently the woman disengaged herself from the arm of the man and walked directly to Rebecca. 'Good evening, Miss Rebecca. Perhaps we should sit down somewhere. We have much to discuss.'

Without doubt Rebecca was exceptionally grateful that Aisha had spoken to her, and in doing so, reassured her of who they were, because after all that had happened to Rebecca during the last few days, she would probably have acted on her inclination to jump into the Danube on seeing them. As she quickly explained to them, the vision of Aisha and Karim so far away from London and dressed as they were would probably have been one shock too many for her sanity. Karim found them a quiet spot in the café below deck, and with the silent efficiency which she remembered so well, organised soup and coffee for them all. He insisted that they all should eat before talking, and Rebecca's hunger asserted itself as a large bowl of goulash was placed before her. She ate without speaking, but couldn't help staring at her companions. Their clothes were completely western, and well-tailored. Both wore wedding rings. Karim had a silver chain across his waistcoat which was no doubt attached to a watch. They both looked the image of a respectable English middle-class couple. True, their skins were darker than most, but curiously not as dark as Rebecca had remembered. She stared at them unselfconsciously, as if she was seeing them for the first time, which in a sense she was. They had been so much a part of the background in the house in Gower Street that she had no more registered their presence than she had registered the furniture. They had become part of the backdrop to her life in that house. True, Rebecca was required to amend her initial opinions of them when she had discovered that they had been shadowing her through the streets of London, but any further curiosity about them or their origins had dissipated when her own problems had taken hold of her psyche.

A calm, quiet voice brought her thoughts back to the present. 'First of all, Miss Rebecca, our names are no longer Karim and

Aisha, but Joseph and Ida. Joseph and Ida Reith.' Rebecca stared openly now as Aisha/Ida reached out to Karim/Joseph and clasped his hand, lovingly. 'Reith is the name we took in honour of your blessed Aunt Miriam and, yes, we are married, Miss Rebecca.' Rebecca looked over the heads of her companions to catch the eye of a passing waiter. 'Wine. Please? Three glasses.'

CHAPTER 58

ONE HOUR AND two carafes of wine later, Rebecca was in possession of the facts about her companions, or at least new facts. The Reiths had taken it in turns to narrate their story, beginning with how Miriam had returned to London from a trip abroad with them both. When anyone had enquired about the origins of the pair she had said 'Most people content themselves with bringing back a carpet from their travels. I brought back those two.' *Bought* rather than brought, it transpired. Miriam had bought the children from their parents rather than see them starved and prostituted on the streets. Nor were they Indian, as Miriam had elected to pretend, but they were Roma – and proud of it. Nor, it seemed, were they siblings, but Miriam decided it was simpler to introduce them to London as such. All her actions had been to ensure that they were safe, well nourished, well educated, and had learnt their roles as 'Indian servants' well. In return they had remained utterly loyal to her even beyond her death. Joseph (it would take a while before Rebecca got used to calling him that, if ever) told Rebecca about Miriam's gift to them and proudly handed over their business card. 'Reith Investigative Services'. Rebecca laughed now, and after a few moments Joseph and Ida joined in. All tension had gone from the strange trio.

'All of which is, obviously, fascinating. But it does beg the question – what are you doing *here*? It cannot be a coincidence that you appear on the same boat as me, so please, tell me what is going on.' The Reiths both fidgeted nervously in their seats, each movement the mirror of the other. Ida nodded to her husband, encouraging him to speak first. 'When your Aunt Miriam first realised that she was ill,' Joseph began, 'she freed us from our bonds to her, and set us up in business.' Rebecca felt a spark of anger rise within her that other people had known that Miriam was ill and she herself had not. 'You have already told me about your business,' she interjected irritated. 'So?' Joseph looked awkwardly at his wife for encouragement, but instead she took up the narrative. 'So, Miss Rebecca, Miriam knew that you were still in danger, especially if – sorry miss – when, you recovered your senses.' Rebecca was paying full attention now, despite the effects of the wine. 'Miriam knew you would be in danger from those who had harmed you and would not want you to recall what had happened. They did not want your sanity jeopardising a continuation of their activities.' Rebecca felt her gorge rise in disgust at the thought that another girl might be placed into the same situation that she had been but with no hope of rescue. It had not even occurred to her. She had been so wrapped up in the horror of her own experience that she had elected to obliterate the wider picture. It was true, if there *was* any way of putting a stop to those vile people she would try. But try what? Who would believe her anyway? Especially once she had been incarcerated in the asylum.

Noisy and demanding thoughts were rushing into her head and crowding everything else out. She felt a hand reach for hers, and a gentle voice call her name. To respond was a struggle, but she marshalled her thoughts once more so she could pay attention. The Reiths waited silently and watched as the myriad emotions flowed over her features. Eventually she felt able to motion them to carry on. It was Joseph who spoke next. 'It was Colonel Burbridge who came up with the plan initially. In fact, it was he who alerted Miriam to the danger.' Lord Hawsley had been trying to use his Freemason network to uncover information about Rebecca. Obviously, he was getting nowhere with his immediate circle, as the Colonel himself soon received an unexpected invitation to Hawsley's lodge. The conversation therein left him in no doubt that Hawsley was determined to uncover Rebecca's whereabouts and that he believed that the Colonel would tell him where she was hiding, Brother to Brother Mason. As it turned out, Miriam had deliberately (and with the Colonel's acquiescence) *not* told him where Rebecca was being hidden. Miriam was no fool, and although she knew that the Colonel loved her, it would be hard for him to betray the vows he had made to Freemasonry if he was placed in the situation of having to lie. Miriam simply did not want to put him in that position. A truly remarkable woman, your aunt. More intelligent than she was ever given credit for, in my opinion.'

Hearing this pronouncement from Joseph made her smile. It was not just their clothes which had changed, but their demeanour and their language. Their opinions were wonderfully in keeping with the respectability of their dress. Rebecca was reminded of the chameleons in Samuel's book of nature which she had studied with such delight back in Ramsgate. 'We are all chameleons,' she mused. 'We mould the beliefs of others by our actions and therefore appear as they expect.' She couldn't help thinking of Professor Farkas and her performance of submission. Had he been fooled? Probably.

Fooled, certainly, but more by his own vanity than her acting.

It was Rebecca's turn to ask questions, and ask she did. Nothing that the Reiths had told her had yet explained why they were here. 'Colonel Burbridge realised that Lord Hawsley would not stop until he had found you, or at least found some way of tracing you. That is where we came into the plan.' Joseph patted his wife's hand and took over the narrative once more. 'It was quite simple. His Lordship needed someone to look for you, so all we needed to do was to ensure that Mr Isaac came into possession of our business card, and we left the rest to him.'

'Joseph disguised himself…' his wife interrupted proudly, 'and sneaked our business card into Mr Isaac's pocket while he was with the Chinaman.' Rebecca had no idea what she was talking about, but gestured to Ida to continue with the recitation. 'Once the effects of the drugs had abated, he took his "discovery" directly to his Lordship at his London club. By that very afternoon we had been engaged to find you. He didn't come himself, obviously. Mr Osborne did that. He explained that he was concerned for the fiancée of his employee, Mr Isaac, and was trying to find you for purely altruistic reasons.' Rebecca found herself weighing every word from the lips of these people whom she thought she knew. Were they the enemy now? The Reiths looked at one another in concern, before Joseph spoke again. 'Miss Rebecca, you must listen to me. The Colonel reasoned that Lord Hawsley would employ someone to hunt for you eventually, and it made sense for it to be us. That way we would prevent him from commissioning anyone else, and we would be best placed to ensure your safety. We made an oath to your Aunt Miriam that we would keep you safe, and this we are doing. Her death has made no difference to our promise.'

Joseph ordered fresh coffee from the waiter and placed it neatly in front of Rebecca. She could not speak, and watched the coffee go cold as she tried to make sense of what the Reiths had told her. If they were the enemy, then they could already have given her location away. Obviously, they could not abduct her from Professor Farkas, so what if someone was waiting for her when the boat next moored? As if reading her mind, Ida spoke. 'If you don't believe us, ask Mr Samuel.' Until that point Rebecca was only half aware of their words, then she registered Samuel's name, or at least that's what she thought she heard. 'Sorry, Kar... Joseph, you did say Samuel?'

'Yes, Miss Rebecca. We went to see Mr Samuel in Paris. To ensure your safety we needed reinforcements, and we know that you would trust him.' Rebecca resisted the inclination to laugh hysterically. There was too much to process here. She felt emotionally drained, her mind was muddied with alcohol and coffee, and now her body was finally succumbing to the exhaustion which had been waiting on the edges of her consciousness for days. The sun was sluggishly making its way over the horizon to herald the arrival of a new day. 'Sleep,' Rebecca muttered. 'I must sleep. I cannot think.'

Leaving her companions seated silently in the salon, she headed back to her cabin where Sofia was sleeping soundly. Rebecca gently edged herself onto the bed so as not to disturb her, and lay down fully dressed next to her. Sofia rolled over and threw her arm heavily around Rebecca's shoulders. Wearied as she was, Rebecca could not sleep like this. She felt both trapped and out of control. She needed to get away.

Remarkably, she managed to do just that. Her ability to float out of her body had returned to her just when she needed it most. She lay in the cabin still as a statue, while her mind extracted itself and took flight. She flew away to Paris and into the past where she had felt safe and secure with Samuel. Had he finished decorating our apartment? She flew further away and back in time to her sojourn with the Waltons. Was their child – Suzanne – already walking? she mused. She flew even further back, to London and her friends. Did they still think of her? From her bird-like vantage point she circled around these memories and all the while she grew stronger. She had friends. Miriam's money would give her freedom. All she needed now was a plan. As she returned her consciousness back to the cabin, Rebecca registered Sofia's weight wrapped around her. Step one of the plan had to be to get Sofia safely back to Vienna and the convent. She looked down at her now numb hand and resisted the desire to raise it to her mouth and start chewing on her nails as she always had done when anxious. 'No. Not any more. I am taking charge now.' With this thought foremost in her mind she extracted herself from Sofia's embrace and pulled her journal from her carpet bag. 'A plan. That's what I need now. A plan.' With her pen poised over a blank sheet of paper she waited patiently for the words to come, then, slowly, she started to write.

Joseph Reith was to be found sipping coffee and watching the river, seated at the same table in the salon where Rebecca had left him and his wife the evening before. It was obvious from his clothing that he had not been there all night, but she could not help momentarily comparing his apparent stasis to the automata in that basement room in Baross Utca. She tried to shake off this image, but not before Joseph had registered the concern on Rebecca's face. He put down his cup carefully and rose courteously to greet her. 'Good morning, Miss Rebecca. Can I order you some breakfast?' As she was about to decline, he called over the waiter – keeping his eyes on him weaving through the crowded tables. He continued to speak. 'I suggest you eat, miss, even if you are not hungry right now. In circumstances like this it is always better to eat when you can. We have no way of knowing when we will get the next opportunity.' When the food arrived, Joseph turned back to the river and sat in silence as she ate. Rebecca was grateful for this as it allowed her to marshal her thoughts before speaking. She hadn't realised how hungry she was, and was grateful for Joseph's quiet thoughtfulness. She watched his profile as she ate. She mused silently. 'He is quite a handsome young man. I had never noticed before. Truth be told,' she continued to herself, 'I don't think I really looked properly.' Suddenly, ashamed of herself for this, she leaned over to Joseph and touched his sleeve. 'Joseph.' He turned and looked calmly into her eyes. 'I am grateful to you both. Truly. I am. Not only for what you have done now, but for what you did before…' She faltered as a fleeting vision came to her of the moment the ceiling of the Egyptian House shattered onto the occupants of the ritual room. She paused. 'I need to take charge now. I want to take charge. It is my life and my destiny and whatever happens now, I want it to be though my actions.' Joseph remained silent and watched as she drew the journal from her pocket. Rebecca read from her notes, while Joseph listened patiently.

CHAPTER 59

WHILE JOSEPH AND Rebecca thrashed out the best route to deliver Sofia to Vienna, and then for Rebecca herself to reach Paris safely, Ida was helping Sofia to dress and had taken food to her in the cabin. It occurred to Rebecca later that day, that the lack of curiosity with which Sofia greeted the arrival of the Reiths should have troubled her, but she had more pressing concerns on her mind. She couldn't allow Sofia's moods to cloud her judgement right now. As soon as Sofia had eaten, she fell back to sleep, allowing Ida to join Rebecca and Joseph in their council of war. 'What you need to understand, Miss Rebecca,' said Ida, quietly, 'is that we must report any change in your location or circumstances to Lord Hawsley. This we do by telegram, and if we fail to do so we risk losing his trust and having him employ someone else to follow you. Someone who would be considerably less scrupulous in their actions.' Ida shifted uncomfortably in her chair. 'His Lordship wants you back on British soil. He doesn't like loose ends and wants this one to – how can I put it – disappear.' Rebecca was deeply unhappy at this, but she saw the sense in their words. She didn't need the repercussions spelled out to her. If she was back in England, Hawsley would do everything in his power to see that she was returned to the asylum – or worse. 'We need to continue to report your whereabouts, that is certain, but we can buy some time. We can delay for around 24 hours, and a day should be enough for you to make substantial headway on your route to Dr Charcot.' Back to Paris and a certificate of sanity, Rebecca continued silently, and my freedom. With that I can claim Miriam's inheritance, and his Lordship and his cronies can go to hell. Rebecca and the Reiths' conversation continued until all possible options had been mapped out.

Some hours later, and after a surprisingly refreshing sleep, Rebecca felt the need for fresh air. The ferry was slowing down for the first stop on its journey towards Vienna. Feeling invigorated, she went on deck and leaned heavily on the railing, allowing the breeze to ruffle her hair. Her mind was clear, and whatever happened now, she felt more in control. That was until she saw the figure on the quayside. It was Stefan.

Reeking of the horse which he had ridden through the night to reach the landing-stage, Stefan came aboard and stood before Rebecca. 'You *must* leave this ship now. You *must* come with me. Please. No time to explain.' His distress moved Rebecca but her immediate reaction was to pull away from him. 'You don't understand.' Stefan was now growing frantic. 'The police are following you. Professor Farkas told them that you have abducted his vulnerable ward and that you are dangerous. We don't have time to argue.' The Reiths arrival on deck, and Stefan's repetition of his plea, prompted Joseph to dash ashore. 'Pack now. Be ready to leave when I return.' Galvanised into action, the three women grabbed their travelling bags and waited anxiously by the gangplank for Joseph to return. Fifteen anxious minutes had passed, and the ferry was making its final preparations to depart before Joseph reappeared on the quayside. Urgently, he motioned them ashore, turning as he did to disappear into the crowd. Stefan went first, pushing his way through the mass of people, with Rebecca hidden behind him dragging Sofia who clutched her hand. Ida followed close behind, and the five were soon absorbed by the crowd.

'You stink, Stefan. You do! Really, really horrid!' Sofia seemed to find it amusing that the smell seeping out of Stefan's pores now pervaded the cramped carriage in which the five fugitives sped north and away from the landing-stage. To be fair it was a strong odour, but a bad smell was so far down the list of Rebecca's concerns that she couldn't help laughing out loud. Stefan had the grace to look sheepish and accept Sofia's teasing. By silent consensus, the group did not speak of events until Sofia had once again fallen asleep. Rebecca marvelled at Sofia's capacity for rest. It seemed to her like Sofia's protective mechanism, and a successful one at that. This girl seemed happy to allow others to make her decisions for her, and her compliance, although useful right now, told a darker story of the events which had conditioned her into such passivity. Rebecca pulled her thoughts away from these musings as Stefan recounted what had unfolded in Baross Utca once Rebecca and Sofia's flight from the house had been discovered.

Rebecca was appalled by what he told them, but by now no longer surprised at the lengths to which people would go to protect themselves. It transpired that when Zoltan had realised that both women had left, the Alienist went into his consulting room, closed the door, and systematically destroyed its contents. 'It looked like a hurricane had swept through. There were books torn apart and thrown all over the floor. The table was turned over and the chaise had been ripped open with a knife,' Stefan said, swallowing nervously and looking over at Rebecca. 'I have never seen such rage.'

The sound of destruction brought Stefan and the servants to the hallway, where they waited anxiously for the tempest to subside. When all eventually fell silent, Stefan knocked on the door. In that moment, all the servants disappeared, leaving him alone in the hallway. (From the look on Stefan's face as he continued, it was not without fear that he had entered the room.) Zoltan was standing in the middle of this carnage coolly smoking a cigarette. He spoke calmly. 'Ah, Stefan, there you are. Be a good man and summon the police.' Zoltan looked around him as if seeing the chaos for the first time. 'Look what the madwoman, Miss Rebecca, has done to my beautiful room. Not only that but she has abducted my ward, Sofia. She must be stopped. It is vital that she is restrained in a secure asylum before she does any more harm.'

Stefan watched Rebecca's reaction as he continued, but her face was by now a mask. Whatever Stefan told her now would only act as fuel to her determination to get away from Zoltan, and to ensure Sofia's safety.

Stefan had done as he was asked, and, once the police had left, had waited for his master to summon him once more. Rebecca could feel her anger rising at this, but her face remained impassive. Stefan's next words were carefully enunciated. 'I did it for you. I did it so that I would know what he was doing. That is why I am here. When you spoke to me in the hallway,' he paused and looked at Rebecca's face for her reaction but she gave none, 'I wanted to tell you, but there was too much to say.' Rebecca was confused. 'Tell me what?' 'I needed to be sure about Zoltan, about what was happening in that house, and, once I knew, I had to find proof.' Rebecca looked over at the pregnant Sofia. 'Your proof is sleeping there.'

'No,' he countered, 'Other things were happening in that house and I had to be sure.' He reached under his seat and, delving into his travelling bag, he pulled out a fabric pouch about the size of a book. 'Photographs. Proof of what sort of a man he is.' As Rebecca made to ease out the contents, Joseph gently stayed her hand. 'Allow me, miss. I don't think that you should see these.' Rebecca stretched her neck and breathed deeply. 'No, Joseph. I need to see.'

The images were pornographic, but more than that, they involved women who looked drugged. The poses were dehumanising, degrading and involved extreme subjugation. Zoltan's exposed form could be clearly seen in a few them. Some of the images were of Sofia, naked and staring blankly into the camera, and had obviously been taken over a period of years as she could not have been more than seven or eight in some. Others contained images of different women. Some were hooded, but others clearly showed their features. Stefan answered the question before Rebecca could ask. 'They were patients of his. I recognise at least three of them. I had my suspicions but no proof.' A hard tone entered his voice. 'I have no money, Rebecca. No rich friends or patrons and no other way of making my way in the world than the profession which I have chosen and believe to be a good one. When Professor Farkas accepted me as a student, it meant that I could study and would be able to support myself as I worked as his assistant. To discover that the man was little more than a loathsome abuser put me in a difficult position.'

'Difficult?' Rebecca's anger kicked in. 'Difficult? You would work for a man *knowing* what he was doing to women and children? Have you no morals?'

Sofia and the Reiths seemed to no longer exist as the conversation between Rebecca and Stefan grew in intensity. Stefan looked intensely into her eyes. 'Have you ever been hungry, Rebecca? I mean really, truly hungry? When you exist for a week on the delights of a roast onion and have no idea when you will eat again?' Rebecca could feel his words taking the heat out of her fury, but it was not cool enough for her to forgive him just yet. 'That didn't make it fine for you to stand by while he did these vile things.'

'Rebecca, please give me some credit. The moment I became aware of what was happening I did not stand by. I needed proof of his activities. The photographs. That was how I could ensure that he would be forced to stop his activities, and, furthermore, he would have to give me a good reference so I could go elsewhere and finish my studies.' The heat of Rebecca's anger now returned. 'So, not to mince words, that makes you nothing more than a grubby blackmailer.' With that she turned her face to the window and refused to speak another word for the rest of the journey.

It had grown cold in the carriage, and by the time the silent group stepped down from it, darkness, and with it large flakes of snow, had begun to fall. They had arrived at their destination, a tiny coaching-inn half embedded in the side of a mountain. Feeling stiff and numb from the many hours on bumpy roads, Rebecca stumbled from the carriage and felt her feet sink deeply into a snowdrift. The strong smell of pine which assailed her nostrils reminded her of happier times walking in the hills above the Mayr Clinic with Sofia. These memories were quickly shattered at the sight of her friend's hand over her pregnant form as she was lifted from the carriage by Stefan.

Rebecca would have been happy to fall straight into bed, but the growling from her stomach alerted her to hunger. She remembered what Joseph had said, 'Eat while you can,' and when the smell of chicken soup started to penetrate her nostrils, she found herself drawn – with the others – into the tiny dining room of the inn. The beams were blackened with age, and the couple who ran the inn had the same patina as the wood from hard work and proximity to fire. They were, however, perfectly kind and hospitable, treating Sofia as they would a child. Their assumption that Stefan was Rebecca's husband, and Sofia their daughter, made it easier for everyone to gloss over any questions which might otherwise have arisen. A strange conviviality fell over the group while they ate and drank that evening, as if they were nothing more than a party of tourists enjoying an off-the-beaten-track experience, rather than a group of fugitives from the law. Once the host and his wife had retired to the kitchen, Joseph began speaking. 'We do not have much time now. Tomorrow I must communicate with his Lordship and tell him that you left for Vienna on the ferry. It would not be too much of a stretch to say that you left the ferry at the landing-stage and we had not realised, so had to continue to the next stop before communicating our failure.' Rebecca pushed her plate of food away from her and, resting her elbows on the table, began to massage her forehead with her palms, finally pushing her fingers through her hair before sitting back in her chair and looking at her companions, one by one. She did not speak. To be truthful she was feeling utterly overwhelmed by, well, everything.

Stefan's voice penetrated her thoughts. 'Rebecca, I am sorry you have such a low opinion of me but I want you to know something.

I followed you simply to give you the photographs. I thought that once you show them to Dr Charcot, anything that Zoltan claims about you can be dismissed. You can ruin the "Good Professor Farkas" and make sure he never harms anyone again.' Rebecca thought about it. Yes. Stefan was right. 'But it will ruin your reputation too, wont it?' Stefan stood, pushing back his chair. 'Yes, it will. But it will be worth it to see that bastard finally fall.'

CHAPTER 60

REBECCA WAS DREAMING. She was back in Ramsgate and could hear voices in the distance and detect the tantalising odour of freshly baked bread. For one moment, she was back in her own bed where she had felt safe. Back when mother was still alive and the secret language of German was one they alone shared in the household. Rebecca sat up in bed and reoriented her thoughts to the present, then reached out for Sofia. The lumpy feather-bed was piled high alongside her and Rebecca patted it gently to find Sofia's form. She froze. Sofia was not there. She was not in the bed. She could see Sofia's clothes hanging neatly on the back of the chair where Rebecca had tidied them away, and her shoes were tucked under the bed next to Rebecca's own.

Suddenly wide awake and with her heart pounding, Rebecca began frantically to dress. Where could she be? Perhaps she had heeded a call of nature, but how had Sofia managed to climb around her while she was sleeping? Dressed now, she pulled open the door of the room and looked along the corridor for any signs of Sofia, any lights. There were none. Fingertips resting on the walls, she made her way along the corridor and then down the ladder-staircase into the dining room. As she reached the bottom she felt the draught from the half open door. Embers from the fire cast enough of a faint glow to make out the shape of the room and see that she was alone. She grabbed a heavy cloak from the rack by the door and seized the lantern from the table, lighting its stub of a candle from the guttering fire. It wouldn't last long but she didn't have time to start searching now. Sofia was somewhere out there and she had to find her. Rebecca could not fail her friend. She had no thought in her head other than getting her Sofia back to the warmth and safety of the building.

She stepped out through the doorway. The world outside was white and sealed, all sound dampened by the snowdrift. Large, sparse flakes were falling silently onto their sisters, making the landscape appear even more strange and alien. Rebecca drew the cloak tighter around her body and held the lantern close to her chest. A sudden memory of a visit to see Holman Hunt's painting 'The Light of the World' sprang into her head. This experience was no romantic rendition like the painting.

It was difficult to walk in the unyielding snow, and her fear of losing the light was increasing. This was hopeless. The sensible thing would be to turn back right now and wake the others. That was when she saw the footsteps. The imprint of a barefoot child almost obliterated by the falling snow. Rebecca turned and followed this trail of breadcrumbs as it led deeper into the forest, willing for respite from the falling snow for long enough to find Sofia still alive. Her vision began to blur from the whiteness around her. It was becoming harder to see. She staggered to a halt to try to get her bearings.

The snow was now falling hard and the wind had begun to howl. The sound of her breath seemed loud and jagged. She looked around her. The impressions of the footsteps had disappeared, obscured by the recently fallen snow. Rebecca could feel the darkness of the forest closing in around her, and sounds of wolves baying in the distance froze her momentarily to the spot. She could not stop now. If Sofia had fallen in the snow and the creatures found her... Rebecca's fear charged her body to action and galvanised her forward. She scanned the horizon for any sign of life, and it was then she saw the building, or at least an area of sky where the stars were obliterated. She began to run towards it and into ever deepening drifts of snow. Each step was exhausting now, and when she finally reached the doorway of the chapel she was grateful for its sanctuary. As she opened the door she felt herself sink to her knees and watched the last flicker of illumination as it left the lantern. In the guttering candlelight, she caught glimpse of a small damp footprint on the stone step, leading down the aisle of the chapel.

Blinking hard to try to shake the darkness from her eyes she called out. 'Sofia, please!' she shouted. 'You must come with me. It's too dangerous for you to be out here on your own.' She pushed hard on the chapel doors to close them, the wind forcing her into the calm of the nave. Her eyes semi-blinded and ears deafened from the onslaught of the blizzard, she half-stumbled through pools of light towards the painted crucifix ahead. She could see no sign of Sofia. Blurrily, she peered into the darkness of the right transept. Nothing. She turned to her left, where a vision met her eyes. Floating before her was a tall and beautiful female figure, illuminated and dressed so perfectly in white and blue, swaying gently, with tears in her eyes. She watched as this vision seemed to turn and look directly towards her, and open her mouth as if to speak, but Rebecca could hear nothing.

Senseless with exhaustion now, Rebecca wanted nothing more

than to reach out to this beautiful woman and ask her if she had seen Sofia, but most of all she wanted to embrace this exquisite vision, and fall into her arms and sleep. She would feel safe here. Taking a step forward, her eyes began to focus, and she saw that this was no woman, this was a statue, and that the illusion of movement came from the multitude of low, white candles around her feet. Rebecca felt her knees give way in exhaustion, and she knelt before the figure of the Virgin. She felt the tears welling up inside her, and the fatigue of the last few months began to wash over her like a wave. 'I'm tired. Tired of running. Tired of other people and their needs. Tired of games and strangeness. I just want to go home.' Despite her exhaustion, she found a smile begin to play around her lips. 'I'm sure that my family would be delighted to come and get me, kneeling as I am before an idolatrous statue in a Christian chapel! If they needed any proof that I had lost my wits, this would give them enough evidence to put me back into the asylum!' She began to push herself up from the cold stone floor, and, as she did so, an otherworldly scream seared through her brain.

Spinning her head around in the direction of the sound, she watched in horror as a cloaked figure flew out of the darkness from the depths of the darkened right transept. A cape billowing around her, Sofia launched herself towards Rebecca, spitting and screaming obscenities. Her face was contorted with rage. Rebecca fell back to the ground and she heard a crack, and felt the searing heat of pain shoot through her arm. Sofia had her hands around Rebecca's throat and was squeezing harder and harder. She saw the faces of the gargoyles on the ceiling above Sofia. They seemed to be watching the scene below, straining their necks and craning their bodies forward as if to get a better view of the violence. Rebecca caught sight of her mother's locket, her most precious possession, given as a lover's gift, once more around Sofia's neck. When she could stand the pain no more, she passed into unconsciousness, the locket still rocking back and forth in her mind's eye.

Some considerable time must have passed as she lay on the floor of the chapel. Her face felt numb and frozen, her body stiff. She listened intently before daring to look. There was a sound of rustling. Could it be a small animal, or the sound of the oil burners? Perhaps she was alone and Sofia had left her for dead? She half-opened her eyes to be greeted with total blackness and Sofia's scent very close to her. Dread overtaking her emotions, she pulled her head sharply away from the scent and the blackness fell away. She had been covered by Sofia's cloak. Taking in her surroundings, she realised that she had been moved from where she fell, and that she was lying on the altar, the crucifix towering above her.

Supine and helpless in the chapel, a fever of fear washed over her in waves. How long had she been here? No-one knew where she had gone. She would die here before she had got a chance to live. Hot, selfish tears began to burn in her eyes. A new rustling sound distracted her momentarily, but before she could focus on it, another sound broke through. A single, female voice chanting. The tune was unfamiliar but felt ancient and harsh. With this sound, every hair on Rebecca's body raised up in fear and protest. The discordance continued, a plainsong which needed more voices to create harmony. This was solo, and it was cold, rasping and inharmonious. Rebecca's fear escalated towards sheer terror and she realised that there was no longer any point in pretending she was still unconscious. The sound of this one-part disharmony grew louder, and the figure from which it emanated moved slowly and inexorably towards her. She tried to move now, only to find that she had been bound hand and foot with rope, and the searing pain of her arm threatened to return her to unconsciousness. She fell back onto the altar, and turned her head towards the sound of the voice.

Sofia was at the doorway of the chapel. Rebecca could see that she was barefoot, and had removed the cloak, leaving her wearing only her white under-shift. The distortion of her slender frame was visible now. The body of her unborn baby pushed the shift outwards and Sofia's breasts were now much larger and more prominent than she remembered them. The figure in white walked calmly down the nave, cupping a tiny candle in one hand, and holding a knife in the other. The glow from the flame lit her face from below and made her look even more vulnerable. She was a parody of a child bride.

Rebecca knew now for certain that Sofia was going to kill her.

She turned away from the apparition which was Sofia, and looked up towards the crucifix, her lips too dry for words or prayer, even if she had known what to say, even if she had any belief in a deity in any part of her being. She closed her eyes tightly, and as she did, she heard the rustling sound again. This time it seemed to be coming from above her. She stared into the blackness above, and saw the dark, calming eyes of Stefan looking back down at her from behind the lectern, his finger pressed firmly to his lips, pleading with her to remain silent.

CHAPTER 61

SUBSEQUENT EVENTS MOVED swiftly, although in Rebecca's eyes the scene played out in slow motion – a scene she would never be able to erase from her mind.

Sofia was moving ever closer towards Rebecca's prone body on the altar. She tried to call out to her, but her voice would not comply. Her eyes pleaded desperately as Sofia gently blew out the candle. 'Time for sleep, my darling. Time for sleep... Goodnight.' Directly over Rebecca now, she grasped the knife with both hands, and as she raised it, Stefan threw himself from the lectern over Rebecca's body, pushing Sofia back. Stumbling down the altar steps into the nave, Sofia began to shriek, a wretched, animal sound of pain emanating from somewhere deep inside her tiny body. Her face contorted in rage as Stefan advanced on her, and she backed away towards the figure of the Virgin. Still clutching the knife, she waved it in front of her in a wide arc. 'Keep away from me! You just want to take me back to Papa! I won't, I won't go.' Stefan backed away, stretching his hand out to Sofia. 'Please, Miss Sofia. You can trust me. I would not do anything to hurt you.'

'You lie! Everyone lies to me. Everyone who said they would

care for me and love me and protect me. They all lied to me, every one of them.' She sagged, the knife now loose in her hand. 'All except one. Virgin Mother never lied to me.' She turned towards the statue. 'Virgin Mother will always love me if I am good. The nuns told me. They promised.' Stefan tried to creep closer to Sofia as she spoke to the statue, but she sensed his movement and whirled around, her face suddenly a mask of calm. She spoke now with a different, altogether more adult voice. 'It's alright, Stefan. I will come with you, now. I just have one more thing I want to do here. Let me give a gift to Virgin Mother and then I will come home with you. To Papa.'

Rebecca watched powerless as Sofia raised her arms to her neck, and for a moment she thought that Sofia was trying to remove the locket. No sooner had she lifted them than she swiftly brought them all the way down, knife in both hands, and pushed the point hard into the base of her distended belly. She dragged the knife point upwards and blood began to pour from her body. She fell onto her knees. Stefan rushed towards her and Rebecca realised it was useless. Sofia's dying voice croaked out into the darkness. 'She gave her only son to save mankind. I give her my child... all I have... all I ever wanted...'

Rebecca tried to move but the pain searing through her shoulder held her to the altar. Unable to turn away from the scene of carnage, she tried to close her eyes to it, but could not. Rebecca watched helplessly as Stefan lowered Sofia's tiny form to the flagstones. He covered her with the cloak as the red seeped out of her body, a rivulet of blood channelled in a line towards the altar. Rebecca was beyond fear. Beyond agony. Beyond thought. Her eyes closed and she allowed the pain to wash over her and unconsciousness to once more carry her away.

It was the movement which woke her. That and the pain in her shoulder. Opening her eyes fully, she saw the redness of dawn curling around the horizon. Her body was ensconced deep in hay and covered over with sheepskin. There were gaps in the wooden sides to the cart through which she could see snow and occasional flashes of vegetation. With difficulty, she pushed herself up into a sitting position, only then realising that her arm had been roughly bandaged and strapped to her body. A hand reached down to her, touching her shoulder. 'Lie down, Miss Rebecca. Sleep if you can.' Incredibly, she did.

The group travelled on through the day, only pausing for food and a run into the woods for a call of nature. Ida and Joseph Reith, unrecognisable in rough cloaks, took turns at the reins or in sleeping. 'We must keep moving.' It was only when night had fallen that the end of the cart was dropped down and Joseph motioned her to descend. 'We will be safe here for the night.'

The 'here' he was referring to was an abandoned cottage, or at least that is how it seemed to Rebecca. 'These are the summer huts of the shepherds. They use them when their flocks are in the high pastures. In winter, they drive them south to the lower pastures.' Joseph helped her down from the cart. 'We are in luck. A few days earlier and the tenant would have been here.' Rebecca's curiosity got the better of her. 'How can you possibly know all that?' Joseph smiled. 'The roses have just been cut back, and there is fresh sheep dung behind the house.' Farkas had been right about one thing. Most people look but do not see. Ida and Joseph certainly saw, and if in the future she could find some way of repaying this extraordinary couple for their loyalty, she would make sure and do it.

The house was tiny, with a mezzanine bed in which the Reiths insisted Rebecca sleep. She lay down carefully, and for the briefest of moments allowed herself to think about last night. The search, the chapel, the death... but the pain in her body would not allow her the luxury of a respite from the horror which had happened. Rebecca's first clear thought was a selfish one. What would happen to her now? The authorities believed her to be an abductor, and an insane one at that. For Sofia to die in such a way would ensure Rebecca's return to the asylum, even if she could manage to prove that Sofia had done this terrible thing to herself. She was certain that Farkas would find a way of persuading people that Rebecca was to blame. Her fear for her own future was soon penetrated with feelings of grief for Sofia. The poor, damaged child. What chance did she have for a happy life? Her mother so broken and a family which rejected her because she was a bastard. Her life could have been so different – and all of this before Farkas got his claws into her. Rebecca's fear and grief were suddenly pushed aside by anger. It was as if a fire had suddenly been given oxygen and burst into life. She was *not* going to give in. No matter what happened now, she would get through this. Somehow. She just needed time to think. A wave of sleep caught her up and she dived into it gratefully. There would be time enough to think, but first she needed to rest.

The next morning, she awoke to the sound of wood crackling in the fireplace downstairs and the smell of cooking. Soon after, the neat form of Ida appeared at the top of the ladder next to her bed, holding a wooden bowl and a spoon. Rebecca looked over at her, seeking some echo of the woman who had been Aisha, but there was none, other than her startling eyes. Ida smiled. 'You must eat.' She held the bowl out towards Rebecca so she could smell its contents, and smiled. 'Chicken soup. A cure for everything. I know Miriam would not have approved of the contents but she would have sanctioned the sentiment.' Ida eased Rebecca up into a sitting position in the bed, and gently placed the bowl on her lap, guiding the spoon into her hands. 'Please. Eat now.' Ida watched Rebecca as she tentatively raised her arm. The pain in her shoulder was subsiding but she now noticed the cuts and grazes on her hands. Rebecca didn't want to look too closely anywhere else as, judging from unpleasant sensations which were trying to get her attention, she was probably black and blue in other parts of her body too. When Rebecca had finished, Ida spoke. 'I realise that you will want to know what is happening, and what is going to happen, but first you need to read this.' She removed the bowl and spoon from Rebecca's hands and replaced it with a letter. There was no envelope, and she did not recognise the writing. She looked up at Ida who tilted her head slightly in response to the unspoken question. 'Yes. I know its contents. I was there when Stefan wrote it.'

The letter was not long and had obviously been written in haste. Emotions carried the sloping letters forward and back and Rebecca sometimes found it difficult to read. 'Dear Rebecca,' it read, 'I write this to you in the brief time I have before you must leave. I know only one thing, and that is I will never forget this night. I want you to run. Leave here as soon as you can and never look back. I will return to Budapest. You were right. I was – I am – a coward. But perhaps you can see me in a different light in future. I will go to the police and report Sofia's death. Her suicide. I will tell them that I was following her on the orders of Professor Farkas and that when I found her she was already dead. I will tell them that no-one else was with her. She came to that place alone. I found her alone. Then, if they believe me, I will return to Baross Utca and tell Farkas about her tragic death. I will confront him with his despicable acts and force him to retract his statement about your abduction of Sofia. If he does not comply, then the disgusting photographs – which I have already sent to Dr Charcot in a sealed envelope – will be opened and Farkas will be exposed for the monster he is. His reputation will be ruined forever.'

Rebecca turned over the page. The letter stopped abruptly. There was no signature. She looked up at Ida. 'There was no time. I know he wanted to say more, but he had to leave. There is only one post-carriage a week in winter here, and if he was to catch it to make his way into the town, then he had no time.' Rebecca folded the letter carefully. Ida leaned forward and covered her hands with her own. 'Sofia's body will be found soon. We had to get as far away as possible before that happens, and can only pray that the hosts at the inn do not connect Sofia with their strange "English" tourists.' Ida stood and walked to the door, and pointed to a pile of rough sheepskin. 'Your new clothes, miss. You must dress. Now. I will help you.'

Half an hour later, a shepherd boy sat on a milking-stool before the fire, watching the remains of Rebecca's clothing burn. 'Only your hair now, miss.' Ida held a formidable pair of shears behind Rebecca's head – obviously intended for separating sheep from their wool – and sliced deftly through the loop of Rebecca's long black hair. She held it in front of her, before throwing it into the fire. 'Don't worry, miss. Your hair will grow again.' She continued to slice away at Rebecca's hair until she stood back, arms akimbo. 'It's not very good, I'm afraid, but to be honest, that's what makes it all the more convincing. Now for a few finishing touches.' Ida bent down and reached beneath the fire, where she brushed her fingers with the cold embers she found there. Rubbing them around Rebecca's ears and jawline, she finished with a final sweep of her face. 'Perfect. I am sure that even your own Aunt Miriam would not recognise you. Rebecca was grateful for the lack of a mirror, for, even though she did not consider herself to be vain, it was probably better if she didn't know what she looked like right now. Rebecca had, at least for the moment, disappeared from the face of the earth.

CHAPTER 62

THE ONE REMAINING object linking the grubby, dark-haired shepherd boy to Rebecca was her travelling bag, and to relinquish this, even to the care of the Reiths, took a lot of persuading. Finally, Rebecca gave in, but not before shedding tears at the thought of letting go of her treasured book. Samuel's gift. She knew that it made sense, but as she watched the horse and cart containing the Reiths disappear around the bend in the road, she realised that she was utterly alone. No-one could recognise her or find her, and although she knew that this was the objective, she was disturbed by the thought of being so completely exposed in an alien landscape.

The Reiths planned to head towards the nearest civilisation and eventually catch a train to Vienna, where they would report to Lord Hawsley that Rebecca had evaded them. It wasn't ideal, but it was the only plan they had for now, and with the more pressing complication of Sofia's death, it would have to suffice. Ida was the unhappiest of the two about leaving Rebecca on the roadside, but as Joseph pointed out, their continued presence with her was now a liability. He went on to remind his wife Rebecca was an intelligent girl – woman, Ida corrected him – and that she would have no problem making her own way down the mountainside towards the village of Saint Anton. They had left her with a few Austrian schillings in a pouch – reasoning that possession of any more would be suspicious – to survive on until they could make contact again and move her to a safe place.

Her walk down the hillside and through the meadows was pleasant enough. She kept the orange rooftops of the village below in her sights, and allowed herself to enjoy the freedom of walking alone, and in trousers. She couldn't – in all honesty – report that she preferred trousers to wearing a skirt, but crunching through the snow and then the damp vegetation, she could certainly see the advantage of this type of clothing. It was very unlikely that any time soon she would be cycling through London in (what felt like) her bloomers. Memories of happier times with Miriam gave her a moment's respite from the more immediate tragic recollection of Sofia's death. Rebecca doubted she would ever be able to look at candles again without it conjuring up visions of the horror in the chapel. She wondered if she would ever be able to forget. No. On reflection, she did not want to forget. She wanted to remember. She wanted to remember Sofia, but a Sofia made more gentle by a better life, a life where her madness had never manifested, or at least one in which she had been cared for and allowed to blossom. Rebecca was not angry at her friend, but at the circumstances which had led Sofia to kill herself in such an appalling way. Had she truly believed that she would die? Perhaps some part of Sofia's mind had honestly believed that she would survive and, somehow, hand her unborn child to the Virgin Mary and walk away, whole. One thing Rebecca was sure of now was her *own* sanity. Even in the darkest moments of her connection with the Angel, she had at no point done any harm to herself or to others. Her mind flew to Ramsgate Harbour and the urchin boy. 'No,' she mused. 'I no longer believe that I caused the boy's death. His death, if indeed he did die, was not a response to my actions.' By the time these thoughts had made their way through her mind she was already on the threshold of the village. She paused. This was going to be a challenge.

As it transpired, her impersonation of a shepherd turned out to be less problematic than she had believed. The whole village seemed to be full of them, or at least so it seemed to her. It was market day, and the village square was packed with people, produce and livestock. She allowed the crowds to carry her through the stalls, and she took in the eventful atmosphere gratefully. Some things do not change the world over, she thought to herself, as she heard snatches of conversation exchanged over a board heaving with vegetables. Gossip was being traded freely even as the price of produce was being debated. The sight of so much food reminded Rebecca that she needed to eat. 'Eat when you can, Miss Rebecca.' Joseph's voice echoed in her mind. This was one piece of advice with which she was happy to comply.

She followed her nose towards a tantalising smell, and found herself standing before a large, round pot, and an equally curved woman holding out a ladle in her hand towards passers-by. 'Süppe? Come, taste my beautiful vegetables!' A rough, male voice made a comment at which his companion sniggered, and was then rewarded by the woman with a swift bang on the back of the head with the ladle. She then looked across and extended the spoon towards Rebecca, but she shook her head, suddenly awkward. She looked up and, seeing a church before her, realised that there was something she needed to do first. She would light a candle. A candle for Sofia. She needed to do it for them both.

It was cool and light within the church. The pews were of pale blond wood, and her eye was drawn down the nave towards the central of three arches in which sat a plain, wooden cross illuminated on either side by simple windows. Slowly she walked down the aisle. She needed to lay the ghost of Sofia to rest. Although her heart was pounding, Rebecca knew that this was the right thing to do, and, after lighting the candle and counting out one of her precious coins into the offering plate, she made her way back to the pews. Rebecca sat down, silently. Unable to bring herself to pray, nor for that matter would she know to whom she would direct any of these devotions, she remained still and in the moment, thinking of Sofia and hoping that at last she had found some peace. Unaware of their existence, tears rolled unchecked down her cheeks.

When Rebecca eventually rose to leave, she realised with a start that she was no longer alone in the church. A tall, stooping man stood, framed and shadowed in the doorway, shepherd's crook in hand. Rebecca rubbed at the tears with the back of her sleeve and tried to walk past him, but he barred her way. 'I am looking for a boy to watch my sheep while I go back up to the high pasture. Is it you?' He spoke slowly, and his intonation was strange, but Rebecca could understand him well enough. She nodded her head, silently. He turned away, and she followed him.

The man, it seemed, had been observing Rebecca earlier on in the marketplace. Thinking that the young man's reluctance to partake of the soup had been the result of poverty, he had decided to follow him and, perhaps, offer him some work. Obviously, this man had no idea that Rebecca was, in truth, a 'her' not a 'him' at all. The disguise, complete with the terrible haircut, was working, it seemed. Rebecca soon discovered that when the shepherd, whose name was Jakob ('Just Jakob,' the man had whispered) had watched Rebecca hand over her precious coin in the church, he had decided there and then that he could trust this boy with his flock. Rebecca learned most of this from the soup-seller the next day, unbidden, accompanied by a large mug of soup and a tear of crusty, warm bread, all part of Jakob's payment for caring for his flock.

Rebecca soon began to look forward to her daily contact with Ana-Marija, the soup seller. It rapidly became the highlight of her days and a stimulating counterpoint to the bleating of sheep. Sheep, Rebecca decided, were utterly stupid creatures, and she would be very glad when she no longer needed to spend time in such close quarters with their noisy, uncoordinated bodies. Jakob had disappeared for the mountains that first day, leaving Rebecca (or Anton, as she had unimaginatively introduced herself) in charge of one of the countless temporary sheep-pens which had sprung up on the outskirts of the village. Rebecca was surprised that sheep needed protecting down here, but, as Jakob pointed out, 'It is two-legged wolves not the four-legged variety I need to worry about down here.' Rebecca nodded, silently, and counted the days (and the sheep) until his return.

Apart from sheep and soup, there was only one other occupation to punctuate her day. Each noon she headed for the steps of Saint Anton's church, where she waited patiently until the church-bells chimed the quarter hour. As the Reiths left her on the mountain track they had looked down the valley towards the shining onion-dome of Saint Anton's church. 'We will come for you. Be at the doors there every day at noon for one quarter hour and we will send word to you as soon as we possibly can.' So, she waited. A week went past, and Rebecca was now becoming accustomed to the gentle rhythm of the village. People left her alone, and she preferred it that way. If only she had a single volume for company she would have been quite content. As it was, the people around her became the characters in her story, and as each day passed she fleshed out their relationships and history. Even so, she was getting bored and, although she didn't want to admit it, worried.

What if the Reiths had been delayed, or something terrible had happened to them and no-one knew how to find her? Even with these dark suppositions Rebecca realised that she had options. She could take the few schillings which Jakob had promised her for tending his flock and make her way across the country and back to Paris. Or, if it was safe, she could go to the next town and send a telegram to Charcot. She had options. For now, she could do nothing except wait and dare to dream once more of life in Paris as a medical student. This desire had now burned its way into her mind. In each moment when fear threatened to overwhelm her, her imaginings of how life could be after rushed in to comfort. To anyone looking at her now they would see nothing more than one of the many scrawny shepherds around the village. There was nothing to distinguish her from the others, nothing of note – and that is just as she liked it.

It was Monday. Another monotonous day, only distinguishable from all the other days preceding it because it followed Sunday – the only day without the market. It was noon and she made her way up the steps of the church and watched a man she did not recognise pin a new notice to the board. He looked at her without curiosity as she wandered up to the board to look more closely. The new addition was a poster. With a sketch of her. In bold letters at the top were the words 'REWARD' and beneath it in a bold print, 'Wanted for child abduction'.

CHAPTER 63

REBECCA'S FIRST URGE was to tear down the notice, and stuff it deep into the pocket of her sheepskin jerkin before anyone else could see it. Of course she could do that, but the result would only be to draw attention to herself. Besides, she realised as she distractedly pushed her way back through the crowded marketplace, there were plenty more of them. Images of her face on posts, in the hands of people, trampled on the ground. Unthinking, she found herself at the stall of the soup-seller, who made note of her early arrival for lunch but, thankfully, seemed too busy with other customers to register Rebecca's distraction. She hid herself away at the back of the stall and crouched down on a wooden stool, heart pounding loud and painfully in her chest. She found herself on the edge of tears; her stoicism in the face of this new blow was being shattered by the turn of events. She could feel the weight of her solitude like a lamb on her shoulders, and her sense of who she was supposed to be, eroding. What if the Reiths did not come for her? What if someone recognised that she was the fugitive with a price on her head, and she was taken back to Hungary? So many questions threw themselves at the windows of her mind and she watched miserably as they pressed themselves onto the glass, muted and desperately clamouring for her attention.

Ana-Marija's rosy face suddenly appeared before her, steaming mug of soup in hand. She stared at Rebecca intently, and Rebecca was suddenly afraid. 'You are early, little one. Why don't you sit back here, out of the way? It's busy today and I need the space.' Rebecca mumbled her thanks and took the proffered soup. Ana-Marija pulled aside a curtain, dropping it in front of Rebecca, hiding her from view. Wordlessly, she ushered Rebecca into the tiny storage space. Seating herself on a lumpy sack of potatoes, Rebecca drank the warming soup gratefully, studying the shadow play of people walking past outside. Her heart was still pounding furiously, and, although nothing had been said, it was obvious that Ana-Marija had registered that Rebecca was not all she appeared to be. She would need to move fast now. She had to leave this place of safety, and with it, the prospect of keeping her rendezvous with the Reiths. Rebecca considered Ana-Marija's actions and faced facts. No matter how kind someone was to her right at this moment, all might change with the prospect of a reward.

Having drunk her soup, she felt better. Fortified. Realising it would be some while before she ate again, she guiltily pocketed a couple of carrots and pushed her way under the canvas behind her, making her way out from the back of the stall. She looked around. All about her seemed peaceful. Normal. That is until she saw a boy handing out more of those wretched flyers.

Rebecca made her way back to the sheep-pen where, only a few weeks earlier, she had hidden away the small pouch of money which Ida and Joseph had given her. Hopefully, it would be enough to get her passage on a cart or a ferry somewhere – anywhere – where she could then try to contact her friends. She considered her options.

Charcot would have a telephone, she was sure. He wasn't the ideal person to contact, especially if the story of her abduction of Sofia had found its way to Paris, but she could talk to him, tell him the truth – or at least some of it. She needed to find a way to get a message to Samuel. Yes. It was a plan. Not the best, but it was all she could come up with in the moment. The critical element was for her to get as far away from this village and its multitude of wanted-posters, to somewhere more crowded where she could hide herself more easily, and from where she could contact her friends.

Arriving at the sheep-pen, she pushed her way through the flock and reached her hand deep into the hay bale where she had hidden her money-pouch. It was still there. Relieved, she wrapped her hand around it. Its velvety texture gave her a sudden confidence. It was a reminder of who she truly was, and a reminder of the fact that she had friends. With the carrots in one pocket and the money-pouch in the other, she pulled her sheepskin hat snugly over her head, tucking away her ragged hair, and manoeuvred her way back through the sheep which had now gathered nosily around her. The sheep pushed their noses through the gate as, out of habit now, she checked the pen was securely closed.

At first, she couldn't work out what she was hearing, muffled as the sound was by her hat and mixed in with the usual hubbub of the market-traders calling out their wares. Then she registered it. Dogs. Lots of them. She saw them moving through the crowded square, driving space before them and straining hard on their leashes. She could pick out at least ten men and dogs, all with their backs to her and moving towards the church. Standing as she was by the sheep-pen, Rebecca was completely exposed. It was only a matter of time now. There was nowhere to hide, and nowhere to which she could run. Rooted to the spot she waited for the inevitable.

Looking back on the events of the hours which followed, Rebecca could still barely believe all that had happened. In the same moment when she registered the hunters, it seemed that the dogs had scented her and – in unison – they changed direction and headed back through the marketplace towards the spot where she was standing. Rebecca watched, almost impassively, as the hunters registered the change in their dog's moods and they themselves began to run. Behind her, the sheep started to bleat agitatedly, and, as Rebecca turned to calm them, the sound grew louder and louder, followed by a pounding in her head which threatened to overcome her. She pulled off her hat to release the sensation, and in that moment, understood that the pounding was coming from outside of her head, in fact outside of the sheep-pen, and outside of the village. She looked towards the mountainside where she herself, only a few weeks before, had walked away from her friends. The mountain pass was now white, and looked like it was moving. She shaded her eyes from the glare of the sun to see the sight more clearly, and registered that it was not an avalanche, but a mass movement of sheep coming down from the high pasture. Hundreds upon hundreds of swiftly moving animals were now on their way down the mountain. As she watched, the leaders arrived in the village and poured into every street, alleyway, and even into houses. The cascade seemed unending, and she watched as the mass moved into the marketplace, demolishing stalls and trampling the unwary.

The reaction of the dogs was startling. At first, they stopped their pull towards Rebecca and then, tails down, tried to hide. Their handlers pulled viciously at their chains, seemingly unaware of the wave of sheep which was about to hit them, and hit them it did, and hard. As did Ana-Marija. Even in the terrible situation she found herself in, Rebecca could not help laughing as she watched her friend land a substantial blow with a skillet on the head of one of the hunters. The scene was increasingly difficult to take in and she watched as hunter after hunter disappeared into the mass of walking wool. She marvelled at the destructive power of these docile creatures when gathered en masse.

With the sound of the frantic bleating of sheep still ringing in her ears, Rebecca's eyes were suddenly drawn to the edge of the marketplace. Two men on horseback were riding hard, and straight towards her. Her body sagged. There was to be no reprieve. She would be taken back to Hungary and condemned to an asylum, or prison. In that moment, she found herself praying for the Angel to be real and for him to come for her. Life would not be worth living now. Her chance for freedom was to be snatched away, never to return.

The horsemen stopped just short of the sheep-pen. Their mounts were frothy with exertion, and, as the first rider leaned down towards her, she did not move. He reached out his hand. 'Can you mount on your own, or do I have to come down there and get you?' Rebecca stared at this man. She had no idea who he was. 'It's me, Rebecca. We don't have much time. It's me, Cornelius.' Rebecca blurted out the first thing which came into her mind. 'You look younger without your beard!' The laughter which erupted from the second rider made her look up at his face properly. It was a beaming Samuel, trying desperately to hold his frantic horse still. 'Quickly! Open all the pens. Let the sheep loose! The more mayhem, the better!'

Clutching tight onto the waist of Cornelius, Rebecca rode away from Saint Anton. Rebecca's first thought as she looked back on the scene of chaos was one of regret that she hadn't been able to keep her promise to Jakob. He would have to hunt the hills for his sheep now. Taking one last look at the village, she turned her face towards the future, and home.

CHAPTER 64

THE JOURNEY BACK to Paris was, thankfully, without further incident. As soon as the sun had set on that first day, the shepherd boy ceased to exist, his clothes burned on the fire in Rebecca's bedroom at the roadside inn where the three travellers were to spend the night. Rebecca had been smuggled into the inn shrouded in a cloak and the excuse of tiredness. The indifferent host had sent her up a meal of stringy chicken and vegetables which she ate with gratitude, nonetheless. On reflection, she mused from her lumpy bed, sniffing the rancid atmosphere, burning the clothes probably hadn't been the best idea. The disgusting stink of sheep fat which permeated the room meant she would have to sleep with the window open, even though leaves were invading, blown in by gusts of wind. She shivered, more through anxiety than cold, but very soon was sound asleep.

Rebecca woke early, hearing birdsong above, and the rumble of carts on the road below. She noticed that her window had been closed by someone, and more fuel (sheep dung she realised with distaste) had been added to the fire. The smell of sheep had, however, now gone, and with it the person who had hidden among them. Samuel had brought with him one of Rebecca's oldest dresses for her to change into, and before retiring for the night, he knocked quietly on the door to her chamber. He said little, but held her close to him and then stood back to reveal a curiously nervous Cornelius holding a tissue-wrapped package. Cornelius had bought her a gift of a beautiful, tasselled shawl which she opened and admired. He then showed her how to wrap it artistically around her head in the manner of a turban so she could disguise her chopped hair. 'I used to watch dear Père's models cover their hair in this way many times. I always felt it gave them a proud, Grecian air somehow.' Rebecca found her voice blocked with emotion, and threw her arms around his neck gratefully.

The next morning, she woke early and dressed quickly. It was good to be back in her own clothes, even though they were now hanging loose on her body. Rebecca pushed her hand through her prickly hair, registering that it would take some time before it grew sufficiently to go without any covering. Scrubbing the grubby glass of the mirror with her sleeve, she saw a young, slim woman appear before her. She had lost weight it was true, but it suited her, she realised. Her skin had started to turn brown, but that would soon fade back to its natural pale hue. She turned her face to scrutinise it in more detail. The turban on her head gave her a bohemian air, one which, Rebecca felt, she could comfortably trade for the loss of her trousers. At least she looked more like herself. With a final tuck of the shawl she was ready to face the world again.

By the second day on horseback, Rebecca had developed the knack of sleeping in the saddle. She rode with Cornelius and Samuel in turn so as not to exhaust the horses, and at the end of that night she fell gratefully into her bed fully clothed. She had never been able to understand the love affair some people seemed to have with horses, and two days in intimate proximity with them was doing nothing to dispel her antipathy. To be fair, these mounts had been ridden hard for days, so there was no wonder that one of them had tried to nip her when she climbed into the saddle on the second morning. Rebecca made a silent promise to herself. Once she was safely home she would stay as far away as possible from all creatures with more legs than she had.

Eventually they arrived, sweaty and tired, at the outskirts of Sargans as the sun was setting, and, while Cornelius trudged into the town to secure their lodgings for the night, Rebecca and Samuel waited at the lake's edge, hidden from view of the road by a copse of dense trees. The horses were slaking their thirst noisily, muscles quivering as flies buzzed around their salty haunches. Rebecca stood stiffly and resisted the urge to pummel her numb buttocks with her fists to get some sensation back into them. Samuel prowled back and forth silently. As Rebecca watched him, she realised that he, too, was changed. He seemed more relaxed, less fragile. He had a new habit too, she noticed. When he was thinking, he played with a ring which was on his little finger. She hadn't seen it before, but registered immediately that it was important to him. 'Did Cornelius give it to you?' Her words came without thought, without filter, and Samuel responded in kind. 'Yes. It was his mother's.' Contained in those words was a lifetime of history, emotion, hope and love. From the first moment she had seen them together, it was obvious to her that they were a couple. Part of her mind wanted to be jealous, but tired as she was, she knew that there would always be room for her in Samuel's heart, and, on reflection, perhaps in Cornelius's too. It was no small thing that he was doing, risking his reputation to be consorting with a fugitive. Rebecca's mind moved from the profound to the more immediate mundanity as her toes began to cramp and she yelped.

When Cornelius returned to them, Rebecca was lying on the ground, with Samuel standing above her grasping her foot. She veered between hysterical laughter and yowls of discomfort. Cornelius found himself a rock to sit on, lit a cigarette and watched them. It didn't take long before all three were helpless with laughter. It seemed the only rational thing to do.

Later that evening, the trio were ensconced in Rebecca's bedroom. Fed, watered and now all ready to sleep, Cornelius changed the convivial mood abruptly. 'Tomorrow we will return to Paris. I will try to telephone Charcot before we leave here so he knows what is happening, but I have no guarantee of being able to get through before we board the train. This is the most dangerous part of our journey now. We will be trapped among other people, with no way of knowing if the search for Rebecca has reached this far.' Rebecca tried hard to focus on his words, but she was halfway to sleep already. She felt herself being guided to the bed where her head sank deeply into the feather pillow. The last thing she saw as her eyes close, was the sight of Samuel squeezing his lover's hand. Rebecca was dreaming before the door closed behind her companions.

Although Cornelius had predicted problems, it turned out to be a peaceful and rather dull train journey. Rebecca ate, slept, ate again and stepped onto the platform at one of the stations to use the conveniences. A change of trains in Vienna was the only time when she felt any anxiety, but there was nothing here to concern her. A busy, anonymous station. That was all. She climbed onto the train to Paris gratefully, and it was with some surprise that she realised she was developing an affinity with the mundane. She reflected that it was probably because her life had recently been so random and strange that she was beginning to find genuine pleasure in the ordinary. Looking out of the window at the conurbations being built around the stations, she imagined how her life would be if she lived in one of those houses. She sighed. Give it a week and she would be screaming from boredom probably, but it was interesting at least to realise that she, as much as anyone, had cravings for what they did not have. She leaned back in her seat as the scenes outside disappeared into darkness and the window reflected its inhabitants. Through the darkened window she watched Samuel, dozing on the shoulder of his lover. Cornelius looked up and smiled at her reflection, then away to the pages of his book. Rebecca continued to scrutinise him. Yes, she thought to herself. I believe he is a good man. I wish them happiness.

Seeing the ease Samuel and Cornelius shared together made her reflect on her own experiences of potential lovers. Sofia? Where did she fit into the equation? No. Not a lover – an encounter – and a tragic one at that. Rebecca knew she was drawn towards men, but they did not seem to be drawn to her. What about Stefan? Was he, could he, become a lover? Was he even interested in her in that way, and, if so, was she interested in him? This was not a question she could answer. A sudden movement of the train jolted Samuel from his sleep, and he looked over at her and smiled, affectionately. What, then, of Samuel? A friend, certainly. A lover, never. She smiled gently back at him. There was one question she could answer for certain. She loved him regardless.

They arrived in Paris late in the evening. The Gare de l'Est was still busy, mainly with freight rather than passengers, but there were enough people around for Cornelius to insist that Rebecca wear her cloak and cover her head with the hood. Too tired to argue, she complied, and watched through its narrowed view the scenes of activity around her as men ferried barrows of goods around the platforms and onto the trains. A series of canary-yellow omnibuses carried them across Paris, and it was only when they were at the doorway to their apartment building that she dragged the hood down. An action which, in turn, pulled her turban from her head. Cornelius bundled her hurriedly into the vestibule. Rebecca was about to protest, when Samuel spoke quietly to her. 'He cares about you because I care about you and he cares about me. Whether he is overreacting or not, please respect his reasons.' Rebecca closed her mouth and followed them up the stairs, too tired to discuss the point.

In the shadow of a doorway opposite, the glow from the bulb of a pipe was the only thing visible. As the trio made their way up the stairs, a man stepped out from the darkness, knocked out his pipe on the wall and headed down the street towards the Salpêtrière. Later that evening he took his usual seat at the bar. 'Good evening, Armand. The usual?' He smiled broadly at the barkeeper. 'No, I am meeting someone. I will have a glass of your best pastis.' As he spoke, a man arrived at the bar, delicately dabbing his top lip with a handkerchief. Armand nodded towards the new arrival. 'He will pay.'

CHAPTER 65

R EBECCA WAS GENUINELY impressed. The apartment, which she had only until now imagined, was large and airy, and, containing as it did the modern conveniences of a water closet as well as running water, positively luxurious. Yes, the decor lacked a woman's touch, and the few pieces of furniture contained in it looked forlorn in such a large space, but, she said happily, she loved it. It surprised her to realise that her friends were waiting nervously for her approval. She didn't make them wait long for it. Expressing her delight, she kissed Samuel with ease, and Cornelius with more formality. Then she set about her exploration of all the nooks and crannies of the apartment, respectfully ignoring their bedroom, but they threw open its doors to her anyway. She was glad of this. Given time, and she felt that it would not take too long, she could imagine herself sharing her life in this apartment with these two men. Certainly, it was not a conventional arrangement, but, she reasoned, she herself was not conventional. She smiled inwardly, wondering if she was treading a path not dissimilar to that which Miriam had taken. When the conventional has no place for you, you must find a place for yourself. Perhaps, just perhaps, this could be such a place.

That evening, they dined quietly, but in style. A fire had been lit to warm the water, allowing Rebecca to take the first hot bath since she could care to remember. While she luxuriated, Cornelius went to the hospital to seek out Dr Charcot. On his return, he smiled reassuringly. 'I have told Charcot enough to ensure his understanding. He has asked us all to present ourselves to him at seven tomorrow morning, so we can talk more fully and in peace.'

Some hours later, the spruced-up trio left the remains of their long – and substantial – meal on the table, and took their wine glasses to relax by the stove. The men seated themselves on the floor and ostentatiously lit cigars. Rebecca decided this could be the perfect opportunity to tell Cornelius about Miriam's inheritance, and with it her dreams of training to become a doctor. Rebecca tucked her feet up on her chaise longue which was, for now, the only comfortable piece of furniture in their shared space. It felt strangely comfortable to have these men around her. They seemed to demand little of her other than her happiness. Certain now that Samuel had not told his lover, it was time to share her secret with Cornelius, and with this sharing show him that she trusted him, as she trusted Samuel.

He said little in response, but she knew that he understood the importance of her sharing this, and he thanked her graciously for having confidence in him. The rest of the evening was taken up with tales told and retold, especially those of how the Reiths had elicited Cornelius and Samuel's help in rescuing her from Saint Anton. As the stories on both sides unfolded, there was no small amount of laughter, and events which had not even been slightly amusing at the time became more comic in the retelling. Rebecca started to relax properly. A small, well-hidden part of her began to peep out from behind its mask and ask if it was time yet for her to be happy. Perhaps, just perhaps.

The next morning, the trio arrived at the Salpêtrière Hospital as instructed, and Charcot embraced Rebecca with considerable warmth. As he drew back to study her face for signs of distress, she was surprised to see tears in his eyes. 'I am so very sorry, Rebecca. That a man in a position of trust should place you in such a terrible situation. It is not acceptable, in fact worse than that, it is deplorable.' He walked her carefully to his inner office, and motioned her to sit in the chair opposite him. Once seated himself, he unlocked his desk drawer and withdrew two envelopes from it, before placing them carefully side by side. Charcot seemed nervous. He poured himself a glass of water and then cleared his throat. 'First and foremost, this is now yours.' He handed a small, fat envelope to Rebecca, and she withdrew from it a document. It was the certificate pronouncing her sane. The confirmation of her freedom.

She read through the certificate calmly and then registered the date at which he had signed this document. Charcot had signed this two months ago. Now she understood his trepidation at her reaction. If he had only handed her the certificate before she had left for the Mayr Clinic, perhaps none of the subsequent events might have occurred. Rebecca composed her thoughts before raising her head to look directly into Charcot's eyes. 'You are not responsible for that which happened to me.' She watched as the tears, which had been brimming in his eyes, now ran down his cheeks. 'I made my own choices then. Now I have this,' she lifted the certificate in her hand, 'I will continue to make my own choices. I am responsible for myself, and no-one will ever take that away from me now.' Charcot withdrew a red handkerchief from his pocket and blew his nose vigorously. Rising from his chair, he came around to the front of his desk to stand before Rebecca. He thrust out his hand towards her. She stared at it in confusion. He waited with outstretched hand. 'Shake my hand, Rebecca. Take it as an equal and forgive my blindness. You are the one of the sanest and most insightful creatures I have encountered in some years... and that includes my students.' Here he looked towards Cornelius, and the tension was suddenly broken. Rebecca rose from her chair and shook Charcot's outstretched hand. Equal at last. Or at least, for now.

Rebecca's appetite had, most definitely, returned. On leaving the confines of the Salpêtrière, they made their way across the river towards the Parc de Bercy and its wine warehouses where they were soon drawn towards the tantalising smells of hot food. Samuel's first choice of venue was rapidly vetoed by Rebecca on account of the plat-de-jour consisting of lamb, but before long they had installed themselves into the depths of a different, but very crowded, bistro. 'Always a good sign,' said Cornelius, contentedly quenching his thirst with a bowl of cider. 'Today is a good day.'

'Yes. A very good day,' echoed Rebecca, unconsciously placing her hand on her bag which now contained both of the envelopes that had been, until that morning, locked away in Charcot's desk drawer. Samuel looked at his partner, quizzically. 'Is there something more?'

'Ah, my dear Samuel, you read me well. Yes. I have some news of my own. Last evening, when I went to see Dr Charcot, he told me that my thesis and its defence has now been accepted. I am no longer a student.' He picked off invisible lint from his lapel in self-deprecation. 'You may now refer to me as Dr Mercier.' Rebecca reached over to Cornelius and kissed his cheek, happily. This time it felt natural. Samuel made do with a vigorous shake of his lover's hand. No doubt he would make up for this with a stronger show of affection in private. 'There is something else. Dr Charcot will, obviously, be taking on another student. He asked me for his opinion on your young companion – Stefan. He will need a new tutor now his own is – indisposed – and Stefan seems keen to return to his native France, so I have put in a good word for him.' Samuel watched with interest as a blush reached Rebecca's cheeks. 'He will arrive for his interview with Dr Charcot next week.' Rebecca tried to break the penetrating eye contact which Samuel was now subjecting her to, and was grateful for the intervention of the waiter who had appeared to take their order.

That evening, Rebecca spread out the contents of the two envelopes which Charcot had handed to her, and with them before her eyes, she tried to assess how she now felt. With the first document, she was now legally in possession of her sanity. Charcot had assured her that he would take care of the situation with Professor Farkas, and with his words she felt secure that the threat from Budapest was now over, or at least would be soon. The contents of the second envelope were more bitter-sweet. It was a vellum card on which Miriam had written by hand. Dated the same day as the last missive which Rebecca had received from her, it simply contained the name and address of her aunt's solicitor in London. Rebecca turned the card over in her hands, tracing the words on the page as if by doing so she could bring Miriam back to life. Leaning into the chaise longue, she looked up at the ceiling. Some hours later, Cornelius and his lover returned home from their evening celebrating, to find her still there. Fast asleep. Samuel gently eased the note from her and placed it on the floor at her side. Cornelius slipped his hand into Samuel's and they stood together in silence, watching over Rebecca as she slept.

Rebecca had no desire to go to England, expressing more than a little anxiety at putting herself in the same country as Lord Hawsley and his cronies, or indeed her own father. Paris was her home now, she explained heatedly to her friends, and she had little or no intention of leaving it any time soon. This opinion she expressed vehemently over coffee in Dr Charcot's office, and was pleased to hear that he agreed. 'It makes more sense for the solicitor to come to you. After all, you are an heiress now, and you will need a solicitor of your own. If he wants your business, make him do the travelling.' Rebecca was amused by his expression, but delighted when, there and then, he telephoned Miriam's solicitor and suggested that Miss Zimmerman would appreciate if he came to her in Paris. Mr Vanderbilt accepted the suggestion with alacrity and offered to present himself to Miss Zimmerman on the following Monday afternoon at a venue convenient to her. Charcot offered his inner office, and the meeting was settled. Thanking Charcot, she surprised herself by saying, 'I would like you to be here, please. That is, if you don't mind.' In response, Charcot kissed her on both cheeks. 'It will be an honour. I will watch over you as a father would a child, and I will do so with pleasure.' As she left the Salpêtrière to shop for furniture, she ruminated on why she had asked him and not Samuel or Cornelius. 'If I am to take charge of my own life I need to trust people, but there is no need for anyone to know everything about me.' Trust, she concluded, meant sometimes keeping secrets. With this at the forefront of her mind, she headed off towards the flea market, and Samuel.

CHAPTER 66

'IT'S A GOOD thing that we have a large apartment, as I fear our darling Rebecca will fill it to the brim in no time!' Cornelius laughed, as the newly arrived furniture was arranged, and rearranged. After the dining table had been shifted by the men for the sixth – no seventh – time on Rebecca's instructions, Cornelius called a halt to events and threw himself down onto the chaise longue. 'Enough! I will waste away with all this exertion!'

'No fear of that,' rejoindered Samuel, prodding at his lover's midriff. 'A little more exercise and a little less mutton would do you good!' This good-natured verbal sparring continued until Rebecca heard the chimes from the nearby church signal a quarter after the hour. 'I must go, or I will be late.' She gathered up the fringed shawl and wrapped it around her head as Cornelius had shown her. It had become a natural movement to her, and at least part of her mind was not looking forward to the day when she would no longer need to wear it. Short hair, if not exactly feminine, was certainly easier to manage.

She walked quickly down the staircase, her shoes clicking noisily on the wooden steps. By the time she reached the ground floor, the concierge, Bruno, was waiting by the door, holding it open for her with a smile. Thanking him with a smile of her own, she made her way into the street, and the sunshine. It was a good day. Breathing deeply of the Parisian air she suddenly coughed, as the richness of the smell emanating from the sewers below caught in her throat. She laughed to herself. 'Perhaps this is the nature of a love affair. You embrace something even though it irritates you.' It was true that the faults of Paris were many. Chaotic, noisy, rude and in some areas downright dangerous, Rebecca realised, nonetheless, that it had her in its thrall. As much as she had loved London, it was for the people she had met there, not the city itself. It seemed cold and aloof beside Paris. Yes. It was a love affair, and one which Rebecca had every intention of deepening with time.

She arrived at the Salpêtrière early and, rather than kick her heels in the corridor of Charcot's office, she decided to walk through into the inner courtyard and find a bench on which she could sit and read. She had acquired a quantity of new books – all in French – thanks to the direction of Cornelius. Not naturally drawn to novels, she was surprised at his recommendations, but Cornelius argued that you learn much about a society from its dreams, so she read Voltaire, Dumas, Flaubert. It was, however, the works of Victor Hugo which most gripped her imagination, reading them as she did among the very streets of Paris which he had described so vividly. Drawing out a substantial copy of *Les Misérables* from her bag she settled herself down to a period of self-indulgence.

A quarter-hour had passed and Rebecca had not moved from her spot, only noting the passing of time by the chiming of the hospital clock. A dark shadow cast on the pages of her book was not enough to disturb her at first, but when the shadow started to cough politely she registered that it was a person standing before her. She looked up from the pages slowly, to see a neatly dressed and nervous-looking Stefan. Rebecca rose suddenly, her book falling from her lap. The ensuing commotion, as both bent to pick it up, was enough to camouflage Rebecca's embarrassment at seeing Stefan so unexpectedly.

'What are you doing here?' she asked, abruptly. 'I have an interview with Dr Charcot. Your friend, Dr Mercier, was kind enough to recommend me for a position as a student here.' Rebecca heard the clock chime the half-hour. 'I am late. Sorry I must go.' Stefan touched her arm. 'Please, will you come back? There is so much I need to tell you – so much to say.' Rebecca nodded as she hurried towards Charcot's office and all that awaited her there.

Two hours passed, and Rebecca was still in Charcot's office. She was stunned into silence and rooted to her chair. Two hours in which Rebecca discovered that Charcot's description of her as an heiress had turned out to be an accurate one. Not only was she to inherit the house in Gower Street, but a substantial portfolio of investments, and, most intriguing of all, a property in France. 'Why France?' she asked Mr Vanderbilt, watching him as he neatly folded Miriam's Last Will and Testament, placing it carefully back into its sleeve. Her question went unanswered. Instead, he pushed his glasses back from where they had slipped to the point of his nose, and unlaced the strings of a hardboard folder which was set squarely on the desk before him. Charcot had vacated his usual seat and was standing by the open window, stroking a mewling kitten which was inelegantly using the weft of his new jacket to make its way up his sleeve and towards his shoulder. Charcot seemed to be paying little attention to the kitten, and even less to the conversation, but Rebecca knew better.

The solicitor sifted through the folder and pulled out a document. It looked old, and it was. 'Pertaining to the aforementioned property in France,' began Mr Vanderbilt, pompously, but not unkindly, 'To wit; one farm, one manor house, one small industrial unit (pottery and quarry), one area of forest, one area of farming land (arable and dairy), and one abbey.' Rebecca's eyes widened, and Charcot turned from the window. 'An abbey?' he queried. 'An abbey,' continued the solicitor. He turned his attention to another page. 'Current inhabitants consist, I understand, of between forty and sixty individuals.'

He paused. 'This property has passed through the matrilineal line of your family for seven hundred years. You will be the sixteenth woman to be the incumbent. Sometimes it has passed from mother to daughter, other times from sister to sister, occasionally to a cousin, but always among the females of your immediate family. You have neither the right to sell this property nor cause it to be broken up or used for any purpose other than that which it already fulfils. The manor house on the land is yours to live in should you wish, but you are not required or expected to have any other involvement in the activities of the community.'

Rebecca was confused. 'What community, exactly?'

'Why, it is a convent, of course.'

He went back to his notes. 'It consists of ten cloistered nuns, and the rest of the numbers are made up of associated laity who live in other buildings nearby.' He paused and looked over at Rebecca. 'Your responsibility is to see that it is maintained and protected.'

Now Rebecca was not only confused, but thoroughly intrigued. 'Where is this place?'

'Fontaine-Daniel. In the Pays-de-la-Loire.' She looked over at

Charcot for enlightenment. He smiled. 'But there's nothing there! Just farms and countryside and more farms!' Removing the now sleeping kitten from his shoulder, he dropped it onto the desk, much to the consternation of the solicitor who made a vain attempt to sweep his papers into his arms before the kitten decided that they would be much better shredded.

Taking pity on Mr Vanderbilt, Rebecca lifted the kitten from the desk and lowered it to the floor. Then, taking a sideways look at Charcot's mischievous face, she moved her attention back to the solicitor. It took some moments for him to compose himself. This effort was aided in no small measure by Rebecca's assurances that she would like him to continue to act for her. He smiled, contentedly. 'I would be delighted, Miss Zimmerman. Your aunt was a delightful woman and I would be most happy to care for your financial affairs with the same rigour and attention as I did hers.'

Another half-hour went by as the solicitor revealed more details about how, where and when Rebecca could access Miriam's finances. However, Rebecca politely but firmly ended the conversation when he asked what her intentions were with regard to the Gower Street house. She did not want to think about it just yet, and certainly was not going to make the journey to London any time soon. He informed her that minimal staff were still in post at the house, and monies had been put aside by Miriam to pay them for a full year. Rebecca did not need to think about it for now. It was the abbey at Fontaine-Daniel which had piqued her curiosity.

After numerous pleasantries and much bowing and offerings of assistance by Mr Vanderbilt, Charcot and Rebecca were finally alone. 'He talks a lot, don't you think?' smiled Rebecca. 'All lawyers do. They love the sound of their own voices, especially if they are bringing good news. Bless them all.' Charcot smiled back at Rebecca and retrieved the kitten from under the desk and returned it to its preferred perch on his shoulder. 'Will you go and visit your new fiefdom?' Rebecca laughed. 'Do you think I look like a lady of the manor now?'

'Perhaps not, but your wealth means you will never have to work, nor, should you change your mind, study. There are other ways of helping mankind than joining the ranks of the medical profession, my dear Rebecca.' His voice was serious. 'You have money now, and with it comes the ability to make choices that are not available to most of us. Think long and hard before you commit to learning medicine. It is an all-consuming, arduous road, and one which grows longer with each new scientific discovery.' His face softened and he rested his hand on her shoulder. 'Young as you are, you have already had experiences which would overwhelm a weaker individual. Perhaps you deserve an easier life now, rather than one which will bring with it more hardship.' The kitten on his shoulder mewled loudly for his attention, and Charcot began to stroke it gently. He scrutinised Rebecca. 'Think carefully before you decide to train as a physician. That is all the advice I can give you.'

Closing the door to Charcot's office, she hurried back to the courtyard. Catching the heel of her boot in the cobbles, she stumbled awkwardly. The square was deserted. Stefan must have got tired of waiting for her. Even though she had not thought about him since they had parted, she was disappointed that he had not seen fit to wait for her. No matter. She had no need of him – nor any man for that matter. She was a woman of independent, and – she suddenly realised – substantial means. She looked down to see one of her heels hanging uselessly. It was, most definitely, time for some new shoes.

CHAPTER 67

B Y THE TIME Rebecca had hobbled back to their apartment, her newly acquired joy had been overlaid with irritation. Entering the vestibule of the building, the concierge jumped up to greet her, and in the process almost tipped the nurse from his lap. Bruno Roger smiled happily at Rebecca in greeting, while Valerie covered her own embarrassment by asking after the health of Cornelius. Rebecca took off her shoes and made her way up the stairs sullenly. 'Everyone around me seems to have someone to love. Maybe I should get a pet, like Charcot.' Her bare feet examined the smooth wood of the stairs and the repetition of step after step up to the apartment partially soothed her testiness. Once at the apartment door, she had regained her equilibrium and was ready to talk to her friends.

This would not be happening any time soon, however, as, when she entered the apartment, she saw that they were not alone. Cornelius and Samuel were seated around the dining table, and their visitor had his back to her. She did not need to see his face to recognise Stefan. Registering her arrival, the three men rose in greeting, Stefan hanging back shyly as she kissed her friends.

Rebecca put out her hand towards him, and instead of shaking it he bowed formally and kissed it. She laughed, then immediately regretted it as Stefan looked up at her crestfallen. 'Forgive me, Stefan. If you saw what I had to do when I was living as a shepherd-boy you would not be too inclined to kiss that hand.' He stood upright, still holding Rebecca's hand, turning it over in curiosity. 'Well, it looks like a lady's hand to me...' He raised an eyebrow quizzically, all tension suddenly broken.

Once again, Rebecca told the story of her time in Saint Anton, and Samuel and Cornelius repeated their involvement in her delivery back to France. Rebecca was struck by how quickly those events were becoming disconnected from reality (and emotion) in the telling. Perhaps this was the root of analysis, she mused, talking about events helps you to dissociate from the pain while they become nothing more than stories. The room had fallen silent, Cornelius opened another bottle of wine and Stefan cleared his throat. It was time for him to speak.

Silently he placed Rebecca's locket on the table. Then he began. He spoke quietly. First, he told them how the police had incarcerated him until Professor Farkas arrived from Budapest to corroborate his story, and to collect Sofia's body. Rebecca was sure that this tale – like their own – had been sanitised and revised, but the way in which Stefan unconsciously touched his ribs told her something more. She, of all people, knew how it felt to have your liberty taken from you, and the fear of not knowing what was going to happen to you. Rebecca understood that Stefan had not undertaken his task lightly, and it could have gone horribly wrong if Zoltan had decided that his student had betrayed him. Zoltan must have confirmed Stefan's version of events, as he was released without charge. At no time did he question Stefan, and nor did Stefan offer any elucidation.

Sofia was buried in the graveyard of the chapel in which she had been found. The verdict of 'accidental death' wiped clean the stigma of suicide, allowing her to be laid to rest in consecrated grounds. Stefan's voice faltered at this point, and he took a sip from his wineglass before continuing. The funeral had been an austere and sad event, with only the pastor to officiate and the two men in attendance. His eyes glazed over in remembrance, recalling how the snow had receded, leaving bare, muddied earth and a grave which was half-filled with water. He shuddered at the thought of Sofia's body being lowered in there. It seemed like a final indignity, somehow. He shook the images from his mind and brought it back to the present, continuing with his tale. 'You can put your mind at rest now. The hunt for you was called off after the inquest. As soon as I got back to Hungary, I packed my bags and returned to France.'

'What of the photographs?' Rebecca asked. Stefan smiled thinly. 'If Professor Farkas suspected me of having a hand in their theft, then he made no indication of it to me.' He pushed his hand through his untidy hair. 'I was just happy to get away from that place. So many things which were impermissible had become normalised in that house. Zoltan Farkas kept vulnerable people in his thrall, and they believed it was acceptable for him to do so. Once you step away, it is like stepping out of the events in a fairy tale. Horrifying and real when you are in it, but once you move away you can see it for what it is.' He stopped suddenly. 'Sorry. I had no idea how much I hated that man. It feels good to be able to express it.'

'What will you do now?' asked Cornelius. Stefan seemed grateful for his interruption. 'Well, thanks to you, Dr Mercier, I have the opportunity to continue my studies under Dr Charcot. It is more than I could have wished for.' Cornelius smiled indulgently. 'Please, call me Cornelius. We are all friends here.'

As Rebecca prepared herself for bed that evening, she considered Cornelius's words. *All friends here.* Her own feelings about Stefan were more opaque. Stefan had put himself at risk both to save her life from Sofia, and then to ensure her safety by sending the photographs to Charcot. It troubled her, and she couldn't quite put her finger on what it was that bothered her so much about him. She concluded that she felt beholden to him by his actions and this was not a feeling which sat comfortably. True, he had not asked anything of her, but this was, perhaps, at the heart of what was so troubling. Her experiences had conditioned her to believe that no-one (or at least very few people) acted in a purely altruistic fashion. With shame, her mind went back to her own response to Sofia's death. It had not initially been one of sadness for her friend, but of concern for herself. She sat on the side of her bed, brushing her short hair. Her train of thought continued. 'It is natural that we should each think of ourselves, our needs, our fears, surely? What was she to make of a man who had put her needs above his own?' Lying back on the bed she watched the shadows play on the ceiling. Her sleep that night was fitful.

Waking early, she found that her nocturnal ruminations about Stefan had dissipated in the heat of a new day. Rebecca felt happy, relaxed and, above all, a feeling of security was starting to wrap itself around her. True, she still had to deal with her father. She knew that Charcot would have already informed Jeremiah Zimmerman of the decision to issue Rebecca with her certificate of sanity. As far as Rebecca's father was concerned, the clock was now ticking on her return to England, to Ramsgate, to Isaac and marriage. Each sphere of influence would exercise its pull, drawing Rebecca into closer orbit until she finally disappeared into a space framed by utter conformity. She would be nothing more than a satellite to the wishes of society until her trajectory decayed and everything she might have been was destroyed. That, she thought – her determination rising with the sun – is *not* going to happen. Whatever I do now will be my choice, and mine alone. Whatever mistakes there will be will be of my own making. With this thought in mind, she knocked on the bedroom door to wake her friends and headed off to the market to buy croissants for breakfast, and to get her shoes repaired. She didn't have access to Miriam's money just yet, and prudence came as second nature to her now.

That being said, once breakfast was over she told Samuel everything the lawyer had shared with her. Cornelius had already left for the Salpêtrière, leaving the two of them to spend the day together. 'So, Miss Zimmerman. You are rich! Mazel tov! You will never need to soil those pretty hands of yours again, nor stain your skin with sunlight, like a peasant!' Rebecca knew she was being teased, but his words made her feel uncomfortable. 'Samuel, can I ask your opinion of something?' She took Samuel's silence as assent, 'What do you think of Stefan?' Samuel began to clear away the detritus of their meal and Rebecca waited impatiently for his response. He sat down beside her, taking his hand in hers. 'What is it you want me to say? He risked his life, his job, and his liberty to save you. Those are not the acts of a common man. I could argue that he did them because they were the right things to do in the circumstances, and perhaps he would not have done them had you not opened his eyes to the reality. On the other hand…,' he continued. 'Samuel, please…' Rebecca interrupted. 'Stop debating like a rabbi!' Samuel smiled and squeezed her hand, then walked over to the open window where he lit a cigarette. 'When someone asks for an opinion it is usually the last thing they actually want. What they desire is for their own opinion to be validated. That is why we usually only ask people we believe will agree with us. So I ask you. What do *you* think of him?'

'I don't know. I don't really know him.'

'So that is the answer. Get to know him. Then you will be able to answer your own question.'

Rebecca smiled. 'How would you like a trip away from Paris, somewhere in the countryside, perhaps?' Samuel smiled in response. '… and, perhaps, take Cornelius and Stefan too?' Rebecca grinned in response. 'Perhaps.'

CHAPTER 68

ONE ROAD LED into Fontaine-Daniel. The same road led out of it. If you were on that road and not going to Fontaine-Daniel then you were, undoubtedly, lost. That piece of information was imparted philosophically by the driver of the carriage which they had hired in Mayenne.

Before embarking on the last part of their journey, the four travellers had indulged in a substantial lunch at the Grand Hotel overlooking the river. Rebecca was starting to regret having eaten quite so much, as the track was narrow and bumpy, and her recently digested meal was causing her some discomfort. She dozed fitfully, unaware of how much time had passed and only waking when the carriage halted. She opened her eyes. It was dusk. The road had ended, and, looking beyond it, she saw a small but well-proportioned manor house surrounded by tall trees. It was not what she had expected. In the style of a Scottish hunting lodge, it came complete with a studded door and an arched doorway.

The companions climbed down from the carriage, and their luggage was handed down by the driver. 'I do hope we are expected,' Cornelius quipped, advancing to look for a bell-pull to announce their arrival. It was, in the event, unnecessary, as the door was opened from within as he spoke. A diminutive woman greeted them with a smile, and stepped aside to welcome them into the hallway. The Scottish theme seemed to be continued here, with half-panelled walls and a vaulted ceiling. She directed each to their own bedrooms, and informed them that a cold meal had been prepared and was laid out for them in the dining room so they could eat when they were ready. A bell pealed a single time, and the woman bowed her head. 'I will leave you now.'

Rebecca watched the small figure walk across the courtyard before being swallowed into the darkness. She shivered. It was cold in the house, and it had the feeling of being uninhabited, although not neglected. Stefan lit a fire and the four friends spent the evening in the comfortable dining room in the glow of its flames and the light of the candelabrum which they carried over from the table. Cornelius began to ask Stefan about his studies, then his history and his family, and Rebecca drew her face back into the darkness and listened attentively.

For a few short moments before her consciousness caught up, Rebecca had no idea where she was. There was a silence around her which she found, not to put too fine a point on it, unnerving. How quickly she had accommodated to sleeping through the street sounds of Paris! She sat up in bed and tried to force her spiky hair to lie flat, then focused her ears to extract anything she could from the silence. Then she heard it. Birdsong. She smiled and went to the window, opening it wide to bring the sound closer to her. Leaning out, she took a deep breath of forest air. It felt good. The view was across the courtyard to the area where last night there had been nothing but darkness. She could now see a low building with a large, central doorway, large enough for a cart to pass through. On either side were smaller doors and, above, four narrow, glassless slits and, before them, people working. That building seemed to be much older than the manor house, made, as it was, of substantial stone blocks. Leading off from each side of the central building were tall, ivy-clad walls. Leaning further out of the window, Rebecca could just see where the walls turned. The building was evidently a gatehouse, and whatever was behind it was surrounded by this wall. It was time to explore.

Dressing quickly, Rebecca made her way across the courtyard. She could now discern what it was that the people were working on. As she approached she realised that they were all women. No-one looked up, or even registered her arrival. Each seemed wrapped in her own world. This space was a physic garden, well-stocked with medicinal herbs – some of which she recognised thanks to her sojourn with the Waltons in the lock-keeper's house. A time several lifetimes ago. She stood silently for a moment, watching the rhythmic movements of the women as they weeded and harvested. There was a harmony here. It felt good. She stretched down to touch a plant which she recognised. Mint. Stroking its leaves with her hand she raised her palm to her face and inhaled the strong and distinctive scent. A low, heavily accented voice spoke to her. 'Black mint. We use it to reduce nausea.' Rebecca turned to find herself staring into the cowl-framed face of a nun. 'When made into a tisane it can help disperse anxiety. Would you care for a glass?'

Rebecca underwent a sequence of emotions as she followed this tall, green-eyed woman towards the gatehouse. Her first feeling was one of irritation. Why was it that no-one here seemed to be paying her any attention? After all, she was the rightful owner! Then a wave of humility caught up with her. She didn't own this place, it had been entrusted to her care. This was a responsibility, not a right. The next emotion to reach her mind was that of curiosity. There were myriad questions to which she wanted answers. Then it was full circle as irritation came around again. This time, it was because the nun had assumed she needed the mint tea to calm down. She wasn't anxious... or was she?

She was shown now into a small, spartan room containing wooden settles along the opposing walls. These benches had a low, age-worn table between them. The nun signalled Rebecca to remain here and, leaving her alone, disappeared through an inner door. Rebecca lowered herself onto the nearest seat, landing with a bump on its hard surface. Her hearing carried her attention back through the open window and she allowed the presence of birdsong to once again fill her mind.

She had no idea of how much time had passed since she had waited here. The garden was now empty, and so was her stomach, judging from the sounds now coming from that region. No matter. She could wait. When the nun finally returned, she carried a small wooden tray. On it was an earthenware teapot alongside two glasses arranged with perfect symmetry. A tiny plate of rose-scented jellies sat between the glasses and she took one, chewing it methodically, à la Mayr. Neither woman spoke, and, seated directly opposite one another, they drank their tea in silence.

There would be ample opportunities for questions and Rebecca got the feeling that this was not the time or the place for her to start asking them. When the pot had been emptied of its aromatic contents, the nun smiled at her. It was a spontaneous, gentle smile of someone who found herself precisely where she wanted to be. 'You have questions. I will, of course, answer all of those I am able.' She rose. 'Let us walk. Perhaps it is simpler to show rather than tell.' Rebecca got up to follow, and stopped suddenly as she registered a change. 'You are speaking English!' The nun opened the door leading back the way they came and beckoned her outside. Her smile widened. 'Yes. I speak English. I could say that it is my native tongue, but that is not strictly true. I am – was – Irish.' More surprises.

'The physic garden you have already seen. Here we grow and prepare herbs to reduce pain of many kinds. Over there...' she pointed to a row of hives in the distance, shaded by tall trees, 'are our bees. Their honey and the distillation of other secretions are used to reduce inflammation and infection. The light for our quarters and in our chapel comes from their gift of wax.' They walked towards the hives, her wide habit creating a pathway through the long grass for Rebecca to follow. The recitation continued. 'Myself, I am rather fond of bees. My mother always used to say that I should tell the bees when there is news, so they can pass it on. I should say that your arrival definitely falls into this category.' Rebecca didn't know how to react to this, and held back from the hives as the nun walked among them, seemingly unaware of the bees as they flew around her. 'Don't be afraid. A bee will only sting if you upset it.' Again, the sudden smile came to the nun's face, bringing with it an aspect of youth. 'A bit like a woman, wouldn't you say?' No response from Rebecca seemed to be necessary, and so she gave none, preferring to let this enigmatic nun continue the tour. She wasn't in a hurry. She could take her time. It was only when these unconscious thoughts knocked on the door of her awareness that she realised it was probably the first time in her life when she hadn't been in a hurry to be somewhere else. It felt, well, right somehow.

They continued walking along the edge of the forest, keeping the perimeter wall to their right. Realising that she no longer wanted to refer to this woman as 'the nun', Rebecca asked to know her name. 'My name, when I lived in the world, was Lorraine Flaherty. When I took my vows the name of Benedict was chosen for me. I joined the order when I was fourteen years of age, and I have not left the confines of these walls since that day. That was more than thirty years ago. For the past seven years, I have had the honour to hold the office of Abbess and Mother to all within its walls.' Rebecca was confused. 'Which walls?' Benedict pointed towards the trees. 'Those walls.' Rebecca peered into the dense forest, and, once her eyes became accustomed to the darkness, she registered what she was seeing. The darkness was impenetrable, and more solid than forest – it was the result of a tall wall. Old and imposing, Rebecca estimated, it was probably as high as a two-storey building. Like the walls around the asylum. She shuddered, but this time she could leave whenever she wanted.

CHAPTER 69

THE ONLY SOUND came from the rustling of leaves in the trees as the women retraced their steps away from the sight of the forbidding barrier and back towards the gatehouse. When they reached the doorway, Mother Benedict turned to her left and Rebecca now followed her along the inner perimeter wall. They turned the corner, continuing to walk alongside the wall towards an arched, iron entrance, deeply embedded in the stonework, and partly concealed by ivy. Extracting a large key from a pocket of her habit, Mother Benedict opened the gate, and presently Rebecca found herself within the cloister. The area within these walls was considerably smaller than she had imagined. At its centre was nothing more than a simple wooden chapel. There was no spire, and it bore more than a passing resemblance to a chalet in the mountains rather than a church. As she drew closer, she noticed that the blackness of the wood from which it was constructed had been darkened from charring. Unusual, she noted.

As they continued along the path from the gate towards the structure, Rebecca could now see that there were other paths radiating out from the chapel. Some went to each corner and some to the centre of each wall. Eight paths in all. The paths to the corners seemed for ornamentation only, while the one which she was now treading was replicated to the two other walls, and she noticed that each of these ended in identical iron gates. The final path led from chapel to gatehouse. This simple symmetry pleased her.

As if reading her mind, her companion stopped on the path to the church and turned to her. 'There are eight paths within these walls. Eight ways in which one can approach this space. Four routes for the body, each with a gate. Four more for the spirit to enter – hence no need for openings.' The sound of a single bell tolled six times. 'I will accompany you back to the courtyard. The bell calls me to devotions and I must leave you. Return tomorrow morning and we can continue your visit here.' With this, she turned around and soon Rebecca was deposited outside the door of the gatehouse with no more ceremony than a cat put out for the night. The door closed firmly behind her, and Rebecca was left alone with her thoughts.

As she walked away from the spiritual building towards the more temporal pleasures of a meal at the manor, she found herself trying to feel resentment at the way in which Mother Benedict was behaving. Although it irked her, she could find none. After all, Rebecca was a visitor, and when she had left this place, the life of the convent would continue undisturbed. Her thoughts were soon invaded. Greeted loudly at the door to the manor by Cornelius, Rebecca put her feelings aside and went indoors to regale her companions with all she had learned.

Their visit quickly settled into a routine. Her mornings were taken up with Mother Benedict, the afternoons consisted of exploration of the forest, and the evenings were spent in noisy companionship. Until now she had not spent any time with Stefan alone, unconsciously preferring to stay close to Cornelius and Samuel. But as the days went by, and with increasing frequency, she found herself walking alongside Stefan as they investigated the countryside around the manor. At first, he spoke little, but each day the ease with which they conversed increased. Stefan had no notion that Rebecca was visiting her inheritance, assuming that this was a trip organised by Samuel. 'It was nice of your cousin Samuel to invite me to come along with you,' he said, shyly. 'How long have you known Dr Mercier?' This sudden change of topic alerted Rebecca to divert the conversation, as she sensed which direction it was heading. She surmised that Stefan was either about to ask whether Cornelius was her lover, or voice his suspicion that he was Samuel's. Either way she had no intention of engaging with the question, and neither did she want to have to obfuscate or lie. Deciding it was better to ignore it, she asked Stefan about himself, in the confident expectation that, as all men liked to talk about themselves, he would quickly forget what he had asked.

She had underestimated his astuteness – and furthermore his training as an analyst. Stefan smiled ruefully at her. 'All you had to do was to say that you did not wish to answer. It would have sufficed.' Rebecca blushed deeply in response. 'I am sorry. It was unworthy of me. At least understand why. After everything which has happened I trust little around me, and even fewer people. Samuel and Cornelius are lovers.' She looked up at Stefan, waiting for his shocked reaction. It did not come. He smiled at her. 'They make an excellent couple. I only hope that I meet someone with whom I can find such a love.' He walked on. Rebecca stayed where she was, deep in thought. 'Did that mean he, too, preferred men, or was he flirting with me?' Her reverie was broken as Cornelius and Samuel caught up with her, sweeping her along with their new-found enthusiasm for the woods.

The next three mornings were taken up with Rebecca's visits to the convent. Each day she presented herself at the gatehouse, and with pleasing regularity, Mother Benedict collected her from there and showed her another aspect of the abbey and its inhabitants. The dairy was an extraordinary affair. A much taller and grander building than any of the others around it, consisting, as it did, of an arched doorway and well-proportioned windows, it now housed a small herd of cows. 'Originally, services for the local people had been held here. Monks from the abbey would come from within the cloister to say Mass, while the great unwashed would enter from the outside. Never the twain shall meet,' she smiled, pointing up inside the building to a mezzanine floor. 'Monks above, peasants below.' She lifted the hem of her habit to avoid a cow-pat. 'I much prefer it as it is. Besides, our little herd give us the most wonderful milk.'

Continuing her exploration of the temporal buildings, Rebecca realised that this was actually a self-contained village. In the days that followed she saw the farm, lime-quarry and pottery – complete with a beehive-shaped kiln the size of a small cottage – but these were of little interest to Rebecca, other than the understanding that they allowed the convent to be virtually self-sufficient. Mother Benedict explained. 'Any surplus, such as ale, candles or honey, is traded with nearby villages for goods or services, but generally we ourselves are capable of doing most of what is needed.' As a testament to this, Rebecca watched as two women walked confidently across the apex of the gatehouse roof, evidently repairing some of the fallen slates. She had still only seen other inhabitants at a distance. Perhaps they preferred to remain apart from her. She was, after all, a representative of the world from which they had willingly withdrawn.

This withdrawal from the world was not absolute, however. There was an infirmary, and it was this that Rebecca was most keen to see. If she were to train as a doctor, this would be useful to her. Unlike the manor house which was within the grounds of the abbey, the infirmary lay outside its perimeter wall. It was a large, rectangular building with a roof which seemed disproportionately large. 'It is one of the original buildings from the time of the monastery. Before we came to this place there was a Cistercian abbey here. It was a much grander affair than that which you now see around you. The outer walls are from that time, as is the farm, the infirmary and the forge. There used to be a much larger church here too, with a spire as tall at the cathedral at Le Mans,' Mother Benedict continued. 'What happened?' Rebecca asked her. 'This area of France has been invaded many, many times over the centuries – by your compatriots I might add – and eventually there were no more treasures to take from the church, so the structures themselves were destroyed. Time and the need for building materials meant that much of what had been the abbey is now part of many a farmhouse hereabout.' She smiled. 'Such is the nature of man. The need for shelter outweighs the need for spiritual succour.'

Mother Benedict led the way towards the infirmary. Once inside the main door, she dipped her hands into the bowl of water placed there, covered by a cloth. When she had finished her methodical hand-washing, she indicated for Rebecca to do the same. As Rebecca took her turn she observed the scene before her. The long, narrow room was quiet and tidy, and the windows were wide open, allowing in the sound of birds, and the warmth of the sun to penetrate the space. There were eight beds, four on either side of a central walkway. Five of the beds were empty, but in the remaining three, the occupants were sleeping. By one bedside an elderly nun massaged the feet of the prone figure, who moaned gently. As Rebecca passed them she realised that the nun was blind. She did not react to the new arrivals, but continued with her gentle, rhythmic movements, humming to herself quietly.

At the far end of the room was a table, and seated there was a bespectacled nun, reading intensely and taking notes. Mother Benedict walked towards her, and the figure rose in greeting, tucking her arms away within the folds of her habit. 'Rebecca, may I present Sister Agatha. She is our infirmarian and apothecary. All of the tinctures and tisanes which we use here are created by her.' Rebecca looked at this woman. She seemed very young to be in such a responsible position. 'I would love to talk to you about what you do.' A brief look was exchanged between the nuns, and Mother Benedict gave the smallest of nods in assent. 'Come tomorrow. Sister Agatha will be your guide.'

CHAPTER 70

SISTER AGATHA WAS a smiling, bubbly bundle of energy. She was short, round, and walked fast, with small, neat steps. Although young, her shoulders were already rounded from years of bending over to plant and pick herbs, and the bridge of her nose was ridged from wearing the glasses which she needed to read. Rebecca noticed that whenever she was deep in thought, she stroked the ridges unconsciously. She liked her immediately.

This vivacious nun began her instruction by showing Rebecca the layout of the herb garden, and it came as no surprise that there were eight beds in all. 'Eight divisions of our day, eight paths to the chapel, eight beds in each ward of the infirmary. The shape of the figure eight denotes continuation, infinity and rebirth and we have eight devotions: lauds, matins, prime, sext, none, terce, vespers and compline. She reeled off their names breathlessly and with a small laugh. 'The number eight has represented harmony since the inception of the order and you will see it repeated all over the abbey.' She pointed to the pattern in the gates and the keystone over the gatehouse door where a rough figure eight had been carved into the rock.

Rebecca still had many questions, but she began with those about the origins of the order. 'It has existed since the days of the Crusades. Our founding mothers were the daughters of money-lenders in Jerusalem. Sent out by their fathers to accompany a group of Knights Templar as security – ransomed one might say – they travelled with the knights as they fought their way west and into Europe.' Rebecca processed this information. 'The order was founded by Jewish women?' Agatha nodded her assent, absent-mindedly dead-heading a marigold and putting it in her pocket. 'These women were much more than vassals to their families, they were educated. Not only were they cultured and articulate, but they were also experts in physic, and it wasn't long before the Knights Templar made use of their skills with herbs as they fought their way from Jerusalem. 'They were skilled fighters, too.' Rebecca looked at her, surprised at this revelation. 'They had to be able to protect themselves. They were accomplished in fighting with both stick and sword. Sadly, these skills were not passed onto us.' Rebecca smiled at the thought of this gentle figure wielding a weapon. As if reading her mind, Sister Agatha spoke again. 'Never underestimate a nun...' Looking up shyly she allowed the phrase to hang in the air. Both women laughed and the atmosphere between them warmed.

'Of course, it wasn't long before love blossomed between these Christian men and Jewish women. That, as you can imagine, transgressed so many vows of both chastity and religion that it became a scandal which reached the ears of the Pope himself. The reputation of these women as healers began to spread, and those who benefited from their ministrations named them the Lady Templars. They were alchemists, Jews, and worst of all, they were women. This could not be tolerated.

'The knights themselves were hunted down, tortured, mutilated then executed. The women and children (for many of these unions had borne fruit) were captured as they tried to flee. The history of our order tells that they were seized by the Pope's men, and taken to him to be tried personally, but he decided to spare them. Their now famous skills with herbs were deemed too valuable, and they were given the choice to die or to convert. They chose to live.'

As she spoke, Sister Agatha continued her perambulations around the physic garden, her hands moving independently of her words as she weeded and nipped, plucked and tidied. She stood up stiffly. Rebecca remained still and silent, unwilling to break the flow of this extraordinary tale. 'The first abbey of Mary the Jewess was founded in lands which became Germany, by the banks of the Mosel. Initially, all the women took the veil and were immured there. Effectively they were prisoners.' She pulled the dry marigold flower from her pocket and, with her fingertips, crumbled it to dust, allowing the fragments to fall back onto the earth. She continued.

'At present, there are around one hundred abbeys such as this one spread through every land touched by the Crusades. Each abbey was founded by one of the original women who had set out as captives from Jerusalem, or by their direct descendants. You will not read of us in any official history of the Church. We are a secret and independent order, affiliated to no other. We are tolerated and protected by the papacy because of our unique value, but we bear allegiance to none other than our sisters and those to whom we provide service.'

Rebecca considered this extraordinary tale. 'So that means I must be a descendant of one of these women.' She thought about the images of battle which had haunted her dreams as a child. Had her mother's bedtime stories prepared her for the moment when she was to hear this history? Was this the reason she had conjured up the phantom of the Angel of Death so vividly?' Sister Agatha stood in silence, watching as Rebecca tried to process her emotions. 'Camomile tisane, perhaps?'

Over tea, Rebecca told Sister Agatha her own history, including in it the Angel, her dreams of battle and the experience of watching her mother die. It had not been her intention to disclose so much about herself, but Sister Agatha's gentle manner and non-judgemental features helped her unburden herself. When she had finished, Agatha took her back to the garden. 'Would you like to see my pharmacy – apologies – the abbey pharmacy? Of course, it isn't mine but I can't help feeling somewhat protective about it. You will find it is a little messy as I am stock-taking, but if you can overlook that, I am sure you would find it interesting.' Rebecca was grateful to the little nun for her compassion, and even more so for changing the tone of their conversation from one so strange, to one which was normal. Rebecca craved the ordinary right now.

The pharmacy was to be found in the roof of the infirmary, accessed via an iron ladder situated in a narrow room beyond the wards. Rebecca realised that she had only been in one of the wards before, when in fact there were eight. Of course there were. Once they had climbed the ladder, she could see that the whole of the roof-space was taken up with herb-drying racks and various retorts and distillation equipment. She picked up a curiously shaped glass vessel which had another glass section within it. 'That,' called out Sister Agatha, as she tried in vain to clear an area on the large table at the far end, 'is a bain-marie, invented by Mary the Jewess herself. Through her, the order has a tradition of scientific discovery which stretches back centuries.'

Giving up in her effort to tidy the table, instead Sister Agatha pulled out a large, heavy volume, dropping it onto the table with a thump. 'This is our pharmacopeia. Each apothecary adds to it, and we share our recipes from convent to convent. I am fortunate here. Herbs grow well in this climate, and the bees collecting nectar from these plants produce a particularly nourishing honey. If you are interested I can show you some of the preparations?' A fascinating afternoon was then spent with Rebecca smelling and tasting a variety of tinctures, and rubbing different salves into her skin. Sister Agatha was obviously knowledgeable, and it wasn't long before Rebecca asked her about her own history.

'I have lived here my whole life. I was deposited on the doorstep of this convent and they are the only family I know. I have neither desire nor inclination to leave the abbey and there is nothing on the outside world which would entice me to do so.' Rebecca couldn't help thinking of Sofia – another soul left in the care of nuns. At least Sister Agatha seemed happy. She looked over at her companion, absorbed in her book, able to indulge in her passion and surrounded by those who shared her beliefs. It wasn't a bad life, after all. Not one which appealed to her, but she now had a greater understanding of why someone would want this seclusion from the world. At least these women had chosen their own path, however narrow it seemed to Rebecca. They were not dictated to by men and that could only be a good thing in her mind.

The companions had only two more days remaining before their planned return to Paris. Samuel and Cornelius were already eager to leave. The sojourn in Elysium had been all very well, Cornelius had said, but he missed the smell of the sewers. Rebecca knew that his comment was only partly in jest, but this place had an air of unreality about it. Ultimately, it was a place to which none of them really belonged. A few more days and it would be time for Rebecca to make her decision about enrolling in medical school.

That evening, Stefan proposed that tomorrow they all walk down to the village which lay outside of the abbey walls. It seemed that while Cornelius and Samuel had spent their mornings reading and lazing around the manor house, Stefan had made himself useful in the village. 'I would like to show it to you. It really is a remarkable place.' Samuel and Cornelius exchanged indulgent looks, and even Rebecca wondered what could be so remarkable about a village in a backwater of France, but she agreed on behalf of all of them that they would go with Stefan. The rest of the evening was spent in companionable conversation about very little indeed. Rebecca looked around her, and, indulging her imagination, she wondered what was really going on behind the eyes of her friends. She sighed, resigning herself to the thought that you could never truly know another person – even if you love them – or perhaps especially if you do.

CHAPTER 71

Early the next morning, Stefan led the way into the village of Fontaine-Daniel, a short walk through the forest but a world away from the tranquillity of the abbey. The village was a scene of bustling activity with construction work seemingly taking place on every building, and new structures being erected further up the hill. Stefan's enthusiasm was infectious, and the group were soon being regaled with the local history. 'This location has been inhabited for six hundred years. First came the Cistercians who built the original abbey in the forest. The village you see around you is new, and was constructed for the factory workers. Here is the factory. In it beautiful fabric is made. French design at its best. As you can see.' He pointed through the mullioned windows of an ancient building which he told them had been the refectory of the original abbey. 'Look in here. Modern, mechanised looms. Technology acquired from England, no less!'

'Damned noisy,' commented Cornelius. 'Don't think I would enjoy working in those conditions.' Stefan responded. 'Yes, you are right! It is not a pleasant sound. That is one of the reasons the owners no longer have children working in there. The workers are on designated hours and they are paid considerably more than any other factory hereabouts. And these,' he turned and pointed towards the lake and the three imposing buildings which edged the roadside, 'are homes built to house those workers. Aren't they wonderful? They are clean, heated, and the inhabitants have access to the river in which they can wash their clothes.' His eyes were shining in his eagerness to share his knowledge.

'The weavers used to have to walk many miles from their homes before beginning work each day. Now they have somewhere close to live.' He smiled at his companions. 'One day there will be a social hall and a church. But right now, the priority is a school.' The companions had followed Stefan into a rudimentary square where another ancient building, similar in style to that of the infirmary, could be seen. 'This was once the abbey forge where blacksmith monks would make shoes for horses, frames for cartwheels and even gates.' Rebecca thought of the iron gates in the inner wall of the convent. They had almost certainly been made here. Stefan was still talking. '... and because the children do not work, they can be educated. Right here. Isn't that perfect? The children of the workers will be taught reading, writing and rudimentary arithmetic and so will have the opportunity to better themselves. No longer will they be forced to work like slaves for a pittance so that rich Parisians can have their finery!'

Cornelius applauded slowly. 'A fine speech. Your Phrygian cap is showing there, Stefan.' Stefan turned to him angrily. 'Was the blood of the sans-culottes shed for nothing? Is education to be only for those fortunate enough to be born into riches?' Cornelius reached out to Stefan and rested his hands on his shoulders. 'My friend, forgive me. In my youth, I too was full of ideas and enthusiasm for change, but as one ages, priorities and an understanding of the human condition changes you.' Stefan's breathing began to calm. 'I truly applaud your sentiments, but I have learned that to change a society you cannot impose your world view on others, but have to let them come to their own conclusions. Change causes ripples around the individual like a pebble dropped into that lake over there.' Stefan pulled himself away from Cornelius. 'You have grown fat, Dr Mercier. I believe that one man can change the world around him. Look at what is happening here. One man – to be accurate – one family, were charged with compassion for the conditions of those who work for them, and through this they have made a difference to all involved.'

Cornelius kept his counsel. It was not worth mentioning that the changes which Stefan was so enthusiastic about had been done by people with money. Money brings power, and with it the choice of how to exercise it – either for personal aggrandisement or for the good of society. However, he had to concede that this family sounded – interesting. People above profits. A thought-provoking concept but one which would hardly take hold in France, he was sure. It would be stimulating to meet them, but, he thought, that was unlikely to happen. Cornelius already knew that neither he nor Samuel would come here again.

He walked in silent rumination as Stefan continued with the tour of Fontaine-Daniel. He had an aversion to paternalism, that was certain, but he was not fond of the anarchy of socialism either. It was hard to be a good man, sometimes. He observed Stefan. He means well, to be sure, but Cornelius couldn't help thinking that Stefan would be much less of a political firebrand if he got some sex occasionally. Looking over at Rebecca as she listened intently to Stefan, he wondered what the future held for these two. Hopefully it contained love. He himself would not turn back the clock for anything. Samuel was his world now, and perhaps Stefan was right; he no longer cared for others as much as he had before Samuel. He walked over to the object of these reflections, and, linking arms with him, drew him closer. Stefan continued to lead them around this curious village, his companions listening politely as he extolled the virtues of its guiding principles.

A week ago, when the companions had first arrived at the manor house, they had given no thought as to its running. Meals were prepared for them, and their beds were made daily. It was only when Rebecca realised that all of this was being done by the nuns that she took a moment to think of the care they were receiving. The linen smelt beautiful, and a sprig of lavender had been placed each night on their pillows, and the food – although simple in preparation – was all fresh and had been well cooked. Rebecca noted how quickly she had settled into the role of a superior, and this pained her. It was hard to think that she had grown so callous so quickly. From that moment on, she chivvied her companions into clearing their plates away, and, once she had discovered the kitchen, sharing the washing-up. Cornelius and Samuel found this newly discovered domestic obsession amusing, while Stefan threw himself into it with enthusiasm. Rebecca realised that this young man did not enjoy leisure, seeming to prefer activity. Between the four of them the chores were soon completed, and when two silent nuns next brought their meal she was rewarded with beaming smiles from both. It felt better to contribute than to receive passively, Rebecca mused. She was also sure that she would have to keep reminding herself of this fact as comprehension of how much money Miriam had actually left her sank in.

The meal that evening ended amicably, and Samuel and Cornelius retired to their room. Rebecca curled up her legs into the armchair by the fireplace. Her eyes defocused and she stared into the fire, watching the flames dance, and listening to the crackle of logs burning. Stefan joined her in the chair opposite, having first placed two glasses of rich, red wine on a low bench between them. For a while neither of them spoke. Rebecca broke the silence. 'How is it that you come to know so much about Fontaine-Daniel?' Stefan took a speculative sip of his wine, returning the glass carefully onto the bench. 'I have been spending my mornings there. On the second day, I wandered over to the school and got into conversation with a man. I thought he was the architect. In fact, he is, but Monsieur Denis also owns the factory. We talked for an hour or more, and he explained his vision for the village to me.' He picked up his glass again, this time cupping the bowl in his hand. 'He asked me for suggestions, and I am honoured to say that he accepted some of them. Soon I found myself there every day, working with the artisans to create the interior of the schoolroom. He raised his left hand, displaying a blackened fingernail. 'I am not very practical, I'm afraid. They gave me full marks for effort but none for execution.' He smiled ruefully. Rebecca remained silent, waiting for him to continue. She sensed that there was more to this recitation than just story, as he had not shared it with the others. He continued. 'After our visit this morning, I went back to say goodbye. Something happened. Something which I didn't expect. Monsieur Denis offered me the job of schoolmaster.'

Rebecca lifted her own glass, letting the light from the fire play through the red liquid. Curious emotions were passing through her mind. Now that she might be parted from Stefan she realised that her feelings for him had grown stronger in the time they had spent together. How did she feel about this news? '… and what about your studies? What about Dr Charcot?'

'I have to think, Rebecca. There is so much I could do here. Perhaps more than I could if I worked as an Alienist. After all, I still have those skills and I can use them to help others. Perhaps being a schoolmaster here, in this unique setting, is an opportunity to be a better man. I only just got this offer. There is more to consider than my professional life.'

Rebecca put down her glass. 'What will make you happiest?' she said, her throat suddenly dry. Stefan mirrored her movement, placing his now-empty glass by hers. 'What would make me the happiest is if you would consent to be my wife. I can offer you little by the way of comforts. The stipend of a schoolmaster is small, but the job does come with a house, and its own plot where we can grow our food. I don't expect you to say anything right now, but please consider my humble proposal.'

He left her alone by the fireside, where she stayed until the fire was nothing more than embers. She shivered. Could she possibly live here as a simple schoolmaster's wife? What about her dreams to become a doctor? If Stefan had fallen in love, it was with an illusion. Rebecca was a wealthy woman now. His feelings for her would inevitably change when he discovered that she was an heiress. Besides, as her husband, he would have access to her wealth. Her thoughts began to shoot out tendrils like ivy and they took hold of her emotions. Did she love this man, and could she trust him? Her accelerated breathing began to slow down and other thoughts started to crystallise. She remembered Charcot's words. Money brings the power to make change. Could this be her path?

CHAPTER 72

IT WAS TO be their last evening at the manor house. In the morning, they would start their journey back to Paris. Cornelius and Samuel were already packed and ready to go, and had decided to spend the day lounging around the house, reading. It seemed that the pull of the forest had released its hold over them. Moreover, Cornelius was complaining that he would be picking burrs from his trousers for months. Spending time in such close proximity with Samuel and Cornelius had made Rebecca realise just how much Samuel had changed. She was no longer the focus of his attention in the way she once had been. True, when Cornelius was not around, their connection felt as it was before – almost – but it was evident to Rebecca Samuel would rather be spending time with his lover. No matter. It was obvious that Cornelius felt the same way about Samuel. Watching them together as they walked through the wood, she had recognised how different they were from one another. Notwithstanding these disparities, the relationship seemed to be working. Samuel was happy to go with the flow, while Cornelius could be – not to put too fine a point on it – quite fussy. Maybe that was the secret to a successful relationship – being different. 'One loves another because of their faults, not despite them!' Samuel had said to her, watching Cornelius stalk off in a huff after snagging his best jacket on a thorn bush. 'Somehow, I don't think he will ever be a country boy!' He laughed, then followed his lover, placing his arm around his shoulder and quickly dispelling Cornelius's darkening mood.

Rebecca spent most of their final day within the convent walls, partly to spend time with Sister Agatha, and partly to avoid Stefan. She had no idea what she was going to say to him. Nor did she feel that she could talk to Samuel about the proposal, as, now he was in love, she felt sure he would be inclined to extol its virtues. She could speak to Mother Benedict, but this did not feel right either. Instead she let the thoughts percolate through her mind as she watched Sister Agatha teach her how to use the bain-marie. She reflected. The more time she spent with this woman, the more she thought about the prospect of her own study. Perhaps she could focus on medical research? Maybe with Sister Agatha's knowledge and access to the ancient pharmacopeia she could test the recipes therein, and help to bring some of these folk-remedies into mainstream medical science.

'Sister Agatha,' Rebecca began, tentatively, 'the recipes in this book – what are they for, exactly?' The nun looked up sharply. 'Pain. Anxiety.' She closed the book with surprising force. 'You must excuse me now. I have some decoctions to prepare.' From the look on the nun's face, Rebecca knew better than to ask if she could stay and watch. 'Thank you for your time,' she said, quietly. Sister Agatha reached out her hand towards Rebecca. 'Forgive me. I spend too much time alone up here.' She guided Rebecca towards the ladder. 'Besides, there are other writings which you would need to see first to understand the work I do here.' Her hands gently stroked the edges of the ancient book. There are things that it is

not for me to explain. You will need to speak to Mother Benedict.'
She smiled. 'If Mother Benedict wills it, then I would be happy to
welcome you here once more and teach you all you wish to know.'
It was obvious now that Rebecca's time in the pharmacy was at
an end. 'I am sure that Mother Benedict will be waiting for you
tomorrow to say goodbye properly. You can ask her then, perhaps.'

Rebecca made her way down the ladder and began to walk along
the infirmary corridor. Her eyes were drawn into the first ward
where she could see the blind nun, carrying a small, earthenware
flask and a drinking vessel. She stood at the doorway watching as
the nun confidently navigated her way towards the only occupied
bed. In it was an emaciated woman, her body propped up with
pillows as she struggled to breathe. Her eyes stared in fear, and
her body convulsed in violent movement back and forth, back and
forth, as if she were trying to raise herself up from the bed. The nun,
now seated at the bedside, turned her head towards where Rebecca
was standing, and, with a slow movement of her hand, signalled
for her to enter. Rebecca walked towards the bed, and the pathetic
creature in it raised her eyes. They locked onto Rebecca's, and she
stretched out her arms. The nun continued to summon her forward,
and soon she was standing by the bed, looking down on this pain-
wracked figure. Suddenly, the woman's hand grasped Rebecca's arm.
She was shocked by its strength, and tried to draw away. Before
she could do so, the woman pulled her close to her face and raised
her skeletal body from the pillows. She strained her sinewy neck
forward and kissed Rebecca's cheek. Tears began to pour from
her eyes. Releasing her grip, she fell back once more onto the bed,
exhausted from the effort. The nun smiled sightlessly at Rebecca,
then, feeling her way to the dying woman's mouth, held the cup
to her parched lips. Rebecca pulled up a chair and sat down, now

face to face with the blind nun, the sleeping woman between them on the bed. Not knowing what else to do she took up a thin hand and stroked it gently as the light outside began to dim.

By the time she left the infirmary, dusk had painted the horizon with a vivid orange hue. Rebecca had remained until the last, tortured breath had left the dying woman's body and the nun had gently covered her face with a sheet. Rebecca turned to close the infirmary door behind her. Once more facing the courtyard to the manor house, she took a moment to enjoy the view of the sky, picked out as it was by the highest branches of the trees, underlined by the darkness of the wall beyond. It was then that she saw a piece of the darkness separate itself and begin to advance towards her slowly. It was the Angel. Hooded, imposing, silent.

There would be no escape now. She knew better than to try to run or hide. A continent had not been great enough to separate her from this apparition. Rebecca waited. Waited for the end. Her mind moved through the images of now-impossible futures, painting pictures of how her life could have been – with Stefan – as a doctor – even as a mother. All the while the figure continued its inexorable advance. Rebecca pulled her shawl around her shoulders and watched, impassively. But then the mask of her fear slipped away from her eyes and instead of looking, she observed. This was no apparition on the path before her. It was, most certainly, a man. As he came closer, the cloak billowed out around his body, revealing a suit. She almost burst out laughing. Since when did the Azriel, Angel of Death, wear a suit?

The figure halted ten paces away from her, and dragged back the hood of his cloak to reveal a face she recognised. It was Osborne, but he had changed significantly since she had last seen him loom lasciviously above her in the Egyptian House a lifetime ago. In the light of the fading dusk she could see his even, handsome features were now distorted. The brow, which had been so smooth and haughty, was now covered in disfiguring lumps and a large, ugly sore leaked from the corner of his mouth. He stood before Rebecca and his features distorted further as he snarled at her. 'You couldn't just stay in the asylum, could you? You had to escape. You stupid woman! Did you really think you could just get away, that we would forget about you? We were never going to let a creature like you destroy what I have spent a lifetime discovering. I wouldn't risk exposure by you. No, no, no little pretty Rebecca. You forced me to track you halfway across Europe. You forced me to do this. First, I used the traitorous Reith's and then your idiot fiancé – but you managed to lose them all. I would have lost you too had it not been for the vocal villagers. You may have thought you could hide yourself away in the convent but I am a hunter, and I have hunted you down. It is better this way.

'You have forced me to finish the job myself, don't you understand? I will make the kill. It ends here, Miss Zimmerman. You cannot be allowed to live any longer. The future of the Temple of Hermanoubis depends on it, don't you see? I will be the one to release you into its light and your power will pass directly to me.' He stretched out his arms and bowed his head, dramatically. Pulling himself upright, he pushed his hair from his face with his damaged hand. He locked eyes with Rebecca and she stared back as his other hand reached deep into the cloak. He pulled out a knife. It was a long stiletto, its blade glistening in the fading light. He smiled.

Rebecca turned to run, but lost her footing on the steps of the infirmary and sprawled face down into the gravel, her face hitting the stones painfully. The sound of a gunshot suddenly reverberated around the buildings, and Rebecca dragged herself to the wall, curling up foetally, covering her ears and pushing her face into the stones as if their permanence could save her. Footsteps echoed on the gravel, and a man's voice called out her name. She peered into the darkness. Two figures scuffled in the gloom. Once more a gunshot sounded, and both figures fell to the ground. 'Stefan!' Rebecca cried out in anguish. Figures were now running from all directions. She got up awkwardly, running as fast as she could towards the prone figures. Osborne was screaming out in pain, blood pouring from the gunshot wound, his viscera visible. The other figure was face down. He was not moving. The stiletto had penetrated his neck. Rebecca turned him over gently.

Looking sightlessly back at her were the open eyes of Isaac Coren. Her fiancé. His expression was of surprise rather than pain, and a momentary gratitude to a god which she did not believe in overwhelmed her. She fell to her knees, her bloody hands held away from her body. A keening broke the silence. It was a moment before she realised it came from her. Then she began to rock. Back and forth. Back and forth.

Unresisting, she was lifted from the ground and carried back to the manor house. 'I'm here, Rebecca. You are safe now.' Stefan pulled her body closer and pressed his cheek lovingly to hers. 'No-one can hurt you now.'

CHAPTER 73

IT WAS THREE days before Rebecca's fever broke. Three nights in which she had raged and raved. Her dreams were populated with battlefields and blood. The Angel stayed away in fear of her as she was now an elemental. Her fury was transported on the wind and the waves. Ancient trees pulled free of their roots and hopeless ships were dashed on the rocks. Buildings fell to the ground as fire flew through their interiors causing rocks to shatter, leaving nothing but rubble. And all the while, the heartbeat of the earth pounded in her ears, forcing her to the ground in expectation that soon, very soon, she would be swallowed up.

On the fourth morning, the tempest abated, and her exhausted sanity crawled up onto the beach of her conscious mind. She had survived the storm.

The first sound she registered was that of birdsong. Her head felt empty of thoughts, as if she had been purged. She was hungry too. Raising her head, she saw Samuel leaning on the ledge of the open bedroom window looking out at the physic garden. 'My goodness,

Rebecca. You gave us all a fright back there.' She felt her heart surge with happiness. The black rings around Samuel's eyes told her that she still had a place in his heart. It was evident from his looks and the flippant tone he used that he had not slept. It was only later that she discovered he had remained by her side the whole time, cat-napping on the bedroom chair and only moving from the room when Cornelius forced him to come away to eat.

Samuel handed Rebecca a glass of cool water and watched her intently as she drank. 'It's fine, Samuel. I am well now, honestly I am.' She could see the anxiety radiating from his eyes and throughout his features. She knew what he feared. He was afraid that he would lose her to madness and might never get her back again.

She pushed herself upright in the bed, enjoying the coolness of the air in the room. 'Where are the others?'

'Cornelius and Stefan had to return to Paris yesterday. We had no way of knowing how long you would be ill.' Part of Rebecca was hurt when she heard the news, while the other, relieved. It would mean that she would have some time alone with Samuel.

Fully awake now, her mind permitted access to her most recent memories. Registering her realisation, and before she could speak, Samuel interjected. 'Isaac is dead. Mother Benedict has written to his sister that he died in a tragic accident. I am sure that among your stepmother's emotions about her brother there will be relief.' He sat down on her bed, and stroked her hair as if she were a child. 'Osborne, is he…?' Samuel interrupted. 'Osborne somehow survived the shooting. He is in the infirmary.'

The short walk from the manor house across to the infirmary building took Rebecca longer than she could have imagined. The fever had not beaten her mind but it had exhausted her body. When she reached the doorway, she paused, resting her hand on the wall where a few days before she had cowered in fear. She didn't have the energy for emotion right now, and so she allowed the birdsong to lift her spirits before she saw Osborne once more. She pushed the heavy door open, and washed her hands as she had been shown. She was greeted by Sister Agatha, who, surprisingly, kissed her on both cheeks before embracing her. 'It is good to see you on your feet. Gentle exercise and light food for a couple of days and you will be yourself again.' Rebecca wanted to reply that she wasn't at all sure who 'herself' really was, but it was too early in the day for such philosophical discussions. Besides, seeing Sister Agatha's reaction alone had worked as a tonic.

Fortified, she made her way into the ward. Osborne was alone. As she entered, she smelled incense, and as she advanced towards the bed she soon realised why. The odour coming from Osborne was revolting. It was a mixture of shit and a strange sweetness which she could not place. His torso was bandaged, but the brown-blackness of blood was wet on the bandages. He was unconscious, but even in this state his face contorted in pain. She stood in silence at the foot of the bed. Even though this man was responsible for so much of the trauma which she had undergone, seeing him in this state gave her no pleasure.

Mother Benedict had joined her. They stood together in silence for a while, and seeing he was starting to wake, she called out to the duty nun who came rapidly to the bedside. His eyes opened, and, seeing Rebecca, his face once more contorted with hate. He tried to speak, but nothing except blood-flecked spittle came from his mouth. 'It is time to leave. You are causing him distress.' As they left the infirmary, Rebecca's anger boiled into words. 'He once tried to rape me! He hunted me down to kill me. What about the distress which he caused me?'

'We are not here to judge. We have one function here. It is time that you learn what it is.'

They walked in silence from the infirmary to the chapel. It was the first time that Rebecca had been invited in, and the only place which she had not seen. The interior was as surprising to her as the exterior. They entered through a central double-door into a room which seemed wider than it was long. Arranged around a central aisle were wooden, high-backed pews. These were not seats but resembled screens more than anything, screens which were divided at intervals by protruding lengths of wood. Between each, a nun could stand for long periods of time, using the armrests for support if needed. Nor were the pews in straight rows like the chapel in Saint Anton, but these were semi-circular. Front and centre of the aisle was an icon. It was a painting of a woman holding, what Rebecca realised, was a bain-marie in one hand, and a stiletto in the other. On its horizon, Rebecca could see the outline of the walled city. Jerusalem. Mother Benedict beckoned Rebecca to come closer to the image. 'Our spiritual ancestor, Mary the Jewess. In one hand, she holds the bain-marie to denote her skills with medicines. In the other, a misericorde.' Rebecca registered with shock that it was the same type of weapon with which Osborne had tried to kill her. 'He stole it from us. It has now been safely hidden away. There will be no more blood on its blade.' Mother Benedict pointed to it once more. 'If a knight sustained mortal injuries on the battlefield, this weapon would be used to speed his journey to God. It was sharp enough to penetrate armour and long enough to pierce the heart or the neck. If that wasn't possible, then the eye would suffice.' Rebecca stared at the icon in horror. Why was it depicted here?

She scrutinised the image again. There was something else. On the ground by Mary's feet, as if scratched in the earth, was a figure eight with a line across its centre.

'Just like that etched on your mother's locket. I expect you noticed.' Rebecca lifted her hand to her throat and touched the talisman which Stefan had returned to her in Paris. Enfolding it in her hand, she mused wryly. 'Yet again, I looked but did not observe.' Of course, she knew the symbol, but as it had always been there around her throat, she had seemingly wiped it from view. Perhaps this is the nature of the human condition. We see the differences, not the similarities, and it was for this reason that she had failed to see that the figure eight with its bisecting line could be found everywhere in this place. Mother Benedict waited until Rebecca looked across at her. 'I need to understand.'

The chapel did not end with the icon. To either side were fabric hangings which Rebecca had assumed were nothing more than decoration. However, Mother Benedict pulled one aside and Rebecca realised that the area of worship with the pews was merely an ante-chamber. In the centre of this hidden space was a large, plain box. It was a dais, shaped like a house with a steep roof. At the bottom of each roof part was a shelf, and on each shelf rested a book. These books were old. There was, Rebecca noticed, space for eight books. One space was empty.

'When the order began, the founding mothers were instructed to pray to the crucifix and observe all the offices deemed appropriate to show fealty to the Pope. You will see none of that here. Nor will you see images of Jesus or saints that would connect us to worship as the authorities would have us do. Even our prayers are our own.

The essence of them is more in what is not said, than that which is said. We pray for a kindness and compassion for all, whether their path is Christian, Jewish or that of Islam. We pray for all regardless of whom they love and how they live. Kindness is our doctrine, and we do not judge.'

She paused. 'Radical thought, even in these enlightened days.' Sister Benedict's eyes closed in on a memory to which Rebecca had no way of ingress. She waited patiently for the nun to continue. 'As the order is a closed one, we were eventually left in peace.'

Rebecca reached out to the books, and a sudden memory came to her of the synagogue back home with its Torah scrolls at the heart of it, loved and protected by the rabbis. Questions. Ideas. Knowledge. She turned to Mother Benedict. 'Tell me more about the books.'

CHAPTER 74

MOTHER BENEDICT REACHED out to the first slim volume and reverentially rested her palm on its wooden cover. 'A book which is not read is dead. The ones you see here are all living books, and as such, have their own special power. It also makes them dangerous to those who would have us live in ignorance. An ignorant population is a malleable one.' She turned to Rebecca. 'Once you have read these words you cannot unread them. They become part of you, and through you they come to life.' She opened the book. 'Contained in here are the words of the anchoress, Julian of Norwich. *The Revelations of divine love.* You would think that a text of this nature would contain nothing to fear, would you not? Julian speaks of the compassionate nature of God, and the female aspect of divinity. It was… is, not a popular theme. Whenever the female divine is evoked, the male hierarchy seeks to suppress.'

She turned the fragile pages delicately, and Rebecca noticed that some of them were charred. Mother Benedict touched them gently. 'Countless unnamed women have died to protect this book. We came by it after the Revolution, when the Carmelites, who were its guardians, delivered it to us for safekeeping. Many were executed, but we believe that some found a way of escaping. Their wish was to return for it one day and so we hold it in trust until such a time as their successors have a home for it. There is no-one outside of the order who knows this book even exists. It is better that way. Better for it to be believed lost than have someone come looking for it who would abuse its contents, or even destroy it completely.

'This one here,' she moved to the next book, 'contains accounts of Hildegard von Bingen's visions.' She pointed to others. 'We also have volumes containing her music and divine revelations. I have no way of knowing how many copies of these texts exist. Once a year a sister from our fellow abbey in Pfalzel comes to copy sections from them. It is a time-consuming process, but a labour of love.'

She smiled encouragingly at Rebecca, then walked around to the other side of the wooden structure, pointing to a vacant spot. This is the space for the pharmacopeia which Sister Agatha guards so fiercely, and this...' – indicating a slim, plain book – 'is the one which you need to read to truly understand the purpose of the order.'

Before Rebecca could respond, Sister Agatha rushed into the room. 'Mother, it is time.' Without another word, Mother Benedict headed quickly down the aisle with Sister Agatha and Rebecca close behind. They headed towards the infirmary.

Once inside, the screams of pain and fury were unnerving, more animal than human. Osborne's limbs thrashed wildly, while his eyes bulged horribly. The blind and, until now, silent nun spoke in an inversion of the words of Sister Agatha. 'Is it time.' It did not seem to be a question. Rebecca had been forgotten as these women shared an unvoiced connection. Mother Benedict spoke. 'It is time.' She turned to Rebecca. 'You must leave now. It is time.' Sister Agatha drew a tiny flask from her pocket and handed it to Mother Benedict.

Rebecca walked numbly from the infirmary. Even after all he had done, she did not wish to see the death throes of Osborne. She felt no animosity towards him, only a dull fear that, with the manner of his death, he could still do her harm. How were the authorities going to react to his death, shot as he had been by her fiancé? Giving in to her anxieties she began to worry at a fingernail, and when that and the skin around it had gone, she contemplated moving onto the next one.

The chapel was still empty. She made her own way past the image of the foundress and into the hidden room. Picking up the history of the order she lowered herself down to the floor, and, using the dais as a backrest, began to read. It didn't take her long as there were only eight pages in this volume. Eight pages in which the vocation of the order was clearly laid out.

Written as a letter from a mother to a daughter, it spoke of the responsibility of living a good life, and the right to make a good death. Rebecca continued reading. As she did, the bell sounded out for prayer, and she could hear the summoned nuns silently enter the chapel. She read on as the sound of plainsong began to fill the space. Her eyes blurred with tears as the music which she could not understand wrapped the writings in a cloak of almost unbearable poignancy. The emotion threatened to overwhelm her. She read on.

The letter told of the dark days of the Crusades, when the only way to die for those mortally wounded was to suffer dreadful, drawn out agonies, or, if they were fortunate, the release of the misericorde. In its place, the Jewish women began to use their knowledge of herbs to give the mercy stroke to their fallen knights. They could die as they had lived, with dignity. These women chose to help their own lovers to die rather than have them die in pain on the battlefield, or to fall into the hands of the enemy and be subjected to agonising tortures. Knowledge of their ability spread, bringing with it more danger in accusations of witchcraft.

Once the Order of Mary the Jewess was created, these women could still be found on the battlefields of Europe, this time with the tacit blessing of the Pope. Like the Valkyrie of old, they came to select who would die. Soldiers soon began to tattoo the symbol of the bisected figure of eight onto their bodies, so the nuns would know who had prepared themselves for this eventuality.

Rebecca allowed tears to escape her eyes, unsure of whether the music or the words had created them. She wiped them away with her sleeve and continued to read.

When she had finished, she pulled the book close to her body, weeping for the knights of ancient times, their Jewish lovers and the knowledge which she now had in her possession. Mother Benedict was right. Words once read cannot be unread. They become a part of you.

Rebecca waited until the last voice had been stilled and the nuns had all left the chapel, before emerging. Mother Benedict was waiting for her, framed by sunlight in the doorway. She turned, and Rebecca followed her. Instead of the infirmary, they headed towards the farm. The sun was shining. Bees hummed and birds sang. Just as they had on the day of her arrival. Nature alone could not lift the stone from her heart today. She had to speak. 'You gave Osborne something, didn't you? So he would die. That's what this place is, isn't it? People come here to die.' She had no better way of saying those words. Mother Benedict seemed not to hear. 'Rebecca. There is pain in this world which you could not imagine. The pain of a mother who brings five children into the world, and they in turn have children. She is now old and the man she loved is dead. She is infirm and can no longer walk. She was a proud woman who now needs feeding and cleaning like a baby. Can you imagine how she feels? Or the once handsome young soldier who now drags himself around the marketplace on the stumps of legs remaining to him as he begs a sou for bread? Or the woman disfigured by disease for which there is no cure? And what of war? There will always be war and it will not be too many years before it returns to France. I can feel it. So much pain, Rebecca. Not all of it visible – and only so many ways in which to endure it. If a man or woman wishes their life to end while they still have dignity, who are any of us to judge?' She turned to Rebecca, lifting the sleeve of her habit until her shoulder was exposed. On it was a tattoo. A figure of eight bisected by a line. 'If my life becomes intolerable to me, with this mark I show that I have elected to choose the time and manner of my own death – and, if I am not able to make that decision, this mark empowers those around me to make that decision with my blessing.' She pointed to the women in the fields around them. 'We all carry the mark.'

The kiln was already lit. Wood burned furiously at its base, and Rebecca had to shield her eyes as the iron door was closed on the physical remains of Isaac Coren. She felt nothing. She wanted to feel something. After all he had saved her life. But the stone in her chest meant that right now, breathing was all that she could safely manage without her emotions splitting her open. Osborne's body would soon follow Isaac's, but she would not be there to watch.

Mother Benedict would write to his wife, explaining that he had died in the infirmary, but nothing more would be said. After all, his syphilis was already visible. No doubt, Mrs Osborne would see his death as a mercy, and, no doubt, simply move on with her life.

Rebecca had a choice. There would always be a choice, she realised, and it was never going to be simple, or even clear-cut. While she raged internally that it had not been for Mother Benedict to decide on the timing of Osborne's death, Rebecca knew that if the gunshot did not kill him, then the gangrene which had already invaded his body would, and if not that, it would be the syphilis. Either way it would be a painful, ugly and demeaning death. At least his syphilis went some way to explaining the mania and obsessions. Ironic really. He was mad. She was sane. He was dead. She was alive. Rebecca made her choice.

As they walked away from the kiln, she turned to Mother Benedict and declared 'I cannot accept that what you do here is right. I will become a doctor, and I will fight for the life of every patient.'

'As is your choice, Rebecca. As it was also your choice to watch your mother die.' Rebecca reeled angrily away from her as if she had been slapped in the face. 'I did *not* choose...' her voice faltered and her inner self called her to order. 'Yes, you did choose. You could have called for someone, anyone to come and help, but you didn't.' Mother Benedict continued levelly. 'I believe that is why the Angel of Death has accompanied you, day and night. Knowing that you did nothing to save your mother is what drove you into the arms of insanity. The knowledge that you deliberately allowed your mother to die has haunted you ever since that time.' Mother

Benedict touched her arm. 'You can free yourself from this guilt, Rebecca. The locket which she wore. The symbol. She wore the bisected eight around her neck.'

The significance came to her in Samuel's voice. '*You shall not etch a tattoo on yourselves.*' She even remembered the chapter and verse: Leviticus 19:28. So, the locket was her way of wearing the mark. Alma Zimmerman, her mother, had chosen the right to die, and Rebecca had, albeit unknowingly, respected her wish to follow this path.

Epilogue

I N THE BEDROOM of her tiny attic apartment in the servants' quarters of Gower Street, Rebecca methodically brushed her long, lustrous hair before looping it up as Sofia had shown her. She could think of Sofia now. There had been a long time when she could not. Looking at her own reflection in the mirror she stroked her mother's locket. It had been many years before she had chosen to wear it once more. Many years of immersion in medical training and the pain and suffering of humanity. Now it was once more visible around her own neck, and unconsciously she traced the bisected figure of eight etched on it. Rebecca had thought long and hard about whether she would ever wear the locket again, knowing as she did what the symbol signified. She looked at it, and at herself, in the mirror. Rising, she smoothed her grey, simple dress. It was time to visit Miriam.

Her life was changing, she mused. Again. For the past few years, Samuel and Cornelius had divided their time travelling between Paris and the Côte d'Azur. Recently, they had settled in the south of France where they now lived with Père and whichever lover was currently sharing his bed. Samuel wrote often to her, and Rebecca had visited them, but the sun there was not to her liking. She felt too exposed, preferring the more muted seascapes of northern France. She holidayed alone by preference, usually staying out of season in the modern and anonymous Grand Hôtel des Thermes overlooking the sea in Saint Malo. She smiled ruefully to herself, looking down at her dark clothing. She had developed an affinity with greyness.

In the end, she had decided against selling the Gower Street house. Keeping the top floor for her own use, she then offered the East End Association for Women's Suffrage a peppercorn rent for the use of the rest of the building. Mrs Burton and Clarissa were the driving force and together had become genuinely formidable, as were the numerous women who arrived daily for help and advice with their toy manufacturing businesses. As Clarissa had pointed out to her recently, 'Food on the table comes first, votes in the box come second.' Now Rebecca had qualified as a doctor, occasionally she would be called upon when one of the women had a 'problem'. Rebecca had to be very circumspect.

It had amused her how many of Miriam's spiritualist friends gravitated back to Gower Street to help with the women's cause. Apart from Mrs Tiran, that is. Or, to be accurate, the recently married Mrs Colonel Burbridge, as she preferred to be known. According to Mrs Thorne, her (now ex) friend insisted that everyone must use her husband's title when they addressed her in future. Rebecca had not actually minded the fact that the Colonel had married someone else. He was a good man. What did offend her was Mrs Colonel Burbridge's insistence that Miriam had communicated with her from the other side via planchette and given her blessing to the newly-weds. Rebecca could only tolerate so much nonsense these days, but she held her tongue regardless. It was too easy to make enemies. Kindness and compassion were her touchstones now, even though there were times when she could cheerfully murder someone. She flinched internally. Kindness and compassion. Kindness and compassion. Even if people have some strange beliefs. Kindness and compassion. If she repeated it often enough, perhaps one day she would truly believe it was possible to live by these tenets.

As she pondered the vagaries of relationships, it was Stefan who inevitably came into her mind. Since that day when she had called out his name, they had corresponded regularly, but not seen one another. When Stefan had returned to Paris after the visit to Fontaine-Daniel, he had gone directly to Dr Charcot to inform him of his decision not to take up his kind offer of a studentship. Charcot was taken aback by the refusal, but quickly found a replacement student in the form of a certain Mr Tourette. Within a few short weeks, Stefan was on his way to Fontaine-Daniel to take up the post of schoolmaster. The weekly letters which he sent to Rebecca were brought to life with stories of the inhabitants of the village, and she soon looked forward to them. Increasingly, it was his opinion she sought out now rather than that of Samuel. Very soon she would visit him. Life was, indeed, changing.

One regret for Rebecca was that there had been no reconciliation with her father. Jeremiah Zimmerman had staunchly maintained his position that Rebecca must return to Ramsgate once she had been declared sane, and even the knowledge that she was now an heiress did little to change his mind. His only concession was that he would not insist on her marrying, and she could remain under his roof provided he controlled her financial affairs. He was quickly disabused of his belief that as a woman she was incapable (or would be unwilling!) to do this for herself, when Rebecca wrote to him from France informing him that she had now enrolled as a student at the Faculty of Medicine in Paris and had no intention of returning to England any time soon. She tempered her response with an expression of hope that her father would be proud of her, but her hope was to remain unsatisfied. Jeremiah did not respond to her letter, nor did he contact Rebecca again.

She was disappointed, but it was his choice and it was up to her to respect it. She could not allow herself to suffer because of it. The understanding that each of us makes our own decisions and must stand by the repercussions had become a recurring theme in Rebecca's life. She fought it at first but now accepted it stoically. Thankfully, Zachary's reaction to her return had been a different one. He seemed delighted to welcome her back into his life – especially after he had ploughed his way through the many letters which she had written to him and had for so long remained unsent.

Miriam had elected to be buried in the Jewish section of Highgate Cemetery. It was unusual, but then, so much about Miriam had been. Rebecca and Zachary travelled there together by train, then walked up the hill to the cemetery gates, enjoying the warm summer sun which accompanied them. They found the road leading up to the entrance jammed with hearses and the accompanying carriages full of black-clad mourners, all waiting impatiently for their turn to go through the gates and deposit their cargos therein. It was a veritable traffic jam, and some of the mourners were becoming quite agitated at the delay. It was not at all the dignified, tranquil place Rebecca had imagined.

The siblings avoided the crush by making their way through a smaller, pedestrian gateway and meandered towards the Jewish section, taking their time to see the various parts of the cemetery and stopping to admire some of the grander plots or commenting on particularly odd or mawkish statuary. Others seemed to be doing the same thing. It appeared that the cemetery had become a fashionable place to visit. As they were in no hurry, they wandered past the chapel, the catacombs, various statues of dogs, horses and obelisks and too many angels to count, then continued their ascent towards the circle of Lebanon with its ancient cedar tree. The sun had gone behind a cloud, and the greyness of graves was echoed in the sky above. As they walked together, Rebecca caught sight of her brother's profile. Zachary had become a good-looking young man. Taller than her, he most resembled his father in his looks, but certainly not in his temperament. Very soon now he would begin his life as an art student. Against Jeremiah's dying wish, and with Rebecca's financial help, Zachary would soon be joining her in Paris. There was room enough in her apartment for them both, and brother and sister would be able to share the space – at least for a short while.

They had reached the entrance to the Jewish section. Compared to the other parts of the cemetery, it seemed cold and lacking in colour. There were no flowers. There were no angels. In fact, there was very little ornamentation anywhere, just row upon row of seemingly identical headstones. The only sign of humanity were the random stones placed on the graves. Names and dates. Dates and names. Occasionally, on a grave at the end of a row she saw the carved sign of a hand, indicating that the occupant was one of the Cohanim.

She squeezed Zachary's arm in recognition of the deep love she felt for him. Even though he was taller than her now, she still wanted to protect him, protect him from harm, protect him from history, protect him from himself. Perhaps it would always be this way.

Reaching Miriam's grave, she allowed Zachary to explain to her the meaning of the tiny stones on the graves, even though she already knew their significance. 'The Talmud teaches that the stones are to keep the soul in the grave, so that the family won't be haunted by the spirit of their dead.' There were such stones on Miriam's grave. Rebecca reached down instinctively to clear them. Suddenly, Zachary put his arm out to stop her. She felt a surge of fear. Fear that with this act he was showing he was still too deep within the shadow of his father and the doctrine espoused by him, to find the strength to liberate himself.

Then, slowly and systematically, one by one, Zachary removed each stone. When he had almost finished, Rebecca realised that she had been holding her breath as he went about this task. She finally exhaled and started to shiver. When the grave was clear of stones, Zachary stood close to Rebecca – her shoulder touching his arm. They stared at the headstone together and, taking a pristine white handkerchief from his waistcoat, he used it to wipe the dust from his hands. 'Better?' Rebecca's shivers subsided and she smiled at him. Looking at his strong face, she replied, 'Yes. Much better.' Stepping forward she placed the single white lily which she had been carrying at the base of the headstone. For the briefest of moments, the sun found its way back to them and they were illuminated by a circle of light. Aunt, niece, nephew. Family. For a few minutes, they stood together in companionable silence with the dead, then walked back to rejoin the living in the bustling river of humanity that was Highgate.

By the gateway, the cloaked figure looked on impassively, motionless and silent.

ArtSpace Gîtes – Fontaine-Daniel

ArtSpace Gîtes is a project in Fontaine-Daniel, France, created by the author of *The Soul Midwife*. Consisting of two gîtes in the heart of the village, its purpose is to bring together professional artists and creatives in an inspiring environment, and visitors who want to experience a more authentic visit to this rural area of France.

Utilising local artisans and craftspeople, the gîtes incorporate the finest Toiles de Mayenne design as well as reclaimed/recycled materials. The village prides itself on its eco-credentials, and has its own bio-organic épicerie selling local produce. The village annually hosts a festival of the earth.

There is a closed order in the convent located close to Fontaine-Daniel. The religious order of Mary the Jewess described in this book is purely fictitious and has no association with or resemblance to them. The order does, however, make great candles.

Come and visit us. Discover the extraordinary village of Fontaine-Daniel and learn about its history – from the Cistercian monks to the founding of heritage fabric manufacturer Toiles de Mayenne more than 200 years ago.

FOR MORE INFORMATION ABOUT:

ARTSPACE GÎTES:	WWW.ARTSPACEGITES.FR
FONTAINE-DANIEL VILLAGE:	WWW.FONTAINEDANIEL.FR
TOILES DE MAYENNE FABRIC:	WWW.TOILES-DE-MAYENNE.COM
ÉCOLE DE CRÉATION:	WWW.ECOLE-DE-CREATION.FR

artspace
gîtes

fontaine daniel

Toiles de Mayenne is a family-owned company

Toiles de Mayenne is one of the last French weavers. From its beginnings in 1806, the factory, which is still independently owned, has developed expertise in the production of high-quality fabrics for use in interior decoration – furnishings, drapes, cushion covers, throws, and more.

The tiny village of Fontaine-Daniel, nestling in a wooded valley, and built over the course of the centuries by visionary architects and workers, still encapsulates the vision of an industrious and harmonious society.

The brand's close relationship with its clients and close attention to service enable it to provide solutions for living well in attractive and individualised surroundings.

TOILES DE MAYENNE
DEPUIS·1806

www.toiles-de-mayenne.com